To keep up to date with Alicia's new releases, sign up for her books and for other news, find her at her website **aliciamontgomeryauthor.com/** or on Facebook **/aliciamontgomeryauthor** and Instagram **@aliciamontgomeryauthor**.

Alicia Montgomery has always dreamed of becoming a romance novel writer. She started writing down her stories in now long-forgotten diaries and notebooks, never thinking that her dream would come true.

After taking the well-worn path to a stable career, she began self-publishing paranormal shifter romance novels in 2016, selling half a million books while downing nearly as many cups of coffee. She's moved so many times in the last twenty years that she's not sure where she'll be by the time this book gets printed, but wherever that is, she'll be somewhere enjoying a sunset walk with her husband J and pandemic poodle puppy Jessica Jones.

ALICIA MONTGOMERY

HORN IN MY SIDE

HEADLINE
ETERNAL

First published in 2025 by Headline Eternal
An imprint of Headline Publishing Group Limited

This paperback edition published in 2025

1

Cataloguing in Publication Data is available from the British Library

ISBN 978 1 0354 3212 7

Typeset in 11.04/14pt Adobe Garamond Pro Std
by Six Red Marbles UK, Thetford, Norfolk

Printed and bound in Great Britain by Clays Ltd, Elcograf S.p.A.

Headline's policy is to use papers that are natural, renewable and recyclable products
and made from wood grown in well-managed forests and other controlled sources.
The logging and manufacturing processes are expected to conform to the
environmental regulations of the country of origin.

Headline Publishing Group Limited
An Hachette UK Company
Carmelite House
50 Victoria Embankment
London EC4Y 0DZ

The authorised representative in the EEA is Hachette Ireland,
8 Castlecourt Centre, Dublin 15, D15 XTP3, Ireland (email: info@hbgi.ie)

www.headlineeternal.co.uk
www.headline.co.uk
www.hachette.co.uk

This is for all my readers who have been with me since the beginning, back when I was a scared new author. You've given me the strength and inspiration to keep writing, and while I'm still scared, I know you'll always be there to catch me.

Chapter One

JASMINE

Jasmine Gonzalez heaved a long drawn-out breath as she surveyed the daunting task ahead of her. Then again, completing daunting tasks was her specialty.

This particular one, however, required the use of a ladder or for her to be about seven feet tall, neither of which she had, or was right now in this moment.

She chomped at her lower lip, staring up at the looming sign atop the large bay window. The letter *T* had come loose and hung upside down, dangling from a single nail at the base, so it currently read "Fantastic ails and Magical Scales Pet Shop."

It was tempting to leave it be, as there were about a million other things that needed fixing inside the shop—the kelpie-tank filters had to be replaced soon, the pens required a locking-spell refresh, the POS system (which was probably older than her) was long overdue for an upgrade—and on and on.

Normally, she could call on the owner of the shop to make small repairs, like fixing the sign, or to purchase supplies like ladders, but he had recently passed away. Vrig had been an elderly orc, who'd hired Jasmine as a cashier almost five years ago when she was new in town and had no experience with either magical pets or working in retail. He'd been a kind boss, as well as her landlord, as he'd offered her the tiny apartment over his garage at a rent that was way below market prices and the place was only a ten-minute walk away from the store.

Vrig had taught her everything he knew, from learning how to handle newly hatched basilisks to predicting when the phoenixes were about to regenerate. She'd come to love the work and caring for all the magical creatures at Fantastic Tails, but her favorite part of the job was matching clients with the perfect pet. Vrig had said she was a natural at it, and for the first time in her life, Jasmine had found something she was truly good at. It worked out for Vrig as well, because over time he had given her more duties, and spent less time at the store, often letting Jasmine open up in the morning and close up at the end of the day.

She, too, enjoyed the increased responsibilities and decision-making powers on the business side of the shop. Vrig seemed happy to allow her to take on more work and even gave her a modest pay bump and a promotion from cashier to manager, though that was more ceremonial as she was his only employee. Still, she loved her routine at the shop, her cozy apartment over Vrig's garage, and even this quiet little town. For the first time in a long while, she was content to stay in one place, something she hadn't felt since she and her father had left their tiny town in the Philippines to move to the United States when she was twelve.

The last five years working at Fantastic Tails had gone by so quickly, she barely noticed it. Heck, she didn't even think about what was to come next, enjoying her life day to day, never worrying about tomorrow—at least, not until Vrig had died.

He was gone now, and she was still here. Truly, she could have left—should have left—when he passed away, but there was no one else to take care of the store and she just couldn't leave the creatures in the shop, not when the authorities were still trying to find Vrig's next of kin to sort out who would inherit his estate. Up until his death, she'd been running the entire operation anyway, so she decided to stay on and figure out what to do, at least until everything was sorted out. As far as she knew, Vrig had never married nor had any children, and had never spoken about siblings or other relatives, so she couldn't provide the authorities with any information. That had been three weeks ago and she hadn't heard anything from the administrator appointed by the probate court since.

Jasmine swallowed the lump in her throat. Some days, she still expected him to come walking in, all smiles as he greeted her, usually bringing her a to-go cup from the coffee shop down the street. Despite his appearance—seven feet in height, shaggy white hair, green skin, sharp tusks—Vrig had been a gentle and kind soul, not only to her and the customers, but to the animals in the shop. There were times when she would even forget he was gone. She'd get an idea and would walk over to the back office where he was usually holed up, then stop halfway, remembering she would never see him there, crouched in front of his computer, glasses perched on his face, always ready to help with some repair or to answer a question she had about a new creature.

His loss left a huge crater in her chest, but at the same time it reminded her of what was to come. It was like waiting for the proverbial axe to fall, wondering day in and day out if some long-lost relative of his would come sweeping in, take over the shop and his house, and kick her out of her apartment.

Of course, there was the option of buying the shop and running it. The thought of it had become more and more appealing since Vrig had died. However, that would mean being tied down for the next few years or so, not to mention the huge financial commitment of taking on a loan. That, of course, would all hinge on Vrig's heirs wanting to sell to her. It wasn't just the business Vrig had owned, but the building and land itself, which was prime property as it was located right in the middle of Main Street. They could shut down the shop and sell everything for an enormous profit and Jasmine would not be able to do a single thing about it.

But there was no use worrying about that, because there were other pressing matters she had to deal with, such as the one right in front of her.

Or rather, *literally* hanging over her head.

If Vrig were here, she wouldn't need a ladder, as he was tall enough to fix the sign. Heck, he could use magic to simply put it to rights.

But he wasn't here, and it was all up to her.

Jasmine drummed her fingers on her arm. She would leave it be for now, but she didn't want *another* sternly worded letter from the Dewberry Falls Main Street Business Association. The board was all about keeping the town's commercial hub immaculate and pristine, so as to attract customers and keep property values high. She could not afford to get on their bad side, not after the last incident that had gotten her a first warning.

"It wasn't my fault those mini cockatrices got out of their pens," she grumbled to herself.

And she had chased all three of the escaped jailbirds up and down Main Street, and thankfully wrangled them back into the shop before they could seriously harm anyone. Since they were the mini variety of cockatrice, their gaze couldn't kill anyone, but it was enough to leave Alice Vanderpelt in a coma for twelve hours.

No, this definitely had to be fixed now. Martha Goodeheart, who served as chairman of the board, was just *itching* to serve Jasmine with a second warning, and once she received three, she would have to pay a hefty fine.

Hands on her hips, she marched back into the shop as a hoppy sixties tune piping in through the Bluetooth speaker on the counter greeted her.

"One fine day, indeed," she muttered to herself.

Though tempted to turn the speakers off, she knew she couldn't. The creatures in the pet shop seemed to like music, at least that's what Vrig had told her in the beginning. "Silence drives them crazy," he'd said. "They all start lookin' at each other and some of the more 'ornery ones pick fights. But the music keeps them calm."

And so they had music piping in 24/7. Initially Vrig had boring elevator music playing, but as she took over more of the store, Jasmine eventually replaced his playlist with her own favorites, particularly those bright, soulful upbeat Motown tunes from the 1950s and 60s.

She rooted around in her purse until she found the black elastic buried at the bottom, then proceeded to braid her long, black hair into a rope so it wouldn't get in her way. Then, she grabbed the step stool under the counter. It would only boost her five-foot-nearly-nothing frame about another foot and a half, which would not be enough. As she tapped a finger on her chin, she spied a large cement block from the corner of her eye. Vrig had used them to prop the door open sometimes. After a quick mental calculation—and a small prayer to her ancestor spirits—she picked up the stool and the block, tucked a hammer under her arm, put some nails in her pocket, then headed outside.

You can do this.

She placed the step stool under the sign, then the cement block on top of it.

What doesn't kill me only makes me stronger.

It might fracture a limb or two, but thankfully the shop had an excellent employee health plan and she'd only have to be at the bone-setter's office for an hour. Two, tops.

Placing her right foot on the first step of the stool, she gave it an experimental wiggle. Hoisting herself up, she set her left foot on top of the block, then the other.

Yes!

But now came the hard part. She actually had to fix the darned sign. At this height, she could maneuver the *T* to its proper position, but she would have to stretch, *really stretch*, her other arm to pull the hammer far back enough to drive the nails in.

Jasmine did not dare look down, even as the stool wobbled. Holding her breath, she proceeded to swing the *T* upwards. It remained upright by some miracle and she considered leaving it as is, hoping it would hold up at least until she got some help—maybe she could call her friend Kap to finish the job tonight, as the tree giant was certainly tall enough to fix this without a ladder. She would have contacted him earlier, but he was still surely asleep, being nocturnal and all.

With a determined grunt, she fished out a nail from her pocket and positioned it as high as she could on the painted wooden letter, about halfway up the vertical stem of the *T*. Pulling the hammer back, she swung it forward to ensure she got enough momentum—then felt the cement block slip.

Jasmine shrieked, bracing herself for the pain when she hit the solid pavement. However, that didn't happen. Her body hit something solid, but it wasn't concrete. Rather, she was pressed up against something rock-hard, and warm, and *breathing*.

Uh-oh.

A loud grunt made her wince. Slowly, she lifted her head and gazed up into luminous purple eyes.

Oh, Mother Goddess!

"I . . . I . . ."

Her entire mouth had gone dry and she could only stare open-mouthed at the tall, green-skinned stranger holding her in his arms. An orc, she guessed, though there wasn't really much doubt, as the sharp lower tusks peeking from between his lips and the elongated ears were dead giveaways. A mane of shaggy hair as dark as a raven's wing fell over his forehead and between his dark purple eyes, which stared right back at her.

"Do you mind?" His low, gruff voice sent a shiver down the backs of her knees.

"Mind? What?"

His eyes darted down to her hands, which were planted—no, gripping—the prominent pectoral muscles under his shirt. As if she hadn't embarrassed herself enough, her fingers involuntarily squeezed them.

They're so . . . hard.

And she wondered if he was hard everywhere.

Also, was he green all over?

Warmth crept up her neck, just thinking about what his skin was like underneath those—

He cleared his throat.

Oh, Mother—

"Sorry!" She pulled her hands away, then began to wiggle in an attempt to free herself of his arms, flailing like a fish caught in a bear's mouth.

"Yeow!" he shouted as her hand smacked against the side of his head. The arm cradling her legs whipped out from under her and she landed on her feet.

"Oh shi—sorry!" She reached up to check where she had hit him, but that was a useless gesture as even on her tiptoes her hand barely touched his chin. "Are you okay?"

"I'll live," he grunted, rubbing at his face.

"I'm really sorry. I, uh, just panicked. Are you sure you're all right?" Thankfully, she hadn't poked his eyes. "Do you want me to look at it? Do you need a doctor, a healer, or a medicine man?" She couldn't quite recall what type of healthcare professional orcs went to.

"It's fine. What in Vorlak's name were you doing?" He glanced over the step stool, which was now on its side, the cement block broken in two beside it. "Don't you know how dangerous and foolish that was?"

She flinched but quickly recovered.

Who the heck did he think he was, anyway?

"Well, if you're *fine*," she began as she picked up the stool, "have a good day, then." *And I'll see you never.*

He snorted. "I came here to see the pet shop."

She froze midway as she reached for the broken cement block. *He was a customer?*

Deciding the cement block was not salvageable, she stood up straight and faced him, craning up to get a good look. About seven feet tall, he blocked most of the sun from her view, his massive shoulders and arms like boulders covered in red-and-black-checked flannel.

"You're looking for a pet? For yourself or perhaps your offspring?" She cringed inwardly, thinking of how she had groped him.

He could be married. With kids.

But he didn't seem that old, perhaps a few years older than herself, but certainly mature-looking enough to have a child or two running around.

"No."

She ignored that tiny yelp of victory from her brain—and other parts of her body.

He could still be married.

Besides, he had been rude to her just two seconds ago, calling her foolish.

Silence stretched between them as she waited for him to follow up and tell her why he was here. Was she supposed to read his mind and figure out what he wanted?

Shrugging, she continued. "Well, sir, if you're not in the market for a pet, perhaps you're at the wrong place." She pursed her lips and used them to point up at the sign, where, sadly, the

T once again swung down from its fixing. "We're a pet shop, specializing in all creatures scaled, fanged, feathered, furred, and everything in between."

"I am at the right place and I don't want a pet."

"You don't? Then why—" An alarming thought popped into her brain. "Sir," she began, her voice firm, but professional, "I don't know what kind of place you think this is, but we strictly offer creatures as *pets*. And not for other purposes."

"I know and—" His dark brows furrowed. "Wait, do you think I want to *eat* them?"

"Or use them in spell-casting or experiments." She crossed her arms over her chest. "You wouldn't be the first to try." She'd seen Vrig deal with such nefarious would-be customers, and while she probably couldn't toss this orc out on his ass, she could scream really loud.

"I'm not here to—" He raked his clawed hands through his messy mane. "I'm Mal."

"And?" Was she supposed to know who he was by name?

"Of the Urduk Horde."

Now that sounded familiar. "Urduk . . . as in—"

"Vrig's horde. I'm his nephew."

A heartbeat passed as she processed the information.

This orc was Vrig's nephew. His relative.

Heat flooded her cheeks. "I . . . I . . . ." Her tongue refused to follow what her brain wanted her to say.

He let out a huff. "And you're Jasmine, right? If I promise not to eat any of the creatures, will you let me inside so we can talk?"

Oh, Mother Goddess, she not only fell into his arms and molested him, but also implied he was a savage creature who devoured adorable pets.

If you can hear me, she pleaded to her ancestor spirits, *please strike me with a thunderbolt right now and erase my existence from this world.*

"Well?"

Unfortunately, she remained earthbound.

Great help you are, ancestors.

"Uh, yeah, okay," she mumbled, managing to gather her wits. "Please, come inside."

She led him into the shop, gesturing for him to go first, watching him to gauge his reaction.

Most people who first entered Fantastic Tails were often taken by surprise by its interior. While the façade looked like any of the other shops of Main Street, the inside had been magically renovated into a space that was four times its size. Half the store was dedicated to the various pet supplies—food, toys, beds, cages, leashes, and the like—as they accounted for most of the store's profits. The other half was where they kept the creatures, two levels of spacious cages, pens, and habitats holding the different pets they had for sale. The lower level had all the landbound and flying creatures, while the second floor was wall-to-wall aquariums filled with all kinds of water and amphibious animals. Vrig had said he'd built the entire thing himself, including casting some of the spells to expand the space.

It was truly a sight to behold, but the gigantic orc simply glanced around and let out a grunt, seemingly unimpressed.

Jasmine pursed her lips, waiting for any other reaction. When none came, she went to the register, as if the massive counter was a shield protecting her.

"Uhm, Mr. Mal, I'm sorry for what—"

"It's fine," he said, tone dismissive as he waved a massive hand. "And it's just Mal. I'm here to settle Vrig's affairs."

And where have you been all this time? she wanted to say, but she bit her lip before the words tumbled out of her mouth. "Oh, I see."

"I travel a lot," he began. "Took the administrator a while to get a hold of me."

"He didn't leave a will or anything. And they said they couldn't find any contact information of relatives in his home or belongings."

"Vrig didn't have any close relatives, only me. He was my father's older half-brother."

"Did you know him before he retired?" Before Vrig came to Dewberry Falls to open the shop, he had been in the Orc Division of the Army Corps of Engineers.

"Not really. Met him a few times when I was a kid before my dad died."

"Uhm, still, I'm sorry for your loss."

He shrugged. "It's okay."

"He went peacefully." Her chest tightened as she recalled the events. "The night before he died, he'd seemed normal, though he mentioned that his arthritis had been acting up so I told him to go home early. The next day, when he didn't show up at all, I went over to his house with some soup. He didn't answer and the locking spell prevented me from going inside, so I called emergency services. The EMTs said he'd passed away in his sleep the night before."

"It was his time."

That's what many of their neighbors had said when they came to offer their condolences. Still, guilt filled her. If she had checked up on him that evening, maybe she could have done *something*. At the very least, if she had stayed with Vrig, he wouldn't have died alone.

An awkward silence passed between them before she managed to swallow the lump in her throat. "Do you want anything to drink? I have coffee and tea."

He shook his head. "No, thank you. I just want to settle things and get going."

"Of course," she said through gritted teeth. *Calm down*, she told herself. He didn't really know his half-uncle, so she couldn't expect him to grieve a near-stranger.

"The administrator mentioned you've been keeping things running around here while they were looking for me, even though you didn't have to."

She gestured to the wall of cages and glass cases. "I can't exactly just lock up the doors and walk away."

"I get that," he said gruffly. "And don't worry. I don't plan to inconvenience you further. Please don't feel that you have to stay."

She'd known this day was coming. Had run the scenarios in her head, about what she would do once Vrig's kin were found, where she would go, her next steps. But to actually have to face it head on now was a punch to the gut.

"Of course," she managed to say, despite all the air leaving her lungs.

"Depending on your employment contract and the shop's finances, I'm sure I could offer you some kind of severance." He frowned. "How did you manage to stay on without Vrig?"

"What do you mean?"

He glanced around. "Running a place like this has to be a headache for accounting."

"A-accounting?" Wait, was he implying she was doing something underhanded? Cooking the books? "I assure you, everything's in order, accounting-wise," she said, her tone chilly.

"I—what? No, I wasn't implying—" He let out an impatient snort. "I—"

"Vrig promoted me to manager two years ago. Since then, I've been running everything, both in the front and back office." Except the store's bank accounts and payroll, of course, but thankfully all their suppliers had been paid up until the end of this month, and her salary had hit her bank account just yesterday, which meant Vrig had signed off on it before he passed away. "I assure you that everything is in order when it comes to the shop's finances."

"I'm sure they are."

"Margins are thin, but your uncle said this was more of a side hobby for him, something to do in retirement to stave off the boredom, so he didn't care about money as long as he wasn't completely in the red."

"I didn't mean to imply anything." More awkward silence stretched between them before he spoke again. "Look, I'm grateful for your help and staying on. But the shop isn't your problem anymore. Since Vrig died here and didn't leave a will, this whole thing has been a headache to deal with. I have a meeting at the law office down the street so I can get some help and hopefully we can get all this sorted out sooner rather than later. They'll be in touch with you for anything." With that, he turned and walked toward the door.

Jasmine could only stare at his large, flannel-covered back as he exited the shop, the door closing behind him slowly in an anticlimactic manner.

Here it was, the axe falling, burying straight into her chest.

Numbness took over her, and for a few minutes she didn't move. It was only the sound of the chirping baby oozlums demanding their midday meal that knocked her out of her trance. Instinctively, she grabbed the bag of birdseed from under the counter and sauntered over to the large cage in the corner.

"Patience," she cooed as she pulled out the feeder.

The colorful little birds flew backwards in circles as they waited for their meal. As soon as Jasmine drew closer, they slowed their flight and flitted toward the front of the cage. She pressed her palm against the bars, and they hovered next to her fingers, warbling a high-pitched tune. Once she'd replaced the feeder, they dove right in.

With a satisfied sigh, she took a step back and glanced at the other creatures around her—the cerberus pup with its three heads on its paws as it snoozed in the corner of its pen, the pair of fenrir cubs play-fighting, the phoenix chirping happily in its cage—and her heart sank further.

Vrig had been selective with his customers and it truly wasn't about money for him. He made sure that potential owners had the right temperament and lifestyle for the pet they wanted; after all, these were living creatures and someone who, say, lived in an apartment and worked eighty hours a week would not be able to handle the responsibilities of training a griffin hatchling or a wily kobold. He refused to sell to anyone who wouldn't be a good owner, and he had a generous return policy for customers who changed their mind, as he'd rather take the loss than risk the poor creatures becoming neglected.

Vrig's nephew didn't mention what he had planned, but he didn't seem interested in anything about the business aside from the books, which meant he would likely close the shop. And if that were his plan, the most logical thing to do would be to sell the remaining creatures to one of those soulless, big-box stores who would give them to just anyone who walked through the door.

I can't let that happen.

While she had been undecided all these weeks, Jasmine knew what she had to do: she had to convince Vrig's nephew—*Mal*, she reminded herself—to sell Fantastic Tails to her.

If she could afford it.

She lived frugally and so she had some savings, but that would not be enough, so she would have to take out a loan. The idea of having to pay back an enormous sum made her break out into a cold sweat, but there was no way she could buy the shop outright.

Jasmine straightened her shoulders. She had to at least try. If she didn't, she would surely regret it. It was another daunting task, but those *were* her specialty.

She didn't know how long Vrig's nephew would be in town, so she had to act fast. Grabbing her phone from the counter, she tapped out a message to Tracy, the manager at the Dewberry Falls Credit Union. She and Tracy went to the same spin class on Thursday nights, and often grabbed a late drink together afterwards.

Got a minute? Can I swing by your office?

Grabbing her purse from under the counter, she gave the shop a once-over before marching toward the door, flipping the Open sign to Closed, then activating the alarm system. As she exited, she spied the stool and broken concrete block outside, reminding her of her unfinished task.

I'll definitely have to ask Kap to come by later. She'd make him a batch of her sinigang soup in exchange.

However, as she picked up the stool, she glanced up at the sign and, to her surprise, the *T* was the right way up.

Huh. How did that—

Her phone's ringtone shook her out of her thoughts. Seeing the familiar name flashing on the screen, she quickly picked it up. "Tracy? Hi. Thanks for calling . . . Yeah, I'm good." She gave the sign one last glance. "Do you have a few minutes? I need to ask you something . . ."

Chapter Two

MAL

Mal's entire body sagged in relief as he finally reached his room at the Dreametime Motel. As the door shut behind him, he leaned back and closed his eyes. It had only been his second day in this little town, and he was ready for all of this to be over. In truth, he'd had longer, grueling days working on various construction sites over the years, but there was something about spending hours lining up at government offices and signing papers all day that was its own personal brand of hell.

Lumbering toward the bed, he stripped his clothes off and placed them on top of the covers, then headed to the spacious bathroom. When he had asked the front desk if they had any vacancies, he didn't even think to request an oversized room, yet they automatically gave him one. Thank Vorlak, because oftentimes when he had to check into a hotel or furnished apartment, he would have to crouch just to fit through the door, or had to put two beds together to get a decent night's sleep, and never mind the usually cramped bathrooms. Though this room was by no means five-star lodgings, he appreciated that he could move around easily and the furnishings could actually hold his weight and size. And after a long day like today, he was glad he could take a hot shower without later paying for it with a crick in his neck.

He sighed and laid a palm against the wet tile, moving his head side to side so the needles of water from the shower head massaged his scalp. Normally, this helped him relax, but his mind was occupied with everything he needed to do and accomplish in the next few days.

He finished and dried himself off with a towel then wrapped it round his waist before stepping out of the bathroom. As he sorted through the clothes in his duffle bag, searching for something to wear that was somewhat clean, he grumbled to himself.

I didn't even want to come here.

Not that he was ungrateful, but he frankly didn't care about this inheritance from some long-lost uncle. Mal had been determined to just ignore the official-looking letter his mother had forwarded to him and let everything go to the state. After all, he'd hardly known Vrig, and it didn't seem right he should inherit his assets.

His mother and stepfather, however, had other ideas.

"He was your family," Morlak, his mother had said. "Your last blood relative on your father's side."

"And there's nothing more important than family," his stepfather, Karak, had added. "Go and settle his affairs. If anything, it is your duty to give him a proper send-off."

Mal could not argue with that last statement. Tradition dictated that every orc who passed away had their ashes spread over the Victory Fields in Ghalad-Dur, the orc homeland, so they could be reunited with their ancestors. And so, Mal made plans to travel to Dewberry Falls, the quiet, northern California town his uncle had been living in for the last twenty years.

Thankfully, Mal had just finished his last job, building a mountain-cabin getaway for some rich warlock. He enjoyed being a contractor, liked the challenge and the variety of jobs and locations on which he worked. Before the cabin, he was in the Caribbean overseeing work on a brand-new luxury resort. They had needed his expertise in the construction of the special suites for magical and oversized creatures. And before that he'd been in Macao, renovating a few of their private gaming rooms and out-fitting them with special anti-cheating spells.

All his jobs were challenging, paid well, and more import-antly, he got in, got the job done, and got out.

Mal mostly worked alone, though he did hire local hands to do the grunt work or special tasks he couldn't do himself. Still, he more or less went through his day without having to interact with other people.

This business with his uncle, of course, was an unexpected and unwelcome intrusion into his plans. He didn't see much of Vrig growing up, except for a few Conquest Day dinners and per-haps one or two of his father's birthdays and, of course, his dad's funeral when Mal was ten years old. After that, Vrig had sent a birthday card every now and then, and Mal hadn't really thought of him much in the last twenty years. His death hadn't been unexpected, as he had to have been at least ninety years old.

This was an inconvenience, but he would treat this like any other job: get in, get it done, get out. So, as soon as he'd arrived, he'd gone straight to Foxbird Funeral Homes to retrieve his uncle's ashes. The director had assured him that Vrig had been given the proper orc funeral rites, but that had entailed his pyre be lit at midnight three days after his death and allowed to burn until morning, so they couldn't wait for his relatives to be found. But, at least now that Mal had the ashes—which had been placed in a white urn that currently sat next to the TV—he would be able to perform his duties as Vrig's heir and spread them over his final resting place back in the homelands.

After dropping the urn back in this motel room, his next stop was supposed to be the local probate lawyer. However, the pet store his uncle owned was on the way to the law office so he decided to stop by and at least have a look. He didn't know what to expect, certainly not the tiny human balancing precariously on top of that Orc-SHA violation of a makeshift ladder, trying to hammer at the sign. Thankfully, he'd gotten to her in time, catching her before she landed on the concrete pavement.

The whole thing had been ridiculous. *She* had been ridiculous, and as soon as he felt her soft body in his arms and her flowery perfume tickling his nose, he knew he had to let go of her. It didn't help that she was a pretty little thing with her large, doe-like brown eyes, deep, smooth golden skin, and that rope of long, lustrous black hair that fell down her shoulders. He wondered what it would be like, unbound and spread out all over—

He groaned. He shouldn't think of her that way.

Yes, he definitely should not have held her so close or for so long, but it wasn't as if he could let her fall and break her leg, no matter how foolish her actions were.

And then those small, perfect fingers dug into his chest, sending a twinge all the way down to his nether regions.

It was the tiniest twinge.

A minuscule one, really.

And it had been forgotten the moment she smacked him in the face.

Served him right, he supposed.

Mal should have been insulted that she had insinuated that he was there for a snack, but he couldn't blame her—his kind had not always been so discriminating in their eating practices. She had looked horrified and chastised when she'd found out who he was, which had not been his intention at all. He had thought the administrator had informed Vrig's manager that he had arrived in town, but apparently she didn't even have a clue that Mal existed.

Of course, he hadn't meant to insult her back by insinuating she was skimming off the top when he asked about the books, but rather that managing a retail outlet with a physical location in general was a hassle, at least from what he'd learned from the business classes his parents had encouraged him to take before he set off on his own. He'd been trying to gauge if his assessment of the business was correct, though that wouldn't have had any bearing on his decision to close the shop and sell the building.

It was too bad, though, because the inside of the store had been well-constructed and planned—the expansion spell made use of the existing space, the handcrafted wooden shelves were sturdy, and the pens and tanks holding the various creatures were crafted with care and ingenuity. But then again, he wasn't surprised—the orcs of the Urduk Horde were builders, after all.

Part of Mal didn't want all that hard work torn down. It had probably taken Vrig a year or two to plan and build everything, plus months to work on the spells. But the fastest way to put this all behind him would be to shut down the shop, dispose of the inventory, and then get the building in selling condition. The land was worth a lot according to the lawyer he'd met, but Mal didn't really care much about the money. Sure, it would make a good nest egg, but he had about thirty years until retirement, and he still enjoyed his work.

Speaking of work . . .

He abandoned his search for clean clothes and, still wearing the towel around his waist, lumbered over to the small desk and table in the corner of the room, sat down, and opened his laptop, clicking on the mailbox icon on the desktop. As emails began to pour in, he scanned the new items, disappointment filling him when the one message he'd been waiting for didn't appear.

He tapped his clawed hands on the table as he hit the enve-lope icon again to check for new messages, just in case, but sadly nothing new appeared in the inbox. As if to torture himself

further, he opened up the starred email he had pinned to the top
of his mailbox from five weeks ago and re-read it once more.

```
From: Grok@OrcHistorical.org
To: Mal@TerraFormBuilders.com
Subject: Re: Following up Re: We have
received your bid

Dear Mal,

Thank you for your follow-up email.
I just wanted to confirm that the elders
have still yet to decide on the bids for
the construction of the new historical
center. Please do be patient. We will
contact all the bidders once the final
decision has been made.

In glorious victory,
Grok of Harvik Horde
Coordinator-in-charge
Orc Historical Society
```

Mal closed the lid with an audible huff. It had been nearly six
months since the Orc Historical Society had closed the bidding
and *still* no decision? How could that be?

*What in Vorlak's name were those doddering old orcs doing all
day? Twiddling their claws and drinking hemlock-root tea while
discussing the Barcid Wars of 1024?*

Scrubbing his palm down his face, he calmed himself. Renovating the old lodge into a brand-new historical center would be
a major undertaking, so it made sense that the elders wanted
to choose the right contractor. Mal's patience, however, grew

thinner by the day. If this were an ordinary job, he wouldn't care; he had dozens of offers at any given time and many of them paid much more and could be finished in a shorter period.

This was, however, an incredibly prestigious contract. This wasn't just any old building, but, rather, the place where their ancestors had gathered and prepared for battle, as well as celebrated their victories, back when the world was new and war the norm. There had been talk about renovating the old central lodge into a historical center for what seemed like decades, but it had never really materialized until now.

Mal knew that if he were alive, his father would have jumped at the chance to work on the job. Competition was fierce among the builder hordes, and Mal worked on his bid for weeks and weeks, tweaking and adjusting numbers and timelines. Every day, he checked his email, his phone, and even the online notifications from his PO box where he had his snail mail sent, hoping to hear word. He delayed starting new projects that were too complicated or would take too long in case the Historical Society picked him and wanted him to start right away.

Mal never put his work life on hold for anything. Perhaps it was his builder nature, but he liked plans. One couldn't simply start any build—from the simplest kitchen renovations to the most complex architectural marvels—without planning. There had to be structure and blueprints and schedules. A plan guaranteed that all would run smoothly and exactly as intended.

Yet this job meant so much to him that he was willing to wait. He'd spoken to Karak about it several times, and his stepfather only urged him to be patient. "These things take time," he had said. "And I wouldn't worry—you crafted a competitive bid. I'm sure you'll get it."

But each passing day he didn't hear back chipped away at Mal's confidence.

What if his bid was too expensive?

What if it *wasn't* expensive enough?

What if—

A knock from outside broke into his thoughts.

Who the hell could that be?

No one knew he was staying here, except the people at the law office, and it was after five o'clock. Besides, they had his phone number and email if they needed to get hold of him.

Maybe I forgot to sign something.

Mal must have read a hundred pages of legal papers and forms today, so it was likely he'd missed one or two. The lawyer had said they had to file a couple of things at the court first thing tomorrow, so that was probably why they were here, after hours. Pushing himself up off the chair, he marched over to the door and yanked it open.

"What did I . . ." A familiar flowery scent tickled his nose. "It's you."

Vrig's manager at the pet shop—Jasmine—smiled sheepishly up at him. "Yes, it's me," she said in that melodic tone of hers. "I—"

She stopped short, her eyes bulging out of their sockets. At first, he thought she was having some kind of seizure, but when he followed her gaze, he realized it was fixed on his chest, bare as he still only wore a towel around his waist. She visibly swallowed as her gaze moved lower.

She was checking him out.

And that twinge down south came back with a vengeance.

He couldn't think about *that*. Besides, what did he expect? He was practically naked in front of her; if the roles were reversed, he too would find it hard to stop himself from checking out her luscious curves—

For Gaku's sake, stop ogling her.

"Jasmine?"

Her head snapped up, her face red.

Clearing his throat, he said, "How did you know I was here?"

That probably came out gruffer than he expected, and she visibly winced, her doe eyes turning wounded, as if she were a puppy he'd kicked. His gut recoiled, much like it had yesterday when she'd done the same thing when he had told her how dangerous it was for her to try to fix that sign without any help or proper equipment. He had repaired it himself with a simple mending spell before he left, just so she wouldn't make another feeble attempt and end up with a broken leg or arm. Because now *he* was responsible for everything and everyone in the shop until he sold it all off.

To her credit, she recovered quickly, a sincere smile once again on her face. "This is the only motel in town, and I know you're not staying at Vrig's house, so I therefore concluded you had to be here," she said matter-of-factly. "I'm just glad you're in 1F and I didn't have to knock on a lot of doors."

She was going to knock on every single door in this motel until she found him? "What do you w—" He cleared his throat. "I mean, what can I do for you?" He could be polite if he wanted to, but it wasn't his initial instinct to do so, not when he worked by himself or with other builders and workers, whose manners were even rougher than his.

Brown eyes blinked up at him.

"I was wondering, Mal . . . do you want to have dinner?"

Both his hearts slammed into his chest. "Like . . . a date?"

Her cheeks and nose reddened under her tanned skin. "No!" She slapped a hand over her forehead. "I mean, I'd l-like to talk to you. For us to talk. And maybe, since I'm guessing you haven't had dinner yet, we can do it over a meal? Or-or not." She clucked her tongue. "S-sorry. Never mind. I shouldn't have come." Slapping her hands over her mouth, she quickly turned on her heel and began to walk away.

Mal stood there, frozen as he watched her. She obviously had something important to tell him, and he'd scared her off, acting like some juvenile who had yet to experience his first coupling.

Run after her, fool.

"Wait! Jasmine!"

She stopped immediately and he reached her in five steps. Slowly, she pivoted to face him.

"What is it that you wanted to speak about?" he asked.

She glanced around. "It's kind of . . . It's complicated."

"How so?"

"I . . . can we please sit down and talk?"

"I'm sure you can tell me what it is you want."

"Yes, but . . ."

"But?"

"We're all alone in an empty parking lot." She gestured around them. "And I'm not exactly comfortable speaking to a stranger by myself. And, like I said, you must be hungry. I think better on a full stomach. My treat, okay?"

He blew out an impatient breath, but had to concur with her, especially on the part about being alone and speaking with a stranger. Besides, he was about to leave her jobless soon, so he supposed he could at least hear her out. "Fine."

"Great! Let's go to the diner next door."

"All right."

"Uhm, Mal?" She bit at her lower lip.

"Yeah?"

"Do you want to . . . maybe put on some clothes?"

He slapped himself on the forehead mentally. "I'll be right back."

After he'd dressed in the clothes he'd been wearing earlier, Mal followed Jasmine to the diner next door. As they walked over, Mal couldn't help but wonder what it was she wanted to talk about. Would she try to stop him from selling the pet shop? He couldn't imagine what else she could possibly want from him.

He sympathized with her, he really did. It was tough losing a job, but she was young and—yesterday's situation aside—was probably smart and could easily land on her feet. Besides, why would she want to be stuck in this town, working for just above minimum wage in a pet shop that barely broke even?

The garish neon sign above the classic chrome diner building proclaimed it as "Pamola's Diner", just in case the cartoon illustration of the smiling winged beast with a moose's head, a man's torso, and an eagle's legs was obvious enough. Mal couldn't help but smirk as the pamola was hardly the jovial creature that sign portrayed it to be. They were mean and vicious, and often took prisoners back to their nests to toy with them before devouring them or feeding them to their young.

When they reached the door, he opened it and gestured for her to go inside, then followed her to the nearest empty red vinyl booth.

"Do you know what you want?" the server, a pinched-faced lamia, asked as she slithered toward them, her long, scaly tail swishing behind her.

Jasmine immediately spoke up. "One special plate with home fries, toast, and eggs over easy, plus a side of pancakes." She glanced sheepishly at Mal. "I like breakfast for dinner."

He put down the menu he hadn't had a chance to read. "Same, but double everything."

"Coffee?"

They both shook their heads.

"Be with ya in a jiffy," she called as she slunk away.

"So," Mal began, "what was it that you wanted to talk about?"

Jasmine placed her hands at the edge of the Formica table and drummed her fingers. "Again, I'm so sorry about Vrig."

"Thank you," he said automatically, because what was he

supposed to say? He hardly knew his uncle, and it wasn't that he didn't care, but this situation was just so awkward.

"He really was a great boss, and everyone around here thought he was a nice guy. He'd been here over twenty years. Did you know that? He was a pillar of the community. Joined the Volunteer Fire Department. Participated in all kinds of activities, especially at the elementary school. He always contributed to fundraisers, plus he would bring the pets to the assemblies. The kids loved it. His death is a big loss to Dewberry Falls."

"Uh-huh." He wondered if she would get to the point before their dinner arrived.

"I know you must have a lot of things going on right now, with his estate and his house and all . . ."

Ah yes, that was another headache he had to deal with, and he hadn't even seen the house yet.

"And they say you shouldn't make rash decisions while you're under emotional stress . . ."

You're the one giving me stress with all this beating around the bush, he wanted to say, but held his tongue, lest she turned those wounded brown eyes on him again.

"But if you don't think it's too soon—a-and I completely understand if you do and you need more time, but I was wondering if . . . if you had thought about what you were going to do with Fantastic Tails?"

Finally. "I have. And, Jasmine . . ." He prepared himself mentally for what he wanted—needed—to say to her. Folding his hands together on the table, he focused his gaze on his intertwined fingers, afraid to look at her. "I have no choice but to close it down. Like I said, I can offer you a generous severance, which should help keep you afloat while you search for another job." Carefully, he lifted his head to meet her gaze, realizing he at least owed her that. "I'm sorry."

"That's why I wanted to talk to you, face to face." She inhaled deeply. "I want to buy the shop from you."

Now *that* he didn't expect. "You do?"

"Uh-huh," she said with a determined nod, her fingers continuing their steady rhythm on top of the table.

"Great," he said, relieved that he didn't have to worry about her losing her source of income. Why, if she could afford to buy the shop, then she probably wasn't hurting for cash in the first place. "That would really help me out."

"But . . ."

He snorted. Of course there was a but. "Yes?"

"Er . . ." Her fingers drummed faster. "I can't quite afford it. Yet," she added quickly. "I just need some time to get the paperwork for a loan together and, uh, save up more money."

"How long?"

"About . . . six or seven months?"

"Six or seven *months*?" he echoed.

"Yeah." She blew out a breath. "I do have some savings, but the loan officer at the credit union said I'd have a better chance of getting approved if I had a bigger amount set aside. Plus, I have to get my business proposal done, then all the paperwork at City Hall, the permits . . ."

Mal was not liking the sound of this. "And how would this work, exactly?"

"Well . . . I would keep managing Fantastic Tails, of course, and you can stay on to sign off on the paperwork, paying invoices and my salary. Vrig also approved any purchases and upgrades, plus made repairs and helped with stocking the shelves."

He shook his head vehemently. "No, absolutely not."

"It's not a lot of work," she pointed out. "You can stay in the back office all day if you want. I can do most of the stuff out front, like ringing up customers. I'll stock the shelves and, if you don't feel like doing it, I'll get the repairs done myself."

He raised an eyebrow at her. "Like you did yesterday?"

"Er . . ." Her cheeks pinked again. "I'll hire someone, then. But I still need you around to sign off on everything because you're the owner now."

"Jasmine, I can't wait around here for six or seven months." He raked his claws through his hair. "If you had the money right away and you could buy it outright, that would be a different story. But I need to settle Vrig's estate and assets, and soon."

"What do you plan to do with Fantastic Tails, then?"

"Close it down, dismantle the building and the enchantments, and sell it."

Don't look into her eyes, Mal ordered himself. *Don't do it*—

But of course he did, and those sad puppy-dog eyes hit him straight in the gut.

Godsdamnit.

"What will you do with the animals?" she whispered in a soft tone.

"Sell them off, I suppose. Maybe to PetWarehouse?"

"You can't!" she burst out. "I mean . . . not to those corporate stores. Do you know how the creatures get treated over there?"

"I'm sorry, Jasmine," he said. "But I really can't wait."

"Those places are terrible. They keep the animals in these tiny cages or in overcrowded pens and dirty aquariums. And then they let just *anyone* buy them."

"It's a pet shop—you're supposed to sell them."

A horrified expression crossed her face. "Do you need the money right away? Is that it?" Her lips twisted. "If you give me a few weeks, I'm sure I can find another way to buy it from you. Maybe talk to the credit union again—"

"No," he said quickly. "But I need to finish dealing with Vrig's estate as soon as possible. I'm a contractor and I have a very important job waiting for me." Well, technically, he didn't have the historical center job yet, but the elders could make their decision at any time and he had to be ready. "Jasmine, I'm the type of person who likes to plan things out. I never make a decision rashly and always like to know what I'm getting into. I need to know that I'm not going to get burned in the end."

"I'll sign a contract if you want."

"That's not what I meant." Orcs weren't big on paper contracts anyway, as they always kept their word. "I don't start any job unless I know the outcome. If a client even feels shady, I decline them. I like guarantees and I'm sorry . . . I just don't think you'll be able to get everything done before I have to go. I can't give you a few more weeks or wait around until you've saved enough money. The sooner I get rid of everything, the better."

"I see," she sniffed, and her eyes turned just a hint watery—which was enough to send a twinge to a different part of his body, namely, his hearts. "Then we don't really have much to talk about, then. If you'll excuse me, I'm not as hungry as I thought I was." She stood up, but not before fishing her wallet out of her purse.

"No, please, put that away," he urged. "I'll get it." She shouldn't have to pay for a meal she wasn't going to eat anyway, especially when she was about to be unemployed. Which, a voice in Mal's head said, was his fault.

She hesitated, then put the wallet away. "Good night, Mal."

"Good night, Jasmine."

He tamped down the urge to chase after her again. After all, he owned the shop now and he could do with it as he pleased. Being Vrig's heir was not a responsibility he wanted or for which he'd asked. He had a life to go back to and a job he enjoyed. Even if he stayed, it wasn't as if he knew anything about running a pet shop.

No, he didn't have a choice. He had to shut it down.

"Hey, where did your girlfriend go?" the waitress asked as she

returned, two trays of food in her hands, plus another one balancing on the end of her tail.

"She, uh, had an emergency."

"Oh, did you want her food to go, then?"

"No, I'll eat it."

Mal finished both plates of food, even though it all tasted
like ash. After paying, he dragged himself back to his motel
room, though this time he felt no relief at being inside. Worse
still, his stomach was tied up in knots, tightening as he stared at
the white urn next to the TV.

Plopping himself on the chair, he let out a half-grunt, half-
snort. He couldn't let some pretty little thing and her big doe
eyes derail him from his plan: get in, get the job done, get out.

How anyone could say no to those sweet brown eyes, he
didn't know. Worse, she didn't even seem to know she was doing
it. Maybe that's how she finagled a job from Vrig in the first
place, though she didn't seem the type to use her womanly wiles.
Perhaps Vrig had seen something special in her and had obviously grown fond of her if he'd kept her around this long. With
his strength and magic, Vrig wouldn't have needed a full-time
manager.

Don't even think about it.

He couldn't stay here and run the pet shop with her. It was a
crazy idea. Aside from the fact that he knew nothing about retail
or magical creatures, there were half a dozen short-term jobs on
which he could work; he could even go home and visit his parents
in Vermont for a couple weeks. But he was absolutely not staying
in this little town, working in that shop, day in and day out,
without a plan or guarantee she'd even be able to get that loan to
buy the shop from him.

He glanced back at the urn, then at his laptop. Opening it
once again, he clicked on the mail icon and waited . . . for
nothing.

Slamming it shut, he leaned back on the chair and scrubbed a hand down his face.

Godsdamnit.

But, Mal supposed, he could hear her out—listen to her proposal, her plan to save money and get a loan. He owed Vrig that, at the very least. But he wouldn't let her convince him to derail his own plans.

I'll go to the shop tomorrow.

And if that email from the Historical Society arrived between now and then, he would take the first flight out to the homelands and find another way to settle Vrig's affairs.

Chapter Three

JASMINE

"There, there," she cooed at the fenrir cub who whined at her when she passed by its pen. "Don't you worry. You'll have your lunch soon. It's not time yet."

The tiny thing was incredibly food driven and eager to please, and she guessed it would make a good pet for someone who wanted to train it. After giving it a scratch on its chin, she continued toward the back office.

Pausing, she gave herself a little motivational pep talk before pushing the door open. Vrig's office was exactly the way it was on the last day he came in. For all the care and effort he put in constructing the front of the shop, this space looked like any ordinary office.

Of course, while it was cramped for Vrig, as he had been seven feet tall, it was comfortable for her petite stature. She walked over to the oversized table, running a hand over the surface, a thin layer of dust accumulating on her fingers. She supposed she should clean in here, but it wouldn't matter anyway. Soon, this place, along with the shop, the building, and the creatures, would all be gone.

Circling the desk, she climbed up the office chair, settling into a cross-legged position. Mal was certainly in his rights to do what he wanted with Fantastic Tails and all of Vrig's assets, and she wouldn't be able to do anything.

But he didn't have to be such a surly grouch about it.

It seemed impossible to her that he and Vrig were related by blood. Most people would look at Vrig and think he was some mean and fierce orc, but really it was the opposite. He spoke in a soft voice and had been so gentle and careful with his words and actions.

His nephew, on the other hand, was very orc-like in nature. Not that she had encountered many of them, but they were known to be a menacing species, and also quite insular. From what she'd read, they often lived in communities that were closed off; in fact, despite its reputation for being a multi-species community, Vrig had been the only orc living in Dewberry Falls.

Jasmine knew she could be quite sensitive to words and tones and that was something she worked on. When she first moved to America, she had found the directness of the people abrasive and, having only learned English in a formal setting, it had been difficult for her to understand the nuances of the language and things like sarcasm and jokes.

Over time, she integrated into her new home, but frankly it had been difficult, not to mention inter-species relations, which added a different dimension to navigating everyday life in Dewberry Falls. But much like her transition to a new country, she had fumbled her way through it and somehow found herself entrenched in this cozy little town. And now she was going to have to start all over again.

This was not, as one of the first American idioms she learned said, her first rodeo. She'd moved and started a new life several times at this point. Her father had first been recruited to work as a nurse at a hospital in Los Angeles, where they stayed for a year before he found a better offer in Miami. They lived there for two years, enough time for Jasmine to finish high school before they relocated again to Pittsburgh in Pennsylvania. She was in her first semester at Pitt when she decided to drop out, as she felt college wasn't for her, and she went to New York, then to Denver, then to San Francisco, staying a year or two in each city before the urge to move overcame her. After two years in San Francisco, she'd decided to pack up her belongings and drive north with no particular destination when her car broke down outside the small town of Dewberry Falls. She had planned to keep driving once her car was fixed, but then she saw the "Help Wanted" sign in the window of Fantastic Tails and Magical Scales Pet Shop.

True, she hadn't meant to stay here this long and she could always start all over again.

I just don't want to, she thought with a petulant pout.

Dewberry Falls had become her home. Why should she have to leave?

Maybe I can find another job.

The boutique down the street always needed a hand during busy days. There were also plenty of caregiving jobs available, or she could walk dogs and clean houses to make ends meet.

Or I could finish my nursing degree.

There was always that option. She could go live with her dad for a bit too; he said she was always welcome to come home— wherever home was, anyway. Currently, Jed Gonzalez was a traveling nurse, but he kept a three-bedroom house in Coreopolis, just outside Pittsburgh. She could go back and ask the admissions office at Pitt about re-enrolling or go to a community college. Starting school again at thirty years old would be humbling, but it wasn't like she would have a choice.

However, the thought of living with her dad again didn't sit well with her, but she wouldn't be able to afford to go to school and pay for rent at the same time. And it wasn't that she didn't love her dad. She did, very much so. But there was an entirely different reason she couldn't live under his roof again.

There was a shadow over their relationship, one he had no idea existed. This looming phantom was of Jasmine's own creation, a secret she kept over the years. Her father loved her, she was sure of that. It was just difficult to reconcile that with what she'd overheard that day after her grandfather's funeral.

It's not fair, Jed had said. *It's because of Jasmine, isn't it? The Inheritance should have been passed to me. I showed—*

Ding ding dong!

The bell signaling someone had entered the shop startled Jasmine, and instinctively she rushed out to the front, calling, "Welcome to Fantastic Tails and Magical Scaa—o-oh!"

She stopped herself in time before she lost her balance, both her mouth and her feet stuttering as she saw who it was—Mal. He stood by the counter, looking tentative, and infuriatingly attractive all at the same time.

Jasmine groaned inwardly, remembering how he had answered the door in nothing but his towel last night. His chest and torso were perfectly formed and his bare arms were like sculpted rock, just as she imagined. It really did look as if he was green *all over*, as that towel around his waist had barely covered his most important bits.

"Hi," he said, knocking her out of her very inappropriate thoughts.

Squaring her shoulders, she walked toward him. "Hello, Mal. Do you want to take a look around? I could show you the back office where all of Vrig's things are." He seemed to prefer the direct approach, so she dispensed with the niceties.

His dark eyebrows furrowed together. "Yeah. Something like that. Jasmine, could we—"

The doorbell once again rang and she snapped into

customer-service mode. "Good morning! Welcome to Fantastic Tails and Magical Scales," she greeted. "How can I help you today?"

A well-dressed, middle-aged cyclops woman took tentative steps inside. "Hello. We're looking for a pet." She gestured to the young boy next her. Jasmine guessed he couldn't have been more than ten years old, at least in human years.

"Mom and Dad said if I got straight As, I could get a pet," the boy said.

Smiling, she bent down to his level. "And did you?"

"Yes," he proclaimed, the single blue eye in the middle of his forehead brimming with pride. "Even in math."

"That's awesome." She quickly glanced up at the boy's mother and recognized the look of apprehension on the woman's face. Children were Jasmine's favorite customers, as she loved the pure happiness and awe in their faces whenever they entered the shop and left with a new pet. However, they often proved to be the most difficult, or at least the adults were, and it was a challenge to find a creature that suited both parent and offspring.

"Do you have any idea of what kind of pet you wanted? I'm Jasmine, by the way."

"I'm Alexios," he said. "I was thinking a chimera," the boy said, which earned an exasperated sigh from his mother.

"Have you taken care of a pet before, Alexios?"

He shook his head.

"Not even a goldfish? Or a hamster?"

"No, Mom and Dad wouldn't let me."

Alexios's mother spoke up. "We lived in an apartment in Bayview City up until July. There was never any space for pets. But then we heard about Dewberry Falls and the fantastic school district, and that the community would be welcoming, so we decided to move here. Best decision we made."

Jasmine grinned at the woman. "I'm glad. This is a great

town. So," she said, turning back to Alexios, "chimeras, huh?" Choosing her words carefully, she began, "They are pretty fun and you can do all kinds of activities with them, but multi-headed creatures can be a challenge for first-time pet owners."

"See, Alexios?" the mother interrupted. "Even she thinks you're much too young to have such a big pet."

Jasmine pursed her lips, stifling the urge to snap back at the mother. She had avoided using the word "kids" or "child" as it sounded condescending. After all, she had first-hand knowledge that children could be independent and responsible too, as she had learned to depend on herself when she and her dad moved to America with no support system. But lecturing the woman or Alexios wouldn't do anyone any good.

"I think a young *man* like you would be up for a challenge." Jasmine mustered a serious, non-patronizing tone. "But owning a chimera is like having three pets at once. You would have to make sure you can give each creature enough attention and prevent them from fighting each other. You also need to teach the lion to hunt, ensure the goat has plenty of space to run and graze, and create the right habitat for the snake. You'll have to use all your extra time before and after school and weekends to take care of them."

His eye blinked, then he glanced up at his mother. "I guess we can find something else," he said, prompting a sigh of relief from the cyclops woman.

"All right, why don't we check out a couple pets? Do you want to look upstairs, at the aquariums? No?" She chuckled when the boy shook his head determinedly. "No pets in tanks, then? Something you can play with, but not too messy?" This time, his mom nodded. "Let's see what we have, then."

She ushered mother and son toward the lower-level pens and cages, showing them different creatures, telling them about the proper care for each one, briefly catching the mom's eye to gauge her reaction. After two rounds of agonizing, the boy eventually settled on a carbuncle kit, a cat-like creature with long ears, blue fur that glowed in the dark, and which loved shiny objects.

After bringing them around to the pet-supply section to pick up some basic supplies and then upselling a toy and treat-box subscription, she rang them up at the counter and placed the kit in its brand-new pen, before walking with them to the door.

"Thank you," his mother, whose name Jasmine learned was Nefeli, said. "For everything."

"No problem. Do you need my help with the crate?"

Nefeli shook her head and gestured to the Mercedes parked in the spot outside. "We can manage."

"Bye, Jasmine!" Alexios waved. "I'll see you soon when I come back to buy litter and food."

Jasmine gave mother and son a final wave as they secured their purchases inside their vehicle, then closed the door.

"Sorry about that," she said to Mal, who had been waiting by the counter the entire time. She could have sworn he watched her while she assisted Alexios and his mother, but then again, what else was he supposed to do? "So, what was it again you came here for?"

He shoved a hand into his hair. "I wanted to talk."

"Oh?" She focused her attention toward the display of various pet snacks on the counter, lining up the edges so they weren't sticking out of the case. "What about?"

"The store. I mean"—he paused, as if to gather his thoughts—"about what you said last night."

She didn't bother to look at him, instead continuing to fuss with the display. "And?"

"I think . . . that is . . . I could . . ." He huffed. "I suppose I could stay around for a bit. To help with the shop."

Her fingers froze halfway as she was arranging the packets to face label out. Her heart soared, but she tamped down the excitement, not wanting to be disappointed. "Oh? But what about that job you were waiting on?"

"Er, actually, I won't hear back from them for a while."

She whirled around, placing a hand on her hip. "So you really didn't have another job lined up."

"I have several, but this one—Look." He took a careful step toward her. "I went through what paperwork I had and spoke with my lawyer. Because Vrig didn't leave a will, it's going to take some time to get his affairs in order and it would be much faster if I was close by to sign off on things and make decisions right away. So I thought maybe I'd stay until all that was sorted and prepare to put the house on the market. In the meantime, you can keep running the shop and get your loan paperwork done."

Jasmine could only stare at him, slack-jawed. "R-really?"

"Yes."

"Oh!" In her giddiness, she leapt forward and wrapped her arms around him. "Thank you!" When he stiffened, however, she quickly let go and took a step back. "Sorry! I was so—"

"It's fine," he said dismissively.

She couldn't even feel hurt by his tone, not with this amazing turn of events. "But really, thank you." Oh, she wanted to cry; in fact, the tears were already welling up and her throat was getting scratchy.

Oh, for the love of the Mother Goddess, Jasmine, don't start.

She took a deep breath to clear her sinuses, and then released it. "I promise I'll have the money and the loan ready in a couple months."

"Six months," he reminded her. "You said six months."

"Yes, six months. Maybe sooner." If she really scrimped and saved.

I guess it's Lucky Three instant noodles for lunch and dinner for the foreseeable future.

Still, it would be worth it if she could stay in Dewberry Falls and own Fantastic Tails.

"If I get word on this job, though, I'll have to leave sooner," he said. "I'd still give you the six months, but the shop would have to be sold by the end of that time period. Would you be okay with that?"

"We can have a contract and everything, if you want, since you need assurances and guarantees," she suggested. "And, I promise, you don't have to do any of the work. I manage fine on my own most days anyway."

"Orcs aren't big on contracts and paperwork," he said. "I'll keep my end of the bargain."

"Right." She believed him, of course, as Vrig always kept his promises, and she only had the most basic employment contract to keep things legal and for tax purposes. Stretching her hand out toward him, she said, "Shake on it, then?"

He hesitated for a moment, staring at her hand as if it were a hot poker, but took it anyway. His massive palm engulfed her entire hand all the way up to her wrists, his grip and the touch of his rough, work-hewn skin surprisingly gentle.

"Six months," he repeated. "Not a day longer."

"Six months," she assured him, staring up into those luminous purple eyes, mesmerized by them, unable to look away. When he cleared his throat, she shook herself out of her daze and withdrew her hand. "You won't regret this."

He snorted. "I hope not."

Chapter Four

MAL

Mal dropped his duffel bag on the ground, stopping a foot short of the porch steps of the Craftsman-style home before him. It appeared to be an original from the 1930s, painted in lemon yellow and white, with a large bay window on the upper floor. Despite its age, the exterior was in excellent condition, not a surprise since Vrig had been a builder. Orcs, especially those from builder hordes, took pride in their homes. It was a testament to their skill and tradition, and known to last forever, which is why their kind were in such demand in the construction business. Custom-designed orc-built homes cost a fortune and increased in value over time. This one would be no exception.

Nonetheless this was *one more thing* he had to do to settle his uncle's estate.

Regret loomed over him like a cloud. While the pet shop was the biggest albatross around his neck, selling a whole house ranked a close second. Maybe he'd be lucky and find someone who would take the lot off his hands, but he doubted someone would buy it as-is. Buyers, after all, would want to see a home they could turn into their own, without the remnants of the old owner. Depending on what he found inside, it would take time to get it ready for selling. He would have to sift through all the knick-knacks and personal items, and then arrange to sell off the furniture, plus dismantle all the enchantments or create new ones. And since he was going to stay here for six months, it only made more sense for him to move into the house—which he owned now anyway—instead of paying for a room at the Dreametime Motel.

I should have left and let the lawyers take care of everything.

Better yet, he should have stuck to his original plan—sell the shop and walk away.

Get in, get it done, get out.

Yeah, right.

He huffed.

This is what he got for letting a pair of pretty brown doe eyes influence him.

Even though he told himself he'd hear out Jasmine's plan, the more he thought about it, the more he leaned toward rejecting her proposal. Indeed, after speaking with the probate lawyer this morning—a crafty nine-tailed kitsune named Howard Nakamoto—it didn't seem worth the trouble to stay.

"If Ms. Gonzalez has a solid business plan, then selling to her makes sense for the business's longevity. Plus, you can stay around town to sign more papers to settle Vrig's estate," Nakamoto had said. "But from a financial point of view, you'd be better off selling the inventory and the shop. The land alone would fetch a tidy sum."

Nakamoto was right. Getting rid of the lot was the practical thing to do, not to mention the Orc Historical Society could call him at any time. He should get into a taxi right now, head to the airport, and leave Dewberry Falls. He had no obligations to anyone, after all.

Yet, as he left the lawyer's office, he found himself walking to

Fantastic Tails. He told himself that he would just be a few minutes. However, seeing Jasmine inside the store, helping the cyclops boy pick a pet while treating him with kindness and respect instead of the usual condescension adults had for children, had struck something in him. Somehow, it just didn't feel right to shut everything down.

And because he'd promised her the six months or until the Historical Society wanted him—and orcs never broke a promise—he was stuck here with the pretty little human day in, day out. He'd be working alongside her, seeing her bright smile every morning, hearing her lilting voice. Smelling her sweet perfume as she passed by, hips swaying, that long rope of hair flicking invitingly down her back.

Gaku help him.

But maybe he'd hear back from the Historical Society before then. At least he hadn't completely lost his head over a pretty face. No matter the outcome, whether Jasmine got her loan or whether he sold to a corporation, he had a guarantee that he would come out on top.

Squaring his shoulders, he picked up his duffel and marched up the porch. As soon as he touched the doorknob, he heard the audible click of the deadbolt unlocking, signifying that it recognized him as the new owner. Just as he'd suspected, Vrig had used a standard blood-based locking spell that would only open for him, or in the event of his passing, his blood heir.

"Hmm . . ."

He jiggled the knob. There was a something about the magic that felt *off*, like it had been worn down. A brute-force counter spell, he guessed. Temporary, maybe lasting only an hour or two, but effective against locking spells. Jasmine had mentioned the paramedics had to break into the house the morning Vrig died. Seeing as there was a large population of magic users and creatures in Dewberry Falls, he wasn't surprised spell-casting would be standard training for an EMT around here.

Now that he was here, he would have to re-do everything to remove the remnants of the counter-spell. Better to start clean, anyway. For now, he disabled it and walked inside.

The interior was just as nice as the outside, and like the shop, it had been expanded from its original size to more comfortably accommodate an orc's larger frame. Dark, masculine colors like mahogany and ochre dominated the main living area, and a well-worn black leather sectional couch sat in front of the large flatscreen TV.

Walking over to the fireplace, Mal spotted a few knick-knacks and two picture frames. The first one was a portrait of an orc couple—Vrig's father and stepmother. The second frame held a photo of two male orcs, an older one who looked to be in his thirties, and a gangly younger teen. They were both smiling into the camera, dressed in their finest furs and leathers, standing outside the Urduk Horde's family lodge in the homelands, likely during a major celebration. The older one he recognized as Vrig. And as for the younger—he knew that lopsided smile anywhere.

Hargoth of the Urduk Horde.

His father.

Vrig was already off to college when his stepmother became pregnant, which explained why he wasn't around during Hargoth's fledgling years. Then he joined the Army Corps of Engineers, so he traveled the world for an extended period. From what Mal's mother had told him, Hargoth had very much looked up to his older brother, and when they did reunite, they acted like best friends, picking up where they left off like no time had passed.

The last time Mal had seen Vrig was at Hargoth's funeral,

and he had been quiet and somber through the whole three-day affair, staying up until the end, watching over the pyre as the last embers died on the final morning. He spoke a few words to Mal and his mother Morlak, promising to come if they should ever need him.

The first three years without his father had been tough, but they'd managed to get through it. Then when he was thirteen, Morlak met Karak and the rest was history. While Mal couldn't ask for a better father figure than Karak, there were times he wondered what would have happened if Hargoth hadn't been killed in that car accident.

Pushing those thoughts aside, Mal made his way toward the kitchen. Like the living room, it was spacious, well-maintained, and sparkling clean, except for a small desk in the corner piled with envelopes and papers. Hesitating at first, he reminded himself that all this was technically his now, and that there might be something in there that could help speed up the process of settling Vrig's estate.

As with paper contracts, orcs did not believe in wills either, and according to ancient law, all assets went to the next of kin, split equally. And because all orcs kept their word, there were no petty squabbles or court battles over inheritance. That, of course, would have been fine if they were in the homelands, but because Vrig lived and worked outside of orc territory, he was subject to the human law, which made it more complicated for Mal to simply take possession of his property as Vrig's last living relation.

All right, let's get through this.

There were two piles on the table. One consisted of bills, junk mail, official letters, bank notices. The other was a mishmash of papers of different colors and sizes. Mal picked up an oversized sheet of yellow paper that had obviously been written by a child's hand using crayons.

Dear Mr. Vrig,

Thank you for bringing us Pete today during
assembly. I learned a lot about the chamrosh,
and he has pretty wings.

Love,
Jenny Green
Second Grade
Edith Hamilton Elementary School

Underneath the writing was a drawing of what Mal assumed
was Pete the chamrosh—a creature with the head of a dog and
wings of an eagle.

There were many more letters and drawings from children on
top of the file, expressing gratitude for bringing all kinds of creatures to the elementary school during various occasions. At the
bottom of the pile were sheets of plain white paper—printed emails.

Of course Vrig still printed his emails.

Most of them sounded like they were correspondences with
his buddies from the army corps, all personal stuff, so Mal put
them aside. However, one particular email jumped out at him, or
rather, the sender's name did.

From: <u>Jasmine.gonzalez@esdamail.com</u>
To: <u>vrig.urduk@fantastictails.com</u>
Subject: Tygre pic

Hey Vrig! Here's the photo I said I'd
send to you. So adorable!!

The photo attached showed Vrig holding his hand up as a
small, blue catlike creature rested in his palm.

Unable to help himself, Mal rifled through the rest of the emails between Jasmine and Vrig. They were all friendly, mostly work-related, with pictures attached of different creatures from the pet shop or repairs that needed to be done. There was one picture that had caught his eye—it was a selfie of Jasmine and Vrig outside the shop, both of them smiling up at the camera.

"Get ouuuuuuuuuut!"

The scream lit up every danger instinct in his body and he whirled around. "What the—" He grabbed the bat that was aimed at his head and pulled it away from the assailant. "Who are—Jasmine?"

Big brown eyes grew even larger as she stared up at him, hands still raised while the rest of her remained frozen. "M-Mal?"

He lowered his arms. "What are you doing here?"

"I . . . I . . ." Color returned to her ashen face as her hands dropped to her sides. "I saw the door open and thought someone had broken in."

His blood pressure went up a few notches. "You thought someone broke in here and you brought a *bat*?" His claws raked through his hair. "What if I had been a robber? Or armed? Next time, call the police." If she had been hurt . . .

Her nostrils flared. "There wasn't any time, and I panicked. But how did you get in here? The EMTs said the counterforce spell they used would only last two hours and then the house would lock itself again."

"The locking spell recognized me as the blood heir since I own the place now."

"Blood—oh. Right." She bit at her lower lip. "I'm so sorry. I was just . . . I thought . . ."

"It's fine," he said with a grunt.

"That morning Vrig passed was the last time I was in here." As her gaze roamed around the kitchen, she ran a finger over the granite countertop. "They took his bo—him away, but I stayed.

There were dirty dishes in the sink and I couldn't just leave them there. I also threw out the trash, and there was stuff in the fridge that would go bad so I tossed that out too. I thought I would do the laundry, but . . ." Her pretty face went blank as all emotion drained out. Or not, and it was something else entirely—the processing of grief.

"Why?" he asked, not knowing what to say.

She snapped out of her trance. "Why what?"

"Why did you clean?"

"I don't know. It seemed . . . It was the right thing to do. Except for that"—she pointed at the desk overflowing with papers—"he liked everything neat and orderly."

From what Mal had seen today, Vrig didn't seem as if he had any other social interactions except for when it was related to the shop or the pets. He was obviously fond of Jasmine as well, and she of him. He was glad that in the final years of his life Vrig was not so isolated or lonely.

She inhaled a sharp breath. "Anyway . . . I suppose you're selling the house too?"

"Yeah. But I'm moving in here for now, while I get stuff sorted."

"I see. Oh." Her shoulders sagged. "I guess you're my landlord now too."

"Landlord?"

"Vrig rented me the small apartment over the garage." She jerked her thumb behind her, pointing toward the window over the kitchen sink. "I have last month's rent check ready, by the way. There's money in the bank. I didn't spend it when Vrig passed."

"R-rent check?" Somehow, his brain was still processing the idea that Jasmine was living here. Well, not here inside the house, but less than twelve feet away from where he too would be eating and sleeping and spending most of his days.

"Uh-huh." She covered her mouth with her hand. "I should have brought the check instead of a bat. Let me get it now."

"No, you don't have to—"

But she was already gone, scampering away through the back door like a spooked rabbit. He could only stand there, trying to figure out what had scared her off. Did she not realize that, aside from the shop, Vrig would have left him the house too? Or maybe she had a different thought—he would evict her the first chance he got.

That would be the rational and logical thing to do; he didn't want to be further tied down here and being a landlord was more trouble than it was worth. Besides, he doubted that Vrig had a rental contract with Jasmine either, and that might complicate things even more when he started looking for buyers. So, yes, he would have to evict her eventually.

However, as his gaze strayed back to the pile of papers, to the selfie of Vrig and Jasmine on top, he knew he couldn't just kick her out of the garage apartment. Jasmine had done right by Vrig all these years, even now after his death. Vrig would want his friend to be taken care of.

I'll tell her she can stay until the house is sold. Which won't be until he settled things with the shop anyway, so it would give her plenty of time to find somewhere else to stay.

The sound of footsteps and a soft *swish* caught his attention. A small, rectangular piece of paper now lay under the back door, likely slipped under the crack. He pulled the door open, but there was only empty air. Up ahead, a light in the small window over the garage switched on.

With a grunt, he picked up the check.

Chapter Five

JASMINE

Jasmine peeked out of the window for the hundred and twenty-fifth time, waiting for any movement from the main house.

Nothing.

She'd been watching it like a hawk since she woke up at six that morning, vigilantly scanning for signs of life.

Maybe Mal was a late riser.

In any case, the coast was clear. She grabbed her purse and keys and hurried to the door, relieved that she would not be running into him. After what happened last night, she needed to spend as little time with him as possible.

A bat, really?

The memory of it made her cringe so hard she had to stop and brace herself against the doorjamb. Once again, Mal had berated her for her foolishness, and while her automatic response was to take a defensive stance, he had been right as she could have gotten hurt if it had been a real robber inside the house. Hopefully, this was not a sign of things to come for the next six months.

Still, for this morning at least, she wouldn't have to see him.

Straightening her shoulders, she marched down the stairway leading out of the garage apartment, locked the door behind her, and made her way to Main Street.

Another beautiful day in Dewberry Falls.

The sun was out, the birds were chirping, the air was crisp and fresh, and she still had time before opening to grab a cup of coffee. As she entered Brew-tique, the comforting smell of coffee tickled her nose. Now that she was on a tight budget, she really should be making her coffee at home.

Just this one time.

And by buying a cup, she would also be supporting a small, woman-owned business, which Fantastic Tails would be soon.

As it was the morning rush, the line to order was long, but moved briskly, and so she was at the front in no time. "Hey, Minerva," she greeted the owner who stood behind the counter.

"Morning, Jasmine." Minerva Morrigan flashed her a bright smile. "Your usual?"

"Yes, please."

"One flat white, coming right up." The screen lit up with her order and Jasmine tapped her debit card on the terminal, adding in a generous tip. "Thanks."

"How's business?"

"Great. Busy, but all good." The witch took a to-go cup from the stack next to her before snapping her fingers. The paper cup floated to her left, toward the espresso machine, which blew a steady mist of steam as the lever moved on its own. While it looked as if the shop was manned by an army of invisible employees, it was actually magic that powered the operation, from the oven that warmed all the pastries and hot breakfast sandwiches, to the tables that bussed themselves.

"You know where to grab it," Minerva said.

"I do. Thanks so much."

She slid down to the end of the counter where customers

picked up their finished drinks. There were a few people lingering waiting for their orders, most of them she recognized as employees of other shops on Main Street. She nodded at them in greeting, thanking her ancestor spirits that it was much too early—and everyone still much too uncaffeinated—to be in the mood for a chat. As she waited, something caught her eye on the bulletin board on the wall—a brightly colored flyer for the upcoming Founding Day Festival.

"Oh Mother Goddess." She slapped her forehead. "I can't believe it's almost Founding Day."

"I know, right?" said the mousey—as in, she had big mouse ears, a black button nose, and whiskers—young woman next to her. Jasmine recognized her as the high-school kid who worked at the frozen yogurt shop on weekends. "It's in a couple of weeks."

The Founding Day Festival was the main summer social event of the year for the residents of Dewberry Falls. For one weekend, the entire Main Street was shut down to vehicle traffic. There were games, rides, and various food trucks set up all over the street. Businesses were also encouraged to set up booths outside their shops, and thus it was the biggest weekend for sales for many of them, including Fantastic Tails. She made a mental note to start stocking up on their best-selling accessories and start planning their specials.

"Jasmine, medium flat white!" Gary, the only other employee who worked in Brew-tique, called.

"Thanks, Gary." She picked up the cup he placed on the counter and headed out with a final wave to Minerva.

Hmmm. So good.

The coffee was hot, and the micro foam perfectly creamy. As she entered Fantastic Tails, she was in the middle of savoring another sip when she nearly choked on the brew.

"H-hello?" she sputtered at the unexpected sight of Mal, standing by the stairs leading to the second level. Dressed in his usual flannel shirt, work pants, and boots, he carried a bag of aquatic pellet feed over one shoulder. His shirt was rolled up to the elbows, showing off the sinewy muscles of his forearms.

A jolt of heat zapped straight to her belly. Oh Mother Goddess, how could one strip of bare green skin affect her? Now she understood the term "forearm porn."

Turning his head toward her, he let out a grunt. "Morning."

The indigo of his eyes startled her. Despite the early hour, they were alert and fixed on her. "W-what are you doing here?" She placed her things on the counter, turned the lights on and the music up, and then strode over to him.

"I thought you said you wanted me to help out around here."

"Yes, but I didn't think you would be here today." The events of last night flooded her brain once more, but she resisted the urge to visibly cringe. "I mean, obviously you're allowed to be here anytime you want."

"So what's the problem?"

Did he have to be so grumpy so early in the morning? "N-nothing at all, but"—she wrinkled her nose—"what are you doing?"

"What does it look like I'm doing?" He motioned to the bag over his shoulder. "I'm feeding the animals. I ran out of the first bag so I grabbed this one from the shelf." Without another word, he trudged up the steps, taking them two at a time.

"Which . . . ones?" she huffed as she chased after him. "And how much?"

"I just started over here." He gestured to the front row of water tanks. "And I dunno, a cup each? I read the directions on the package."

She pressed her lips together, then blew out a breath. "You should have waited for me. I have a system to keep track of everything."

Side-stepping him, she marched over to the tanks, reaching

for the clipboard hanging on the shelf. She pointed to the page on top. "Each tank and each type of creature has a specific time and amount they need to be fed, which also changes depending on how many of them are in the tank."

"I didn't see that."

She bit at her lip as she read through the list. "Okay, it's not too bad. The luscas got their breakfast a little too early and the kelpies should get another cup, but other than that everyone in this row should be fine with a cup each." She nodded at the bag he held up. "Do you mind?"

Hefting it lower, he opened the top so she could scoop a cup and drop the food into the kelpie tanks. The hungry little fellows galloped toward the surface, sucking up the pellets as they drifted downwards. "There you go."

Mal scratched at his mop of ink-black hair. "They make automatic feeders for tanks these days. With timers and everything."

"I know. Vrig used them before, but I prefer to do it myself. My system works."

"Doesn't seem efficient. You have the information about how much each tank gets and when. Just program the feeders once and you won't have to worry about doing it again."

"It isn't always about efficiency." She hung the clipboard back on the hook, then proceeded further down to the next row of tanks. "This way, I can perform a check on the animals and the individual aquariums first thing in the morning, in case any of them got sick overnight or if there's something wrong with the tanks."

"But you have cameras all over the place and in the individual pens."

"You've already checked the pens? What time did you get here?" She was pretty sure she had started checking the house for signs of him the moment she woke up.

"Around five a.m.?"

"You've been here since five in the morning?"

"I'm an early riser," he stated.

"Right." She took another clipboard hanging from the next row. "Now, the creatures in this section are all herbivores, so they'll need a different type of feed. It's that tub up there."

"This one?" He plucked the white plastic container with a cartoonish depiction of a smiling seaweed-like mascot on the label from the high shelf behind him.

"Yup."

When she held out her hand to take it, he shook his head. "I'll do it."

"I can manage it." She'd been doing it on her own all these years, after all.

"Just tell me how much each one gets."

"But—"

"This is still my shop, right?"

"Yes." But he didn't have to rub it in her face.

"It'll be faster if I help you. Besides, what if you couldn't come in and I had to do this by myself?"

Well, he had a point there. "All right, you can help with the feeding."

Mal trudged to the nearest tank, which contained a four-legged creature with a bulbous head that had two horns protruding out its sides and tusks peeking from its mouth. A long, fish-like tail swished behind it as it approached the front of the aquarium.

"How many cups for this guy?"

"Don't get too—!"

Before she could stop him, he tapped his foreclaw on the tank. The creature let out an angry grunt before ramming its head against the glass. The tank was shatterproof, but the poor thing was still upset.

Mal jumped back, nearly colliding with the shelf. "What in Vorlak's name is that thing?"

"It's a makara. Very territorial, especially at this age."

"People actually want to buy that thing?" he asked in an incredulous tone.

"Once they imprint on an owner, they make excellent house guardians, and are very good with young children. They're one of our bestsellers." Bending down, she peered into the glass to check on the makara. "Don't worry," she cooed. "That big guy didn't mean to scare you."

He blew out a breath. "*He's* scared?"

"She," she corrected. "Can you give me half a cup, please?"

"Fine. Here you go."

Being an amphibious creature, the makara's tank consisted of a floating island surrounded by water. Jasmine poured the contents of the cup Mal handed to her into a chute above the tank, letting the pellets pile on top of the sandy beach area.

"He made that, didn't he? Vrig, I mean."

"Yes." Her gaze remained fixed on the creature as she carefully approached the pile of food. After a few sniffs, she began to chomp down heartily. "I suggested we start stocking makaras since they're in demand. So he designed and crafted this tank. They come to us as eggs and we take care of them until they're about eight weeks old. At around ten weeks they start imprinting with their surroundings and their handlers permanently."

To her surprise, Mal had bent down next to her. "How old is this one?"

"We've had her about seven weeks, so her owner will be stopping by in a couple of days to pick her up." Her focus changed from the makara to Mal's reflection against the glass, his indigo eyes tracking the creature as it dove into the water after finishing its meal. With his face relaxed and the scowl gone, he looked even more striking. She glanced down at his lips, even the pointy little tusks protruding from between them, wondering if they hurt when he kissed someone.

A hot flush crept up her cheeks, and Jasmine quickly stood up. "Er, let's keep going, shall we?"

They continued down the next rows of aquatic creatures, with Jasmine explaining to Mal every creature's dietary needs. He didn't say much, just small grunts and "hmms" here and there, but for some reason, she couldn't help but feel he was judging her.

After an hour, they'd finished the entire floor and she hung the last clipboard back onto its hook.

"All done," she declared. "See, with my system everyone gets what they need, when they need it."

"What about you? When do you get what you need?"

She spun around to face him. "Excuse me?"

"I mean, you need rest. You don't work every day, do you?"

"Of course not—we're closed on Tuesdays."

"Who takes care of the pets?"

"We work with a gnome temp agency that comes in and makes sure all the creatures are fed and the pens are cleaned." Gnomes were trustworthy, after all, and known for their love of animals.

"Ah, that's smart."

"And efficient," she emphasized, using his own words. "Once Vrig installed their magic door, they just come in when we need them and take care of everything."

He tapped a claw at his chin. "Hmmm."

"What is it?"

"The filtration system on the tanks, how old are they?"

"Er, probably as old as the shop?" she answered sheepishly.

"What?" His eyes widened.

"I've been asking Vrig for about two years, but he always says the shop doesn't have the budget to upgrade it. So I clean and change the filters out more often."

Mal's mouth pulled back into a line. "Vrig was not hurting

for money. He owns this lot and paid off the mortgage on his house last year, plus he has no other debt."

"I don't know anything about the house," she said. "But our expenses are quite high. Food alone is about sixty to seventy per cent of the costs."

"And you want to own this place, when it's barely making a profit?"

She opened her mouth, then quickly pressed her lips together. His tone sounded familiar—too familiar.

Why are your grades so low, Jasmine? You'll never get into a good nursing program.

Jasmine, why didn't you finish your degree?

You could be making so much more money as a nurse, Jasmine.

Her father, of course, had meant well. After all, he had given up his entire life in the Philippines, leaving behind everything and everyone he'd ever known, to give her a better future in the United States.

"Jasmine?"

She snapped out of her trance. "It's not all about the money, you know."

He let out an impatient snort. "Maybe I should check on those accounts."

"Maybe you should." She cocked her head toward the staircase. "Everything's in the office back downstairs."

"Fine." Turning on his heel, he lumbered away from her.

Once his frame had disappeared down the staircase, Jasmine found she could breathe again and released her pent-up outrage with a quick exhale.

Mother Goddess help her.

Vrig might have pinched a few pennies here, but not to the detriment of the animals in his care. Would Mal be as miserly as a troll? She sure hoped not because she'd had a troll boss before, and it had been unbearable.

Six months, she told herself. He'll be gone in six months.

Jasmine had no choice but to put up with him for now. Once she got her loan, he'd be gone and she'd own this place clear and easy, with no meddling orc to mess up her system, make "helpful" suggestions, or send her judgy looks.

Hopefully, she'd be able to make it through the next couple of months without taking a baseball bat to his head for a second time.

Chapter Six

MAL

Mal pushed away from the desk and the monitor, and began to massage his temple with his thumb and fore claw. He'd just finished looking at the accounts and . . . things weren't looking great.

Just like the house, the computer unlocked for him since it recognized him as the new owner of Fantastic Tails. The first thing he did was examine the books. It wasn't terrible, but the shop barely made any money. Vrig didn't take any salary or withdraw any profit. He didn't need to as his mortgage on the house was paid off and his pension was more than enough to live on. Jasmine's salary was pitiful, and perhaps the only reason she could live off it was the below-average rent Vrig charged her for the studio over his garage.

Why she even wanted this place, he didn't know.

She loved the shop and the animals, that was for sure. It was evident from how she cared for the various creatures and gave each one special attention. She barely had to look at her clipboards as she explained what they required. There was something about the way she spoke and moved that had him mesmerized.

The animals, too, were naturally drawn to her, even calmed by her presence.

Yes, she seemed born to run this shop. It just didn't make any sense from a business standpoint *why* she would want to. It would struggle if it continued like this, and she would be forced to cut corners or obtain more loans or even take a lower salary. And if things didn't improve, then she might be forced to shut down the entire thing.

I could still sell everything.

Get in, get it done, get out.

It might even be the best thing for Jasmine, to mitigate her losses. Legally, there would be nothing she could do about it if he sold the lot tomorrow. She had no idea how orc law worked, and technically they weren't subject to it since they were outside the homelands.

However, Vrig would be disappointed, and so would his father, not to mention his mother, stepfather, and basically all of orc society would shun him if he went back on his word now. He himself couldn't stomach the idea of breaking a promise. So he would have to stick to their agreement.

In any case, whether he sold the shop to Jasmine or to another company in six months, he'd still come out on top. But somehow, the thought of leaving her on her own to pilot what was essentially a sinking ship didn't sit quite right with him.

Not like I could do anything about it.

At this point, the barest minimum he could do was keep his word, occasionally helping out as she'd said. He could also stop charging her for the apartment, but she would probably shoot down that idea. Jasmine didn't seem the type to accept charity, even in the form of free rent. There was nothing else he could do, and he wasn't about to invest in the shop himself.

Of course, he could make things easier for her.

A few upgrades here and there wouldn't hurt.

He could do some of the work himself, plus use his contacts in the industry for materials. He'd done a job for a finfolk family and met the architect who constructed their home—a huge aquarium mansion half sunken into the sea—who could probably get him a discount on some high-quality water filters that wouldn't need to be replaced so often. Taking his phone out of his pocket, he typed a quick message to the contact on his phone that he had saved as "Bob Hallow Architect."

The locking spells on the pens upstairs also needed refreshing or even an upgrade. Vrig was a master builder and spell-caster, but probably hadn't kept up with the latest developments in the craft. Mal knew of some newer incantations that would help improve the security of each pen.

Rising from the chair, he made his way out of the back office, making a mental list of the things he could do. With everything that had happened in the last couple of days— finding out about Vrig's death, coming here, sorting out the legal stuff—it was actually a relief to have something to do. Building was in his blood and soul, and he truly was happiest when he was busy.

There was no sign of Jasmine, though he could hear her shuffling about upstairs, probably "correcting" any other mistakes he'd made. He hadn't meant to mess things up, but he'd been bored waiting for her to come in this morning, so decided to start feeding the aquatic animals, not knowing she already had a system in place.

Looking at the rows of pens and cages, he rolled up his sleeves. He'd leave mealtimes to her, but this—spell-crafting and building—was his specialty. Starting with the first row, he ran his hands over each cage. They all had the same kind of old-fashioned locking spell, something an old-timer like Vrig would have used. It was effective, but over time it needed to be refreshed every six months. He would also have had to weave in an addendum spell to give Jasmine access, likely using a drop of her blood or a lock of her hair to activate it.

Mal had recently begun using a newer spell, one he learned at a week-long spellbinding seminar last year. His clients had all been pleased with the more advanced magic, as it only required refreshing after a couple of years and it was transferrable, which reduced the need for Mal to travel back to their location. The owner, if they were magically inclined, could also take possession of the lock or have a local trusted warlock or even a sorcerer refresh it for them. That might have been bad business for Mal, since he couldn't charge a maintenance fee, but spell-casting had never been his favorite part of the job anyway.

He stood in front of the very first pen—one that contained a cerberus pup snoozing in the back—and wrapped his hand over the latch. He whispered the words, allowing the magic to flow from his soul to his fingers. Orcs were not powerful magic wielders like witches and wizards, but his ancestors were able to harness what magical affinity they did have toward their strengths, like warfare, hunting, farming, or in his case, building.

As the magic began to settle, he murmured Jasmine's name, conjuring up an image of her in his head. That's all he needed to ensure she could open the pen without any trouble. Carefully, he twisted the latch, opening the door a crack to test it, then closed it again.

Satisfied with his work, he moved to the next pen, or rather, a cage. There were three or four flying creatures in it, but he couldn't quite recognize what they were.

Shrugging, he placed his hand over the latch and began to recite the spell, repeating what he'd done with the cerberus pen. As he said Jasmine's name, he once again thought of her, though this time, his mind wandered to the first time they'd met, when she'd fallen into his arms. How soft her body was against his, and her big brown eyes—

A low vibration from his pocket interrupted his thoughts. Quickly, he fished his phone out. The caller ID on the screen read "Bob Hallow Architect."

"Hey, Bob," he greeted.

"Mal, it's been a while. How are ya, mate?"

"Doing good. Yeah, it has been a long time. How are the kids?" He recalled Bob liked small talk, so even though Mal wasn't a fan of idle chit-chat, he understood that it was part of doing business.

"Growing like weeds. The little one, Maureen, is just about ready to start walking. Tristan's almost as tall as me, and he's only fourteen. Wife complains he's eating us out of house and home. And Katy, she's a firecracker, that one. Came in second in her last karate tournament in Canberra—"

"Yeah, that sounds great. You must be so proud." He closed the door behind him. "So, listen, remember that job we worked on in Caithness?"

"For the finfolk fam? Sure do. What about it?"

"I was wondering if you could put me in touch with your water-filtration supplier?"

"You working on another aqua mansion?"

"No, nothing that big," Mal chuckled. "Just a couple of aquariums."

"Ah, I see. Yeah, I can send you their number and give them a heads-up."

"You will? Amazing. Thanks, Bob."

"Anything for you, mate. I'll text you the number." There was a crash in the background, followed by a cry. "Whoops, I think little Maureen just discovered the corner of the coffee table. Gotta go. Great talking to you, Mal."

"Thanks so much, Bob."

Mal sighed with relief. *One call down, and—*

A shriek coming from the main floor sent every nerve in his body into full alert.

Jasmine!

What in Vorlak's name could she have done now?

Mal nearly ripped the office door off its hinges as he raced out to the main shop floor. "Jasmine, what's going—"

A feather landed on his nose as a flying blur whizzed right above his head. The urge to sneeze was unbearable, but thankfully he managed to brush off the plume in time. "Jasmine?"

"Help me!" She scrambled up to the counter, desperately grasping at something perched on the shelf above her.

"What did you do?" he roared.

"This isn't my—Just grab the other one, and whatever happens, don't let them go outside!"

The urgency in her voice spurred him into action. He followed the first creature he saw into the main room, spying it above a shelf full of soft chew toys near the back. As he stomped over to where it was, he grabbed a bug net hanging from the display, ripping off the plastic packaging.

"Here, here, little one," he called.

"Don't stare at it," she warned. "They're mini cockatrices, so they can't kill you, but they can put you in a coma."

"Cocka—" He rubbed a hand down his face, not even wanting to know *why* they stocked these animals. "All right, come here you . . ."

As the creature jerked its rooster-like head side to side, he avoided its gaze, focusing on its lizard-like body. Holding his breath, he quickly swatted at it, but it moved too fast, the bug net smacking against the shelf.

"Fuck!" Mal swung around to follow the animal as it flew across the room. He dashed over, net raised high and swung. "Gotcha!"

It let out an angry cry as it struggled against the net. He was just congratulating himself as he put it back in the pen when he heard Jasmine's cry once more.

"The door!"

Jasmine's eyes widened as the front door opened a crack. With a snap of his fingers, Mal shut the door and locked it. The would-be customer outside pushed repeatedly, but it didn't budge.

"We're closed!" he shouted, running toward Jasmine, who remained on the counter. "Is it still up there?"

She nodded to where a long, scaly tail hung down from the top of the shelf. "Cockatrices actually can't fly very high, but once they get up there, they don't want to come down."

"I see. I should be able to get it." The shelf was only a foot taller than him, so he easily reached up, grasped the tail and pulled the cockatrice down, ignoring its angry squawks.

"I got it!" Jasmine opened her arms.

"No!" His hearts stopped as she caught it. "Don't look—"

"I'm fine." The cockatrice ceased struggling as she placed a hand over its eyes.

"Do you have a death wish or something?" His stomach twisted at the thought of what could have happened if she'd caught it from the wrong end. "You could have been hurt, you reckless fool."

She clucked her tongue. "I told you, it can only put you in a coma."

"Only a coma?" Gaku help him, he might not survive the next six months.

"Besides, cockatrices have never been a problem for me. There, there now," she soothed. "Let's get you back to your cage, huh?"

"What do you mean 'never been a problem'?"

She shrugged her shoulders. "It's weird, but their gazes don't affect me for some reason."

"They don't?" That was weird indeed. Full-sized cocktrices— about the size of an ostrich—truly could kill anyone.

"Yeah. That's why we started stocking them. Vrig originally

ordered one for a customer—a gorgon lady from Oregon. Apparently, they have a high-pitched song that gorgons love that only they can hear, plus they already wear these special glasses that prevent them from turning anyone into stone. I was cleaning the cage one day, and I didn't know what it was and Vrig tried to warn me, but I looked it in the eyes and . . . nothing."

"You didn't fall into a coma?" Mal asked, puzzled.

"No. Maybe I felt a little sleepy, but aside from that I was fine. This gorgon lady was so happy she recommended us to her family and friends and now we get orders every couple of months, so Vrig always made sure we have one or two ready since they take forever to hatch. Anyway, can you help me?"

"Huh?" The revelation that Jasmine was immune to cockatrices still had his head reeling. "Help you with what?"

"Getting down from here?" With both her hands secured around the cockatrice, she had no way to safely lower herself to the floor.

"Right." Without a second thought, he took hold of her waist and plucked her off the counter. The scent of her sweet perfume teased his nose, their gazes locking as he set her down, their bodies brushing together in the briefest of touches. Her pretty plump lips parted as she inhaled sharply, and his hands lingered on her for a second longer than necessary—and perhaps, a second shorter than he wanted—before dropping to his sides.

"Th-thank you." Moving past him, she trotted over to the cockatrice cage to return the creature to its home. "I don't know what would happen if they got out again."

"Again?"

The cage latched closed with an audible click. "Er, yeah . . . about that . . ." Jasmine bit at her lip. "They escaped a while back and kind of, er, ran across Main Street."

"They already escaped before?" What else had happened here on her watch?

"The delivery guy was new, and he accidentally dropped the cage as he brought them inside. The door was propped open and—*whoosh!*" Her hands gesticulated dramatically, fingers fluttering toward the outside. "Vrig and I had to chase them down, but not before one of them stunned Alice Vanderpelt into a coma. The Main Street Business Association gave us a first warning. Once you get three, you have to pay a fine." Her dark eyebrows knitted together. "What I don't get is, how did they escape this time? Refreshing the locking spells was the last thing Vrig did before he passed. They shouldn't need one so soon."

Vrig wouldn't have forgotten or done a shoddy job. "Maybe the locking—"

That call from Bob came as he was finishing the spell and Mal couldn't recall saying the final words to complete it.

Mother Trakku.

But not even the Great Orc Mother of Creation herself could help him out of this mess.

It was his fault.

"Mal?" She cocked her head to the side. "What were you about to say?"

The urge to avert his gaze to avoid those big brown eyes was strong, but he didn't dare. He refused to lie to her. "It was me. I was in the middle of upgrading the locking spell for the cockatrice cage when I answered a call."

The expression on her face shifted from confusion to realization and then to displeasure. "So you're telling me it's *your* fault the cockatrices escaped."

"Yes."

"And yet your first thought was that it was something *I* did?" Those soft brown eyes turned ablaze. "B-because I've been messing everything up at this point, right?"

"Jasmine, no—"

Her nostrils flared. "If you'll excuse me, I need to finish some work upstairs." She turned on her heel, hands balled into tight fists, then stomped up the stairs.

Something hot stuck in his throat and his belly churned and twisted. Was there anything lower than dirt? Because that's how Mal felt right now. He scrubbed his palm down his face and groaned aloud.

He'd screwed up, big time.

Chapter Seven

JASMINE

Jasmine took in a deep breath, inhaling the savory and sour sharpness of the soup inside the pot. Okra, sliced radish, shishito peppers, and eggplant floated to the top as her wooden spoon stirred the contents. Sinigang was a favorite comfort food, bringing up memories from her childhood she desperately did not want to lose, of afternoons sitting in the kitchen, watching her grandmother bent over the stove as she dropped the ingredients into the large pot. The compound they lived in was home to multitudes of Gonzalezes—uncles, aunts, cousins, and second cousins and even more distant relatives. Sunday dinners were sacred for the clan and always held at the ancestral house where her grandfather and grandmother lived. While most individual families had their own houses within the compound, Jasmine and her father had moved in with her grandparents after her mother had died giving birth, and so her Lola Marisol had practically raised her.

Jasmine used a fork to poke at an okra floating on the surface. Much too firm, but that was no problem as she had some time before Kap arrived, so she turned the heat down. It was still light outside, and he wouldn't be waking up until the sun began to set. She'd messaged him this afternoon, asking if he wanted to have dinner at her place. Even though he'd been in the middle of his sleep, he'd managed to reply with a thumbs-up.

It would be nice to have him around. They weren't confidants who shared everything, not that Jasmine ever had that kind of friendship with anyone, but she just didn't want to be alone with her thoughts and the chatty tree giant would ensure she wouldn't even have time to think about what had happened this afternoon.

Instead of cringing, outrage bubbled up in her chest like the soup on her stove. Sure, she hadn't exactly made the best decisions in her life and she did screw up every now and then, but to have Mal scold her like a little girl when it had been his fault in the first place? That was completely uncalled for. She could barely hold in her anger, and the only reason she didn't tear him a new one was she remembered he was still technically the owner of Fantastic Tails and her landlord.

Jasmine considered herself a patient person, but she had her limits. And this was only day one.

Would she even make it to six months?

Maybe she wasn't cut out to be a business owner.

Maybe I should just give up and leave.

A knock at the door jolted her from her thoughts. Looking out the window, the sky was painted in the pinks and purples of dusk, which meant Kap should be rousing from his sleep right about now. Perhaps he woke up early.

Or he was hungry.

Kap survived mostly on takeout and pizza and couldn't cook to save his life. The prospect of a home-cooked meal would definitely be a good incentive to come over sooner.

"Coming!" she called as a second knock came. She scurried down the stairs and threw the door open. "You must be starving if—Mal?"

For a split second, she thought she was imagining things. No, it was definitely Mal. He stood in front of her door, his humungous body filling up the entire frame.

"Uh, good evening, Jasmine."

Refusing to look him in the eye, she focused on his chest instead. He was the last person she wanted to see right now. She'd spent the rest of the day upstairs at the shop while he remained on the ground floor, as if they'd drawn a border between the two levels that neither dared to cross. Fortunately, she had some granola bars stashed up there or she would have starved come lunchtime.

"What are you doing here?" Of course, he did own the house and the garage, so he had every right to be outside her door.

"May I speak with you, please?"

Her first instinct was to slam the door in his face. However, the words caught her off-guard, not to mention the tone of his voice—somber, maybe even penitent—and the way his shoulders hunched over made her pause. Glancing up, she met his purple gaze. "Speak about what?"

"I want to apologize for what happened today."

Now *that* she didn't expect.

"I'm sorry," he continued. "I'm really sorry. I messed up and you're right."

Was she hearing him correctly? He was actually apologizing? "Right about what?"

"I jumped to conclusions. That it was your fault."

"That's fine." Her fingers fiddled with the hem of her shirt. "You probably think I can't do this. And maybe I can't."

"No, no." He shook his head. "I don't think that at all."

"You don't?"

"I don't, but . . ." He scratched at his head with a claw. "Have you ever run a business? Do you know what's going on? Specifically, with the shop?"

"What do you mean?"

He hesitated for a moment. "It's not doing too well. Barely makes money most months, and Vrig didn't take a salary or withdraw any profit, but he didn't need to with his pension. Once you take over, you could probably make it work for a few months, maybe cut a few things here and there. But one major expense or repair could put you behind."

"I know that." Or she had an inkling, at least. "I didn't have access to the books, but he was always transparent about the costs, especially when I asked about doing some upgrades or hiring more staff. Like I mentioned when you asked about the water-filtration system, he told me there wasn't enough money for anything extra."

"And you still want to run this business?"

"Yes, I do." The words came out of her mouth without hesitation.

His eyebrows knitted together. "Why?"

Why indeed?

"I know it may seem foolish to you, since there's no guarantee I could even keep the shop if I bought it. But . . ." Jasmine pressed her lips together, then blew out a breath. "Have you ever felt like you had to do something? Want to do it so bad that there's no alternative and you couldn't see yourself doing anything else?"

His face sobered. "Yes."

"That's how I feel about Fantastic Tails. And this town even." She wrapped her arms around herself, rubbing at her elbows. "I've always felt like I never belonged anywhere, even as a kid. Then my dad brought us to America and everything here was strange and new. We moved around a lot before I could even settle down and plant roots. But when I arrived here in town and started working at the shop, I don't know . . ." While she hadn't meant to make such a confession, it all spilled out of her and she couldn't stop. "It felt like what a home should be."

Mal didn't respond for a heartbeat. "I think I understand."

"You do?"

"Yeah." He ground his teeth together, his tusks gnawing at his lips. "Look, if you're determined to run this place, I'll do my best to help you while I'm here, okay? And I hope you accept my apology."

If it were possible, her jaw would have unhinged itself and dropped to her feet. "I accept."

"Good. And for the record, I don't think you're incapable of running a business. I'm sure you'd be successful at anything you tried."

"Thanks." She let out a sigh. "I just wish it were easier. I've been going cross-eyed trying to figure out the paperwork to get the loan started."

"You're smart. You'll figure it out. And I promise, when—not if—you secure that loan, I'll buy you a bottle of champagne."

"I'll hold you to that."

"An orc keeps his word."

There was the smallest tug at the corner of his mouth, but before she could remark on it, their gazes locked once more. The indigo in his eyes intensified, making it impossible to look away. A bead of sweat trickled down between her breasts, and she recalled how big and warm his hands had been on her waist earlier today when he'd picked her up from the counter. And how she had slid along his long, hard body . . .

"Yo, Jasmine, I'm starving! Is that soup ready yet?"

Though Mal's large frame blocking her view prevented her from seeing the speaker, she recognized that voice. "Hey, Kap."

"'Scuse me, passing through."

Mal's entire body stiffened before he stepped aside.

"Thanks, man." The tree giant was more or less the same height as Mal, though not as wide and definitely much hairier, with long, dark locks flowing down past his shoulders and fur peeking out from the sleeves of his uniform shirt and the top of his collar. His light-yellow eyes darted curiously from Jasmine to Mal. "I didn't realize you'd invited another guest."

"Kap, this is Mal," she introduced. "He's Vrig's nephew and the new owner of Fantastic Tails. And the house, of course."

"I'm Kap." He held out his hand. "Sorry for your loss, man. Vrig was a cool guy."

"Thanks," Mal muttered, shaking his hand.

"Are you staying for dinner?" Kap asked.

"No—" he began.

"He was—" Jasmine said at the same time. After a beat of silence, she spoke up. "I mean, there's enough food." Hospitality was practically embedded into her soul; back in her grandparents' house, if a neighbor or friend came by on a Sunday night, they would automatically be invited to stay for dinner. Her ancestor spirits would riot if she didn't at least offer. "Won't you join us?"

"No, I've already eaten. Jasmine, I'll see you tomorrow." Without another word, he turned around and lumbered back toward the house.

Jasmine bit her lip, torn between calling after him and staying put.

"Oh man," Kap exclaimed, sniffing the air. "I can smell that sinigang from here. Are we ready to eat?"

She smiled at him wryly, and put her boss out of her thoughts. "Almost. C'mon, let's go inside."

Jasmine climbed the stairs, Kap lumbering behind her. Thankfully both the stairway and the apartment above the garage had been expanded to accommodate orcs, so Kap didn't have to bend down or hunch over to fit inside.

"The rice is ready." The small rice cooker on the counter puffed out steam, the green "Keep Warm" light turned on. "But the sinigang needs a few more minutes."

"Oh boy." He rubbed his hands together as he lumbered over to the stove. "Yum. Just like home."

"Home" for Kap was the suburbs of Chicago, where his grandparents had settled after they immigrated from the Philippines. Kap was second generation American, as he and his parents were born in the US. Friendly and affable, Jasmine had basically heard his entire life story ten minutes after they first met at Brewtique, a few weeks after she'd first arrived in Dewberry Falls.

Jasmine had had to come into the shop at five a.m. to check on the makara eggs, so she had stopped to grab a coffee when Kap walked in after his night shift with the Dewberry Falls Police Department. Though she recognized what he was—a kapre or tree giant—she'd been surprised to see one of his kind here. Back home, they had neighbors who were tree giants, but they rarely mingled with humans. They mostly kept to themselves, barely leaving their nesting grounds. He must have realized she was staring at him, and though at first she was scared he would tell her off, he actually introduced himself and they'd been friends ever since.

"I think the okra's done, so let me put in the water spinach then we can eat soon. Could you please get the table ready?" As she began to drop handfuls of the leafy green vegetable into the pot, Kap busied himself with grabbing the plates, utensils and then scooping the rice into a serving bowl before sitting down.

"Here you go." Jasmine placed the pot on the table and sat down, folding her hands together to give thanks to her ancestor spirits. "Let's eat."

"I've been looking forward to this since I woke up." Kap's eyes greedily took in the food as he served her some rice. "So, seems I've missed a lot in the last couple days. Who knew Vrig had a nephew?"

"Maybe if you were awake during the day, you'd hear all the gossip."

He raised a dark eyebrow. "Is there gossip?"

"What?" She hoped her tone didn't sound too defensive. "No. No gossip."

Kap scooped some soup into a bowl and then handed it to her. "So, tell me about this Mal."

"There's not much to tell." But she did owe her friend a recap of what had happened the last couple of days, so she told him everything, including her agreement with Mal.

"Wait, you're going to own Fantastic Tails?" He swallowed a mouthful of food. "That's great, Jasmine. That means you'll stay, right?"

"I don't own it yet," she reminded him. "And yes, if everything goes through—the loan, the sale, etc.—I'll be able to stay here in Dewberry Falls."

"Good. 'Cause you're, like, my only friend around here."

"No, I'm not."

"I mean, the only friend who can cook adobo and sinigang," he said with a chuckle. "But seriously, once you own the place, maybe your dad will stop harassing you about finishing your nursing degree or moving back to the east coast."

While Kap had been quick to share his entire history with Jasmine, she had been more cautious, though after a couple of years, he had picked up on a lot of things.

"My dad doesn't harass me," she protested.

He took a hearty sip of the soup, tipping the bowl into his mouth before placing it back on the table with a loud plonk. "Look, I like Tito Jed." Kap had met her dad last year when he'd come to Dewberry Falls for a visit. "But he's gotta lay off. Nursing's not for you, and he needs to accept that."

"That's easy for you to say—your parents have always supported you. I bet your grandparents were harsh on them."

"Yeah, they were. My dad's parents especially. Their dream was for him to become a lawyer or doctor, but he wanted to run a business instead. Then he got engaged to a tree giant—oh man, they nearly disinherited him. But he loved my mom so much so he defied them again. And see, now he and my mom own one of Chicago's biggest Asian grocery stores. Look, I'm sure your dad had good reasons to come here, but parents can't impose their dreams on their children."

Talking about parents always brought up that one thing Jasmine hated to think about. But ever since the possibility of losing everything she'd built in Dewberry Falls came about, she had no choice, really. Even talking to Mal about finding that place where she belonged brought it to the forefront.

She always thought that her father had come to America to give her a better life. That's what he'd told her and what everyone assumed. While partly true, she knew the real reason, and this was the secret that loomed over her head, casting a cloud over their relationship.

It was just after her grandfather's funeral, when she was about eight or nine years old. She was helping clean up the kitchen when she'd overheard her father and uncle arguing outside the door.

"*You know why you weren't chosen, Jed.*"

"*It's not fair,*" Jed had said. "*It's because of Jasmine, isn't it? The Inheritance should have been passed to me. I showed the most aptitude for it.*"

"*It's not her fault, you know, but Papa had no choice.*"

Yes, they left for America for a better life, but Jasmine knew it was also because Jed couldn't accept that he had lost what was rightfully his.

And he'd lost it because of her.

Or rather, because of what she was *not*.

"Jasmine, are you okay?"

"Uh, yeah." She swallowed hard. "I think I made the soup too sour."

"What are you talking 'bout? It's perfect. Just like Dad's." He poured himself another bowl. "I can take home the leftovers, right?"

She chuckled, glad Kap was here to keep her company for tonight. "Of course you can. Now, did you solve that case with Mrs. Palmer's missing ring?"

Kap groaned. "Oh, right. Turns out, her pet crow had taken it."

"Really?" She, too, poured herself another bowl, burying thoughts of the past deep inside. "Tell me what happened."

Chapter Eight

JASMINE

The next few days at Fantastic Tails were relatively quiet and normal for Jasmine. She arrived at work, went through her usual routine of checking on the animals, ordering stock, packing and sending out their online orders, preparing their subscription boxes, and of course, entertaining customers. In all that time, she hardly saw Mal at all. He continued to come in before she did in the morning and mostly stayed in the back office, emerging only to get lunch or leave for the day, usually an hour or two before she closed up. He would wave or nod to her, but didn't speak, and there was a distinct impersonal coldness about him that she could perceive.

Jasmine supposed she should be grateful. He was no longer trying to tell her what to do or how to run the shop. Still, after their talk, a small part of her had hoped he would be more pleasant to be around.

Or that he would be more around *her*.

There was a moment, after he'd apologized and told her that he believed she could be successful, that she thought maybe he was going to lean down and—

Don't be silly.

Mal was her boss and her landlord. He was only staying for a short while, then their business relationship would be over, and she would never see him again.

"Argh!" She tapped furiously on the "enter" key on the keyboard of the computer, but the program refused to load. "What the—*oh.*"

The pop-up on the screen flashed: "Authorization Code Required for Additional Orders." Jasmine had been attempting to order more stock for the upcoming Founding Day Festival, but since it was over her usual amount, she needed Vrig's code.

Or rather, Mal's code.

She propped her hip against the counter and groaned. There was no getting around this one. She would have to go to him.

Jasmine ignored the sinking feeling in her stomach. She raked a hand through her loose locks, pushing her hair away from her face. She'd had a late start this morning and didn't have time to blow dry it, so she'd left it down. After spending a minute searching for a rubber band in the drawer under the counter, she found none. With no other delaying tactics available, she decided to put on her big-girl pants and go to Mal.

I can do this.

Her feet somehow made the trip all the way to the back office without retreating or stopping. With a hesitant knock, she called out, "Hello? Mal?"

"Come in."

The hinges creaked as she pushed inside. "Hey, Mal. Uh, good morning."

"What is it?" He sat behind the desk, eyes glued to the computer screen.

"I need your code." So, this was how it was going to be for the next few months. No pleasantries, all business. She told herself she preferred it that way.

"Code?" His head turned toward her, his purple gaze pinning her to the spot. "What code?"

"Your master code for our ordering system. I can't finish up because it's over the usual monthly amount."

Mal frowned. "Why do you need to order more stuff this month?"

"It's for the Founding Day Festival."

"And?"

Oh right. He had no idea what that was. "Every year Dewberry Falls has a big festival to celebrate the founding of the town. During that weekend, there's a big parade and Main Street is closed to cars and the businesses go all out. It's one of Fantastic Tails's biggest weekends in terms of sales, so I have to make sure we have enough stock to keep up with the demand."

"I see." Rising from the desk, he circled it to lumber toward her. "All right, let's get you that order."

He followed her as she led him to the counter in front. "Just enter it there."

Bending down, he tapped the keyboard. "There."

The bright chirp from the computer told Jasmine the order had gone through. "Whew. Thanks, Mal. Today was the last day for me to order to get everything in on time."

"You're welcome." He drummed his claws on the table. "Jasmine, I—"

Ding ding dong!

Jasmine immediately shifted into customer-service mode as the familiar bell rang out. "Welcome to Fantastic Tails and—Oh." She smiled at the woman who strode in. "Good morning, Mrs. Howard."

Ellen Howard was the principal at Edith Hamilton Elementary School. Petite and middle-aged, she was a pleasant woman and Jasmine enjoyed chatting with her whenever she and Vrig had gone to the assemblies at the school.

"Good morning, Jasmine," she greeted. "And you must be Mal, Vrig's nephew."

The orc eyed her suspiciously. "How do you know who I am?"

"Small town, I'm afraid," she said with a chuckle. "We all loved your uncle and he'll be missed. He was so active in the community. I'm sorry for your loss."

"Thank you," Mal murmured.

Sensing Mal's discomfort, Jasmine switched topics. "To what do we owe this visit? You're not looking for a pet yourself, are you?"

"Goodness, no." She placed a hand over her chest. "I'm much too busy for that. Maybe when I retire. I'm here for an entirely different reason. The school assembly."

Jasmine glanced at the calendar hanging on the wall behind the counter, noticing the big red circle around one of the dates. "That's on Friday, isn't it? I'm sorry, I completely forgot about it." Mrs. Howard would be disappointed with what she was about to say, but Jasmine had no choice. "You're going to have to cancel, I'm afraid. I can't do it on my own." It would be too much work for one person, trying to handle the animals and talking to the kids.

"That's understandable given the circumstances." Her eyes darted to Mal. "I don't suppose you'd be willing to help, Mr. Mal?"

"Just Mal, ma'am," he said. "And how would I help, exactly?"

"Vrig used to come to the school assemblies at Edith Hamilton Elementary," Jasmine explained. "He would bring a couple of the animals and talk to the kids about them. He loved it. It was his favorite thing. We would even close the shop for the morning just so we could go."

"And the children loved him," Mrs. Howard said. "They'll be disappointed if we cancel. They look forward to it every year. But I suppose it's understandable."

"Yeah," Jasmine said. "I'm sor—"

"We can do it."

Jasmine's head snapped toward Mal. "What? You want to do the assembly?"

"If you do the talking, I'll handle the pets."

"Me? T-talk?" She swallowed. "Vrig always did that, and I just helped out." The thought of speaking onstage in front of about a hundred people made her palms clammy and her throat seize.

"You talk to kids all the time," he pointed out.

"As customers."

"Think of it like that, but a lot of them at the same time."

Mrs. Howard clapped her hands together. "It would mean so much to the children if you did come. The parents too, as we do invite them to come to these presentations."

That was, of course, one of the benefits of doing these assemblies. Parents, after all, were the final decision-makers when it came to purchases and it wasn't unusual for a couple of them to show up days after the assembly to shop for a pet, their little ones in tow.

Two pairs of eyes looked at her expectantly. How was she supposed to say no? "I guess I could do it."

"Wonderful. The children will be thrilled." Mrs. Howard beamed at them. "So, you already know the place and time, right?"

"Yes, ma'am," Jasmine said. "We'll be there."

"Thank you so much. I will see you both then." With a last grin and wave, she headed out.

"Oh Mother Goddess, why did I agree to that?" Jasmine wrung her hands together. "How do I even begin to prepare?"

"You'll do fine." His intense purple gaze caught hers. "I've seen you around kids. You're a natural, just like with the animals."

"Vrig was the one who was onstage while I stayed in the back, handling the pets. I've never been good at public speaking."

"Never been good or never tried?"

"Well, I never had to, except at school when I was a kid maybe."

He grunted. "Look, I don't like being the center of attention, either, but how about I stand next to you through the entire thing? Would that help?"

"Y-you would do that?"

"I have to be there anyway to assist you in handling the animals, right?"

"Yeah."

He inhaled sharply. "I think Vrig wouldn't want us to cancel."

A tightness in her throat formed. "I agree," she whispered. "All right, let's do it."

"Okay, how does this work?"

"Work?" She cocked her head to the side. "What do you mean?"

"Like, how do you choose which creatures to take and how do you transport them?"

"Transporting them is easy," she said. "We have extra crates for them, and Vrig and I used to put them in his truck and drive to the school."

"Gotcha. I'll bring the truck over tomorrow. Which ones are you taking?"

"I don't know. Vrig usually chooses."

Mal walked around the counter to stand next to her. Despite his towering height, she didn't feel crowded at all. "Well, you're the boss. Or you will be in a couple of months, which means you have to make the decisions."

He was right. Once she owned Fantastic Tails, she would be making all kinds of decisions. "All right, I'll think on it. I'll have to figure out what I'm going to say." A kernel of doubt planted itself inside her. "What if I pick the wrong ones? Or what if I choose a boring pet and the kids tune me out?"

He gestured around them. "You've been in charge of choosing and stocking the pets here for the last couple of years. You know each by heart, what they need, what makes them tick. I'm sure the young ones will love whichever ones you show them."

"I'll try."

"You'll do great," he said, sounding much more confident than she felt right now.

"Thanks." She smiled up at him, and to her surprise, he returned it. Her pulse did a little dance, as this was the first time she'd seen it, and it made him look even more striking. But then again, he also looked handsome when he frowned, and that tiny line appeared between his eyebrows. And when he did that thing when he was thinking hard and his brows furrowed.

Jasmine averted her gaze, hoping he hadn't noticed her staring.

Get a grip, Jasmine. And stop crushing on your boss.

Clearing her throat, she averted her gaze. "Uhm, I should get back to work."

"Yeah." He took his phone out from his pocket. "And uh, I actually need to go run an errand. I'll see you later."

Oh Mother Goddess, she couldn't possibly still be attracted to him? His shifting moods left her dizzy, from his anger at the cockatrice incident, to his coming to her door to apologize, then treating her coldly the last few days. He'd done so many one-eighties that she wasn't sure which way he was facing now.

He was just being nice, she told herself. Mal had offered to help her because he didn't want to disappoint the kids at the school and Vrig. She had to stop assigning meaning to the things he did, as their relationship was strictly professional and nothing more. In any case, she had more things to worry about, like getting over her stage fright. Just the thought of being up there with all those little faces staring up at her had her sweating bullets. But she'd already promised Mrs. Howard they would come, so she would just have to suck it up and get through it.

"Nervous?" Mal asked as they waited in the wings of the Edith Hamilton Elementary School auditorium.

"Yeah." Jasmine wiped her damp palms down the front of her slacks, then adjusted the hem of her white blouse. Hopefully, her outfit was okay, as she usually wore jeans, a shirt, and sneakers to these things, but she would be onstage today, so she wanted to look presentable at the very least. To her annoyance, a lock of black hair had escaped from her chignon bun, and no matter how many times she tucked it back, it kept slipping out.

"Don't be," Mal assured her. "You'll be fine."

Easy for him to say, since he wasn't going to be speaking in front of a crowd. Jasmine took a calming breath, reminding herself this was just like talking to a customer in the shop. Besides, she'd seen Vrig do this about half a dozen times by now. All she had to do was copy what he did.

". . . and now let's give our guests a warm welcome!" Mrs. Howard announced from the stage.

"All right." She straightened her shoulders. "Here we go."

Jasmine's knees wobbled as she took her first steps onto the main stage, but fortunately, she managed to get to the middle without embarrassing herself. Mal, meanwhile, pulled a cart that held the three carriers they had brought in from Fantastic Tails.

The students, who came from the second and third-grade classes, cheered and applauded, their excitement palpable.

Mrs. Howard raised a hand and a hush fell over the auditorium. "Everyone, this is Miss Jasmine, and this is Mr. Mal. He's Mr. Vrig's nephew and he's helping out today."

While most kids who first saw an orc might have been intimidated by Mal's size and fierce tusks, they all clapped when Jasmine gestured to him. After all, they knew Vrig as a gentle giant, so it was no surprise they offered a warm welcome. Mal, on the other hand, had the most adorable, bewildered expression on his face. Unsure what to do, he did a little wave.

Mrs. Howard handed Jasmine the microphone and gave her a thumbs-up sign. Slowly, Jasmine turned to face out into the audience. "Good mor—" The screech of the feedback cut into her greeting, and she cringed visibly. Clearing her throat, she tried again, but sound refused to come out.

What felt like hundreds of pairs of eyes—though in reality there were maybe about forty kids in total—looked up at her eagerly. Sweat formed on her palms, and she gripped the mic tighter, praying it wouldn't slip from her grasp. Her breath turned loud and heavy to her ears and she resisted the urge to curl up into herself.

As panic rose up in her chest, she turned to Mal. As if sensing her discomfort, he gave her an encouraging nod, then mouthed *you can do this*. While this didn't get rid of the butterflies in her stomach, they did cease fluttering madly. With a grateful smile, she turned back to the audience.

"G-good morning."

Okay, Jasmine, first two words out.

"As you know, Mr. Mal and I run the pet shop on Main Street, Fantastic Tails and Magical Scales."

And first sentence done.

"And today we've brought along a few friends to show you all."

Introduction finished.

"Let's start, shall we?"

Now we're moving.

Mal proceeded to open the first cage, which contained a tiny, furry creature that looked even tinier in the palm of his large hand.

"This," she began, "is a tizzie whizie and his name is Daryl."

Jasmine had chosen the tizzie whizie because it was cute and easy to handle. Yesterday, she'd sold one to a couple buying their first pet together, so she could easily rattle off the same spiel she had given them. "Tizzie whizies come from the Lake District in England and were first discovered by the boatmen who worked there. Mr. Mal, if you please?"

Mal stepped forward and stretched his arms out, murmuring a few words. When he opened his hands, a yellow bubble began to grow from his palms, forming a dome-like enclosure. She'd remembered Vrig doing something similar when he cast spells. Though she always tried to make out what he said she never could and guessed it was in the orcish language. This time, however, she couldn't concentrate on what Mal was saying as she was mesmerized by the sight of his forearms. He rolled up the sleeves of his flannel shirt, showing off the sinewy muscles there. The veins under his green skin pulsed as he held the dome aloft, and heat curled in her belly.

Get it together, Jasmine!

She quickly averted her gaze and turned to the audience. "Tizzie—*ahem*—tizzie whizies have a furry body and are a little larger than an average hedgehog. They have a long tail and small wings which allow them to hover, much like a bumble bee or a hummingbird."

As if on cue, Daryl floated up, his bushy tail wagging back and forth. The children gasped and clapped. Jasmine then rattled off a few more facts about the tizzie whizie, though not many of the kids seemed to be paying attention as their eyes were glued to Mal, who had grown the dome to over five feet now, extending it over the stage so Daryl buzzed around over the children's heads. That suited her just fine, as without the pressure of all those eyes watching her, she managed to get through the rest of the speech unscathed.

Once they'd finished with the tizzie whizie, Mal put him

back into his cage before hauling out the next one—this time, a large crate about two feet tall and three feet wide.

Jasmine's grip on the microphone relaxed. Vrig had brought this particular type of animal the previous assembly and she'd helped him with the presentation, so it was still fresh in her mind. "Now, some of you may remember Bruce from the last time Mr. Vrig was here. Bruce is now living on a farm up in Oregon, but today we have Bruce's little sister, who was born a few weeks ago. Everyone, meet Cora the laelaps."

Mal opened the crate and whistled. A large dog trotted out, similar to a greyhound, though she had white fur with brown patches shaped like stars all over her body and a single one on her forehead. Cora sat down at full attention, facing Mal, pointy ears raised.

"Cora looks like a normal dog, but I assure you, she's quite special. Laelaps are hunters and they never fail to catch their prey." She took something out of her purse—a worn fox stuffie—and waved it around. Cora's gaze followed it with keen interest, though she remained seated on her hind legs. "Mal, can you cover Cora's eyes, please?"

Mal retrieved a handkerchief from his pocket and wrapped it round the laelaps' head.

"Can I have a volunteer?" Several hands shot up and Jasmine picked out a little girl from the center row. "Hi, what's your name?"

"Kaylie." A small, anxious face stared up at her, then at Cora. "Sh-she looked smaller from the audience," she whispered.

Jasmine put the mic down. "It's okay, Kaylie. Cora is nice and well trained." She held up the mic again. "Now, Kaylie is going to help me by hiding this stuffie." She handed it to the girl. "You can place it anywhere you want in the school, Kaylie. Pick a good hiding place, okay?"

The girl's face lit up. "I will."

"Good. Mrs. Howard will help you." She ushered the girl off-stage toward the principal and faced the audience. "Okay, while Kaylie picks out her hiding spot, let me tell you some interesting facts . . ."

Jasmine had been the one to compile the research about the laelaps, so the words flowed out of her easily. In the middle of her speech, though, she locked eyes with Mal, who shot her a small smile and her heart did a little jig, causing her to trip over a few words. Heat crept up her cheeks, and thankfully Kaylie came back before Jasmine embarrassed herself further.

"So, Kaylie, did you hide the stuffie in a super-secret place?" She nodded.

"Let's see if Cora can locate it." She signaled to Mal, who removed the scarf from Cora's eyes.

"Cora," he commanded, "find!"

Cora was gone in a blur of brown and white.

"Why don't we count and see how long it takes Cora to find the stuffie? Ready?" Jasmine raised a hand. "And go!"

The entire auditorium began to count, with even the teachers and parents joining in. By the time they reached forty-five, the doors in the back flew open and Cora came galloping in, her long legs making quick work of the aisle leading to the stage. Everyone cheered as the laelaps approached the front and leapt up—straight at Jasmine and Kaylie.

"No!" She stepped forward, ready to shield Kaylie from the seventy-pound canine about to crash into them. Before she could even brace herself for the impact, Mal dove in front of them and caught Cora. A cheer went up from the audience.

"Are you okay?" Mal turned to face Jasmine, a squirming Cora in his arms, fox stuffie in her mouth.

"Y-yeah, thanks. Kaylie?"

"I'm g-good, Miss Jasmine." She crept around from behind her, her eyes growing to the size of the moon. "Thank you, Mr. Mal."

"No prob, kiddo." Mal placed Cora on her paws and whistled, and she immediately sat down.

"Whew, that was a close one," Jasmine said. "Wasn't that awesome? Kaylie, where did you put the stuffie?"

"In the boys' bathroom," she said, wrinkling her nose. "I thought the smell in there would stop her."

There were a few "eww"s and "yuck"s from the crowd and laughs from the adults.

Jasmine chuckled. "Good thinking, Kaylie, but like I said, nothing will stop a laelaps from finding its prey, not even a stinky bathroom." Another laugh rang out. "After today, Cora will be headed to her new home on a ranch in Montana, where she'll be living with a wonderful family with three kids. So, say bye-bye to Cora, everyone." As the children waved and shouted their good-byes, Mal led Cora back to her pen. "And thanks so much for volunteering, Kaylie."

"Thank you, Miss Jasmine, Mr. Mal." She waved at them before following Mrs. Howard as she led her back to her seat. "So, now we have our last friend. His name is Felix, and he's a carbuncle kit."

Jasmine had gotten the idea to bring the carbuncle from the little cyclops boy and his mom. It was unlikely that any of the parents watching would want to buy a tizzie whizie or laelaps for their child, but a carbuncle kit was the perfect starter pet for any child. That and they were adorable and had luminescent fur, a must for kids who were afraid of the dark. A little marketing and publicity never hurt, after all, and she especially needed it now, if the shop's finances were as dire as Mal said they were.

"Let's say hello to Felix!"

Felix, however, wasn't keen on cooperating this morning. Mal placed his carrier on the floor and opened the gate, but the little creature remained inside.

"Oh dear, I think he's a bit shy." She looked up at Mal, unsure what to do.

His eyebrows did that furrowing thing. "Do you have any treats?"

"Oh, good idea." Reaching into her purse, she found half a dental treat she had stashed in there when she was rushing to get home after playing with the tygre cubs. She placed it in front of the open crate. A few seconds later, Felix came out, sniffing at the treat before he began to munch on it, his bushy blue tail wagging and ears twitching happily.

Jasmine went through her speech, talking about the carbuncle. At one point, she asked that the lights be dimmed and sure enough little Felix began to glow, eliciting "ooh"s and "aahh"s from the children. When the lights turned on, Mrs. Howard waved to her and pointed at her wristwatch, indicating that she should wrap it up.

"Looks like we're almost out of time. Let's say bye to Felix."

Mal opened up the crate door, but instead of heading inside, the little kit decided to run up the orc's arm instead. The orc jumped back and nearly tumbled, but caught himself in time. The carbuncle, however, circled his neck before settling round it, like a fur scarf. Mal grunted and frowned.

A burst of giggles broke out from the kids and Jasmine had to bite her lip hard to stop from laughing. "I don't think Felix is ready to go home yet."

The kit let out a chirp of agreement, and the lines between Mal's eyebrows deepened. He tried to brush him off, and though he unfurled his bushy tail, Felix crawled down to his arms and snuggled in before closing his eyes for a snooze.

A collective "awww" rang out from the audience. Jasmine had to admit, it was a cute sight, especially now that Mal's frown had been replaced by a bewildered expression.

"Thank you, everyone, we'll see you next time," Jasmine said.

As applause broke out, she let out an internal sigh of relief. She couldn't believe she'd made it through this without embarrassing herself. Looking over her shoulder, she glanced toward Mal who was placing the sleeping kit inside the carrier.

After shutting the door, he turned to her. "Thank Vorlak we're done."

"I don't know, Mal . . . You looked the height of fashion with a fur scarf," she teased.

He flashed her a wry smile. "I'll be sure to bring my matching heels and purse next time."

Wait, did Mal just . . . crack a joke?

Before she could react, he lifted the cage, placed it on top of the others, then pushed the cart backstage.

She trotted after him, doubling her steps to keep up with his longer strides. "Thanks so much, Mal. I couldn't have done this without you."

He stopped pushing and swung around to face her. "You did great, Jasmine. What did I tell you? Here, let me."

"Let you—" Her breath hitched as he reached out to her, the soft pads of his fingers brushing her cheek as he tucked back the annoying lock of loose hair behind her ear. Her heart stopped at the contact, and she couldn't help but stare up at his indigo eyes.

"There," he said, his voice so gentle, it made shivers crawl up the back of her knees.

"Jasmine, Mal, thank you so much," Mrs. Howard called from behind.

Spell broken, she turned to face the principal. "You're welcome, Mrs. Howard. I hope that was okay. I'm no Vrig, after all."

"No, and you don't have to be. You did wonderfully. I'm sure Vrig would have been proud."

"Jasmine, ma'am," Mal interrupted. "If you'll excuse me, I have to load up the truck and return the cart to Coach Jennings."

"Of course, Mal, go ahead."

The orc gave her a curt nod, then went back to pushing the cart toward the exit that led out to the parking lot.

"Thank you again," Mrs. Howard repeated. "The children and parents were thrilled."

"You're welcome." Jasmine especially hoped the latter truly were thrilled enough to visit the shop.

"By the way, a few of the parents and teachers sent me photos they took during your presentation and have also shared them on their social media and tagged you."

"They have?" Taking her phone out, she saw notifications lighting up the screen. "Oh wow."

Fantastic Tails didn't have much of a social-media following. Vrig never set them up, and so it was up to Jasmine to create and maintain the accounts. With her being so busy managing the shop, she only had time to post a few photos and flyers for sales here and there, and to answer direct messages when they did come. Kap had been bugging her to do more, but she didn't really see the point.

But now that some accounts had tagged Fantastic Tails, several photos began appearing on their feed. There were a few of the animals, but she noticed something else—a lot were of Mal. One was of him catching Cora, the laelaps looking majestic as it leapt into the air. It already had fifty hearts. Another one, of him with the sleeping Felix snuggled against him, had a hundred hearts.

"That's amazing," she said. "I should thank the parents."

"They're eager to meet you and Mal. Some of the teachers too, especially the women." Her eyes darted toward the exit. "He is a fine specimen, if you don't mind me saying."

"Er . . ."

"If only I was ten years younger." She sighed. "Anyway, can I bring out a couple people to say hi?"

"Uh, sure. We'll be in the parking lot."

"Thanks, Jasmine."

As Jasmine scrolled through her feed, she had to agree. Mal was, indeed, a *very* fine specimen. The one with Felix in his arms showed off those muscled forearms she'd been ogling herself, not to mention that the top button of his shirt had come undone and gave a little peek of a well-formed pec. The top comment on the photo was three fire emojis.

She put the phone away before she started drooling. Besides, she had to focus on what was important—all those eyes on their accounts. While she didn't know much about social media, she knew enough that this had the potential to become *big*.

"Mal." She jogged toward him. "Wait."

Done loading the truck, Mal latched the gate with a firm *click*. "What is it? I need to wheel the cart back to the gym then we can head back to the shop."

"Uhm, about that. We can stay a couple minutes, right?"

"Why?"

"Well, some of the parents and some teachers want to meet with you."

"Me? Why can't you do it?"

"It's just for a little bit. They want to thank you," she reasoned. "Oh look, here they come." A group of about ten people was approaching them. "Just say hello, please? Parents are one of our biggest customers. You said you'd help me, right?"

"I guess?" He let out what sounded like a half-grunt, half-sigh. "Fine."

"And I'll take a few photos for our social media account too. I forgot to give my phone to Mrs. Howard before we started."

"But—"

"There you are." Mrs. Howard waved a hand as she trotted toward them. "Mal, I have a few people here with me who want to say hello."

It didn't escape Jasmine's notice that they were all women, of course. They flocked around him, like bees to honey.

"Hello, Mr. Mal," one of the women drawled, offering her hand. "I'm Marie Lamont, first-grade homeroom teacher. Kaylie's my student."

"Er, hi. And it's just Mal." He shook her hand.

Jasmine whipped out her phone, ignoring the acidic ache forming in her chest as she began to take photos of Mal and the women. They were all young, fit and attractive, and eyeing Mal like he was the last meal on earth. When one of them leaned her head close to Mal's as he bent down to take a selfie with her, Jasmine gritted her teeth. Mal, however, seemed oblivious to the female attention. He was pleasant enough, answering their questions and posing for selfies with them.

Once they were done, Jasmine asked them for any photos they took during the assembly and for permission to post them on the shop's socials. A few of the women also promised to stop by in the next few days, as well as during the Founding Day Festival.

As they drove back toward Main Street, Jasmine checked the tagged photos again. The photo of Mal and Felix now had two hundred and fifty hearts, and the Fantastic Tails account's followers—*Oh Mother Goddess*—had doubled.

She snuck a glance at Mal. It wasn't as if she was the one who'd taken and uploaded that photo of him. But it did give her an incentive to start being active on social media, get the word out about the shop. Who knows, it might even get a few more people through the door. Increased foot traffic wasn't a bad thing, after all, even if they just came in to get a glimpse of Mal.

Her thoughts went back to the women from earlier who were attempting to flirt with him. Did he really not notice? Or was he just being discreet? Anyone could easily find out who he was and slide into his DMs, and Jasmine would never know.

She touched her cheek, remembering how his fingers had brushed against it when he tucked back her hair. Thoughts of those women faded as a warm and fuzzy sensation filled her chest. It also made her think of things she had absolutely no business thinking about.

Jasmine cringed inwardly. This silly crush had to go away, somehow. It wouldn't do her any good and would just distract her from her goals. Fighting against the urge to look at him, she focused on the road ahead.

Chapter Nine

MAL

Mal stopped halfway as he placed the large bag of kibble on a shelf, feeling eyes on him.

"Are you taking another picture?"

Jasmine raised her phone higher, hiding her face. "It's for our Picstagram account." *Click.* "The, uh, label looks good facing out. It's an indie brand and they love exposure like this."

He shrugged and put the bag on the shelf. "Anything else you need me to do?"

"No, we're good." She ran her fingers down the long braid of dark hair over one shoulder, then twirled the ends. "Thanks for getting those bags up there. I couldn't have done it without you."

Those brown doe eyes held his gaze, sending his hearts into a gallop. When she'd asked for his help this morning, he couldn't say no. In fact, he found himself unable to say no to any of her requests.

Can you finish the new locking spells, Mal?

Yes, Jasmine.

Can you change the hay in the griffin pen, Mal?

Of course, Jasmine.

And Gaku help him, he actually liked doing all those things for her. Jasmine could ask him to hunt down a hydra and nail its head to the wall and the only question he'd ask was if she wanted a six-headed or nine-headed one.

How had he got himself into this situation?

Mal had felt guilty after the whole cockatrice incident. She'd been right—he did initially think it was her fault. So, he went to apologize. She didn't have to accept it, but she graciously had, and had told him about why she wanted to run the shop. He'd been so caught up in her story, her passion and the animated way she spoke, and her brown eyes and her pretty lips, that he could only focus on her. She had been so magnetic and for a brief moment he'd been tempted to hold her in his arms and kiss her.

Then *he'd* showed up.

Kap.

The name sent an acrid bubble up his throat. She didn't mention she had a boyfriend. It was none of his business, of course, as he and Jasmine had a completely professional relationship. Still, it stuck in his craw, knowing another man was in her home, sharing a meal with her. He couldn't even stare him down as he was as tall as him, a rarity for Mal. He was also a cop, based on the uniform and marked cruiser parked on the curb. Where did Jasmine find this guy?

Mal had paced around the kitchen most of the evening, a bolt in his chest tightening at the thought of them together. The window had been too far away for him to see anything, though the lights had been on the entire time. Thank Vorlak that after an hour or so he had heard Jasmine's door open and close. When the cop car drove away, the tightness in his chest loosened, but the pressure remained there.

She had a boyfriend. It was best to avoid her, so that's what he did for the next few days. Sure, he treated her cordially, but he refused to get further caught up in her orbit. But then the assembly happened, and all that resolve went out the window.

Despite her worries, Jasmine had done an incredible job. She'd been confident, chose the perfect animals to present, and the children adored her, which Mal already knew would be the case. And much to his own chagrin, Mal had been riveted the entire time.

Since then, he found himself seeking her company in the shop or following her with his eyes. When she wasn't around, he wondered where she was and what she was doing. Many nights, he would glance out his kitchen window, watching the light in the apartment above the stairs, waiting for it to turn off at ten thirty—her bedtime, he assumed. For some reason, Kap never showed up after that first night, and though he tried to squash it, he clung to that glimmer of hope that maybe he wasn't her boyfriend.

"I should get back to my work," he declared.

"Of course," she said. "I'll be at the counter in case anyone needs to check out. Sorry to have disturbed you, especially when I know you're busy with work."

The truth was, he didn't have much to do, at least not for his contracting business. Since he'd arrived in Dewberry Falls, he'd been replying to emails, checking in with his accountant, or working on bids for jobs that would start in six months or so. But mostly he spent his days in the back office twiddling his claws, waiting for that email from the Orc Historical Society that might never come.

"All right." He soaked in the sight of her, as she looked lovely in the morning light today. "Just holler if you need anything."

As he strode back to the office, he couldn't help but feel eyes on him again. Swinging his head around, he saw two women standing by the firebird cages, staring at him. "Can I help you?"

They looked at each other, then one of them, a petite blonde, spoke up. "You're, uh, Mal, right? The orc?"

"Yeah."

"Can we take a picture?" the other one burst out.

He held out his hand. "Give me your phone. Did you want to pose next to the firebirds?"

"Firebirds?" the first one said. "No, we want a selfie. With you."

"Me?" The request took him by surprise. "Why?"

"Duh, you're Mal," she replied. "Please? Do it for the 'gram?"

Now he was even more confused. "What's the 'gram?"

"Picstagram, of course."

Ah yes, the social-networking app. He had an account for his business, but he outsourced the management to some young marketing whiz. All he did was send pics from his jobs and the kid took care of posting them, plus forwarding any job enquiries from the direct messages to his email.

"Please?"

"Uh, sure, I guess." Jasmine would not like it if he were rude to the customers.

"Great! Scooch down, please? We're not as tall as you."

Mal did as she asked, bending down to about their height. The two posed on either side of him, then the blonde stretched out her hand, phone in hand, the screen flashing as she took several photos. "Thanks so much, Mal. We'll tag you in the photos, okay?"

"You're welcome." It still confused him why they would want a selfie with him or how they knew who he was in the first place. "If you'll excuse me, ladies, I need to go."

"Thanks, Mal," they chorused as he walked away.

Mal shook his head. So strange. Of course, he'd noticed other unusual things around the shop lately. There'd been an uptick in the amount of people coming in the last couple of days, but he figured they were nearing some kind of high season, perhaps due to that festival coming up.

Still . . . his gut told him something was up.

As soon as he was alone in the office, he pulled up the Picstagram app on his phone and searched for the Fantastic Tails and Magical Scales account.

The profile featured the store's logo and address, all the usual stuff. When he scrolled through the pics, however, what he saw was definitely not usual. Mixed in with photos of the pets and flyers for their promotions were pictures of *him*.

He recognized the ones pinned on the top, which were from the school assembly, when he caught Cora the laelaps and when he held the snoozing Felix in his arms. After that, however, were photos he didn't even know were being taken of him. There was one of him fixing the squeaky wampus cat pens, oil can in hand as he sprayed the hinges, while another showed him refilling the amikuk tanks. He refreshed the feed, and sure enough, a photo of him with the kibble bag on his shoulders popped up.

New product alert! Our friends at Ethereal Balance just sent us their latest offering—mandrake-flavored canine kibble. Our fenrirs, blue foxes, and raijus go crazy for this one, so get it while it's in stock. #etherealbalancemandrake #fantastictailsandmagicalscales #dewberryfallsmainstreet #petshopcalifornia

The caption seemed innocuous enough, but the photos were more suspect. Yes, the label was definitely at the forefront, but Mal took up most of the real estate in the picture. It didn't show his face, but his back and shoulders were prominently featured. Hearts started popping up on the post and a comment came in with a sweating emoji that said "Zaddy Orc."

Zaddy—

He groaned aloud. While he may not be social media savvy, he knew enough from working around the young guys on his previous jobs to know that these were what people called "thirst traps."

He rose and strode out of the office, searching for Jasmine on the shop floor and found her at the counter with a customer, ringing up their purchase. He took deep breaths as he waited for her to finish, and as soon as the customer left, he marched toward her.

"Jasmine."

"Mal?" She looked up at him with those big, beautiful eyes looking all innocent.

Yeah, right.

He planted his hands on his hips. "Explain the pictures, please."

"Excuse me?" A hand landed on her chest. "What pictures?"

He held his phone up to her face. "These pictures. Zaddy orc?"

"I . . . er . . ." She bit at her lip, color rising under her tanned skin. "Well, you see . . . those pics from the assembly—which I didn't take, by the way; the shop was just tagged—kind of went viral."

"Viral?" he said, incredulous.

"Viral for Dewberry Falls, anyway. It's gotten about fifty thousand hearts the last time I counted?"

"Fifty thousand—" He scrubbed a palm down his face. "Fifty thousand people have seen my photos?"

"At least."

He glanced around them. "Is that why those women wanted to take selfies with me? Or why that teacher from the assembly has been by twice in the week to buy chew toys? Does she even have a pet?"

"Maybe? Er, I'm sorry, Mal." She took in a gulp of air, face flushed. "I shouldn't have been using your photos as thirst traps. I'll take them down and untag you right away."

"Thank you," he said, relieved.

"It's not that I'm objectifying you or anything." She grabbed her phone out from the drawer under the counter. "Sure, your photos have been getting a lot of hearts and comments from single women, but they've been boosting our algorithm, so more people are seeing and following our account. Families, couples, and even people who own non-magical creatures have been coming in too. We've had ten sign-ups for our monthly subscription box and they're not even from Dewberry Falls. Sales are up fifteen per cent in the last five days."

"Fifteen per cent?" He couldn't believe it.

"Yeah." Jasmine's thumb raised to tap on the screen.

"Wait." He gently wrapped his hand around her wrist. "Don't."

A dark eyebrow raised. "Don't?"

"Don't delete the photos."

"No?"

"I mean . . . I guess it's fine," he muttered. "You can't exactly control what other people are commenting nor are you forcing people to buy stuff they don't need."

"Yeah, they're just finding us via the algorithm."

"And it's not like I'm naked in any of the photos."

Her eyes widened and he swore her pulse jumped under his palms. Which reminded him that he still held her delicate wrist, so he dropped his hand to his side.

"Er, yeah." She lowered her gaze. "You're fully clothed in all of them, going about your day."

"It's fine if you want to keep up the pictures you already have. Just tell me if you're taking and posting more photos of me, okay?"

"Sure. Of c-course," she stammered. "I didn't mean . . . Again, I'm sorry for violating your privacy like that."

"Apology accepted."

"I appreciate it." She clucked her tongue. "Oh, I almost forgot, there's something I wanted your help with."

Yes, Jasmine.

Of course, Jasmine.

Do with me as you please, Jasmine.

Gaku help him, he was a goner.

"Er, sure."

"Let's go upstairs."

He followed her up to the second level, doing his best not to stare at her shapely ass. He remembered how perfectly outlined it was when she wore those slacks to the assembly. And that frilly and proper blouse, along with her hair in a bun, stirred up all kinds of naughty secretary fantasies. Mal had to remind himself many times they had an audience, otherwise, he would have been sporting a semi the entire time.

She led him to the back corner to a room marked "private." Jasmine had previously explained to him that this was their hatchery. As Fantastic Tails did not do any breeding, purchasing eggs and hatching saved them a lot of money. Tanks with incubating lights lined several shelves on the wall, though currently, only one was occupied with a clutch of basilisk eggs. Jasmine gestured to the middle of the room, where a single wooden crate lay on top of a table.

"This," she began as she took the lid off, "is what I need your help with."

A single egg lay inside the box, resting on a bed of hay. Slightly smaller than a football and covered in pearly blue scales, it glinted under the overhead lamp.

"What is it?"

"It's a carcinos egg," Jasmine said.

He frowned. "Really?"

Carcinos were basically crabs, except they had four claws, and instead of a hard shell, their bodies were covered in beautiful shiny scales that came in a variety of colors.

Jasmine continued. "One of our suppliers said he had an extra one and gave it to me for fifty per cent off. They're expensive to purchase as full adults, so I thought I'd try to hatch one."

"I see."

She cocked her head to the side. "What's wrong?"

"Nothing. I mean . . ." He leaned in for a closer look. "A couple years back, I helped this guy install a massive custom-made aquarium in his house. Turns out, he was one of those crazy collectors. Loved carcinos. Already had two other tanks filled with them. One day, he showed me about a dozen or so eggs he was incubating." He paused. "I don't recall the eggs themselves being scaly." They had been smooth, like a normal egg. "Or this big. They were also orange, not blue."

"According to the internet, carcinos come in all kinds of colors and sizes. Maybe this is a different species?"

"Perhaps." Though his gut told him something else. Still, he didn't want to contradict her, lest he end up having to apologize again. Besides, when that guy told him how much a single carcinos cost, his jaw had nearly hit the floor. Selling this one carcinos would probably pay their water bill for a couple of months.

"Okay, so what do you need my help with?"

"I don't think any of our hatching tanks will be big enough for this one." Tapping her chin, she slowly spun around, looking at each tank in turn. "Maybe . . . Do you think you could build a bigger one? And I'd like to put it downstairs."

"Downstairs? Why?"

"I've been scrolling my feed on Picstagram to check out what other pet shops are doing on their socials." She snapped her fingers. "I thought, what if we did a series of posts to follow the hatching process? It'll be good content, plus if we set up the tank downstairs, people could come visit and see the egg for themselves. Think of the foot traffic." Her eyes shone with excitement. "We might be able to find a buyer once it hatches too."

"That's not a bad idea." Genius idea, actually.

"And I won't have to post so many photos of you," she said with a laugh. "So, what do you say, Mal? Will you build a hatching tank downstairs?"

"Yes, Jasmine, I'll build you a hatching tank."

Oh, he was a goner all right.

"Yay!" She clapped her hands excitedly. "Come, I have a few ideas." Before he could stop her, she picked up the box and trotted out of the hatchery room. Once downstairs, she settled it on the floor in an empty space between the pens. "There you go," she cooed.

Mal blinked.

What in Vorlak's name was that?

The egg had wiggled as Jasmine spoke to it.

"Did you see—"

Jasmine spoke at the same time. "So, what do you think of building it right—"

Ding ding dong!

Before Jasmine could start her welcome spiel, a booming voice rang out. "Hey, Jasmine. Hey, Zaddy Orc."

Mal's blood pressure skyrocketed.

This fucking guy.

"Kap," Jasmine greeted, waving him over. "What are you doing here? It's like ten o'clock in the morning."

"Yeah, had to work overtime today, big case." He yawned, scratching at the fur on his neck. "Those pics of you are fire, Mal. Glad you finally took my suggestion, Jasmine."

"Suggestion?" Mal gritted his teeth, looking accusingly at Jasmine.

"Kap's been telling me to be more active on social media, to help promote the shop," she explained. "So? Did you solve the case?"

"Still working on it. But I just remembered I haven't thanked you for dinner the other night." He held up a white to-go cup in his hand. "So, I got you your favorite brew."

"Aww, thanks. That's sweet of you," she said, accepting the cup.

"No worries, I owe you, like, twenty more of those for all the times you've cooked. Mal, you should join us sometime."

"Join you?" Now that had taken Mal aback. If he went out on a date with Jasmine, he would never invite another man to be a third wheel.

"Yeah. Jasmine's an amazing cook."

"I'm just okay." She waved a hand in the air, as if swatting away Kap's compliment.

"You're too modest. Vrig used to come too. He loved Jasmine's arroz caldo. It's like a rice porridge with ginger and scallions . . . yum." He rubbed his stomach. "Anyway, I need to crash, guys. Have a great day, yeah?"

"Bye, Kap," Jasmine said as he headed out the door.

That bolt that had seemingly lodged itself in Mal's chest since the day he'd met Kap loosened even more. He and Jasmine appeared close, but not in the romantic-relationship way close. They didn't hug, much less give each other a kiss goodbye. When Kap didn't come back to Jasmine's after that first time—he could now admit that he waited and listened for his car every night— Mal just thought maybe he didn't spend the night during the weeks he worked the evening shift at his job. But seeing them now, they acted more like siblings than lovers.

"He's a tree giant."

"What?" His head snapped toward Jasmine.

"You'd been staring so intently at him, I thought you might burn a hole through his head," she said, chuckling. "People around here who first meet Kap are always wondering what he is, but are usually too polite to ask. But really, he's cool about that stuff."

"I don't think I've ever met a tree giant." Nor had he heard of them either.

"Well, technically he's half tree giant because his dad's human. But, tree giants, or kapre, live in the forests in the Philippines. Kap's grandparents immigrated here, but his mom was born in Chicago and so was he. It's weird, really. Their kind don't usually leave their homes, much less the country."

Weird, indeed.

"I was pretty shocked to see him here in Dewberry Falls. Afraid even, because tree giants aren't known to be sociable. But anyway, we've been friends ever since we met."

Just friends?

"Uh, yeah?" Her eyebrows drew together. "Just friends."

Mal mentally slapped himself on the forehead, as he realized he'd said that out loud. "Er, yeah, that's good. Good to have friends." Relief, however, sluiced through him and that bolt lodged in his chest disappeared. "Er, so, I should start measuring the space for the hatching tank."

"Yeah, sounds good. Thanks again. I should put this back to keep it safe. If my calculations are correct, it'll be a few more weeks before it hatches."

"Here, let me do that," he said, picking up the box. He followed her back upstairs to the hatchery room and replaced it on the table. "Will it be okay in here?"

"Yeah, they're surprisingly easy to take care of. It just takes a lot of waiting. My supplier said we can it move around, as long as we're careful." She reached into the box and adjusted the hay under the egg, her hand brushing over the scaly surface.

What the—

He could have sworn the scales on the egg glimmered under her touch, but it had been so fast, so he wasn't sure.

"Did you see that?"

She stared up at him. "See what?"

"Nothing." Must've been a trick of the light.

She brushed her hands together. "Okay, Clawed is safe."

"Clawed?"

"Yeah, that's what I was thinking of naming him. You know, like the French name 'Claude' but spelled with a W-E-D: a play on 'claw'." She shaped her fingers into crab claws, snapping them together. "Or Clawdia, if she's a girl."

"Will we be able to tell?"

She laughed, her voice like tinkling bells that made his insides all warm. "We'll have to wait, I guess. But, Mal?"

"Yeah?"

Brown doe eyes softened. "Thank you."

"You're welcome."

She flashed him one final smile before she left.

Yup. Fucking goner.

Chapter Ten

JASMINE

"Three . . . two . . . one . . . And we're done!" Erik the spin instructor called out from the front of the class as the music changed and the flashing lights slowly faded away. "You all were amazing. Give yourselves a round of applause."

"Whew!" Jasmine took a swig from her water bottle as she wiped her forehead with a towel. "Finally."

"Was that only forty-five minutes?" Leila, the girl on her right, panted. "Felt like hours. I don't know if I'm cut out for this. I could barely keep up with the routines."

"Don't worry, Lei," Tracy, who was on the other side of her, said. "It gets better after a few more classes."

Thursday was Jasmine's weekly spin class at the Jotunn Gym and Fitness Studio, but she hadn't attended the last three weeks, being so busy with the shop. However, when Tracy had messaged her this morning asking if she was ever coming back, Jasmine decided to go, plus she'd already paid for the classes anyway.

So, she took the bus to the strip mall in east Dewberry Falls where the gym was located and met up with Tracy, who brought Leila to the class. With her petite stature, pointy ears emerging from a nest of wavy brown hair, and pearlescent skin, Jasmine had immediately recognized her as a pixie, even with her wings tucked away under her exercise clothes. She had a friend back in high school who was a pixie, and she said they only unfurled their wings when they needed to fly because they were so big, but also extremely sensitive.

"It's tough being the newcomer." Jasmine patted her on the hand. "I've been doing this for six months, but I improved after, like, three weeks. After my first class, though, I thought my legs would fall off."

"Let's cool down, shall we?" Erik called. As the house lights above turned on, the blue glow from his eyes disappeared. His pure white hair was slicked back with sweat, though because he was a frost giant, the tips of it were flecked with little ice crystals. "Okay, stretch those arms up . . ."

Jasmine slowed her legs and followed the cool-down routine. She was exhausted, but in a good way. She looked forward to this spin class every week, not just for the cardio, but for the duration of the entire class, she didn't have to think about anything else. It was her "me" time and stress relief. Besides, ever since she'd moved to Dewberry Falls, her life for the most part revolved around Fantastic Tails. She loved managing the shop, but all she did was wake up, go to work, come home, go to sleep and do it all over again the next day. It was actually Vrig who suggested she take up a hobby or exercise, as he was worried she was getting too stressed out.

Oh, Vrig.

Grief was a funny thing; Jasmine had never known her mother and even though she was sad about not having her around, it didn't quite hit her as hard as the loss of Vrig. The pain of her grandmother's death, however, remained fresh in her memory, though over the years, the pang didn't hit as often. Vrig was probably the first friend whose death she'd experienced, and with it being so recent, she would still think he was sitting at home or inside his office before she was reminded that he was gone.

At least, though, for the first time since he passed, she didn't quite have that sense of foreboding that left her on tenterhooks all the time. In fact, the last two weeks had even felt, well, normal. Though the initial boom of sales from the assembly and their sudden social-media success had died down, sales were still steady. In fact, they'd made more money in the last week than they had the same time last year, plus gaining more followers and hearts on their posts, thanks to Mal's cooperation. While she avoided posting pictures that objectified him, his photos still garnered the most attention. It was hard to believe how much had changed in the last month since he'd arrived.

And now he only had five more months before he had to go.

A different pang hit her in the chest, one that she desperately wanted to go away. Despite her best efforts, she was still crushing on her boss. How could she not? They were together for six days a week. Plus, she spent the last couple of days watching him hammer and saw and drill, his sweat covering his brows and bare forearms as he built that tank for her.

Yes, Jasmine, I'll build you a hatching tank.

Not build *a* tank, but build *you* a tank.

She shook her head mentally.

I'm putting way too much meaning in his words.

Besides, it was just an ordinary tank, at least from the bits and pieces that she'd seen. He had most of the area sectioned off and hidden with a special soundproof barrier so as not to stress out the animals with the construction noise. Jasmine was reluctant to go inside or take a peek, lest Mal think she was micromanaging him, plus he was doing this as a favor, so she wanted him to have the freedom to do what he needed without interference from her.

"Unclip yourselves from the pedals," Erik instructed as he swung his legs over his bike and landed gracefully beside it. "Bend down, stretch out, put your hands together as you rise and take a deep breath and expel it, pushing out all the stress and worries from your body."

Jasmine shoved thoughts of Mal aside as she followed the frost giant's instructions. When she inhaled, she gathered all her troubles—the fear of losing everything she had built here in Dewberry Falls—and expelled everything out. Last night she'd started on her business plan for the shop, not to mention that she'd managed to live so frugally in the last four weeks that she'd already saved a big chunk of money.

Erik clapped his hands. "Goodnight and thanks, everyone. See you next week."

"I am beat," Jasmine declared. "I need a shower and bed."

"Shower and bed?" Tracy's nose wrinkled. "But what about our post-workout drink?"

"You know I can't, Trace." She was the manager at the credit union where Jasmine was hoping to get a loan. "I'm on a budget."

"You've already missed the last three weeks," she whined. "Please? Just one drink?"

"Ooh, I could use a drink," Leila piped in. "Can I join?"

"Sure, but Jasmine's being a party pooper and wants to go home."

"Please come, Jasmine," Leila urged. "We don't have to go anywhere fancy. There's a new place on Main Street. I heard they're doing half-price drinks for ladies on Thursdays to get people in."

"Is that the one with the hot gargoyle bartender?" Tracy asked.

Leila chuckled. "That's the one. C'mon, Jasmine, you can do one drink. You deserve it."

Jasmine paused. "You know what, you're right." She'd been

making her own coffee every day, taking her own lunch to work, eating instant ramen for dinner every night, plus she'd cut down on her streaming subscriptions. Having one martini—half price, at that—wouldn't break her budget. "One drink."

"Hooray!" Leila raised a fist in the air triumphantly.

After a quick shower, all three girls piled into Tracy's car and drove down to Main Street. Jasmine told herself that she was also saving on bus fare, as she could walk home after.

"Here we are," Leila announced as they entered through a door with the sign "Cedar Grove Grill" above. After telling the hostess they were only coming for drinks, she directed them toward the back. They made their way across the modern-looking dining room, past the sleek black tables and elegant lighting fixtures, to the bar where a small crowd had already gathered.

"Looks like we're not the only ones who've heard about the half-off specials," Tracy said.

"Or the hot bartender." Leila nudged Jasmine with her elbow and pointed to the bar, where a tall figure held up a metal shaker in his hand. Though Jasmine couldn't make out his face from here, from his gray skin, the large horns poking out of his forehead, and of course, the clawed, bat-like wings protruding from his back, he was definitely a gargoyle.

"Half the women in town seem to be here," Tracy muttered. "We'll never get close enough to grab a drink."

"Maybe we can go somewhere else?" Jasmine suggested.

"Aww, c'mon, the line is moving." Leila pointed at the crowd. "Why don't you girls wait here? I'll try to wiggle my way to the front." She gave a dramatic shake of her long locks, sending shimmery dust flying all over.

"You don't have to—"

But the pixie was already gone.

Tracy rolled her eyes. "Sorry about that. She can be like a dog with a bone when she wants something."

"No worries, she seems really nice."

"Yeah, Leila's cool overall. Listen, would you mind waiting for her here? I need to go to the bathroom."

"Sure, go ahead." She waved her friend away, then took her phone out of her purse to do some work. First, she checked on the shop's social media sites to make sure she didn't miss any urgent direct messages. Then she opened the app for the security cameras inside the shop to check on the creatures. She was scrolling through the second-floor live camera feed when she heard a familiar voice.

"Jasmine?"

She looked up from her phone. "Mal?" Yup, sure enough, there he was, towering above her. "What are you doing here?"

"Dinner. Just finished." He raked his claws through his mop of messy hair. "And you?"

"Er, I went to my spin class, then my friends wanted to get a drink."

Mal's purple eyes darted toward the bar—and the bartender—his lips thinning. "I see."

Jasmine cringed inwardly. She couldn't even deny that she was here to see the gorgeous gargoyle. What would he think of her?

Ancestor spirits, she prayed. *Do you guys do time travel? I'd really like to go back to before I agreed to come here.*

"I got the drinks!" Leila cried, raising her small hands, which miraculously held three martini glasses without spilling. "Oh my gods, Jasmine, that bartender really is as hot as they said. I'm so glad we came here."

Actually, ancestor spirits, how about we start from scratch? Like, to before the Big Bang happened? That was probably the only way to erase this embarrassing moment from existence.

"Here." The olives in the glass sloshed around as she handed a glass to Jasmine. "I—Oh, hello." The pixie's eyes widened to occupy half her face as she gaped at Mal. "Jasmine, who's your friend?"

"Leila, this is Mal," she introduced. "Mal is my, uh, boss."

"Is that so? I'm Leila. Nice to meet you, Mal." She flashed him a bright smile.

"Same," he replied. "I was about to go home, so—"

"Oh noooo!" Leila shoved the second drink at Jasmine then hooked her free hand around his forearm. "You can't possibly be going. We just got here. I can get you another drink. Or you can have mine."

"Er, I'm okay, thanks."

Jasmine's stomach twisted like a pretzel at the sight of Leila so close to Mal, her body pressed up against his side. This stupid crush was getting out of hand because she was now feeling so jealous of another woman flirting with Mal that she wanted to throw up.

"Hey, I'm back—hey there." Tracy's gaze flicked down to Mal and Leila's linked arms. "I thought you said we were going to meet a hot gargoyle bartender?"

Oh, for goddesses' sake, can we stop talking about the gargoyle bartender for one minute?

Leila introduced Mal and Tracy. "Mal doesn't want a drink, but he can keep us company." She dragged them over to the nearest empty cocktail table and set her drink down, then released his arm, much to Jasmine's relief. "So, Mal, you're an orc."

"And you're a pixie," he replied.

Leila laughed aloud. "Yup, I am. I've never seen an orc before, much less in Dewberry Falls. My family's been here for almost a century now."

"Leila's clan was one of the original Founding Families," Tracy said. "As in, the Founding Day Families."

Mal's nose wrinkled. "Jasmine told me about the Founding Day, but not about Founding Families."

"Let me give you a primer, then." Leila took a swig of her martini. "Nearly one hundred years ago, ten families escaping persecution from the larger world came together and founded Dewberry Falls as a place where all races, species, and creatures could live in harmony. They wanted this town to be a sanctuary for those who may not be accepted by the humans—no offense, Tracy, Jasmine."

"Oh, don't worry. I know how cruel they can be—even to other humans," Tracy replied.

"Anyway, that's the short version of the Founding Day. Isn't it cool?" She fluttered her eyelashes at Mal. "Orcs don't really travel much or mingle with non-orcs, do they?"

"No, I'm afraid not. Listen, ladies, I should head home. I have an early day."

Leila pouted. "So soon?"

"I'm afraid so."

"Seeing as you're new in town, Mal, you'll probably want someone to show you around." She grinned up at him, then her gaze flicked toward Jasmine. "I mean, unless Jasmine has already been doing that?"

Jasmine swallowed the tightness in her throat. "N-no, not at all."

"Oh, great." She snapped her fingers and a card appeared in her hand. "Here's my number. Call me anytime, okay, cutie?"

"Er, sure." Mal's eyes darted to Jasmine. "I forgot to tell you I finished the tank. You can look it over when you get in. Enjoy your drink. I'll see you tomorrow."

Jasmine sipped her martini, watching his retreating back from over the rim of her glass. Why did he have to choose to eat here of all places?

"Your boss is gorgeous, Jasmine," Leila said. "Even hotter than that bartender. I hope he calls me."

"Why didn't you ask for his number, then?" Tracy said. "This is the modern age, you know. Guys don't always have to make the first move. You don't have to sit around waiting for one to come courting."

"Courting?" She laughed. "Oh, you sweet summer child, I'm not looking to get courted." She licked her lips. "I want some of that legendary orc dick."

Jasmine choked on her drink. "E-excuse me?"

Leila's voice lowered. "Don't you guys know? Orcs have, like, these huge dongs." As if to emphasize her point, she held up both her hands and formed a circle with her fingers. "Actually . . ." She pulled them apart, leaving a gap between them. "More like this. And they have ridges on them."

"Ribbed, for her pleasure?" Tracy piped in.

"Yeah. I've never tried it myself. Seen the photos, though."

Jasmine wiped her mouth with a napkin, hoping it would hide the blush on her face. It was probably too late, as now she couldn't stop thinking about Mal naked and what his cock looked like.

Not that she would ever see it.

"You okay, Jasmine?" Tracy asked.

"Er, yeah." She took a healthy swig of her drink, the warmth shooting straight to her belly, making her limbs all as loose as rubber bands. Or maybe it was the thought of Mal's big—

"Oh, speaking of dicks, I dated his jaguarman once . . ."

Tracy sent Jasmine an apologetic look as the pixie waxed poetic about the male anatomy of her former conquests. She returned it with a wry smile and a raise of her glass, then downed the rest of her drink, trying not to think about facing Mal tomorrow.

Turns out, Jasmine didn't have to worry about seeing Mal at the shop the next day. She arrived thirty minutes before opening time, but she could tell he wasn't there. Normally, the lights would all be on, but it was still dark when she stepped inside Fantastic Tails.

Huh.

She never bothered to check the house before leaving, because nine times out of ten, he was always here first. While it was unusual, perhaps her ancestor spirits had heard her prayers and made him sleep in.

Or maybe he stayed up late texting Leila?

Her stomach churned, but she put those thoughts away. If Mal wanted to text Leila until four a.m., he could do that and there was nothing Jasmine could say or do about it. She was only his employee, after all.

As soon as she hit the light switch, her attention was immediately drawn to the center of the room. Gone was the construction area and in its place was a cloth covering what Jasmine assumed was the hatching tank, cordoned off with a rope and makeshift poles. Mal mentioned he had finished it last night. He must have been working late, because when she'd left for the day, he'd still been at it.

Ding ding dong!

"Welcome to—Mal."

"Jasmine," he greeted as he trudged inside. "Er, sorry, my morning call ran late." He shoved his hands into his mop of hair, pushing it back, the muscles on his forearms flexing. Instead of his usual flannels, he wore a black T-shirt today, perhaps due to the temperatures rising the past week. The material stretched over his wide chest and trim middle, clinging to what she guessed was a perfect set of abs.

Don't ogle him, don't ogle him, Jasmine repeated. *And definitely don't look below his waist.*

She wished she had never learned about orc dick. It had taken all her might not to start searching on the internet the minute she got home last night.

"Have you had—" A loud buzzing sound interrupted him, and he fished his phone from his pocket and glanced at the screen. "Sorry, excuse me." Without another glance at her, he marched toward the back office, the door slamming loudly as he hurried inside.

Mal had never been the type to get distracted by his phone. He never scrolled his feed when he was bored. He never even texted as far as she could tell.

Did he make an exception for Leila?

Jasmine rubbed at her chest, trying to ease the pressure building there. If they were talking, that wasn't her concern, she reminded herself sternly. And if they decided to sleep together, that was *definitely* none of her business, even though the thought of it made her want to lose her breakfast.

Oh Mother Goddess.

If it wasn't evident before to Jasmine, it was now: she had to get over this crush. Pronto. With a determined huff, she strengthened her resolve to draw a clear line between her and Mal, one that she would never cross.

Jasmine busied herself with work, taking care of the creatures, entertaining customers, answering emails and messages, and accepting deliveries. Still, her stupid brain wouldn't stop reminding her that Mal hadn't left the back office all afternoon. Sure, he'd emerged at lunchtime, but he looked distracted as he walked out the door, phone in hand. He hadn't even asked her if she wanted anything from the café or bakery, not that she ever said yes because she did pack her own lunch. No, he just walked out, eyes focused ahead, not even giving her a second glance.

Was he ignoring her because of last night?

Or because he was too caught up texting Leila?

"Argh!" She curled her hands into fists and looked to the heavens. How in the world was she going to get over this little crush?

Focus on work, she told herself. *Five more months and he'll be gone.*

Besides, she had more important things to worry about. For example, Founding Day was about two weeks away and she still had to think of what promotions to do, how to decorate their booth outside, and to start designing the flyers and coupons she would be giving away. Determined to focus on her tasks, she worked on the designs for flyers and their booth for the next few hours.

Feeling her eyes start to strain from staring at the screen for too long, Jasmine pushed away from the computer. She quickly glanced at the door to the back office, then scolded herself, before deciding to head upstairs. All the creatures up here had been fed and their tanks cleaned this morning, so she really didn't need to be there, but it was a good way to stretch her legs and reminded her why she wanted to do this in the first place. Frankly, she'd been so busy with the uptick in business that she'd been neglecting the animals. As soon as she approached the kelpie tank, the little horse-like creatures galloped toward her.

"Hey there," she greeted, pressing her fingers against the glass. "You all must be lonely." The tank usually held about ten kelpies at a time, but now there were only three. "Don't you worry—we'll find you some good homes."

Big corporate pet stores always kept their tanks full, and pens occupied, as nearly empty cages and aquariums weren't attractive to customers. However, Jasmine never ordered new kelpies without making sure all the current ones were first sold off, even if it didn't look aesthetically pleasing. Besides, the supplier Fantastic Tails worked with didn't overbreed their stock, so it took a while to get new ones in.

Seeing as it was almost time for her to close up, she checked on the other animals and went through her closing routine. She had finished cleaning up the mini wyrm habitat when she heard a voice behind her.

"Jasmine?"

Her heart stuttered in her chest at Mal's familiar baritone. With a quick breath, she turned to face him. "Yes, Mal? Did you need something?"

"No." He rubbed at the back of his neck. "Just wondering where you were."

"Oh."

"And if you had a chance to look over the hatching tank?"

"Not yet. It was still covered when I got in. I didn't know if you wanted me to take a peek. And I didn't have much time when I got in."

"Do you want to see it now?"

"Sure."

She followed him down the stairs, and with him a few steps below her, his shoulders and back were directly in her line of sight. Her fingers itched to reach out and run her hands over the muscles, to feel their hardness and then scratch her nails into his scalp while nuzzling at his neck to breath in his male, musky scent.

Bad Jasmine, she scolded as she stiffened her arms to prevent them acting on her impulses. She had to remember that line she had drawn today, and her vow never to cross it.

When they reached the main floor, Mal gestured for her to walk ahead of him. "Take a look."

Grabbing the corner of the cloth, she pulled it off—and let out a startled gasp. Jasmine had expected a normal aquarium with four glass walls. But this was a work of art.

The tank stood on a raised wooden platform so its contents would be at eye level. But instead of leaving the side panels unfinished, he had carved designs on them. Leaves, vines, and flowers crawled along the wooden surface, while different creatures frolicked among them. One side had "Fantastic Tails and Magical Scales" written in the same font as their sign.

She ran a finger across the carving of a dog leaping over a fallen tree trunk, marveling in the detailing of its body, which was when she noticed that it wasn't just any normal dog. From the star-shaped markings on its fur, this was obviously Cora the laelaps.

Jasmine also recognized the other animals from the shop. In one corner was Felix the carbuncle, curled up and taking a snooze, while Daryl the tizzie whizie buzzed overhead. The makara that had attacked Mal that first day stood under the front opening, guarding the precious egg inside. And of course, their favorite escape artists—the two mini cockatrices—were perched on top of a vine.

The interior was even more breathtaking. Similar to the makara habitat, half of the tank was filled with salt water to mimic the ocean, with waves that pushed against the sandy shore. Lush greenery and large rocks occupied the other section, and planted on the beach was the carcinos egg. The lighting Mal used overhead showed off the beauty of the egg, the blue pearly scales shining even brighter than she remembered.

Her breath caught in her throat as a beam of light moved across the surface of the egg, making it sparkle and the scales ripple like a wave. Did Mal use some special type of bulb to give it that effect? Whatever it was, it was mesmerizing, and she struggled to tear her gaze away.

"Mal, this is amazing."

"I wanted to finish it." He strode over to her, stopping when they stood side by side in front of the tank, catching her gaze in the reflection of the glass. Superimposed over the egg, his eyes appeared more royal blue than purple.

"Finish it?"

"Yes. I knew you needed it fast. I did say I would build you a hatching tank."

Her heart tripped over itself at his words. Jasmine recalled him saying that the other night when she asked him to do it, but she'd brushed it off and concluded what he meant was that he was doing it for the shop.

Yes, Jasmine, I'll build you a hatching tank.

But she didn't think—or didn't dare hope—Mal meant that he really was doing it *for her.*

"Stayed late last night," he continued. "And I was hungry by the time I was done. So I went to catch a quick bite at the Cedar Grove Grill."

Oh Mother Goddess, the reminder of last night's debacle with the hot bartender flooded into her brain. *One ticket to Cringe City, please.*

"Yeah, about that. Just so you know, I don't usually go to places like that." Better to bring it out in the open, otherwise she'd never be able to face him again. "I mean, Tracy and I always have a drink after our spin class, but not lately. And we certainly have never been to that bar."

"Oh, I see." His mouth pursed. "It's none of my business, of course."

Glad he thought the same way she did. "And I only met Leila last night for the first time, in case you were wondering and wanted to ask me about her."

"Ask you about Leila?"

"Yeah. But I mean, you've been texting her and everything, so I assume—"

A loud vibration made him start. "Sorry," he murmured as he patted his pockets, searching for his phone.

Jasmine's heart plummeted. Was that Leila calling to ask why Mal hadn't texted her in the last five minutes?

"Jasmine, are you okay?" Mal had found his phone, but didn't pick up the call or even glance down to check the caller ID.

"All good. You should probably answer that."

He tapped at the screen without looking at it. "I'm not texting or talking to Leila."

"You're not?"

"No." He slipped the phone into his back pocket. "A former client called me last night and asked if I was free to do some remote consulting work. So, we've been on the phone, working out the details. It's good money, but he never lets up. He's been calling me all day about his ideas, and he can't stop. Then he gets anxiety over this project, and I have to talk him off a ledge."

"I had no idea."

"That's what this job is, I'm afraid. Part contractor, part therapist." He snorted. "So, I'm not talking to Leila. Or any other woman."

"Oh." A heavy weight lifted off her, and she felt so light she could float. However, she swiftly yanked herself back down to earth. "I mean, if you were, it's totally none of my business."

"But I'm not."

"She's pretty. I wouldn't blame you if you did ask her out."

Jasmine made a motion to brush past him, but Mal extended his arm out. She collided right into the steel-like limb as it caught her around the waist and lifted her up to press her against his hard body. Her stomach swooped as his mouth came down on hers. It only took half a second for the kiss—she and Mal were kissing!—to register in her brain, but after that, she was one hundred per cent all-in.

His mouth was ravenous, devouring hers like he hadn't eaten in days. The tree-trunk-like arm around her waist tightened, the force of his kiss bending her backward like they were on the cover of a historical romance novel. He was the big bad duke dressed only in breeches, while she was the damsel spilling out of a low-cut gown who was trying to resist him. Except Jasmine wasn't trying to resist him at all, not even a little bit. No, she poured her entire being into returning his ardent kisses.

His tongue licked at the seam of her mouth and she opened up to him, parting her lips. Their tongues danced together, tangling in an urgent rhythm. Her breath came in short gasps as he seemed determined to kiss her harder and devour her. His tusks were set wide apart enough that they didn't harm her, but they did graze her cheek. They were smooth and blunt and surprisingly pleasant against her skin.

She gasped into his mouth as he bent down and hauled her up higher, pressing her back against the glass wall of the aquarium. Hooking one hand under a knee, he wrapped it around his waist. She didn't need further encouragement to do the same with her other leg, her hands clinging on to his meaty shoulders, the muscles responding under her touch.

Digging his hips into her, he pinned her with his lower body, a significant bulge pressing insistently against her. Significant didn't even begin to describe it. She shuddered as the ridge of his erection hit her at the right angle, hinting at things to come.

Oh Mother Goddess. They were going to have sex. Right here and now, against the beautiful tank he made *for her*. That wouldn't just be crossing the line; no, it would be coming in like an invading army and knocking down border walls.

Squaaaaawwkkk!

Mal's lips froze against hers, then tore away. Slowly, he placed her back on her feet, then stepped back. Jasmine wasn't quite sure if she should curse or thank the creature—probably the cockatrices or the kinnari—for interrupting their kiss.

"I'm . . . Jasmine . . . I'm sorry. I shouldn't have done that."

Chapter Eleven

Mal should not have kissed Jasmine. He was an idiot of the highest order. But he couldn't help himself.

Mal had no idea that she assumed he'd been texting with the pixie from last night. Why would he? He was not interested in Leila. When Jasmine casually suggested he go out with her, something inside him snapped and he gave in to his impulses.

Should he not have kissed her? Yes.

But he didn't regret doing it. After weeks of wondering, he finally knew how she tasted and how perfectly her curves fitted against his body.

"You-you don't have to apologize."

"I'm your boss. I shouldn't have—"

"If you think you forced me, Mal, y-you're wrong." Despite the tremble in her voice, she sounded resolved. "I let you kiss me—I wanted you to."

He let out an internal groan. She was not making this easy. "And I've been wanting to do that for the longest time." Since he met her, really. "But I wasn't sure . . . You were so . . . I couldn't . . ." The scent of her perfume hung in the air, doing something to the synapses in his brain so it refused to send the proper signals to his tongue. When he managed to collect his thoughts, he said, "We can't do this, Jasmine. There can't be anything more than a professional relationship between us."

Disappointment passed across her face, but was swiftly replaced by a serious expression. "You're leaving in five months."

"I have to. Sooner if I hear back from that job."

"You don't have to explain anything, Mal, really." The fact that she sounded so resigned when her hair was disheveled, and her lips were still swollen from their kisses made him feel like an absolute heel. "And don't think I let you kiss me because you're my boss. I'm still planning to buy this place from you, legally and fairly."

"No—no! Of course I don't think that's why you kissed me." Gaku help him, why was this so hard? "It's not you, Jasmine. You're beautiful and kind and warm. Anyone would be lucky to be with you. It's not right, knowing I can't offer you more than a few months of fun."

A dark eyebrow cocked up. "And what if I want to have some fun?"

She was *really* not making this easy. "I'm not that type of guy, Jasmine. And I can't stay here."

The atmosphere grew thick around them as that truth hung between them. After a heartbeat, she broke the silence.

"You didn't want to come here in the first place. This isn't your home."

"It's not that exactly." He searched for a way to explain it to her. "Remember what you said to me a couple weeks ago? About how Dewberry Falls, and the shop feel like home to you?"

She nodded. "Yeah."

"For orcs, home isn't a place. We believe we have two homes: our homeland where our people sprang from and our heart-home—ashak'roca—which we carry with us wherever we are. It's a state of mind where we are at peace and are content, and for me, that's my work. I love my job, not just because I'm paid well, or I get to travel the world. It's because it fulfills me, and as a builder orc, it brings me closer to my roots. My father was a builder, you see. He died when I was ten years old."

"I'm so sorry, Mal."

He flashed her a grateful smile. "I'm the last of our line, which is why I inherited all of Vrig's assets. When I'm working, it's like my dad's here, even now that he's gone." He paused, trying to construct the words in his head so that she would understand. "This job I'm waiting on, it's not just any normal constructing job. It's the renovation of our historic center back in Ghalad-Dur, the orc homelands. It doesn't pay much, but it's not about the money."

"It's about your legacy," she said in a soft voice. "Your traditions. And working on it would make you feel closer to your father."

Mal shouldn't have doubted that Jasmine would understand perfectly. "If he were alive, he would have done everything he could to get that job. Maybe we would have worked on it together too."

"Oh, Mal . . ." Her small, soft hand covered his. "I've no doubt that would have made him happy."

"He'd be so proud if I got the job."

"I think he'd be proud regardless." Her grip tightened on his hand before she let go.

"This job would take up all my time. I'd have to move back to the homelands until I was done, maybe two or three years, though from experience it'll be closer to five. I would also need to leave the moment I hear from them. That's why I can't guarantee you anything more than a couple of months of fun." And she deserved so much more than that.

"You didn't have to explain all that, but thank you. Truth be told, I'm *not* that type of girl, either. If we got involved and you had to leave . . . it would be too hard, emotionally."

Her admission sent his hearts soaring, but at the same time, wrapped him in fear.

"Besides, you're right. We should keep our relationship professional. Anything more would muddy things between us," she added.

Her words did not give him relief, nor did they ease the ache of wanting her. Perhaps he'd always want her, but regardless, this was the right decision for both of them. "Agreed."

"We should forget this happened."

"Yes, we should." Though that was highly unlikely for him. The taste and the feel of her body would haunt him for the next few months. Possibly for years to come. Even now, his raging erection refused to abate, and the following nights would be spent dreaming of her as he stroked himself to what he knew would only be a temporary state of relief.

"I'll head h-home, i-if that's okay." She scooted to the counter and grabbed her purse. "Would you mind closing up? The upstairs is done, but—"

"I'll take care of everything down here."

"Are you sure—"

"Yes. You have a system." He nodded at the clipboard by the first row of pens. "I won't mess it up."

"Th-thanks."

Jasmine scuttled out the door like she had the devil after her. And who could blame her? This whole thing was awkward, and it was entirely his fault for giving in to temptation and kissing her.

Mal let out a resigned grunt as he grabbed the first clipboard off the hook. In a couple months, he'd be gone; maybe he'd even hear back from the Historical Society sooner. At this point, he was desperate for any word. Losing the bid would be disappointing, but had always been a possibility. At the very least, he could line up his next job and leave Dewberry Falls—and start the process of forgetting Jasmine Gonzalez.

Mal checked the time on his watch, making sure he left the house so that he would arrive at the pet shop after noon. In the last week, he'd done his best to avoid Jasmine. He still went to Fantastic Tails every day, because he'd already made a long list of things he wanted to do around the shop. Despite his resolve to stay away from her, he'd made a promise to help, and an orc always kept his promise.

So he'd stuck to his early schedule, arriving before she did in the morning and usually stayed late or left before she did, so they hardly ran into each other. Neither had planned it that way, but that's how it turned out, as if they had an unspoken agreement to stay out of each other's way. However, every single night, he sat in the kitchen, waiting until the light in the garage apartment switched off at ten thirty on the dot.

Today, however, he'd had to stay home because of a conference call, which didn't finish until ten a.m. That was the time Jasmine was usually busiest on the main floor. To avoid running into her, he decided to head to Fantastic Tails during lunchtime. She usually locked up and went to eat her lunch at the park. He could not risk seeing her again. It would just be too awkward now, after their kiss. Maybe once things went back to normal, things could return to the way they were.

Not that he knew when things would go back to normal. Perhaps they never would, and they would have to tiptoe around each other for the next five months. The very idea of it had tempted him into calling the Orc Historical Society directly to ask if they intended to pick him or not. Thankfully, he spoke with his parents again, and he decided to follow his stepfather's advice to just leave it be for now.

With the "Closed" sign displayed on the window, Mal breathed a sigh of relief and headed inside—he promptly locked eyes with Jasmine, standing behind the counter, brown doe gaze wide with surprise.

"M-Mal," Jasmine stuttered. "You're here."

"Uh, yeah." He rubbed the back of his neck. "Meeting ran late. No lunch today?"

"I, uh . . ." Her gaze flicked toward the tank. "I was worried . . ."

"Worried? Is something wrong?" With his long strides, he crossed the room in no time. "Everything seems fine . . . Seals are holding . . . The base is steady." He gave the tank a thorough inspection. "I could probably touch up that one corner." His fingertip ran over the rough spot he'd missed with his sander.

"No-no, it's all fine," Jasmine said as she appeared beside him. "I know this sounds weird, but I just didn't want to leave it alone. So, I quickly ate my lunch and decided to stay and do some inventory."

"I see."

The seconds of agonizingly awkward silence stretched between them. Just a week ago, he'd had her pressed up against the glass and—

"Well, I should—"

"Do you—" she said at the same time.

Another uneasy pause.

"Have you—"

"Did the—"

Mal let out a huff. "I'll be in the office. I'll take care of that corner later."

"Okay."

Mal cursed to himself as he retreated. Straying away from their unspoken agreed schedule had caused this encounter, so from now on, he would never come in late.

Mal coasted along for the next week, keeping busy and away from Jasmine, that was, until the weekend of the Founding Day Festival. It was early on Friday when he noticed that Main Street already buzzed with activity. Usually, at this hour all the businesses were still closed, or their owners were just trudging into their shops and restaurant to start their mornings.

Today, however, employees and shopkeepers hustled about, placing tables in front of their storefronts, decorating their display windows, and hauling out their wares from inside. Brew-tique had put a makeshift bar outside with an enchanted coffee machine pumping out small cups of espresso, while a magical register rang up orders, mostly from other Main Street employees looking for a jolt of caffeine to jumpstart their early day. A banner was strung across the street, from the library to the general store, with the words "Happy Founding Day, Dewberry Falls!"

Mal nodded and acknowledged the people who waved or greeted them. The restaurant workers in particular recognized him. Not much of a cook, he'd already eaten at every single eatery on Main Street at least three times. Thank Vorlak everyone was rushing today so he didn't have to engage in small talk, though he picked up his pace so he could get to the shop sooner. When he got to Fantastic Tails, the door was wide open, and to his surprise—and annoyance—Kap strolled out, carrying a large table.

"Morning, Mal," he greeted much too cheerfully at this hour.

"Kap." The only reason he managed a neutral reply was because Jasmine had confirmed the tree giant wasn't her boyfriend. Still, his first instinct was to demand to know what he was doing here, though he pivoted to a more casual, "Did you change schedules at the department?"

"No, still the same, but I took off early. Jasmine asked me to help her set up for the festival."

A gut-burning sensation churned in his stomach at the idea that Jasmine would ask Kap and not him.

You know why she didn't ask, he told himself. Not that the reminder helped the jealousy swirling in his gut.

Kap placed the table down on the pavement, then covered it with a red tablecloth slung over his shoulder. "This is your first Founding Day Festival, right? You'll love it. It's fun. There's food trucks, games, rides, and the big parade tomorrow. And—Hey, Jasmine, is this okay?"

Mal froze as awareness of Jasmine's presence washed over him when she strode out of the shop. Then, a different kind of awareness located lower on his body came over him as he saw what she was wearing—cutoff denim short shorts that showed off her tanned legs and a tight shirt that stretched across her generous breasts. Instead of its usual braid, her long, lustrous hair was pulled back into a high ponytail that swung behind her like a waterfall.

"That's fine—Mal." Brown doe eyes grew twice their size. "Good morning." The awkwardness between them was palpable from the way her dusky cheeks tinted pink, and as she averted her gaze, he knew she was thinking of that torrid makeout session.

Miraculously, not all his brain cells had left him, and he managed to croak back, "Good morning, Jasmine."

"I thought you said you were going to change into something more appropriate." Kap pressed his lips together.

Jasmine fanned herself. "It's only seven fifteen and I'm already sweating. Forecast said temps are gonna soar this afternoon." Her arms crossed under her chest, pushing up her breasts so invitingly that Mal had to stifle a groan. "Do you have a problem with it?"

"Er, I'm just . . . concerned."

"*Pffft.*" She waved a hand at him dismissively. "I've seen worse. At least I don't have to be in a bikini top, like the girls doing the charity car wash."

Mal was glad too, because he'd probably end up embarrassing himself in front of half Dewberry Falls if he saw her in swimwear.

"I, uh, don't want you to get sunburned or anything. I heard the UV index's gonna go through the roof today," Kap said. "Right, Mal?"

Kap obviously wasn't concerned about Jasmine's skin health, but rather worried that she'd get harassed. For once, he agreed with the tree giant, but he wasn't going to say anything.

"I'll put on sunscreen," she snapped. "But I'm not stupid. I know what you're implying. Stop with the protective big-brother act, Kap. I can do what I want, and if people take issue with what I'm wearing, then that's their problem. I'm gonna go get the flyers." She huffed, turned on her heel and marched inside, her hips swaying provocatively. It took all of Mal's strength not to ogle her denim-covered ass.

Kap frowned. "Sometimes I swear she doesn't realize how much attention she gets. Not that I think of her that way. I'm just concerned and maybe a bit old-fashioned, but that's how I was raised, you know? And Jasmine's dad made me promise to look after her. Should we hang around her, to keep an eye on things? That way, if she gets into a sticky situation, one of us will be within arm's reach."

"Oh no." Mal raised his hands defensively. "I'm not getting into this. She's an adult and we need to respect her right to do what she wants." Even if the thought of another male looking at Jasmine in that outfit made him want to punch a hole in the wall.

"I suppose you're right," Kap said, resigned. "She's really mad at me, huh?"

"I'd say so."

"Good thing I have my secret weapon." He plucked something from his back pocket—a candy bar. "Here's a tip. If you ever piss her off, a couple of these'll help smooth things over."

"Er, thanks." Not that he ever planned on getting on Jasmine's bad side again. He'd already learned that lesson. "I should head inside."

"See ya, Mal."

With a wave to Kap, he strode into the store, nearly colliding with Jasmine.

"Oops!" she cried, staggering backwards, arms desperately waving like wings to stop herself from falling over while simultaneously holding on to the flyers in her right hand.

Mal reached out and caught her by the shoulders, though he let go of her like a hot coal once she'd steadied herself. The memory of her skin was still stamped in his mind, and he didn't need a reminder.

"Th-thanks." She clutched the flyers against her chest.

"No, it was my fault."

"It's not—" she began.

"I'm sorry—" he said at the same time.

She cleared her throat. "Uhm, yeah, so it's the Founding Day Festival weekend."

"Yes. I see you roped Kap into helping you."

"Yeah, usually Vrig's here, but now I need the extra pair of hands."

"Right." Mal could have helped her—if he hadn't been avoiding her these last couple of days.

An awkward beat passed. "So, do you need any help—"

"N-no. No." She shook her head. "I'll be fine, Mal. Really. Fridays aren't usually crowded."

He hesitated, but trusted she knew better. "All right. But at least let me give out breakfast."

"You don't—"

"I got it," he assured her. "Your system really is well written and organized."

"I—Thanks, Mal."

She scampered away from him and headed out, leaving Mal alone. He fought the temptation to follow her with his eyes and instead trudged upstairs so he could check on the creatures.

For the rest of the day, Mal kept himself busy with one or two things on his to-do list, and of course, checking on the carcinos egg and the hatching tank. He'd meant to keep it simple and functional, but the egg was much too exquisite to just sit inside a plain terrarium. Inspired by Vrig's work on the makara habitat, he'd recreated carcinoses' natural environment as best he could. The carvings on the side were a last-minute addition. At first, he'd added a few vines and flowers, but as he worked on it, he thought of all the creatures in the shop and it just grew from there.

While he didn't want to meddle in Jasmine's business, if one or two of his chores happened to be something that allowed him to peek outside—like oiling the squeaky door hinges or replacing the lightbulbs in the display window—then he told himself it was just coincidence. As Jasmine predicted, it wasn't busy at all that day. She spent most of the day sitting on a folding chair behind the table, chatting with people and giving out flyers, and coming inside to ring up purchases from customers. When he left at five o'clock, she was clearing the table and most of the other shops were packing up too.

Confident that she had everything under control, he showed up near noon the next day, as his client-slash-therapy patient went an hour over their designated thirty-minute meeting. By the time he entered Fantastic Tails, it was, to put it mildly, a madhouse. The shop was filled with more people than he'd ever seen before, loitering around the pens and peering at the pets inside, walking up and down the aisles of pet food and accessories, and scrambling up the stairs to the second floor. The animals didn't seem to appreciate the extra activity, if the many unhappy, cranky squawks, squeals, caws, and growls were any indication.

Where was Jasmine?

Good thing Mal was about two feet above everyone's heads, so he quickly spotted her in the back, by the chamrosh cage. He waded through the crowd to reach her.

"Thanks for stopping by," Jasmine greeted a couple as they walked away, then quickly turned to the family next to her. "So, you wanted to see the water horses, right?"

"No, no." The young boy stamped his feet. "I said I wanted an alicanto!"

"Right," Jasmine replied, flustered. "Why don't I show you—Mal?"

"What's going on?"

"It's the post-parade rush," she explained. "Everyone's tired and cranky, looking for a respite from the heat, so they head into the shops. We don't usually get this many actual customers, but everyone's been finding us on their Picstagram feed."

"Look, it's the orc!" someone stage-whispered behind them. "Do you think he'll pose for a selfie?"

Jasmine winced. "Uhm, the pictures of the hatching tank and the carcinos egg have also gone viral." She nodded to the middle of the room, where a stream of people snaked around the tank, waiting to get close to it. "I had to make everyone line up."

"I said I wanted an alicanto!" the boy screamed at the top of his lungs.

"Miss, can you please help us? We've been waiting for so long," the woman next to the boy—his mother presumably—said. "My husband and I want to go grab lunch."

"Yes, ma'am, of course."

"Finally," the husband said with a cluck of his tongue. "These little shops are so inefficient. I told you, Gina, we should have gone to PetExpress."

Jasmine's shoulders sank. "I'm really sorry for the wait."

"You should be." He snapped his fingers at her. "Now where's this bird my son's been harping on about?"

Mal's temper hit the roof. "Get out," he said in a deadly tone, pointing to the door. "You're not welcome here."

"I b-beg your pardon?" the man sputtered. "Where's the manager?"

"I'll do you one better." Folding his arms over his chest, he shot the man his most menacing look. "I'm the owner."

"And this is how you treat your customers?"

"When they disrespect my employees, then yes. Now get out," he growled.

The man harrumphed. "Fine. Gina, Ethan, let's go. We'll spend our money elsewhere."

The couple dragged away the boy even as he screamed his displeasure. Mal watched them walk out to ensure they were truly gone. "Are you okay, Jasmine?"

"Yeah. Thanks for dealing with that." Her lower lip trembled. "I hate rude customers; they just ruin my day."

He tsked. "You can't let them walk all over you."

"I try to be as polite as I can, but it's tough. Especially with the store's policy about not selling to people who might not be good owners."

"It's a smart policy." But it was also one of the main reasons the shop wasn't doing too well, though he understood why Vrig enforced it, and Jasmine refused to change it even now that he was gone.

Her hands gestured around them. "The extra foot traffic has been great for the store overall; it's also brought in the worst people. They just don't seem to get the concept that these are living beings, not toys they can just play with when they feel like it and then put away."

He snorted. "The customer isn't always right. If any more give you trouble, send them to me."

"Th-thanks, Mal." The smile widened. "For having my back."

"Of course." He would always have her back, no matter what.

"Actually, why don't you go outside and man the table, and I'll take care of things in here?"

"What? No, you don't have to—"

He held up a hand. "I'm still the owner, aren't I? Now, go."

Mal didn't much like crowds, but at least the one inside the shop wasn't out of control. The initial scene had been jarring as it was always so calm and serene on normal days, even during the busy weekends. The foot traffic was good for business, but the animals had to be under a lot of stress. So, he spent most of the afternoon directing the flood of people, asking them not to get too close to the animals or bang on their tanks or rattle their cages. Much to his chagrin, he also ended up posing for numerous selfies. It only got busier as the day wore on and he felt bad that Jasmine had to keep going back and forth inside to ring up customers, so he took over the register.

"Hey, are you the new owner of Fantastic Tails?" said a friendly masculine voice.

"Yeah?" Mal straightened up from where he crouched down behind the screen of the POS system. The first thing he noticed about the man were the large horns curling out from the top of his head and the pointy ears emerging from a nest of long, dark reddish hair. Since Mal was about a foot taller than him, a quick glance down at the thick fur and hooves of his lower half confirmed what he was—a satyr. "And you are?"

The satyr extended his hand over the counter. "Nick Amherst. You're Vrig's nephew, right?"

"Mal of the Urduk Horde." He shook the man's hand firmly before letting go. "Can I help you? Were you looking for a pet or . . ."

"No, no. I just wanted to come by and convey my condolences. Sorry it took me so long, though."

"Thank you. But how did you know Vrig?"

"We were on the same squad of the Dewberry Falls Volunteer

Fire Department," Nick explained. "He was a great guy. Even went on a few calls over the last couple of years. Not that we get a lot of fires around here to respond to. Such a big loss to the community."

"Yeah, he was a good person." Strangely, while Mal hadn't spent any significant amount of time with Vrig as an adult, being in Dewberry Falls, working around the shop, and living in his house had given him a sense of what Vrig must have been like. He regretted never reaching out to his uncle.

"I'm sorry for your loss." He paused for a beat. "Say, Mal, have you thought about joining the volunteer fire department?"

"Me?"

"Yes, definitely." Nick gave the counter a healthy pound of his furry fist. "A big strong guy like you, you'd be perfect."

"I'm afraid I'm not planning on staying in Dewberry Falls," Mal explained. "Just until I get the shop, and the house sold. Couple of months maybe. Seems like a waste to train me when I won't be around too long."

The satyr waved away his objection with a flourish of his hand. "Not at all. And we could use every hand we can get even if it's just for a couple of weeks. The training's not that hard and some of the stuff you learn, like the CPR and basic fire-safety certification, can be useful in real life."

"I'm already certified in both. I'm a contractor."

"Great! You'll be able to start sooner, then."

"I'm not sure I have time—"

"Our squad trains every other Thursday night and the entire department does one Saturday a month at a nearby Fire College."

"I'm quite busy—"

"The schedule is flexible, especially if you're a business owner. We really only get a few calls a week, mostly 'little old ladies whose cats get stuck up a tree' type of thing or accidents, which is why we don't have a full-time fire department. If we do get a big fire, Bayview and the other major cities around will send their trucks."

"Uh . . ."

"Listen, before you say no, why don't you give it a think? Sleep on it?" He slid a card across the counter. "Here's my number. Call me if you have any questions. You know, Vrig loved volunteering at the fire station. He said it kept him young."

"I . . . Okay." He picked up the card, if only to appease the insistent satyr.

"Great!"

"Hey, Mal—oh, Nick?" Jasmine exclaimed as she came up to them. "It's been a while." She opened her arms toward him.

"It's my favorite pet-shop manager." He bent down to accept her hug. While the embrace only lasted three seconds, it was enough for jealousy to once again rear up in Mal.

"Sorry I haven't been by since the funeral. How are things here?"

"All good." Her gaze flicked over to Mal. "Have you two met?"

"Yup, stopped in to introduce myself," Nick said.

"I'm surprised to see you here, since you're usually so busy with all the festival activities. Nick's part of the Founding Families," Jasmine explained. "Your float looked amazing during the parade, by the way. I loved the golden-vines theme."

"Yeah, that's my cousin Flora's work. She's super talented when it comes to art stuff, plus she's still sore about losing to the MacGregors last year." He glanced around, his long ears twitching. "Wow, it's really busy in here, huh? Good for you."

"Thanks."

He checked his watch. "I need to get going. But, Mal, I'll see you soon, eh?"

Jasmine's nose wrinkled. "See you soon?"

He winked at Mal. "He's going to join us at the fire station."

"I haven't—"

"Really? That's awesome, Mal. Vrig loved being a volunteer firefighter. He always said it kept him young."

Nick sent him a grin. "I should get going. See you at eight p.m. on Thursday at the fire station on Garland Avenue."

"See you, Nick." Jasmine waved at him as he ambled out the shop. "So, Nick convinced you to sign up for the volunteer fire department, eh?" she said with a wry smile.

"I . . . guess?" He slapped a palm on his forehead.

Jasmine chuckled. "Satyrs are known for their silver tongues, though I think Nick upgraded to the gold one. He could sell water to a kraken."

Had she ever been convinced by Nick's sweet talk? Not that it was any of his business if she had. The satyr was charming and handsome, and more important, he lived here. Him and Jasmine would make the perfect Dewberry Falls power couple.

He wondered if satyrs were fireproof.

"So how were things in here? Everything okay? You seemed pretty busy."

"Yeah, but I handled it fine."

"Thanks for calming down the animals." Her fingers brushed away the stray locks of hair that stuck to her neck and chest. She looked gorgeous in her linen sundress and Mal groaned inwardly each time a beam of sunlight lit her up from behind, showing off the shadows of her curves.

Jasmine let out an unhappy huff. "All those people in here at the same time must have been frightening for them. I feel so stupid and selfish now, just thinking about business and forgetting their comfort."

"Don't beat yourself up about it." Mal resisted the urge to reach out and console her. "It happens. You can't please everyone all the time. You have to find a balance and give yourself grace if you make mistakes every once in a while. But you have to know, you're doing a great job, Jasmine."

Her face lifted up, brown eyes softening as their gazes locked, sending his hearts galloping. Her luscious lips parted as a short gasp escaped her mouth. Awareness sparked between them, ready to burn up the room.

"Uhm, I should go back outside," she said, breaking the spell. "The crowds will be thinning soon. There's a big concert in Town Square tonight so most people will head there early to secure a spot. You can head home if you want."

"No, I can stay until you close up."

"It's fine, r-really. I'll be okay."

Clearly, the awkwardness between them had ramped up and she was giving him an escape from it. "I'm going to check on the hatching tank before I go," he said. "Had to tell off some punk troll kid and his friends for trying to open it."

Jasmine massaged the bridge of her nose. "Oh no. I forgot about the egg, too. I'll just—"

"Excuse me, miss?" A white-haired woman tapped her on the shoulders. "Can you help me find the treats for luscas, please?"

Jasmine snapped to attention, going into customer-service mode instantly. "Yes, of course. Right this way."

As she led the woman away, Mal strode over to the hatching tank. He checked the glass to make sure there were no cracks and double-hexed the lock on the front opening so that anyone aside from him and Jasmine who attempted to open it would get a nasty rash instantly. He'd love to see that teen troll come back and try to pull that stunt again.

Don't you worry, little one, he said to the egg as he crouched down to its level. *I won't let anything happen to you.*

"Did those kids damage it? How's Clawed or Clawdia?"

As Jasmine's form materialized on the other side of the glass, a brief flash of blue light filled the tank.

Was that—

"Mal?"

"Huh?"

"The tank," she repeated. "Did those kids break anything?"

"No, thank Vorlak." He rose up and circled the tank to reach her side. "I reinforced the front opening lock with a double hex. Better put up a 'do not touch' sign."

"Thanks, I will." She cocked her head. "Are you all right?"

"Yeah. All good." He dusted his hands on his pants. "Are you sure you're okay?"

"Yup, I can close up. You should probably head home or get some dinner. You haven't eaten all day, I bet."

"Neither have you," he pointed out.

"I did. Scarfed a sandwich sometime after noon."

"That was hours ago. Why don't I wait for you, and we can grab something at the café?"

"No, I have leftovers at home."

Mal told himself the rejection of his invitation didn't sting, and he was only being polite when he asked her anyway. "All right, I should go. Have a good night, Jasmine."

"You too, Mal."

As he turned to leave, he gave a last glance toward the hatching tank. He still wasn't sure what he had seen just now, but his gut screamed that this was no ordinary carcinos egg.

Or, perhaps, Jasmine wasn't quite what she seemed.

Chapter Twelve

JASMINE

"Thanks for your purchase," Jasmine said to the father and son duo who had bought the last of their kelpies. "Come see us again."

She waved as they exited the shop, the son holding the door open for his father as he carried out a brand-new tank under one arm and a bag full of goodies in the other.

Sunday of the festival weekend was Jasmine's favorite day. Most people were burned out after the frenzy of Saturday's activities, so now almost everything was winding down. The morning was still busy, but after lunchtime, the crowds waned. She didn't mind the slowdown, as they already had a blockbuster day yesterday, earning about fifty per cent more than last year if her calculations were correct. She was glad she'd followed Kap's advice and had T-shirts, mugs, and stickers made that featured cute cartoon drawings of different creatures, as those had practically flown off the shelves. However, she did draw the line at his suggestion of making shirts with Mal's face on it that said "Zaddy Orc."

Speaking of . . .

Her gaze drifted outside to where Mal stood beside their table, handing out flyers to passersby. She hadn't expected him to come today, but she should have known better. Even though he didn't have to, he came to her rescue yesterday. The crowds pouring in had been overwhelming and that rude father was the icing on the cake. When he'd gone all protective and growly her insides turned to mush. Her feminist side protested at his white—green?—knight act, but well, all other parts of her were screaming, "Yes, please, can I have some more?" like some Victorian-era orphan.

Oh Mother Goddess, I'm supposed to stop crushing on him.

That had been the plan from the very beginning, but that soul-searing kiss against the hatching tank pushed her further away from that goal. That had been over two weeks ago, yet it remained fresh in her mind—his firm lips, the way he moaned into her mouth, his large hands gripping her, the humungous bulge that had pressed up against her stomach. Just the thought of it had her core clenching tight.

Legendary orc dick, indeed.

Even now, as she watched from behind the display window, her eyes were drawn to his muscled back, her fingers hankering to dig into them again and feel them moving under her hands. Mal, as if sensing her ogling him, turned toward her. She leapt backwards, heart jumping into her throat. Did he see her? Warmth crept up her neck and she rushed behind the counter, hiding her face behind the computer screen, praying Mal wouldn't come in.

The rest of the afternoon saw even less customers, and by five o'clock, Jasmine decided to start closing up. She began with the pens and cages downstairs, dropping in dinner for those who needed it and cleaning out all the trays. After a quick wash of her hands, she climbed to the second floor to start with the creatures there. With nearly half their stock gone, she zipped through her work. As she was hanging up the last clipboard, she heard the heavy steps of Mal's boots trudging up the steps. She froze, her brain scrambling for an escape route.

Calm down, she told herself. *It's only Mal.*

"Hey, Mal." Her tone was casual and cool. "What—Oh, you didn't have to bring that up here. I could have asked Kap to come before his shift."

Mal carried the table from outside over one shoulder. "It's fine," he said in a gruff voice. He planted it on the floor so forcefully, the legs scraping the wood made Jasmine's teeth hurt.

Was he angry about something? Maybe he wasn't happy she refused his offer of dinner last night. She was tempted, but a) she didn't have the budget to eat out right now, and b) the two of them having dinner together would feel too much like a date, which would really put a crimp in her "stop crushing on your boss" plans.

"Mal?" she called as he pivoted toward the stairs.

"Yeah?"

"Thank you." She couldn't figure out what else to say, except that she hated that feeling stuck in her gut right now, knowing he was mad about something. "For coming in today. You didn't have to—"

Crash!

Mal's indigo eyes grew to the size of saucers as fear gripped Jasmine's chest.

"*The tank,*" they said at the same time.

Though Mal had bigger strides, Jasmine was faster. She raced down to the first floor, stopping short when she arrived on the main floor.

"Oh no," she cried. "Mal . . . your tank."

Shards and bits of glass littered the floor as one of the tank walls had been completely shattered. Stepping around the debris carefully, she gasped when she looked inside.

"What is it?" Mal's boots crunched on the glass as he drew closer. "Is the egg broken?"

"Yes. I mean, no, not quite."

Large chunks of pearly blue scales littered the floor of the aquarium, but the pieces were completely clean. Mal reached inside and picked up a shell shard. "Looks like it hatched."

"Yeah, that's what I figured."

He held up the piece to his nose, sniffed, then grunted.

"What's wrong?"

"Nothing. I mean . . ." He glanced around them. "A newly hatched carcinos couldn't have done this damage. It takes a few days for their exoskeleton to harden."

She bit at her lip. "So the egg wasn't a carcinos?"

"Unlikely."

"Do you know what it is?"

"No."

But she had a feeling he had a suspicion. Anyway, that didn't matter now. "Would it have crawled out—Oh no!"

Mal's head whipped toward where she was looking—one of the panels of the display window had been broken too. "Fuck," he cursed. "I noticed the reinforcement spell wearing out—I meant to fix it this week."

"We have a bigger problem, though," she pointed out. "The carcinos, or whatever it is, is out there."

"Mother Trakku." He rubbed a palm down his face. "All right, let's go find our escaped jailbird."

Did he think it was a bird, then?

"Okay," he began as the door locked behind them. "Let's split up. You stay on this side of the street, and I'll take the other."

She held up a hand. "But how do we know what we're looking for?"

"We'll probably know it when we see it."

"True." As he turned to cross the street, she called out to him.

"Wait, Mal! We have to be discreet. If the Main Street Business Association hears about this . . ."

"We'll get a big fine." He clenched his jaw. "Okay, we'll keep it as quiet as possible."

"Thanks, Mal."

Jasmine began her search next door at the dry-cleaners. Pushing the door open, she entered Main Street Dry-Cleaning and Laundry, her heart pounding as she waved at the owner, Mrs. O'Shea.

"Hello, Jasmine," the sweet, elderly woman greeted. "How are you? Did you have a good Founding Day Festival?"

"We did, thanks for asking, Mrs. O'Shea." Hopefully her voice sounded casual.

"What can I do for you? Did you want something dry-cleaned or pressed? We're still offering a ten per cent discount for all employees on Main Street."

"Not right now. I was wondering . . ." Oh Mother Goddess, how was she going to do this? "Have you seen anything strange going on around here? Anything unusual outside?"

The woman laughed. "This is Dewberry Falls, dear. I'm not sure what you would categorize as strange and unusual."

"Right." She forced out a laugh.

"Is there anything wrong, dear?" Concern creased her face. "You look flushed."

"Er, you see . . ." Her brain scrambled for an explanation. "We had one of our windows broken."

Mrs. O'Shea gasped. "Oh no. Do you have any idea who it was? Have you filed a report with the police?"

"No, not yet, ma'am. I think it might be just some kid. I'd like to speak with them or their parents before I get the authorities involved."

"How generous of you." She clucked her tongue. "All right, dear. If I see anything or anyone suspicious, I'll call you."

"Thank you, ma'am."

Jasmine went to every business on her side of Main Street, from the general store, the brewery, the bakery, and even the gardening store, asking if they had seen anything weird or out of the ordinary. By the time she reached the last store, the Glitter and Gold Jewelry Emporium, the sign in front had been turned to "Closed."

"Oh no."

She pressed her nose up against the glass, trying to peer inside, but didn't see any creature crawling around nor were any of the windows or display cases broken. The employees of Glitter and Gold always locked everything up tight at closing time and they also had a top-of-the-line security system. If anyone—or anything—broke in, they'd know right away. Still, she wished she had come here first, before they closed up. Her fingers itched, wanting to do something like break the window to check inside, but she didn't want to spend the night in jail.

Defeated, she trudged back to the shop. When she arrived at Fantastic Tails, Mal was already waiting outside.

"Any luck?" she asked.

"No." He shook his head. "Let's go inside and regroup."

Unsure what else to do, she followed him into the shop, stomach roiling at the sight of the broken glass on the floor. "Your tank . . ."

"Will be fine," he said. "I can fix it later. But we have bigger things to worry about."

He was right.

"So, what do we do now?" she asked.

"For starters, something we should have done first. Check the security cameras."

"Duh." She slapped a palm on her forehead, then ran behind the counter. Tapping the keyboard of her computer, she pulled up the footage from the main floor and played it. "Darn."

"What's wrong?"

"I didn't adjust the cameras when you started building the hatching tank." Turning the screen toward him, she played the footage. "You can see the glass shatter but not what broke out."

"And the display window?"

Jasmine's fingers flew over the keyboard and hit play when she found the right video. She *tsk*ed as a dark blur flew through the glass. "Too fast for the cameras to capture it."

"It definitely flew, though."

"Something with wings, then. A griffin?"

"Didn't see a tail. Phoenix?"

"They don't hatch from eggs—they regenerate from ash. Could the carcinos or whatever it is have just flown off? Is it gone from Dewberry Falls? Are we too late?"

"It's possible. But what do you think?"

She shrugged and leaned against the counter, elbows planting on the top and burying her face in her palms. "I have no idea."

A gentle, heavy hand landed on her shoulder. "Jasmine, I need to ask you something."

She lifted her head up. "What is it?"

"What does your instinct tell you?"

"Instinct?"

"Yes." His lips pressed together, tightening around his tusks. "Do you ever get these feelings or ideas and they turn out to be right?"

"Sometimes, but doesn't everyone? And I'm not always right."

He let out a grunt. "How about with the animals here? Do you feel particularly close to them? Like you seem to know what they want or what's wrong with them."

"Well, it's not that hard," she said. "They want food and a safe place to live. And if they act out of the ordinary, they're usually sick." She thought for a moment. "But there was this one time . . ."

"Yes? Go on?"

"We special-ordered this hybrid basilisk, right?" Her fingers clutched at the ends of her braid. "When she arrived, I just knew something was wrong. She wouldn't eat or move around her tank. The supplier said she was fine when he left his farm. The vet we called in said we probably needed to switch her food. But I didn't agree. Like, I could tell she was sick, just from the way she looked at me, as if she were asking for my help."

"What did you do?" he asked in a gentle tone.

"I looked back through the delivery company's records and I hounded them all day until I got a hold of the warehouse in Spokane where the basilisk stayed for one night on the way here. Turns out, they were also holding some weasels in the same warehouse."

"What?" he said, incredulous. "Weasel odor is deadly to basilisks."

"I tore them a new one. Thank the Mother Goddess I found out that day and was able to administer the antidote in time." Thinking about the whole thing infuriated her again. "But what does that have to do with anything?"

Mal's expression turned serious. "Jasmine, I believe you have an affinity for animals. Not just because you love them, but because you're in tune with their nature on a metaphysical level. A kind of magical link with them."

"M-magic?" She couldn't have been more surprised if he'd told her he thought she was a mermaid or a vampire. "That can't be."

"I noticed it not only with the egg but other things. Let me show you." His humungous palm engulfed her hand, the calloused skin rough and warm against hers. Lifting their entwined hands, he led her away from the counter and toward the oozlum cages, where four of the little feathered creatures flew around backwards in circles around the cage. Letting go of her hand, Mal placed his palm against the side of the cage.

"See?"

"See what? There's nothing happening."

"Exactly. Now." Circling her wrist, he placed her hand in the same spot. "Look."

The oozlums slowed, then flittered toward her hand. Their claws clung to the bars, stopping right by her fingers, chirping happily.

"They always do that," she said.

"Not for me." He pulled her hand away and replaced it with his, and the creatures went back to their usual flight path. "The other animals act the same way too."

Jasmine could only stare at his hand, her mind whirling like the oozlum's reversed flight trajectory.

"Surely you've had other experiences in the past?"

"Yes, but I . . . How come I didn't notice? Do you suppose Vrig could tell?"

"It's possible. Perhaps he didn't say anything because he thought you knew." He scratched a claw on his chin. "But aren't you human? Do you have someone in your family tree who wielded magic? An ancestor maybe?"

Her lungs squeezed the air from her body.

An ancestor.

"Jasmine? Are you okay? You look pale. Do you want to sit down?"

She lifted her face to meet his gaze. "No." Her lungs decided to work again as she took in a deep breath. "But I might have an explanation. In my family, we have something we call The Inheritance."

"Like money or property?"

"No, nothing like that." She didn't know quite how to explain it to an outsider, but she had to try. "The Inheritance isn't a physical thing. It's a gift. See, my grandfather was our town's medicine man. An *albularyo*, as we say. He could heal people by whispering spells and making herbal cures from plants."

"He had magic, then?"

"Yes. According to family legend, one of my ancestors, Emilio Gonzalez, received this power from a goddess or spirit. She disguised herself as a poor, sick woman who walked into town one day. No one would help her except Emilio, who took her in, nursed her back to health and gave her food and clothing. After three days, she returned to her true form, and as a reward, gave Emilio the ability to heal sick people and lift curses."

"So you have these powers now."

She shook her head. "No, I don't."

"You saw—"

"No, no. I can't. It's not possible." She stopped to catch her breath, as her heart was pounding as if she were running a marathon.

Or running away from her past.

"There was a catch, you see. The Inheritance could only be wielded by one person in the family at one time, passed on from one male heir to another, and chosen before the current holder dies. Naturally, only someone with male children could inherit, or else the magic would be lost forever once the current holder passes. When my grandfather died, my dad's younger brother inherited it. So, it's impossible that I have it."

"But you still have magic in your line? Couldn't it be possible you have it?"

"No."

"Even just—"

"Haven't you been listening?" she said bitterly. "I can never wield that magic; it will never pass through my line. It's only meant for the male members of my family. My father lost out on The Inheritance because I was unlucky enough to be born a girl."

And that was it. The secret she kept all these years, carried around with her, forming a looming shadow over her relationship with her father. Jed never said it outright to her face, he would never, of course, but she had overheard that snippet of conversation, and it became clear to her.

It's not fair. It's because of Jasmine, isn't it? The Inheritance should have been passed to me.

"First of all, that's a bunch of hydra dung. It's not your fault." Mal snorted. "Are you sure no female has ever received the magic? Or that it can't be shared between two people?"

"As far as I know, never."

"Or the men in your family didn't want to share it with the female offspring."

"Whether it's true or not, the family legend stands. There's only been one albularyo for every generation and they've always been male."

"Hmm." Mal's nose wrinkled.

She narrowed her eyes at him. "What is it?"

"Orcs have this belief, you see." He held her gaze, eyes turning luminous purple as he spoke. "We aren't traditional magic wielders, but our ancestors held on to what little magic they had and cultivated it, used it, shaped it to meet our needs. Somehow, this magic wove itself into our DNA, at least that's what our orc scientists say. It builds and spreads, multiplies as you use it. Perhaps the same thing happened with your family, a little bit of magic bleeding into the next generation's soul each time it passed on, giving all of Emilio's direct descendants the potential to wield The Inheritance, even the women. Regardless, you have some magic in you or an affinity for it, finely tuned for all kinds of creatures and powerful enough to draw them in or become immune to them."

"Like the cockatrice."

His lips spread into a smile. "Exactly."

Jasmine pressed a hand to her chest. "This is . . . a lot to process right now." But what Mal was saying made sense somehow. Perhaps that's why she was drawn to the shop, the animals, maybe even to Dewberry Falls.

"Take your time, think about it."

"Not right now. We have to find the carcinos—or whatever hatched from that egg." She chewed at the inside of her cheek. "How can I use my m-magic to find it?" She tripped over the word, as it felt strange on her tongue.

"I'm not sure, but maybe you can let your instinct guide you. Every creature inside here has magic and leaves a trace. See if you can connect to that."

"All right." She walked out toward the middle of the room, to the broken tank. Thank goodness the beautiful platform hadn't been destroyed, though she did notice something at the corner, right where the carved cockatrices were sitting on the vine. The wood there looked darker, as if it had been burned.

Huh.

She ran her finger over the scorch marks. "Still warm." Closing her eyes, she focused on the spot.

Suddenly, a gust of wind came from nowhere, loosening strands of her hair from her braid. Something flittered across the darkness behind her lids. Glittery and shiny . . . like gold and diamonds.

Her eyes flew open. "I know where it is."

Not bothering to wait for him, she marched outside, retracing her steps down Main Street, to the last shop at the end.

"Glitter and Gold Jewelry Emporium?" Mal, who had been trailing behind her the whole time, read out. "You think Clawed or Clawdia came here?" When she sent him a teasing smile, he shrugged. "We have to call it something. So, why here?"

"This was the last shop I visited, and they were already closed by the time I arrived. I didn't see any broken glass inside, so I thought it was all good, but I had this feeling, like I needed to go in there." She should have followed her instinct. "We could probably wait until morning, but I'm worried he or she might be hungry or thirsty. Or they could hurt themselves."

"Yeah." He put his hand on the door. "Huh."

"What's wrong?"

"I don't feel any magic protecting this place. No locking spells, no shields, or wards. You'd think they'd at least spring for a burglary hex, considering what they have in there."

"They have one of the best electronic security systems on the street. Kap told me about it because he had to respond to a call from them one night when someone tried to break in. There's a silent alarm inside and the entire place locks down once it's triggered. But more important, every item they sell has a curse on it, so if anyone tries to take a piece without paying, they immediately start growing boils on their skin and their teeth fall out and other nasty stuff."

"I see. That makes it easier, then."

"Easier for what?"

"To break inside."

"Break in—" She lowered her voice to a whisper. "Break inside? Are you mad? Didn't you hear what I said about the curses and your teeth falling out?"

"We're not stealing anything. Nothing that doesn't belong to us, anyway," he reasoned. "And we don't need to break in—we're just breaking Clawdia out."

"Clawdia? You think she's a girl?"

"She did choose to hide out in a jewelry shop."

Wow, another joke. But this wasn't the time for laughter. "All right. What do you propose we do?"

"Come with me."

She trailed behind him as he led her to the rear of the jewelry store. Like Fantastic Tails, there was one metal door that served as the back entrance and one window that was above the bathroom sink. A camera mounted on the wall pointed at both.

"One sec." Mal held up a hand, then a yellow dome appeared over them like an umbrella. "It's the same one I used for the tizzie whizie. It generates a magnetic field that disrupts all kinds of electrical signals. Prevents me from getting electrocuted, but in this case"—he nodded at the camera—"it'll make us appear invisible, at least to the camera lens."

"That's amazing." She had no idea he could do that. "But you said we were breaking Clawdia out. How do we do that?"

He gestured to the window. "I can also disrupt the tripwire signal to the alarm with this same magnetic field. But my magic isn't infinite. I can only hold up the shield and stop the signal for so long—you'll have to be quick."

"You want me to climb in and find her?"

"No, no." Mal shook his head. "Draw her out. Call her."

Fear and doubt washed over her and her knees trembled. "How am I supposed to do that?"

"Use your instinct, think about the things you do at the shop. Or how you knew that basilisk was sick." His purple eyes bored right into her. "You can do this, Jasmine."

She didn't respond right away. How could she, when his words of faith shook her to her very core. "I—Okay, let's do this." It was worth a try.

He flashed her a smile. "Ready?"

She rubbed her hands together. "As I'll ever be."

Mal reached up, digging his claws under the window to pull it wide open. "Now, Jasmine."

Still unsure what to do, Jasmine raised her hands up. She tried to imagine . . . whatever it was in there and draw it out.

Come out and play, Clawdia.

Here, here, Clawdia.

Pspspsps?

Oh Mother Goddess, this was stupid. She dropped her hands to her sides. "I'm never going to—"

"Shhh!" Mal hissed. "Do you hear that?"

"Hear what?"

"Something's crawling around in there." His face strained tight, the veins on his temples bulging. "Keep going."

Okay, Jasmine, you can do this.

Rolling up her metaphorical sleeves, she raised her hands to the window once more. "Come on, Clawdia. Time to come home."

Closing her eyes, she tried to picture Clawdia in her mind's eye. First, she was a dark blob, formless and free. Slowly, though, the blob began to take shape. The lower half stretched into five legs—no, four legs and a long tail. Then wings sprouted out from the top half as the head morphed into its true form, slowly forming an outline before the details appeared to her.

The shock struck her like lightning.

"I know what Clawdia is," she whispered.

"What—Fuuuuck!"

A small, dark blur flew out from the open window and straight into Jasmine's arms. About the size of a golden retriever puppy, it let out a happy chirp and blinked up at her with shiny blue eyes that matched its scaly body. Small horns dotted the middle of its head, going all the way down its back, where two wings sprouted on either side.

Mal gasped. "Is that a—"

"Dragon," she finished. "Clawdia is a dragon." The cheeky little thing batted her long lashes at Jasmine, as if she was saying, *Yup, I'm a dragon all right!* "I can't believe it. How did—"

"Let's figure that out later." The yellow magnetic shield above them flickered. "I can't hold on to this much longer."

"Oh, yeah. Sorry." She clutched Clawdia closer to her chest as Mal led them away from the cameras. By the time they walked around to the front, the yellow dome had faded away. They hurried down Main Street, sprinting as fast as they could all the way to the shop. As soon as they were inside, Mal stumbled forward.

"Mal!" Shifting Clawdia to her right side, she slid her left arm around his waist then guided him toward the counter. "Are you all right?"

He heaved. "Yeah . . . need to catch . . . my breath." Planting his elbows on the countertop, he leaned on it and took a deep breath. "Is she . . . okay?"

Releasing him, she wrapped both arms around Clawdia. The baby dragon snuggled up against her shoulders. Sharp talons dug into her skin and the horns poked at her neck, but Jasmine didn't mind the discomfort. "Yeah, she's good."

Mal pushed himself off the counter. "A dragon. I kinda suspected it, but never really thought it was possible."

"My supplier must have mixed up Clawdia's egg with his batch of carcinos eggs," she deduced. "Or he didn't know what it was."

"If he did, he wouldn't have sold it to you for such a low price."

"Have you ever seen a dragon before? I've only watched videos of them." Jasmine had never encountered one, much less had one in the shop. They were much too expensive and there were only a handful of dragon breeders in the world.

"A couple of times. Had some clients who owned them." He peered at Clawdia. "She should grow to about the size of a German shepherd. Human selective breeding over generations reduced their size, though there are rumors that wild dragons as large as buildings like in ancient times still exist."

Jasmine had heard of that too. "Clawdia's ancestors must have been huge."

"Likely. So, are we going to keep calling her that name?"

"Of course," she replied matter-of-factly. "She does have claws. Anyway, I think she's hungry. I'm gonna go find her something to eat. Do you know what dragons like?"

"Not a clue."

Turns out, dragons were not discerning at all when it came to food. After placing her in an empty pen, Clawdia happily gobbled up the banana Jasmine offered her, as well as a jar of peanut butter, half a tub of yogurt, and an entire sample bag of Ethereal Balance kibble. As soon as she finished eating, she curled up into the blanket in the corner and closed her eyes.

"She's finally asleep." Unable to help herself, Jasmine took her phone out and snapped a photo of the snoozing baby dragon.

They knelt down side by side, looking over the side of the pen, watching over Clawdia. Adrenaline poured out of Jasmine as the day's adventure finally caught up with her. She was tempted to crawl back to the counter—and all the way home—but she managed to get to her feet. Mal stood up as well.

"We should close up," she said. "I hate to leave her alone . . ."

"I can stay with the hatchling," Mal offered.

"Are you sure?"

"She shouldn't be able to escape." He had already reinforced the pen and fireproofed it while Clawdia ate. "But just in case, someone should be here. I'll grab the sleeping bag in the office."

"I'll stay. You shouldn't—"

"It's fine. You can stay tomorrow if you want."

"I—Okay." She didn't have the strength to argue. "I'll help you close up."

Heading to the counter, she turned the lights low and was about to lower the volume of the music when she paused. It was one of her favorite songs by a sixties girl group, a sentimental and corny love ballad. On a whim, she turned up the volume, humming along as she began to arrange the counter and clean up the receipts and other clutter on top.

"All done," Mal said as he approached her. "I also found the sleeping bag."

"Thanks, Mal. Are you sure you're gonna be okay?" Rounding the counter, she went over to his side.

"Yeah, I'll be good. I've slept in worse places."

She shot him a skeptical look. "Really?"

"I once had to share a bunkhouse with bunch of ogres after a ten-hour day. They served wildebeest and bean stew at the mess hall for dinner."

"That doesn't sound pleasant at all," she said with a grimace.

"A sleeping bag on the floor isn't so bad. You go on ahead home and get some rest."

"All right. We also have some pillows. Let me go scrounge them up. They should be in the hatching room." Before he could protest, she ran upstairs, returning moments later with a pillow under each arm.

Mal was spreading out the sleeping bag right by Clawdia's pen. "Thanks," he said as she handed him the pillows.

"Yeah." She glanced down at the sleeping dragon through the slats of the pen. "Actually, Mal, I'm not leaving."

"No," he grunted. "I told you—I'll stay here and you can go home."

"Why can't we both stay here tonight?" Her hand waved at the spread-out sleeping bag. "There's more than enough space." Mal's face had such a comical deer-in-headlights look, she had to bite her lip to keep from laughing. "We're just sleeping together." Jasmine discovered that it was possible to blush even when one had green skin. "I mean, sleeping *next* to each other." Clucking her tongue, she grabbed the pillows back and placed them side by side, a respectable space between them. "See?"

"Sleeping on the floor isn't comfortable," he pointed out.

She rolled her eyes. "Mal, I used to sleep on the floor in my grandmother's house for my afternoon naps as a kid." On hot afternoons, her lola would place handwoven palm leaf mats on the cool floor of their veranda where she and her cousins would lie down for their siestas. It was one of her fondest childhood memories. "I'll be fine." Before he could protest further, she kicked off her shoes and sat down on the sleeping bag, crossing her arms over her chest, as if daring him to haul her off. "I'm tired and it's been a long day. Can you please turn off the lights and turn down the music so we can sleep?"

"Fine," he grumbled, then lumbered to the wall with the light switch.

Jasmine plopped her head on the pillow with a big sigh, then turned to her side, facing away from where Mal would be sleeping. The room plunged into complete darkness, but only for a moment, as the glow from the remaining carbuncle kit a few pens away provided some illumination. The music grew quieter and the familiar clunk of boots drew closer, then the sleeping bag tugged and shifted as Mal lay down next to her.

Though adrenaline drained from her body, Jasmine's mind refused to let her sleep. Also, while she did treasure those memories from her childhood, lying on the floor as an adult who was used to sleeping on a bed for the last twenty years was a different matter. Had she known she would be camping out on the shop floor tonight, she wouldn't have worn a romper. She grumbled to herself as she tugged at the fabric riding up her butt.

Rolling onto her back, she glanced over at Mal. With his eyes closed and breath steady, he was seemingly fast asleep, much to her envy and annoyance. She held her hands up, scrutinizing them in the blue light of the carbuncle's glow.

I have magic.

It was strange to think it; she probably wouldn't even be able to say it aloud. Should she call her father and tell him the news? Or would that make him resent her further? While she was excited at the prospect of learning about her newfound abilities, she didn't want to risk making that black cloud over their relationship grow larger.

She took another peek at Mal, sighing inwardly. Today had been an emotional rollercoaster, mostly because of him. But he was also the reason she'd discovered her magical affinity. He was such a contradiction, and she would never figure him out.

Not that she would ever get that chance, seeing as he was leaving.

Turning back on her side, she hugged herself, ignoring that twisting in her gut. Mal would be gone in a few months. Forever. The time would come when she would see him walk out the door for the last time.

Pushing those thoughts away, she closed her eyes and allowed her exhaustion to take her into a deep sleep.

The light behind her eyelids slowly brought Jasmine back into a state of wakefulness. As her eyes fluttered open, the first thing that came into view was the big green blur in front of her eyes. She blinked away the bleariness until Mal's face materialized clearly.

Apparently, he slept like a rock because he was still in the same position as last night. She smiled to herself as her gaze traced the features of his face—the strong chin, his full lips, his pointy mouth tusks, and the arch of his dark brows. A lock of hair had fallen between his eyes, and before she knew it, she was reaching out so she could tuck it away—

His eyes flew open. Jasmine's heart careened into her ribcage, fully waking her. But before she could pull her arm back, he caught her wrist. She gulped and opened her mouth, intending to apologize. Instead, a low moan escaped her lips.

A flash of desire burned in his purple eyes, and he let out a soft growl as he pulled her to him, rolling her onto her back so he could cover her body and meld his mouth to hers.

Oh Mother Goddess.

Though they'd only kissed that one other time, his lips felt like coming home after a long journey. And unlike that first kiss, which had been torrid and desperate, Mal's mouth moved with a languid, sensual motion that slowly built up the urgency inside her. While she liked the excitement of their first kiss, right now the unhurried quality of this one was just right for this relaxed morning.

Her hands ran up the sides of his face, cupping his jaw as he continued his leisurely exploration of her mouth. She curled her fingers onto the back of his head, digging them into his scalp, which triggered a low groan from Mal, making him deepen the kiss. Feeling even more adventurous, she moved her hands down, over those rock-hard shoulders she'd been drooling over these past weeks, digging into the muscles.

He tore his mouth away from hers, moving lower, pressing kisses down her jaw and trailing down to her neck. His tongue licked at the sensitive spot where her neck met her shoulders, sending her moaning and her hips bucking up. His lower body pressed down on hers, and his erection brushed against her, the heat radiating from him enough to set her body ablaze. Parting her knees, she cradled the bulge between her thighs, rubbing up against the ridge until he too was moaning into her mouth.

"Mal," she breathed. "Oh, Mal."

He caught her mouth with his once more in another slow, sensual dance, their tongues twining in a passionate tango. She could do this forever, get lost in his kisses and never come up for air. So when he pulled away, she let out a protesting moan. "Mal, don't stop."

"I have to, ashak'a," he said against her mouth. "You know why, even though I can't stop thinking about you or forget our kiss. I'm sorry. I don't want to make this difficult for you."

Her heart clenched. "There's nothing to forgive, Mal. I can't stop thinking about you too."

"Jasmine . . ." He brushed a claw down her cheek. "What are we going to do?"

Her last thoughts before she drifted to sleep last night came back to her. About how she would never see him again once he walked out the door for the last time. Yes, it would be hard on them both when he did leave. But four and a half months was a long time. "Mal, can't we just see where this goes?"

"What do you mean?"

"You're not leaving right now, are you?" Sitting up, she pulled him so they sat on the sleeping bag, facing each other. "Why don't we enjoy our time together, no matter how short or long that would be and not worry about the future?" She forced out a laugh. "I mean, maybe it'll turn out there's nothing more than this initial attraction between us. Things could fizzle out naturally."

"Or they could end in disaster."

"Only if we let it. But shouldn't we make that decision for ourselves?" Her fingers laced into his. "Mal, we're adults. We can do what we want, even jump into bed together."

"So, like friends with benefits?" His nostrils flared. "I told you, I'm not that type of guy. I won't use you just for sex and discard you when I'm done. You deserve so much better than that."

Her lady parts begged to differ, but she understood where he was coming from. "And I would never do the same to you, either, Mal. I respect you too. You told me before you're the type of person who likes guarantees. When you think about it, knowing that this thing between us has an expiration date *is* like a guarantee. We know what to expect and we can walk away from each other without any hurt feelings while still respecting each other. And at the end of the day that's enough for me."

He closed his eyes and brought her hand to his lips, nuzzling it. "Jasmine. What am I going to do with you, ashak'a?"

"You could kiss me again—*Ohh!*"

He did just that, hauling her back into his arms, shifting them around so she straddled his hips. When his erection brushed up between her legs, she moaned and pressed herself down, cursing this stupid romper once more. Still, she was a resourceful girl, so she ground down on top of him until he was panting into her mouth.

"Jas—Stop, oh!" Mal's huge hands spanned her waist then hauled her up as he rose to his feet. "Not here. It's too . . . weird." He set her down.

"You're right." They had been so caught up in each other, they had forgotten where they were. "I don't want to traumatize the—" She suddenly remembered why they had slept here in the first place. "Clawdia!" she exclaimed, brushing past Mal and hurrying to the baby dragon's pen.

"What's wrong?" Mal asked as he followed her. "Is the hatchling okay?"

Peering inside the pen, she let out a relieved sigh. "She's still sleeping. I can't believe I forgot about her." Or, rather, she had been too distracted by Mal's kisses. "Good thing she's not awake yet."

"Yeah, she's basically a newborn," Mal explained. "She'll probably be spending most of her day sleeping, at least for a while. But she'll wake when she's hungry."

As if on cue, Clawdia's eyes opened, the bright blue eyes immediately training on Jasmine. The dragon sat up and then let out a mournful chirp. Jasmine couldn't quite explain it, but a strange jolt shot through her, leaving a distinct note of displeasure. The image of a feather and a lion's tail appeared in her mind.

"She wants out." Reaching inside the pen, she lifted Clawdia up into her arms. "Hey there, did you sleep well?"

The dragon snuggled against her neck.

"Sweet baby." She patted the dragon's back. "That pen still

smells like griffin, huh? It's okay. We'll get it all cleaned up before we put you back in there."

"Can you hear her talking to you?" Mal asked. "And can she understand you?"

"Not quite." Jasmine paused, unable to explain it even to herself. "See, when I work with the creatures here, I guess what they want and need. I never really thought about it, but my 'guesses' always turn out to be right. I assumed it was something I developed while working here. Like, when you do something over and over again and you get the hang of things."

"I understand," he said. "That's how you learn any skill."

She shifted Clawdia to her other arm. "But with her, it's a little different. We don't talk to each other, not like the way you and I do. She sends me images in my head. Like last night, when I was reaching out to her, she was showing me where she was. I was getting these images of something shiny and glittery." She smiled down at Clawdia. "Guess you were right about females and jewelry."

"Dragons are attracted to treasure," he said. "As I suspected, you can link with creatures mentally."

"I guess so. But this has never happened with any of the other animals in the shop."

Mal rubbed at his chin. "Compared to everyday creatures, dragons are high up on the magical scale. That may explain why you're having these more vivid 'conversations' with her."

She blew out a breath. "It's all too much, Mal. I don't know what I'm supposed to be doing. What if I make a mistake? What if I get one of the animals hurt if I don't understand what they're trying to tell me?"

A warm hand landed on her shoulder. "You don't have to do anything, Jasmine. The magic is there, within you. It always has been. The goddess spirit gave your ancestor that power for a reason, because he was a good man. And I'd like to believe that it would only manifest in you because you're also a good person and deserving of it."

His words plucked at an emotion deep in her chest. "That's kind of you to say."

"You should keep doing what you're doing. And yes, magic is a skill. The more you use it, the more you'll develop it."

Clawdia wiggled around before Jasmine could respond. The image of bananas and kibble appeared in her head. "Hungry, are we? Let's get you some food."

Jasmine managed to find some apples in the fridge inside the office, while Mal opened up a new bag of kibble. Instead of putting Clawdia back in the pen, they lay her down on the sleeping bag instead. As the baby dragon happily munched away, Jasmine grabbed her camera and snapped a few photos.

"Our followers are gonna go wild when I reveal that Clawdia's a dragon. And—" She put her phone down as blood drained from her face. "Oh no."

"What's wrong?" That tiny line between his eyebrows appeared.

She bit at her lip. "I can't possibly post pictures of Clawdia now."

"Why not?"

"It just occurred to me. What if the company I bought her from sees the photos, realizes their mistake and demands her back? I mean, dragon eggs must be worth a hundred times more than carcinos eggs. What if they sue me for her or for the money?"

"Do you want to return her, then?"

Something fierce burned in her chest. "I . . . I don't know. No." She shook her head. "I mean, I—the shop—bought her fair and square. It wasn't our mistake. But, since you own Fantastic Tails, that technically means *you* own her. You could give her back or even sell her if you wanted to."

Indigo eyes searched her face. "But what do *you* want, Jasmine?"

The question caught her off guard, so she didn't know what to say. Or rather, she was afraid to say it aloud because she couldn't remember the last time anyone asked her what she wanted. "Could we . . . keep her? For now at least?"

"Yes, Jasmine. Whatever you want." To her surprise, he planted a kiss on her temple.

"Thank you." Scooting closer to him, she lay her head against his chest, his arm coming around her, as they continued to watch Clawdia gobble up the pile of kibble.

"Jasmine?"

"Hmm?"

"If we're going to do this, we should have a few ground rules."

"Rules?" She looked up at him. "Like what?"

"We shouldn't have sex right away."

Her spine stiffened. "You don't want to have sex with me?"

"Of course I do." His voice turned low and raspy. "I want you in my bed, your sweet body under me, moaning my name while I make you come over and over again."

Oh Mother Goddess, the temperature in the room spiked a few hundred degrees.

"But not right away," he emphasized. "I want to take you out. On a date."

"Oh. Okay."

"And we should have at least three dates before we become intimate. Get to know each other and then decide if we really want to sleep together."

That was actually . . . sweet. "All right."

"Good." Shuffling on his knees so that he faced her, he engulfed her hands in his, then stared down into her eyes. "So, will you have dinner with me, Jasmine?"

Not even the Mother Goddess herself could have stopped the grin from forming on her face. "Yes, Mal, I'll have dinner with you."

His smile reached all the way to his luminous purple eyes. "Friday night, seven p.m.?"

"You want to wait until Friday? Why?"

"Apparently, I have to go to the fireman training on Thursday," he said in a dry tone.

"But why not tomorrow when the shop is closed? Or tonight. Or Wednesday? Or now? We can go on a lunch date. Why, that's four dates right there."

"That's cheating," he told her sternly. "And we should wait at least one week between dates."

"You're going to wait three weeks before we have sex?"

"Yes. I told you: I want both of us to be sure."

Jasmine sure hoped orc dick was worth the wait. "Fine, Friday it is. I'll have to ask my boss if I can leave a couple hours before closing time so I can get ready. He's a real grump, you know," she teased, bumping him with her shoulder.

He threw back his head and laughed—a real, honest-to-goodness laugh that, for some reason, Jasmine swore made him look even more handsome. "I'm sure I can convince him to let you go early."

Chapter Thirteen

MAL

Mal regretted waiting five whole days for his date with Jasmine. The anticipation was unbearable, not to mention, he agonized over the decision, wondering if they were making a mistake. But it had been difficult to say no to Jasmine, not just because she was insistent, but because he wanted her too much. Kissing and touching her had felt so right, even as his brain screamed this was a bad idea.

But they were both going into it as mature adults, and more important, they respected each other. At the end of this—and he knew it would end, even though his gut roiled at the thought—they would walk away from each other without any fuss.

At least that was the plan. However, the more he thought about it, the more doubt crept in that he would be able to let go of her once their time together was over. In the last few years, he'd mostly had short-term flings and a casual encounter here and there, and what he felt for Jasmine was so different.

So, Mal counted the days until their date, all the while spending time at the shop with her as if everything was normal, though each time she came into the office to chat or he passed by her all he wanted to do was haul her into a private corner and kiss her senseless.

Thankfully with Fantastic Tails being closed on Tuesdays he didn't have to see her for one day, though he kept looking out the kitchen window to her apartment, fighting the urge to knock on her door to see what she was doing. Of course, he'd already memorized her day-off routine as he'd often observe her come and go the last couple of weeks. Usually, she slept in, then went for a walk before coming home with a bag of groceries. She never left the house after that, so he guessed she spent the day cooking and watching TV shows before going to bed at exactly ten thirty p.m.

The next two days were more torture, trying to ignore that all he could think about was their date. When Thursday evening rolled around, he was about ready to burst with anticipation, but at least he had an excuse to leave a little early—his first day of training with the Dewberry Falls Volunteer Fire Department. He hated to leave Jasmine alone to close up, but business was slow anyway, and she practically shooed him away, promising to text him when she finished up and got home safe.

After a stop at home to get changed and have a quick dinner, he headed to the fire station, which was about a fifteen-minute drive away. When he arrived, there was one car parked in the lot behind the building, and the lights were already on inside.

"Hello?" Mal called out tentatively as he entered. "Anyone here?" His voice echoed through the cavernous building. He'd never been inside a fire station before, but it was just as he'd imagined, albeit smaller. There was a large red-and-white fire truck parked right in front of the wide sliding garage doors, a row of uniforms and helmets hung on a rack next to it, and tools and other gear were lined up on the opposite wall. He walked toward the nearest doorway to the right, which he assumed was an office of some kind.

"Hi, I'm here—Oh, hey," he greeted Nick, who sat on a worn couch in the corner of the office, reading a book. "I'm here."

The satyr's eyes flicked up, then returned to his book. "So you are."

He waited for Nick to continue, but he remained seated, ignoring Mal. For someone who had all but twisted his arm to volunteer, Nick sure acted like he didn't care that Mal had actually shown up. "When do we start?"

"Soon."

He let out an annoyed snort. "And when—"

"Hey, what's up—Mal, you're here!"

Mal spun round, his jaw dropping at the sight of *Nick* entering the room. "What the—" His head whipped back to the second—or first?—Nick on the couch, whose gaze remained fixed on his book.

"I see you've met Ian," Nick chuckled as he ambled toward him. "My twin brother."

Ah, now the other satyr's demeanor made sense. "I'm Mal," he introduced himself. "Nice to meet you."

"Don't be rude, Ian." Nick circled Mal and grabbed the book from his brother, who sent him a dirty look. Still, he got up and took Mal's hand.

"Ian Amherst." Though he looked and sounded like Nick, his stiff and distant air was the complete opposite of his twin. "So, Mal, did you want to be here or were you strong-armed by my brother to join us?"

"I was convinced without a chance to say no." Mal sent Nick a sly look.

Nick grinned. "And yet here you are. Ian, Vrig was Mal's uncle. He's the new owner of the pet shop."

Something shifted in Ian's expression. "I see. Vrig was an incredible person and I was glad to have known him. My condolences on your loss."

"Thank you."

"I'm really glad you're here. I honestly thought you wouldn't show up." Nick chuckled. "I think I hear the others coming. Let's go out and you can meet them, then we can get started."

They headed back to the main hall, just as four figures were making their way in from the parking lot.

"Hey, guys!" Nick clapped his hands together. "Come on, don't dilly-dally, I want to introduce you to our newest volunteer. This is Mal. He's new in town."

"And he's Vrig's nephew," Ian added.

"Vrig's nephew, eh?" An older man with white hair and a handlebar mustache—the only human of the crew, it seemed—came forward, his hand already out, which Mal took. "Jim Halloway. Welcome and my condolences. Vrig was a fine citizen of Dewberry Falls. I bet he'd be proud that you're taking his place."

Mal didn't have the heart to tell him that he wasn't staying for long, so he put that thought aside for now. "Er, thank you."

"Jim's our chief," Nick explained. "He was an actual fire-fighter back in Seattle."

"Took early retirement when my wife passed," Jim explained. "I didn't want to stay in Seattle, but found that I couldn't leave the job behind."

Nick gestured to the figure to Jim's right—a brawny mino-taur with shaggy brown hair and bright green eyes. "This is Rafe Kincade—after you, he's our newest volunteer."

Rafe let out a chuff and nodded. "Nice to meet you, Mal."

"Likewise," he replied.

"And this is Vendrush, or Ven."

Lanky, blue-skinned with a bright red mohawk, and long mouth tusks, Ven was obviously a troll. "Good to meet you." He took Mal's hand in both of his and shook it vigorously in an unusually friendly way, at least for a troll. "Glad to have you here."

"Er, thanks," Mal said as he extricated his hand from the troll's grip.

"Finally, we have Sterling." Nick indicated the last man, or rather, wolf man.

"Wonderful to meet you, Mal." The posh British accent coming from the lupine head was bewildering for a moment, but Mal managed to keep his expression neutral as he took the furry, clawed hand Sterling offered. "And, please, if you're about to make a joke about a London werewolf in America, I'm afraid I've heard them all," he chuckled.

"I won't," he said. "Great movie, though." He glanced around. "It's just us?"

"There's about thirty volunteers in total," Jim explained. "Each squad trains biweekly and then we all do one Saturday a month at a fire college in Yuba. Keeps things organized."

"Now we're all acquainted, let me welcome you to Squad Thirteen," Nick said.

"Thirteen?"

Nick laughed. "It's a lucky number for satyrs, and since I'm squad captain, I chose the number."

"We're still working out our name," Sterling added. "I voted for Fire Howlers."

"And I wanted to call us Ash Kickers," Ven chimed in. "Like kicking ass? Get it?"

"I don't know how we can call ourselves anything since we've never responded to a real fire," Ian said.

"Anyway," Nick continued. "Should we start, Jim?"

Jim cleared his throat. "Ven, could you please help get Mal outfitted in the proper gear while we do some warm-up exercises?"

"Aye, aye, Chief." Ven gave him a salute. "C'mon, Mal, I'll show you where we keep the extra gear." Mal trailed behind Ven as he led him toward the back. "So, you're Vrig's nephew, huh?

That's cool. I mean, Vrig was a great guy. I loved hearing stories about his time with the Army Corps of Engineers. I wish I could travel the world too. What do you do, Mal? And where did you live before you moved to Dewberry Falls?"

"I'm a contractor," he said. "And, well, I don't really live any-where. I go wherever I can find jobs."

"Wow, you travel a lot too?" Ven's eyes widened. "That's amazing." His eyebrows drew together. "I'd leave Dewberry Falls if I could, but my mother and sisters won't let me."

"Won't let you?"

"Yeah, my mother's the head of our cadre and I'm the only male in the family. She won't let me do what I want." He sighed as they stopped outside the door at end of the hallway. "I know she's worried about me and all, but . . . Oh sorry, I don't mean to bore you with family drama." The troll gestured for him to enter the room, then led him to an empty locker. Mal placed his wallet and phone inside, checking his notifications quickly for a message from Jasmine. Once he saw her text saying she had reached home, he sent a quick reply and closed the locker. "What next?"

"Let's get you outfitted with the proper gear." Ven helped him pick out everything he needed—helmet, jacket, pants, boots, and gloves, then showed him how to put it all on.

"You look great, man," he said, giving Mal a thumbs-up as he stood in front of him in the complete uniform. "Jim will prob-ably want to go through a couple dress drills—that means putting all this stuff on and off over and over again. We have to practice until we can do it in under two minutes. He'll go easy on you since it's your first day, but make no mistake, he takes his position seriously even though we're a volunteer crew, and he expects us to work as hard as professional firefighters. C'mon, let's go back outside."

Sure enough, once Ven and Mal joined the others, Jim started them on rapid dress drills. While it seemed simple enough, the bulky gear was tricky to put on, and it took Mal a few tries to get everything in the correct order quickly. He felt like a fish out of water, and he envied how the others got their gear on in under two minutes while he struggled.

"Don't worry," Nick assured him with a grin. "It just takes practice."

After a few more tries, Mal succeeded in getting the gear on properly, though it still took him more than five minutes. Then, the real work began. For the next two hours, Jim had them doing hose deployment skills—unloading and loading the hoses, pulling and laying them out, connecting them to the hydrant, advancing, and other techniques in how to properly handle the hose. Mal first stayed on the sidelines to observe how it was done, but eventually Jim had him joining in.

"The only real way to learn is to do it," the chief said.

Being the new guy, he did get some razzing from the others, but Mal understood it was all in good fun, and a way to release the tension. Jim didn't let them take it too far, though he did get in a few jabs himself.

"That's a wrap. Great job, everyone," Jim said at the end of the night. "And we're happy to have you onboard, Mal." They all cheered. "Thanks for being a good sport, even though we gave you a hard time. It only means we like you."

"Sorry I called you butterfingers when the nozzle slipped from your hands." Sterling patted him on the back.

"And that I said you were slower than two sloths fucking," Ven said.

"It's all right." It wasn't Mal's first time to be the new guy, and on tight-knit crews like this, he knew that you had to have thick skin to earn respect.

"So, now that we're done," Ven said with a long sigh, "should we all head to the Salty Dog?"

"Of course," Nick replied. "Mal, you should join us."

"Join you?" he asked.

"Yeah, we go to this bar called the Salty Dog after training for drinks."

Mal shook his head. "I don't think—"

"C'mon, man, just one drink," Nick countered. "It's a tradition."

"But—"

"Helps with team bonding, right, Chief?"

Jim nodded. "I'm not forcing you or anything, but getting to know your fellow firefighters outside of the firehouse is an important part of boosting morale and building the team."

"You gotta come," Ven added. "Please?"

"Ian's our designated driver," Nick said. "He'll drive you home after."

Mal grunted. "All right, one drink." It was early still, and besides, if he went home now, he'd probably just spend the evening looking at Jasmine's window.

After a short drive to a strip mall not too far from the fire station, they all arrived at the Salty Dog. It was a standard sports bar that served beer, alcoholic drinks, and a variety of bar food. The staff seemed familiar with the fire crew and a waitress ushered them to a corner table and quickly took their orders.

Mal squeezed in between Ian and Rafe, as he observed they were the most reserved among the others, while the rest tended to be talkative and loud. Still, the rest didn't ostracize the two and even included them in the conversation. The pair of them chimed in with nods or grunts, or in Ian's case, an occasional roll of the eyes.

When the waitress came back with their drinks, Jim spoke up. "I wanted to welcome Mal once again. And of course, let's raise a glass to Vrig. He wasn't just part of our crew, but also our friend. To Vrig."

Everyone raised their glass. "To Vrig."

"Hey, do you guys remember that time when Vrig had to climb up that tree to rescue that cat, only for it to turn out to be a kite?" Sterling said.

"I would have been pissed at the old lady that called it in," Ven replied.

"But Vrig took it all in his stride." Nick clucked his tongue. "That was Vrig, though. Cool and calm, never let anything bother him."

"He loved doing the parades and the school visits," Ian chimed in.

"Which you're glad for because that meant you could stay inside the truck and not interact with anyone," Nick said.

His twin huffed. "I still don't know how you talked me into doing it. But yes, Vrig was happy to entertain the kids."

"Yeah, and they loved him," Ven added. "He had a gentle soul."

A sense of pride went through Mal, and partly remorse that he hadn't thought of his uncle more in the past few years. While he never had a chance to get to know him when he was a kid, as an adult, Mal could have picked up a phone or even hopped on a plane to see his uncle anytime. It would, perhaps, be one of the greatest regrets of his life.

"So, Mal," Jim began, "you're taking over the shop for Vrig?"

"Er, kind of," he said. "For now."

"That shop is so cool," Ven said. "I took one of my nieces there for her birthday. She got a water horse. Say . . ." He looked around slyly. "That hot lady manager still working there?"

Mal's blood pressure shot up and he ground his teeth.

"You mean Jasmine?" Nick interjected. "Yeah, I saw her during the Founding Day Festival."

"Damn, I wish I had gone to Main Street, then." Ven pouted. "My mother kept me busy entertaining guests at home. Wouldn't even let me join the parade."

"That mother of yours . . ." Nick shook his head. "Not that it would have done any good. Jasmine's way out of your league, kid."

"You're not even playing the same sport," Sterling joked.

"Aww," Ven sulked. "She's so nice too. Great with kids."

Mal took a sip of his drink, trying to control his annoyance. But he could hardly blame Ven, as Jasmine was, indeed, hot.

"Must be nice working with a gorgeous woman all day," Nick said with a laugh. "Not that you'd try anything, right, Mal? You're much too professional for that."

"Actually, we are seeing each other," Mal stated. "We're going on our first date tomorrow." He supposed there was no use denying it, as he was planning to take her out on a very public date.

"Whoa!" Ven nearly choked on his drink. "Sorry, man, didn't mean to say . . . I didn't . . . She's hot, but . . ."

"It's fine." The kid hadn't known, after all. No one had.

"You actually asked her out?" Nick's expression was that of surprise, and maybe a hint of envy. "Good for you." He slapped Mal on the back. "Jasmine's a great gal."

"Cares a lot about the creatures," Sterling added. "And a lovely person."

Ian and Rafe didn't say anything, only nodded their agreement.

"Great worker, from what Vrig said, and he had good instincts," Jim added. "I hope things work out for you. A good woman is hard to find these days. After I lost my Rebecca, I didn't want to date anyone."

"Believe me, we tried," Nick said.

"Not your fault," Jim added. "No one could replace her in my heart."

"Maybe your luck with the girls will rub off on the rest of us." The satyr gestured around him. "In case you didn't notice, we're the perpetual singles club over here."

"It's tough out there for us non-humans, even here in Dewberry Falls," Sterling sighed.

Rafe just huffed.

"I don't particularly care for dating these days," Ian said in a dry tone. "And, Nick, you change girlfriends like you do your underwear."

Nick winked at Mal. "What can I say, no one woman can pin me down. But, anyway, good luck on your date tomorrow. Where are you planning on taking her?"

Mal pressed his lips together, contemplating what to say, but Ian spoke first. "Oh, leave him alone. He's under enough pressure already."

"Hey, I wasn't—" But he was silenced with a look from his twin. "Fine. It wasn't like we were going to show up or anything. You are one lucky orc, Mal. Jasmine's a treasure and Vrig really did trust her a lot."

Mal didn't know what to say so he took a sip of his beer, praying that someone would change the topic. Thankfully, Ian started to tell another story about Vrig, and everyone's attention shifted away from Mal and his date. He caught the satyr's eye and sent him a grateful look, which he returned with a nod. The conversation around him faded away as he stared into his beer, anticipation building as he realized it was less than twenty-four hours before his first date with Jasmine.

Finally, Friday came and, as Mal promised, he let Jasmine leave early. She had fussed over Clawdia, but Mal assured her the hatchling would be fine and he'd feed her dinner and play with her before settling her in for the night. Neither of them had had to stay with her in the shop after that initial night, and once they'd set up a brand-new, non-griffin-smelling pen for her, she seemed content by herself. As for the old hatching tank, Mal planned to rebuild it and repurpose it as a showcase piece for the shop. Jasmine could do what she had originally planned for the carcinos egg but with another reptilian or egg-laying creature.

Mal's hearts pounded loudly in his chest as he made the quick walk to her doorstep. He knocked on her door, throat tight with anxiety and excitement.

"Jasmine," he burst out as soon as the door opened. "You look beautiful."

That didn't even come close to describing her right now, but using words were becoming increasingly difficult. Her hair fell in shiny waves down her shoulders and back. He didn't know much about makeup, but he could tell she wore just enough to comple-ment her already gorgeous features. The red dress she wore wasn't particularly revealing, though the color suited her tawny skin.

"Thanks." A shy smile lit up her face. "You look nice too."

He gave the hem of his jacket a self-conscious tug. "This is the only suit I own."

"I'm glad you ditched the tie." Her eyes fixed on the exposed skin where he'd left the top button open, then quickly looked away. "I mean, I didn't dress for a formal occasion or anything like that." Her throat bobbed. "So, where are we going?"

"Blackbyrd on Main Street. I hope you don't mind that we're not going too far, since I didn't want to drive."

"It's a nice night for a walk, anyway. And I love that place, but I've only been once. Their burnt Basque cheesecake is divine." She chewed at her lower lip. "Mal, Blackbyrd is pretty expensive for a first date. Are you sure you wouldn't rather go to the diner or maybe one of the other restaurants on Main? Harpy's Café is good too."

"I already made reservations, and don't worry about the cost."

"But—"

"I asked you out," he reminded her. Besides, he'd been watch-ing her scrimp and save the last couple of months, so he wanted to treat her to something special tonight. He held out his arm. "Shall we?"

She looped her arm through his and they strolled toward Main Street in comfortable silence. Mal breathed in the warm night air as a breeze carried some of Jasmine's perfume and tickled his nose.

"Welcome to Black—Oh, hello, Mal," the host, an older man with salt-and-pepper hair, greeted.

"Good evening, Karl. How are things tonight?"

Karl waved at the fully packed dining room. "Busy, but we're all good. So, reservation for two, right?"

"Yes. This is Jasmine."

"Hello, Jasmine." The host beamed a smile at Jasmine then stage-whispered, "It's usually a table for one, just so you know." Karl winked at Mal, as if saying, *I have your back*, which he didn't mind at all. Mal had been coming here almost weekly, and he liked the charming human.

"Should we wait? We're a bit early—"

"No, of course not." Karl clucked his tongue. "This way, please."

He led them to a table in a cozy corner, which had been set up with a vase of red roses. "Here you go. Your server will be with you in a moment. Is there anything else I can do for you?"

"We're good."

"Have a great dinner, then." With a final wave, he sauntered back to his station.

"Wow, look at you, already a regular," Jasmine said, her tone lighthearted.

"Not really. I eat out a lot here on Main Street, though," he replied. "I don't cook. I mean, I can follow a recipe and everything, but I'm traveling ten months out of twelve, living in hotels and bunkhouses, so I never need to cook."

"Oh, that's right. You work all over the world. Must be exciting, seeing all those places."

"I don't get to do much touristy stuff, mind you. I get in, get the job done, and get out." Saying the words sounded almost alien to him now and it had been a while since he'd thought about his mantra. Though he'd had extended jobs before, the most he'd ever stayed on one site was about four months.

"So all you do is work?"

"Yeah, I mean, that's what they pay me for."

"Do you have any examples of stuff you've done?" She placed her palms on the table and leaned forward. "That tank you made was amazing, but I'd love to see more."

"Sure." Mal took his phone out from his pocket and tilted the screen toward her. "Let's see . . . Here's the last job I did. It was a mountain cabin for a warlock. He wanted it to actually float on top of a mountain." He flipped to the next photo in the album. "Here's a room I designed for a resort down in St. Lucia." Mal had to smirk, thinking of that one. "It was a challenge because I had to make the furniture big enough for centaurs."

"Centaurs?" she echoed. "They like going to the Caribbean?"

"Oh yeah. It's a booming market." He flipped through the album. "Ah, this one's a bank in Switzerland. Not much to see, I'm afraid, as I mostly did anti-theft and security spells. They want me back next year once I've perfected my fraud detection wards."

"Mal, I had no idea." She leaned back in her chair, an astonished expression on her face. "Your work . . . it's amazing. I can see why you like it so much. You're incredible."

He put his phone away. "Thank you. But you've seen Vrig's stuff. This is just standard for orc builders."

"You're too modest," she admonished. "You should be proud."

A young woman appeared and handed them two leather-bound folders. Based on her pale skin, green hair, and the fin-like appendages sprouting from her hair, Mal guessed she was a water nymph.

"Good evening, sir, madame." Her voice had the soothing, bubbly quality of her people, almost as if she were underwater. "I'm Seren. I'll be your server this evening. Please have a look at our menu. We do have some specials . . ." She rattled off the list in a crisp, efficient manner. "If you don't have any questions, I'll come back in a bit to take your orders."

"Everything looks good," Jasmine said as she peered at the menu. "What should I order?"

"Whatever you want," he replied. "Except for the cheapest thing on the menu."

"But what if that's what I want?"

"Then I'll order another one and you can take it home."

Her jaw dropped. "You wouldn't."

"What do you think?" he challenged. "I told you, this is my treat. So get what you want."

In the end, Jasmine ended up ordering the sea bass for her main, while Mal ordered his usual—Wagyu steak (rare), fries instead of mashed potatoes, and green beans and cauliflower.

"I'll be back with your salads," Seren said as she sauntered away.

"How have you been?" he asked once they were alone.

"You see me almost every day, Mal," she said with a chuckle. "I'm doing fine. The shop's doing great. I finished looking at the sales figures from the weekend and we made out like bandits."

"But I mean how are *you*? And how are you coping with your newfound magic?"

"Ah." Her gaze dropped to her lap for a second. "It's a bit overwhelming, to be honest. Before, I went about my day, trying to figure out what each pet needs. But now I seem to be spending an extraordinary amount of time trying to focus and concentrate and see if I can communicate with them." She let out a long sigh. "I hate to say it, but it was almost easier when I didn't know I had these abilities, and I was just guessing."

"Perhaps you're overthinking it."

"Could be. Maybe. Probably. On the upside, I think the phoenixes are figuring it out and they've been asking for more birdseed."

"They're also high up on the magical scale." Mal paused. "I'm sorry you're feeling so overwhelmed, Jasmine."

"Why? It's not your fault."

"But it was because of me that you discovered you had magic." He clasped his hands on the table. "Listen, maybe I can help."

"Help? How?"

"I can teach you a few things."

"Don't we have to have the same type of magic for you to train me?"

He scratched at his chin with a claw. "Normally, you would have to train under someone with the same powers. I imagine that's the case for your family?"

"Yes. All males who want to inherit start working with the current albularyo as soon as they turn thirteen."

"I can't train you to use your magic, but I can help you learn about how magic works. At its core, magic is all the same. While you can't use the same spells as me, I should be able to give you tips and tricks on how to tap into your magic."

A hopeful gleam shone in her eyes. "That would be amazing, Mal. Thank you."

"Don't thank me yet. I might be completely wrong about being able to help you."

"Still—"

"I have appetizers for you," Seren interrupted, placing two identical dishes on their charger plate. "Foie gras quiches with poached pears."

"Are these for us?" Jasmine asked.

"Yes, miss."

"I think we're supposed to have just the house salad included with our mains. We didn't order these," Jasmine said. "Please don't charge us for them. I hope it's not too late to send them back?"

Any other woman would have taken advantage of Mal's generosity, but not Jasmine. She didn't want him to pay for more than they'd ordered, but really, one extra appetizer would not break the bank. Before he could reassure her, though, the server spoke up first.

"Oh no, no, miss." The nymph shook her head, her fins fanning. "These are compliments of Chef Lucien for Mr. Mal." She turned to him. "Chef wanted me to say hello to you and your lady friend for him."

"Please send our thanks," Mal said.

Jasmine shot him a wry smile. "Not really a regular, huh?"

The rest of the meal was pleasant, and Mal was glad he'd brought an appetite because then he was only half distracted by Jasmine. Under the elegant lighting, her skin glowed even more, and he recalled how soft and smooth she had been when he'd last held her. And with each "oooh" and "ahh" when she took a bite of the delicious food, his eyes were drawn to her lips, the memory of how they tasted still fresh in his mind. A few times during the meal, he had to adjust his pants, as his semi-hard erection pressed up against the fabric painfully.

Gaku help him, would he be able to survive two more of these dates when he could barely get through one without fighting the urge to maul her?

"That was delicious." Jasmine patted her mouth with her napkin. "I'd lick that plate clean if we weren't in public."

The image of Jasmine's pink tongue popped up in Mal's head, making him groan inwardly.

"Dessert?" Seren asked as she returned to check on them.

"Yes. The burnt Basque cheesecake."

"Excellent choice. Two forks?"

"Two orders." He caught Jasmine's gaze, sensing her objection. "I'm greedy. I need my own."

"Very well." She picked up their plates. "I'll clear these for you and get back with those cheesecakes."

"Mal . . ."

"What?" He shrugged. "I *am* greedy and want my own dessert. If you don't stop complaining about how much everything costs, I'll order four more slices."

"Fine," she said, resigned.

"Good girl."

Her pupils blew out as a sexual charge filled the air.

Huh.

Mal never figured her for the type who loved praise. Neither was he, but he filed that little gem away for now. He took a sip of his water. "So, I noticed you still haven't posted photos of Clawdia." Jasmine also didn't take her out of her pen during store hours, opting instead to visit her in the back office when she took a break.

"Yeah . . ." Her fingers twirled in her hair. "I'm still worried. She's so young. I don't want her to be stressed if anything happens."

"I know. That's why I spoke to my lawyer on Tuesday."

"You did?"

"Yeah." Howard Nakamoto had been more than happy to do the consult. "He said that we don't have to tell them about Clawdia. If they do realize their error and contact us, we're not obligated to return her. We're legally entitled to keep her as a free gift. As long as we have the receipt and proof of payment and delivery, she's ours. It was their mistake."

She pressed a hand to her chest. "That's wonderful news."

"And if they do try to take her back or demand payment, I'll take them to court. Don't worry, it won't be the first time I've had

dealings with the law. I've had to sue clients for breach of contract before."

"But what do we do with her now?" She folded her hands in
her lap. "Soon, she'll outgrow that pen. Then you'll have to
decide."

"Decide what?"

"Are you going to sell her? I'm sure someone would pay a lot
of money for a baby dragon."

"Do you want to sell her?"

She hesitated. "That's not my decision, is it? You own the
shop."

"And soon you will, when you buy it."

"Oh Mother Goddess." She buried her face in her hands. "I
didn't even think about that. If the bank sees her as an asset on
the balance sheet, the price'll go up. I'll never be able to afford it."

"Jasmine." He placed his hands on the table. "Jasmine, please
look at me?"

Spreading her fingers, she peeked at him between the gaps.

"Jasmine, Clawdia is not an asset. She's a dragon."

"I know that."

He made a decision. Actually, it wasn't much of a decision as
it was the truth. "She's yours. From the moment she called out to
you, asking for your help, she was yours."

"Mal, what are you say—"

"I'm 'giving' her to you, though that point is moot because she
was never mine to give away. Whether or not you end up buying
the shop, you can keep her. I mean, you want to, don't you?"

"Of course," she breathed. "More than anything."

"Then I'll sign whatever you need me to sign, and we can
make it official. I'll have your back, no matter what."

"You can't possibly . . . Mal, that's too much. What if—
What are you doing?"

Mal had stood up in the middle of her babbling and walked

to her side of the table, knelt down to her level, then planted a kiss on her mouth. She froze for a moment before her lips softened, accepting his kisses. When he pulled away, her eyes were glazed over, her breathing heavy.

"No more protests. You've hit your quota for the evening." Returning to his seat, he sat back down.

"Mal, this is really generous of you," she said. "Thank you so much."

"You can thank me by taking good care of her, but I have no doubt about that."

Jasmine practically sparkled with joy, and Mal would have given her a hundred dragons to keep her like this.

"Dessert is served," Seren said as she set down the two plates in front of them. "Enjoy."

They ate their cheesecakes, their conversation mostly light and pertaining to the shop and the creatures. After he'd paid, they walked back. The air was now even more pleasant thanks to the cooler temperatures.

"So," Mal began as they stopped outside her door, "will you go out with me—"

"No."

"No? You didn't even let me finish."

"I don't want you to."

His stomach plummeted. "I understand. This is why we said we would wai—"

"No, no." She shook her head vehemently. "We agreed on three dates, but not that *you* had to do all the inviting. So, Mal, will you go out with me?"

"Huh."

She cocked her head to the side. "What's wrong?"

"I don't think a girl has ever asked me out."

"What? Orc ladies never ask orc men out or something? Do your people approach dating differently?"

"We have our own courting rituals, which are somewhat different from modern conventions. Traditionally, we win our life mates by besting rivals. And not just the men, but women too."

"What? You fight each other?"

"You could say that. In the battle hordes, if a female is interested in a male, she must fight for him. She'll compete with other rivals and then hand-to-hand combat with the male himself."

"You're not teasing me, are you?" she asked, eyeing him skeptically.

"No, that's really how it happens."

"What, so you've had women duel for you?"

"No, not me personally," he clarified. "And that's in battle hordes. I'm from a builder horde so we try to outdo each other by making furniture or building barns."

Her mouth pressed together tight. "I can't even strike a nail into a board correctly."

"I remember," he said, barely keeping the corner of his mouth from tugging up.

"Does this mean you won't go out with me?"

Mal laughed. "Of course not. And I'm only teasing you. Orcs don't fight each other for mates anymore. And yes, I will go out with you. Where do you want to go?"

"I have an idea, but it's a surprise." The corners of her mouth tugged up.

"Surprise?"

"Uh-huh. And you won't be paying a single penny this time."

"Jasmine . . ."

"Nuh-uh." She wagged a finger at him. "Remember what you said earlier tonight? You invited me so you pay, and now I asked you to go out, so it's my treat."

"All right." He let out a resigned grunt. "But don't go crazy or anything. It's not like I eat at fancy restaurants every night."

"Sure, Mr. Regular," she said, sticking out her tongue at him playfully.

The sight of her pink tongue made his cock twitch. "Try that again," he rasped. "And see where it gets you." Bracing one hand against the wall, he crowded her, forcing her to press up against the door.

"Mal . . ." she sighed. "Please."

The single word broke his already tenuous self-control and he swooped down to lock their mouths together. She responded without hesitation, lips moving against his in a soft rhythm. His hand cupped her cheek carefully, making sure only the pads of his thumb touched her soft skin. To his surprise, she tilted her head, so his claws gently scraped the sides of her face.

She clutched at his shirt, the fingers digging into his pecs as she moaned into his mouth. His hand moved lower, tracing her cheek with his fore claw, moving downwards to rest on her neck.

Mal pressed up against her, pushing her back to the door. Soft breasts crushed to his chest, and the heat of her body only intensified the ache building in his groin. Everything around him faded away—only Jasmine existed, her lips, her body, and the sweet intoxicating scent of her perfume.

As their lips and mouths grew desperate, the throbbing of his erection grew more insistent. Reluctantly, he pulled away a fraction of an inch. Releasing her tight grip on his shirt, she lay her palms flat on his chest. She could probably feel his hearts thumping madly against his ribs, but he didn't care.

"I've been waiting to do that all night," he confessed.

"I've been waiting for *you* to do that all night," she murmured, her breath warm and soft against his. "Do you want to come up for coffee?"

He leaned his forehead against hers. "I want to, but I'm not going to."

"Why not?"

"You know why." To emphasize his point, he brushed his erection against her stomach, making her gasp. "Jasmine, the moment I have you alone, I won't be able to help myself. I'm gonna tear all your clothes off and take you on the nearest horizontal surface. Or maybe I won't even wait to get you on your back. I'm climbing up the walls with wanting you."

"Mal, I want you bad too," she breathed.

"But we agreed to wait." And an orc always kept his word. Pushing away from the door, he took a step back and shoved his hands into his pockets. "Good night, Jasmine. I'll see you tomorrow."

She tucked a loose curl behind her ear as she straightened herself. "Good night, Mal."

He waited for her to disappear through the door, listening for the sound of her footsteps as she climbed up the stairs before heading to his own house. Once inside, he waited by the kitchen window, only going up to bed once he saw her light turn off.

Chapter Fourteen

JASMINE

"So," Jasmine asked, "was dinner okay?"

"Okay?" Mal's voice pitched higher. "You're kidding, right? It was phenomenal." His hands waved at the empty dishes and bowls in front of them. "How did you even get a recipe for kuj'ata stew? Or buy kuj'ata meat in the first place?"

She flashed him a mysterious smile. "I have my ways."

Jasmine had begun to scheme their second date even before their first one ended. While she certainly couldn't afford to take him to Blackbyrd or another fancy restaurant, she could whip up a meal that would knock his socks off. After all, her lola always said a way to a man's heart was through his stomach. In this case, she wasn't trying to get into Mal's hearts, but into his pants.

Her grandmother would roll over in her grave if she found out how Jasmine was using those cooking skills she'd passed on.

Initially, she'd planned to prepare one of her specialties—either lasagna or caldereta, Filipino beef stew cooked for twelve hours. However, she had to step up her game if she wanted to beat Chef Lucien's cooking. After a whole day of research, she found a recipe for a traditional orc dish, kuj'ata stew. It was actually similar to her beef stew, so she scoured the internet and found the ingredients from a specialty website, then paid extra for express shipping. When Friday rolled round, she told Mal before she left the shop that she would be picking him up at his door at seven o'clock. She arrived promptly, shopping bags in tow, and proclaimed that she was making him dinner at home.

Leaning back in his chair now, he patted his stomach. "Don't tell my mother, but I think it's better than hers."

"Thank you." All the effort had been worth it, especially hearing Mal's words of praise as well as his satisfied groans throughout the meal. "And no, I won't tell her. If she's anything like my lola she probably wouldn't speak to you for days."

"Definitely. Thank you, Jasmine." His purple eyes shone with warmth. "This . . . this was special. It's nice to have a bit of home when you're far away."

"I know what you mean." As she cooked for him, she had told him stories of her grandmother. It had been good for her too, reliving all those memories. "So, are you ready for dessert?"

"There's dessert too?" His face lit up.

"Of course. There's always room for dessert. It's not an orc recipe, though. I couldn't find any online."

"Yeah, orcs aren't into sweets. We eat fruits and berries, maybe the occasional honeycomb snack."

"But you're an exception, right?" she teased. "You did demand a whole dessert for yourself last week. You have a sweet tooth, don't you?"

"Guilty as charged." He licked his lips. "What did you make?"

"It's one of my favorite recipes my grandmother passed down to me. Coconut and corn pudding, or maja blanca. Why don't we have it in the living room? You go on ahead. I'll bring it over."

"All right."

Jasmine took the metal pan she had stashed in Mal's fridge

when she arrived and then cut the contents into squares. Once plated, she garnished the maja blanca with coconut curds she'd made herself.

Holding the two plates up, she sauntered into the living room, walked over to him, then leaned down to hand him his plate. "Here you go."

She didn't miss the way his eyes briefly dipped down to her cleavage. In fact, she'd been watching him all night as *he* watched her. She'd deliberately worn her sexiest and shortest dress with a deep V-neck that would show off her breasts and her legs. While he thought she wouldn't notice, she definitely saw him ogling them that morning they were setting up for the Founding Day Festival.

"Th-thanks." His eyes scooted respectfully above her neck. "This looks delicious."

And so do you.

When he asked what to wear, she told him to dress more casually. So tonight he wore a pair of jeans and a tight black polo shirt that showed off his muscled arms. He looked so good that the moment he opened the door she almost dropped her bags of ingredients and jumped him right there.

Stupid three-date rule.

Jasmine had already decided that, while she wasn't going to break their agreement, perhaps she could bend it just a little. While waiting was a good idea, she was going to honest-to-goodness expire if she didn't get *something* tonight. Besides, next week was date number three and she just wanted a little preview of things to come. After all, she might need a little extra mental preparation—and several rounds of prayers and offerings to her ancestor spirits—to be able to take on what Mal was packing between his legs.

"Oh." She bounced on top of the couch, knowing it would make her breasts jiggle. "You changed the sectional?"

"Uh"—he swallowed audibly—"yeah, it was pretty worn out so I ordered a new one. I mean, I'm probably going to regret it when I have to get rid of it once this place sells, but I couldn't stand sitting down on those lumpy cushions."

"I see." The oh-so-casual reminder that he would be leaving in a few months slid off her like water on a duck's back, though a small knot formed in her stomach. She quickly pushed that thought aside. "If I haven't said it yet, thank you, Mal, for helping me with my magic."

"Of course."

As Mal said, their magic was very different, not just in type. Mal's skills were miles ahead of hers and there were things he could do that she could only dream of. But he reminded her that he had basically been using magic since he was a teen when he was apprenticing with his stepfather, plus he continued to grow his skills by attending regular spell-casting workshops and seminars and through using them every day for his job.

While he wasn't able to teach her how to use her magic directly, Mal helped her pinpoint her main weakness. Just as she had thought initially, knowing she actually had magic made her second-guess herself even more. It was easier before, as all she had to do was to make an intelligent guess based on her observations. If a fenrir cub was whining, then it was sick, hungry or tired, and her first guess would always be correct. Now, however, it was hard to tell if she was using her magic or her gut, and that only made Jasmine doubt herself.

For example, earlier that week, she had been trying to figure out why the luscas were swimming lethargically. From her experience, it was one of three things: the water in the tank was too warm, they were stressed by the customers, or their diet needed to be changed. However, she was so overwhelmed with trying to tap into her magic for the correct answer that she couldn't decide, fearing that she would choose wrongly.

Jasmine thought she was a hopeless case, but Mal made her see that it was her *approach* that was the problem. "Your magic is part of you—it always has been," he had told her. "But when you're new to it, your body and brain just haven't realized it yet. Just do what you always did and trust your first instinct."

After that, she began to relax more and trust her instincts and her magic. It had only been a week, but Jasmine was beginning to feel more confident in her abilities and that was all thanks to Mal.

"And those greedy phoenixes definitely wanted more birdseed each meal," she confirmed. "And my turkey sandwich too."

He chuckled. "Hopefully you won't regret this."

"No, not at all." She took a bit of the pudding, the flavor of coconut bursting on her tongue before swallowing it. "I used to think I had this bond with the animals because I loved them. But now I know I really *can* connect to them. It's weird and hard to explain, but I like to think of it as a deep empathy. And if anything, my affinity with them just confirms what I already know. Much like every other species on this planet, pets just want to feel safe."

"It makes perfect sense when you explain it that way. By the way, have you told your dad?"

"No, not yet." She shoved a generous spoonful of pudding into her mouth before quickly changing the subject. "Have you tried the maja blanca yet?"

"Oh, no, sorry. I was, er, distracted." Once again, his gaze fell to her chest. "By your explanation of your cleava—your powers." Mal's eyes shot upwards, and he quickly took a bite. "Oh wow, that's amazing. That coconut flavor really comes through and the sweetcorn adds a different layer to it."

"It's my favorite dessert. My grandma and I would literally make it from scratch from the coconuts in our backyard, scraping the meat and squeezing the milk ourselves. This version uses the canned milk, but it tastes almost as good."

"It's delicious. Thank you for making it."

"My pleasure. And I love making this dish. It makes my entire apartment smell amazing."

Jasmine waited for Mal to finish his plate, then reached for it. "Here, let me get that and put it away."

"No, no, please." He stood up. "I'll help you clean up."

"Mal . . ."

"You cooked. It's only fair I clean up. You relax."

"All right. But I'll still help, okay? I can't just sit out here and wait while you wash dishes."

"Okay, you can help."

Heading back to the kitchen, they began clearing the remainders of the meal. Mal did most of the major cleaning, like pre-washing the dirty pans before stacking them in the dishwasher and wiping down the table and counters while Jasmine put away the leftovers. She did take the opportunity to brush up against him when she could, like reaching over to grab the covers for the plastic containers or the paper towels hanging over the sink. To her delight, he didn't discourage her or flinch when they did "accidentally" touch. Rather, she heard his sharp intakes of breath.

"Thanks again for dinner," Mal said as he hit the start button on the dishwasher. "I—"

Jasmine had sidled up against him, practically trapping him against the counter. "I was wondering . . . we could have a second dessert."

A flash of desire sparked in his purple eyes. "Jasmine . . ." He shook his head. "You know we agreed—"

"Yeah, I know we shouldn't have sex yet. But that doesn't mean we can't do other stuff, right? We just . . . won't go all the way." Oh Mother Goddess, she sounded like a horny teenage boy. However, she did feel like one, because she was going to explode if they didn't at least get to second base tonight.

"What do you mean?"

"Let's just enjoy each other's company tonight without any pressure."

His eyebrows drew together in doubt. "I told you I can't control myself around you."

"Yes, you can. I know it. Besides, I'm gonna need a preview before we go to the main event."

"Preview?"

She nodded at his crotch. "If you haven't thought of how different we are, I have. A lot. I've never been with anyone, uh, your size."

Realization dawned on his face. "It's never been a problem before."

"Yes, but I'm gonna have to know what I'm dealing with in order to prepare myself. You can't just expect me to . . . hop on the Mal train without knowing what I'm in for."

"I see." He *hmm*ed. "That sounds logical."

"And practical." She laid a hand on his arm. "So, yes?"

"Yeah," he said, his breath hitching.

"Good." Taking his hand, she led him back to the living room, then sat him down on the sofa. She sent him a sensual smile as she stood between his knees. Her hands went to the straps of her dress, then slowly lowered them down her arms, pulling the fabric down her torso to reveal her naked breasts to him. No bra for her tonight.

"Fuck." Mal's eyes grew to the size of saucers. "Oh fuck, oh fuck, your nipples and breasts are perfect."

"Do you want to touch them? Kiss them? Put them—"

"Come here."

She let out a whoop as he grabbed her waist and placed her on his lap, his eyes stuck like magnets to her chest. "Please, Jasmine, can I . . ."

"You can do whatever you want, Mal."

Bending his head, he pressed his mouth between her breasts, taking a deep breath. His mouth tusks grazed her sensitive flesh, sending goosebumps crawling down her arms. "You smell incredible," he moaned against her skin. "You feel incredible." Twisting his head to the side, his tongue flicked out at her nipple. His calloused hands slid up her torso to cup her breasts, his claws gently raking on her skin, making her shudder. He teased her nipples with the pads of his thumb, then dipped his head down to take one between his lips, tongue lashing out at the stiff bud.

"Mal!" Her fingers dug into his shoulders to steady herself. "More."

His hands slid under her dress and adjusted her, so she was pressed up against his erection. With only her panties and his jeans between them, he felt even larger than she remembered. A sense of panic left her throat bone dry, but the fear disappeared as Mal sucked her nipple deep.

She arched her back, pushing more of her breast into his wet, warm mouth as she rocked against him. His hips started bucking up, meeting her in a slow, sensual rhythm. It was all too much, and while she was tempted to grind on him until they both came, she wanted something else first.

"Mal," she groaned. "Let me see you."

Grunting, he released her nipple. Jasmine slid backwards, balancing herself on his knees, watching intently as he popped the buttons of his jeans. Reaching into his underwear, he pulled out his cock. Rising from a thick nest of hair at the base, it was a darker color green than the rest of him and sizable, but not like Leila's rather graphic two-handed depiction of them. However, her fingers of *one* hand would definitely not be able to touch, so that would be a challenge. One thing Leila did get right were the ridges. Oh Mother Goddess, they were thick, adding to the already substantial girth of his cock. Starting under the head, they grew in size along the shaft, stopping above his heavy sack.

"Mal, can I . . ."

"Yes," he said in a guttural tone.

She gripped the shaft without hesitation and gave him a firm pump.

"Oh fffuck. Don't stop."

Initially, she thought the ridges would make it difficult to caress him, but after a few strokes, she soon got the hang of it. The shaft swelled under her touch, pulsing and if it were possible, growing even more.

A clear liquid dribbled out the tip, flowing over the head and dripping down her fingers. At first, Jasmine thought he had ejaculated, but Mal's body remained still, his eyes shut tight.

"Pre-cum," he explained in a rough voice. "To help our partners." Opening his eyes, their gazes locked and his pupils blew wide with desire. "Our ridges can be . . . difficult to accommodate."

"It acts like lube?"

"Exactly," he breathed out, as if he'd been suffering from lack of oxygen.

So, male orcs made their own lubricant. "How efficient." At least she didn't have to worry about not having enough on hand for their third date. Her thighs tensed up, anticipation stretching taut within her, threatening to snap.

More. She needed more from him.

She licked her lips as she stared at the sticky liquid covering the head of his penis and her fingers. Without any hesitation, she bent down to lap it up with her mouth.

Something that sounded like her name gurgled from his mouth, but she wasn't sure, nor could she hear as blood pounded in her ears in excitement. Opening her lips, she drew the tip inside her mouth. Unable to help herself, she looked up at him, their eyes locking. The pure, unadulterated pleasure and awe on his face encouraged her. So, she lowered her head to take more of him inside, sending his eyes rolling back into his head.

Turning back to her task at hand, she began to pleasure him with her tongue, first swiping at the hole on the tip, then swirling it around the head. Unfortunately, she wasn't even halfway down when she reached the limit with his girth and her jaw was starting to ache. So, she released him but then slid her tongue up and down the hard shaft, teasing at the ridges. They must have been very sensitive because Mal's grip on the sofa cushions tightened, his talons ripping into the buttery soft leather.

Her clit throbbed, and her inner muscles clenched in desperation. At the same time, she reveled in the power she had over him, watching him gripped by pleasure and all because of her.

"Jasmine, stop. Oh please . . . Stop or I'm gonna come if you don't."

It was tempting to continue, but she released him. "We don't have to stop, Mal. I want you to come." She cupped her breasts. "Do you want to do it here? Or anywhere else?"

Heat flashed in his indigo eyes, but before she could say anything, she was on her back, facing the ceiling. "What—Mal!"

He was on his knees on the floor, head between her thighs. Flipping her skirt up, he yanked her panties to the side. "Let me taste you, Jasmine. Please. I want to taste your pretty pussy."

"Yes," she breathed.

The pad of his finger ran up the seam of her sex as his lips trailed upwards. He found her slick entrance and prodded gently. "Watch me, Jasmine. I want you to see me while I eat you."

Her cheeks burned, but she managed to lower her head. Mal's mouth descended on her mound, mouth covering her sex as his tongue snaked at her slick folds. Jasmine's eyes rolled all the way to the back of her head as he lapped at her, the pressure gathering up inside her.

"Delicious," he mouthed against her. "Give it all to me, Jasmine." Hooking his hands under her knees, he hauled them up and planted them over his shoulders. "Yes." Now his large hands reached under her, cupping her ass to lift her up, those claws of his scraping deliciously at her flesh. "So wet. You'll be able to take my cock so well."

When his mouth found her clit, she nearly screamed. He drew the bud between his warm lips, then used his tongue to flick at it, over and over again. That pressure that had been building up exploded as he pushed her to her climax. This time she did scream, her fingers shoving into his hair and tugging so tight she feared she would rip the strands from their roots.

"There, there, ashak'a," he cooed as he eased her down on the couch. "You did so well." He planted a kiss on her slick lips, then eased his hands out from under her.

Once the feeling returned to her limbs, she sat up so they were face to face, her on the couch and him on his knees before her. "Your turn," she said, reaching down to wrap a hand around his shaft. Taking his hand, she said, "Show me how you like it."

Desire flashed in his eyes as his hand covered over hers. He moved slow first, squeezing her fist to tighten her grip, the muscles on his veiny forearms tensing. Then he increased the pace, steady and rhythmic. His cock pulsed and throbbed under their combined touch, the tip pulsing as more of his pre-cum leaked out. His face twisted in pleasure, mouth tusks digging into the flesh of his upper lip. When he increased the strokes, she knew he was close and sure enough, the tip erupted with a burst of creamy white cum.

"Jasmine," he growled. His cock continued to spurt with his seed, splashing her fingers, shooting at her thighs and panties. He let out one last groan and collapsed against her, burying his face against her neck. She held him there, wrapping her arms around his torso, breathing in the scent of his sweat and male skin.

Heartbeats passed before he pulled back. "One second . . ." He whipped off his shirt. "Sorry for the mess. Let's clean you up."

"Huh?" His words didn't reach her ears because she was too busy ogling his muscular chest and perfect set of *eight*-pack abs. Why did she wait this long to have him take off his shirt?

He smirked at her. "Here, let me."

It was oddly romantic, how he cleaned up the mess he'd made all over her. After discarding the shirt, he sat back down on the couch, then pulled her onto his lap so she faced him. Beautiful purple eyes stared into hers.

"Jasmine, that was . . ."

"Thank you." She kissed him on the mouth. "Just so you know, I've already made up my mind about our third date. I'm sure I want to have sex with you, in case you had any doubts."

"Me too." He wrapped his arms around her, pulling her to his chest.

Jasmine sighed and snuggled against his bare chest, breathing in the scent of his cologne mixed with sweat. She could get used to this, but it was getting late, and she needed to get some sleep. "Mal? I should head home."

"You could stay—"

"No." Lifting her head up, she met his gaze. "Thank you for offering. But I don't want to stay the night yet." She had already tested his self-control to its limits, she didn't want him to break their agreement or torture him further. Besides, she wasn't sure *she* could stick to the three-date rule either if she stayed.

"Yes, of course. Besides, I need to wake up at three a.m. tomorrow."

"Three? Why?

"I'm going to Fire College," he stated. "It's down in Yuba."

"Yuba? That's two hours away."

"It's mandatory, so I have no choice."

"Ugh." She lay her head on his chest again. "I'm starting to hate Nick Amherst."

"Me too." His chest rumbled as he grunted. "But you know . . . I'm kind of liking being part of the fire department."

She smiled against his chest. "Really?"

"Yeah. I miss working with a crew. And with me being the new guy, it reminds me of back when I was an apprentice."

"Do they haze you?"

"Some ribbing here and there, nothing I can't handle." He smoothed a hand down her back. "And everyone had these stories about Vrig. He was a good man, and I'm sorry I didn't reach out enough over the last couple of years."

Though they had talked casually about his uncle in the last few weeks, Jasmine had never heard him speak about his feelings on his death. Slipping her arms around him, she gave him a squeeze.

They lay in silence for a minute or two, neither speaking or moving. "I really should get moving." But she didn't want to.

"I know." He pressed a kiss to the top of her head. "Will you be okay tomorrow by yourself? It's the shop's busiest day."

"I'll be fine, Mal. Please take care of yourself. I don't want you hurt."

"That's always a possibility when dealing with fire, but the training's going to be conducted in a controlled environment with all the safety precautions in place."

She knew that, but still . . . "Promise me you'll be careful."

"I will."

Sliding off his lap, she straightened her skirt and pulled up her dress straps. "No, no, don't get up."

"I should walk you—"

"I'm ten steps out the door. I'll be fine."

He got up anyway and tucked his softening cock into his pants. "Like you said, it's only ten steps away."

Mal walked her to her door—still shirtless and terribly distracting. "Good night, Mal," she said before stepping through her threshold. "Stay safe tomorrow."

"Thanks. I'll see you Sunday."

"See you."

Instead of closing the door, Jasmine left it open a crack, watching his large form retreat. The intensity of tonight's events was off the charts. Would she even survive their third date without completely combusting into a pile of ashes? That orgasm broke her apart completely, and he had only used his mouth. She wasn't a phoenix, so she wouldn't be able to resurrect.

She leaned her head against the doorjamb and rubbed her palm on her chest. Perhaps she shouldn't worry so much about the physical aspect of their next date. He would be leaving in a little less than four months, and she wasn't about to think she could make him stay. Mal was the type who, when he put his mind to something and set a goal, pursued it relentlessly until he achieved it.

You were the one who suggested this whole thing.

True. In the past, she'd only had two serious relationships that eventually came to a natural end. This would be similar, only this time, she and Mal knew in advance that it *would* end. This way neither of them had to think of the future, only enjoy the present. And she told herself that would be enough.

Jasmine glanced at the clock on the wall for the hundred and twenty-fifth time, willing the hands to go faster. Then she looked at the calendar next to the computer, willing the day to change from Wednesday to Friday. Sadly, as she discovered, time travel forward was not one of her magical abilities. In fact, she almost wondered if someone had cursed her so as to actually slow down time to ensure Friday never came.

Something had definitely shifted between her and Mal. An

air of anticipation hung between them as the days drew closer to their third date. Each time they would lock eyes, a spark threatened to ignite. She couldn't stop thinking about their interlude last Friday, partly regretting it. Now that she'd had a preview of what sex with him would be like, she couldn't think of anything else except his mouth and his hands and of course his ridged cock, imagining how it would feel inside her.

But then there was also a light atmosphere whenever they were in the same room. Being around him was easy and free, natural even. They spent the days at Fantastic Tails going through the usual routine, though now they opened the shop together in the mornings and he always made sure she was never alone when she closed up. Aside from doing casual repairs around the shop, Mal also helped out with customers and the creatures of course. When they were putting out breakfast the other day, she noticed that he didn't even look at her clipboards anymore, as he'd already memorized what each and every one of them needed.

Today, however, Jasmine was alone, as Mal had a lot of work for his consulting job, which he preferred to do at home. So after grabbing coffee with her at Brew-tique and walking her to the shop, he headed back. Without his presence, the shop felt vast and empty. A few times, she almost expected him to come out of the back office to tinker with the cages or come plodding down the stairs after checking on their newly hatched basilisks, but then she remembered he was back home and she was alone.

The afternoon trudged on and much to her relief closing time arrived. Once she finished her rounds of checks on everyone, she headed to her final stop.

"Hello, Clawdia," she cooed as she approached the pen beside Mal's desk, a bowl of food in one hand. The hatchling immediately reared up on its hind legs, her talons clicking loudly against the metal bars as she pawed at them. Visions of kibble danced in Jasmine's head.

"Yes, I know. You're hungry, but you need to wait."

When Clawdia heard the word "wait", she sat back. Much to Jasmine's surprise, the hatchling was responsive to training and was obedient to commands. She'd watched a few videos online and read articles about how to train domesticated dragons, and many trainers compared them to dogs, except that dragon owners needed extra fire insurance. It was one of the reasons she didn't want to take Clawdia home yet, as she couldn't afford the additional rider.

"Good job." Opening the cage, Jasmine set the bowl on the floor. "Come, Clawdia."

The baby dragon scrambled out of the pen and dove into the bowl. Jasmine snapped a few photos and videos as she happily devoured the meal. One in particular had her giggling—a piece of kibble had been stuck on top of Clawdia's snout and she went cross-eyed trying to lick it off with her long, snake-like tongue. She saved the video in a folder she called "Best of Clawdia."

Jasmine bit her lip as she scrolled through the folder. She still hadn't shared any photos or videos of the dragon on their social media. That was another reason she didn't want to take her home yet. It just felt too good to be true that Clawdia was *hers*. Like one day someone would come and just take her away. It was one thing for her to keep Clawdia, but putting her out there could expose her and she didn't want to catch the attention of the original hatchery from which she'd bought the egg.

A vision of Mal's face appeared in her head. "He's not here, he's at work," she said to Clawdia. "I know you haven't seen him since Monday. I miss him too."

She let out a sad chirp.

"He'll be back tomorrow, don't worry. You wanna play ball?"

Her ears perked up at the sound of the word "ball".

"All right, let's play."

Clawdia was much too young to get the concept of "fetch",

so playing ball with her mostly meant that Jasmine tossed the ball, Clawdia caught it, then refused to give it back until Jasmine chased her all over the room. Still, she was learning fast, which was a good thing because it was important for dragon owners to be able to control their pets, for everyone's safety. In a year or two, Clawdia's dragon fire would be able to do more than just leave scorch marks on the wooden floor. She'd be able to set whole houses on fire, and if Jasmine didn't train her correctly, the authorities could take her away.

If she ever got to keep her that long.

I'll have your back, no matter what.

Mal's words from the other night rang in her head clear as a bell. A smile tugged at her lips as she recalled how he had consulted a lawyer about Clawdia. Aside from the fact that it probably cost money, that he even thought to do it without her asking touched her deeply. He'd already proved to her that she could count on him, so maybe she should allow herself to believe him.

Nervous, she picked up her phone again and opened the "Best of Clawdia" folder, scrolling until she found the photo she wanted. It was one of Mal holding Clawdia, the little hatchling looking up at the orc, her big blue eyes shining with clear adoration. After only a brief bout of hesitation, she pressed her thumb on the share button, then tapped out a caption.

So . . . turns out, it wasn't a carcinos. Welcome to the world, baby Clawdia! #babydragon #hatchling #notacarcinos #oopsies #fantastictailsandmagicalscales #officialmascot #clawdia #maltheorc.

Her lips twitched at that last one, but it was probably time he got his own hashtag since it was pictures of him that got the most likes anyway. After a quick prayer to her ancestor spirits, she hit "post".

There.

No going back now.

Something hit her feet and a small ball plopped down next to her. "Are we done playing 'make Jasmine chase you around'?" Clawdia let out a warble. "How about—"

A piercing siren interrupted her and made her jump, though it quickly faded off, as if it had zoomed away. Clawdia clung to her leg.

"Don't worry, it's just an emergency vehicle," she assured the hatchling. Bending down, she picked her up. "It's really loud, huh? Must be hard on your sensitive hearing, plus we don't have any soundproofing spells in here, like in the shop." She made a mental note to ask Mal if there was anything he could do about that.

A vision of fire popped up in her head.

"Oh no, no. Please, baby, no more testing out your dragon breath." Clawdia had already burned two blankets, a unicorn stuffie, and she'd singed one of Mal's fingertips. "How about—"

The hatchling placed its paws on her chest then lifted her head to lick at Jasmine's cheeks, as if to say, *listen to me.*

"What—"

The heat around her intensified.

"Oh Mother Goddess." That was definitely Clawdia. She'd always used pictures and feelings to communicate with Jasmine before, but never anything as strong as actual sensations. But what was she trying to say?

Another loud piercing wail echoed from the outside, followed by another, both eventually fading into the distance.

Flames danced in her head, growing in size.

"Wait. Are you trying to tell me there's a fire somewhere?" Dragons were fire breathers, and as she learned from Mal, elemental magic was always connected. In the same way wyrms could seek out the nearest water source or kamaitachi hopped on cyclones to traverse long distances, was it possible dragons knew when fires were ablaze?

A strange feeling crept into her stomach as Jasmine pressed

her palm to her chest, surprised at the loud thumping from her heart. Surely they wouldn't call Mal to help with any fire. He was the new guy, had barely had two days of training. However, the pressure in her chest increased.

"Let's get you back to your pen, Clawdia. It's time for bed."

After settling the hatchling back in her crate, Jasmine quickly closed up the shop and rushed outside. Another fire truck zoomed by, its sirens wailing like a banshee, the words BAYVIEW CITY FIRE DEPARTMENT emblazoned on the side. If Bayview had sent their trucks, that meant there was a major fire somewhere.

Maybe it was over in Morristown and they cut through Main Street to get there faster.

Still, her chest contracted, and it was hard to breathe. Unsure what to do, she jogged down to Brew-tique. The sign in front proclaimed it as closed, but she ignored it and threw the door open.

"Minerva!" she called to the witch, who was behind the counter, head bent down as she scrolled on her phone. "Do you know what's going on?"

Her head snapped up. "Aren't you on the Main Street Business Association group chat?"

"Yeah." She hurried inside and crossed the dining area, stopping right on the other side of the counter. "But I put it on mute a couple months ago. I couldn't stand Martha's passive-aggressive tirades. What's happening?"

"Three-alarm fire." Minerva slid her phone over to her. On the screen was a picture of a building with smoke billowing out the window. "Out by Maple Avenue. Blue Skies Vista."

Jasmine knew exactly which area that was. That part of town was barely Dewberry Falls, a fancy new neighborhood with big townhouses and a modern apartment complex with complete amenities. The buildings popped up like mushrooms last year, and because of how quickly they finished construction, there were rumors that the developers had cut corners.

Oh no.

"Jasmine?" Minerva's voice was filled with concern. "Are you okay?"

"Yeah, one sec." With shaking hands, she slid her phone out of her purse and dialed Mal's number.

Pickuppickuppickup.

"You've reached Mal of Urduk Horde at Terra Forma Builders. I can't come to the phone right now, but if you leave your name and number, I'll get back to you as soon as possible."

While his low baritone would normally soothe her, Mal's disembodied voice was like a portent of doom.

"What's wrong, Jasmine?" Minerva came over to her side and placed a hand on her shoulder.

"It's Mal." She quickly explained to the witch about how he joined the volunteer fire department. "I know they're all technically on call during emergencies, but you don't think they'd send him out there? He's only had one day at fire college and that was last Saturday."

"It's a major fire, though," the witch pointed out. "They're probably calling everyone in, even the ladders from the nearby towns."

Jasmine's throat turned dry as a desert. "Let me try Nick." Despite her numb fingers, she managed to tap out a quick message to the satyr. After a few seconds, there was no reply, not even the bubbles indicating the receiver was typing a message popped up. So she called his number.

"Hey, this is Nick," came the smooth voice from his voicemail. *"You know the drill."*

"Argh!" She really was starting to hate Nick Amherst.

"Mal will be okay," Minerva assured her. "There're tons of trucks responding to the fire. He probably won't even get near the blaze. They'll likely keep him at the back, turning on the hydrants or something, or maybe putting blankets on people. Why don't you sit down? Want a chamomile tea or something?"

"N-no, I'm fine. But thank you."

Jasmine worried at her lip. If only she had a car, she could drive over to Blue Vista and see what was going on. "Minerva, does anyone on the group chat have any news? Like . . . injuries or—" Her throat closed up before she could finish the sentence.

"No, no one knows anything. Emergency services and law enforcement are probably keeping things under wraps for now."

"But—Oh, wait." A thought struck her. Fumbling with her phone, she managed to dial a number from her contacts.

"Hello?" came Kap's voice through the speaker.

"Kap! Sorry for the early call, but I just had to call someone. Please tell me you're awake."

"Yeah. What's up?"

"Have you heard anything about the fire on Maple Avenue?"

"That's why I'm already up and ready to head out. Station's all abuzz. Hands-on-deck kind of situation, you know?"

She felt the blood drain from her face. "It's that bad?"

"Yup. With these things, P.D. has to come in to direct traffic, crowd control, you know, for general public safety. Listen, I have to—"

"Wait, don't hang up. You have to take me there."

"There? To the fire?"

"Yes."

"You know I can't do that," he protested. "I could lose my job, plus it's not safe for you. Why would you want to go anyway?"

"Kap . . ." She took a deep breath. "Mal's down there as a volunteer fireman. He's not picking up his phone. Couldn't you just say you were giving me a ride? I don't need you to get me into the site. I just need to be there."

"I . . ." He hesitated. "All right, fine. I'm already in the car."

"Great! Come pick me up at Brew-tique."

"See you in five."

After a quick thank you to Minerva, Jasmine dashed outside to wait for Kap. It was the longest five minutes of her life as horrible thoughts and visions of what could happen—or was happening—to Mal filled her head. Her anxiety somewhat eased when she saw the familiar cruiser approaching. She didn't bother waiting for him to invite her inside.

"Thanks." She clicked on her seatbelt. "I appreciate this. I owe you one."

"I can't believe I'm doing this," he moaned. "Are you sure you want to come? Maybe I should drop you off at home. Have you thought that maybe Mal's just sitting on his couch, twiddling his thumbs?"

"He would have answered my call or texted me by now." It wasn't like Mal to just ignore a missed call from her, even if he was working. "Please, Kap, we're wasting time."

The tree giant put the car into gear. "Jasmine, you're a wreck. Is there a reason why you're so worried about him?"

"No. I mean, he's my boss . . ."

His eyes flicked over to her, then steered back to the road ahead. "Lie. You literally just turned red as a tomato."

"Okay, fine." She blew out a breath. "We're dating, okay?"

"Good for you," he said without missing a beat. "I was wondering when that was going to happen."

"What?" She stared at him, slack-jawed. "What do you mean?"

"Jasmine, I'm a cop. Observation and deduction skills, remember?" He tapped at his temple. "But also, you guys have been eye-fucking each other this entire time. And he definitely wanted to deck me when I showed up at your place for dinner."

"Deck you?"

"Yeah, he was jealous."

"You're crazy. I'd only known him three days at that point."

"I'm a guy. Trust me." His expression quickly changed from lighthearted to stormy. "We're here."

As Jasmine turned her attention outside, her heart leapt into her throat at the scene before them. It was pure chaos, to put it mildly. Half a dozen fire trucks took up the corner of the street where an apartment complex stood, thick, fat curls of smoke rising to the heavens as fire clawed at the blackened windows and walls. Even from inside the car, her nose burned with the sharp stench of burning wood.

"Oh Mother Goddess." An invisible fist wrapped around her chest and squeezed. "Mal . . ."

"I'm sure he's fine," Kap said, sounding confident. He parked the car in the closest open spot. "Stay in here, Jasmine."

"But—"

"I said stay!" The low, unearthly growl from the tree giant sent a shiver through her. "I'll ask around about him, okay?"

The loud slam of the door closing made Jasmine start. She stayed in the cruiser, watching the blaze engulf the looming structure, her stomach twisting with worry. The fire was much, much worse than in her imagination. It was like a movie—no, a nightmare where she couldn't do anything to stop the horrors. A crazed feeling ripped through her.

Calm down. Everything's going to be fine. And—

A loud crack sent all the hairs on the back of her neck standing up. An involuntary gasp left her mouth as she watched the collapse of the east corner of the building, screams and shouts filling the air.

Jasmine flew out of the car like the devil was on her tail, running into the wave of people scurrying away, as if she were a salmon swimming upstream. She crossed over the cordoned-off scene marked ominously with red-and-white tape that read, "FIRE SERVICE EMERGENCY PERSONNEL ONLY."

Lost in a sea of identical uniforms and heavy, soot-streaked gear, Jasmine couldn't tell which one of them was Mal. There were a few who were almost seven feet tall, but from their gait and stride, she could tell they were not him.

". . . I can't believe he went inside!"

"That orc must be crazy."

The word "orc" perked up her ears. Turning to the direction of the chatter, she found two firefighters in full gear, braced against the side of a fire truck, exhaustion and worry etched on their dirty faces.

"Excuse me, did you say 'orc'?" she called. "Was it Mal of Urduk Horde?"

"I don't know his name," one of them said. "He's not from our ladder, though."

"Did he make it out of the building?"

"Didn't see him come out," the other one replied.

Jasmine's stomach turned to stone and moisture gathered at her eyes. But she gritted her teeth, fighting against the tears and wave of emotions threatening to overwhelm her. This was not the time to break down.

Spinning on her heel, she bounded toward the blaze. With the confusion around her, no one noticed or questioned her presence. As she drew closer, the familiar sight of the Dewberry Volunteer Fire Department truck came into view, parked closest to the building. Her heart sprinted in her chest as she rushed forward, stumbling through the mess of firefighters and emergency workers. The hiss of water and crackling flames only added to the panic clawing at her.

Oh Mother Goddess, ancestor spirits, please let him be all right.

"Jasmine! Jasmine!"

She whirled round. "Nick!"

The satyr galloped toward her, stopping a few inches away, his hooves kicking up dirt. "What are you doing here? This area is for emergency personnel only." He reached out to put a hand on her shoulder. "Let me—"

"No!" She put her hands up defensively. "I want to see Mal. He . . . he made it out, right?"

"You know about—" He shook his head. "Damned idiot charged right in when he heard some lady and her two children were still trapped on the third floor." He heaved a breath. "Tried to stop him, but he wouldn't—"

"Just tell me if he made it out," she interrupted, her fingers clawing at his arm.

"Huh? Well, yeah, he did." Nick pried her hands off. "He did that magic umbrella forcefield thing and got out before that one section collapsed. Rescued the mom and kids too."

The relief she felt was indescribable. "Where is he?"

"EMTs should be checking him out. Jasmine, you really should—"

She was already dashing toward the group of ambulances parked behind the fire trucks, her vision blurring through the tears stinging her eyes. A big indistinguishable blob appeared ahead, seated in the back of an emergency vehicle. Wiping the moisture away with her fingers, she slowed her steps, her heartbeat slowing down to a normal pace as soon as her gaze landed on Mal.

"Mal . . ."

His head snapped toward her, his purple eyes bulging. "Jasmine? What are you—Ow!"

"Sorry, sir," said the young EMT who was dabbing at a nasty scratch on his arm with a cotton pad. "If you could please sit still, I'll be done in a second."

"Er, yeah. Sorry about that." He sent Jasmine a sheepish grin. "And thank you."

"Just doing my job. And there you go." With a last swipe of the cotton pad, the wound completely disappeared. "You're very lucky, sir, that you got away with only minor cuts and burns." He looked over his shoulder at Jasmine. "You should probably take him home, ma'am."

"Y-yeah. Sure."

Mal stood up, the ambulance bobbing up behind him. With his giant strides, he reached her in three steps.

She spoke first, scared to raise her voice above a whisper. "I heard the fire trucks . . . Clawdia said there was fire . . . Minerva told me about the apartment building . . . Nick said you went . . ."

Oh.

Mal's big, strong arms came around her, crushing her against him. Pressing her nose against his chest, she took in a deep breath, not caring if he smelled like smoke and sweat. No, to her, he smelled *alive*.

"And you came all the way here?"

"I had to," she murmured against his chest. "I needed to know you were safe."

A soft rumble vibrated against her cheek as he said, "Let's get out of here."

Chapter Fifteen

MAL

Mal pulled into the driveway, then cut off the engine of the truck. "We're here."

Jasmine remained still, her gaze fixed outside the window. Tension seeped out from Mal with a long exhale, relieved that she finally looked like her usual calm self. The sight of her earlier, hair disheveled, face pale, and tears streaking down her cheeks, had both shocked and frightened him. He still could not believe she'd charged into an active fire scene, just to make sure he was okay.

Mal had just finished his work for the day when the text alert came about the fire on Maple Avenue. Nick had signed him up for the alerts as soon as he joined, but he mentioned that he didn't have to respond until he had attended at least one more Thursday evening training session. However, when the alert said it was a three-alarm fire, he knew there was no way Dewberry Falls's one truck could handle it.

Figuring he could help in some way, he drove over to the scene. Good thing too, because the fire was massive. With the training still fresh in his mind, he had managed to assist in setting up the hoses and other equipment and in giving basic first aid to the injured victims. He had been helping an old man who had sprained an ankle when the man told Mal about his neighbors who were trapped inside, a single mom and her two daughters. Mal had tried to tell someone about them, but everyone was too busy trying to control the blaze before it spread to the nearby buildings.

It was then he decided to go in himself. Thankfully, the mom and kids were only on the third floor, and he managed to get them out safely, encapsulating them in his magnetic shield before the collapse, and escaping with only minor injuries himself.

For a brief moment, though, he almost thought he wouldn't make it. And as the heat washed over him and the debris rained down, one single thought permeated his brain.

"Jasmine?"

She started, head whipping toward him. "Huh?"

"We're here."

"Here?" Doe eyes blinked slowly. "Oh."

"Yeah." Reaching out, he brushed at a spot of dirt on her cheek. Before he could pull away, her hand covered his, pressing his fingers so his claws raked her skin. Jasmine turned her head slightly so she could brush her lips against his palm. The intimacy of it sent his hearts into a nervous flutter.

She opened her eyes, as if shocked by her own actions. "I'm sorry. And sorry for overreacting today—" Scrambling away from him, she flattened herself against the passenger side door, gaze averted to her lap.

"No, don't be sorry for that. Jasmine, look at me." Brown eyes like translucent marble met his. "Thank you. But you didn't have to go all the way there."

"Of course I had to. Mal, I was so worried."

He scuttled toward her. "I'm here—nothing happened. Jasmine."

A small, relieved smile tugged at her mouth. "Yeah, thank the Mother Goddess." She took in a deep breath then exhaled. "Well, I'm—*mmph!*"

Mal couldn't help himself as he covered her mouth with a kiss. The impact of it all—the adrenaline rush, his brush with death, Jasmine worrying over him, and the feeling of being alive—punched him in the gut, and that energy had to go somewhere.

Her mouth opened in a moan, allowing him to snake his tongue between her lips to taste her and breathe her in. Small hands came up to grip at his shoulders, pushing him back on the seat so she could settle onto his lap. The skirt of her dress hitched up around her thighs invitingly.

"Mal, I don't want to wait."

"Hmmm?" He sought her lips again, unwilling to stop kissing her until he'd had his fill. Maybe by next week, he'd let her lips go.

"Mal." Her hands cupped his jaw to pull him away and grab his attention. "I said, I don't want to wait."

"Wait for what?"

She bore down on him, her heat rubbing over his half-swollen cock, her panties and his pants and underwear the only barrier between them. His shaft twitched at the sensation, growing impossibly large in such a short amount of time, and he went dizzy from the lack of blood in his brain. Or maybe it was just Jasmine.

"Our third date. Mal, please. I need you *now*."

His hearts crashed together. "I don't want to wait, either." Excitement pulsed through him, and his erection surged. "Let's go inside."

"Mal—Oh!"

Flinging the door open, he slid out the driver's side, all the while keeping Jasmine's legs wrapped round him as he marched them in through the back door.

"Please, Mal," she whined. "Now, now."

"Jasmine, I want to take my time and go slow—" Her fingers dug into his scalp, giving his hair a healthy tug.

"Take me here, Mal." Reaching for the hem of her top, she whipped it over her head.

Mal groaned at the sight of her gorgeous tits encased in black lace. "Jasmine, we're almost—"

"Now." Her tone was demanding. "I need to feel you inside me now."

"Jasmine, I . . . I didn't buy any condoms yet." He'd meant to pick some up, but since Friday was still days away, he hadn't thought he'd need them so soon.

"It's okay. I'm on the pill," she said. "Please, Mal . . ."

Fuck. With a hoarse grunt, he placed her on the kitchen countertop so she sat facing him. "Here? You want me to give you my cock raw, right here?"

Her pupils blew out. "Yes. Quick and rough. Slow later."

The fact that she was shaking with need and could barely put a whole sentence together only made him even harder.

"Yes, Jasmine." He slid his hands up her thighs, pushing her skirt up, claws trailing across her skin. "Whatever you want, Jasmine." Hooking the tips of his talons into the waistband of her panties, he tore through the fabric as if it were wet paper, leaving her pretty pussy bare.

His mouth founds hers in a rough kiss as he unzipped his pants. Taking out his now painfully erect cock, he spread his natural lube around her nether lips, coating her with the sticky substance to ensure she was wet and ready for him. Hauling her closer to the edge of the counter, he notched the tip of his ridged cock against her flesh. Her breath hitched as the head prodded at her.

Mal gritted his teeth as he pushed in. She was tight, too tight, and he could barely stop himself from coming right away.

Slow, he told himself. *Take your time.*

Jasmine, however, seemingly impatient with his pace, pushed her hips at him and let out a needy whine.

"I know, ashak'a," he soothed. "Can't go too fast yet. Just give me a second." Bracing himself, he rocked into her, stretching her. The first couple inches, he was sure this wouldn't work, but eventually, he managed to ease all the way in. Still, she felt impossibly snug around him.

"Relax, Jasmine." Bending his head down, he nuzzled between her breasts, breathing in her sweet perfume. Moving up, he licked a path to her neck, his mouth teasing her flesh until she was squirming. "That's it." Her passage eased. "What a good girl you are. You take my cock so well."

"Mal—Mal!" She squealed as he pulled back and thrust into her, her eyes glazing over. "Oh, Mal . . . you . . . incredible. Please. Now."

Mal really liked this incoherent-with-lust version of Jasmine. Encouraged, he began to pound into her. Her pussy walls squeezed at him, the friction and heat driving him to fuck her harder, not caring about the burning in his thighs as he continued his punishing pace.

"That's it, Jasmine," he growled into her ear. "You're doing so good. I've been dreaming about you for weeks. Wondering how that sweet pussy would feel around my cock. You like it, don't you?"

She whined in agreement. "Yes . . . Mal . . . oh please, oh please."

"Look at me."

Her gaze lifted, brown doe eyes filled with lust locking with his. Slipping his hands under her ass, he lifted her higher, her knees digging into his hips at just the right angle so he could shove up into her, right where he knew the ridges of his cock would hit her G-spot.

She braced her hands on his shoulders, hips pistoning

downwards to meet his thrusts. "Don't . . . stop . . . Mal . . . gonna . . ." Her nails clawed into his skin, which would probably leave a scratch, but he didn't care. In fact, he relished the idea of her marking him.

"That's it, Jasmine," he said as he drilled into her. "Make yourself come on my cock."

Her entire body seized as her inner walls gripped at him, then began to convulse. She screamed his name, babbling some sort of prayer to the Mother Goddess and ancestors as she writhed in his arms, shaking with pleasure.

Seeing her come so beautifully broke his control. Gripping her hips tight, he bucked into her, working harder than he'd ever worked before. Pure pleasure burst from the bottom of his spine, his balls tightening as he came hard. Jasmine's knees released their grip on his hips, and he set her back down on the counter. His palms slapped loudly on granite as he braced himself, his breathing coming in short gasps as his hearts continued a steady, pounding pace in his chest.

She buried her face in his neck. "That was . . ."

"I know." Despite his limbs feeling like wet noodles, he managed to wrap an arm around her waist. "Was that what you wanted?" He kissed her damp temple.

"Oh yeah."

"Good." Holding his breath, he withdrew from her, his seed spilling between them, a few drops spurting upwards to hit her belly. "Ahh." He made a move to remove his shirt, but she stopped him.

"No, don't clean it up." Her eyes darkened. "I like it."

His still-hard cock throbbed again. "We should shower, though. The fire . . . I must stink."

Her nose wrinkled. "I was too busy being horny to notice."

Mal let out a laugh, then picked her up. "Come on, let's wash off together."

He carried her all the way to the bathroom in his bedroom. Despite the fact that he'd just had the most powerful orgasm in his life, the sight of Jasmine's wet, slippery naked breasts were enough to get him hard again. Thankfully, the steam in the shower hid his erection. While he wanted to take her again, he knew she had to be sore. Though she tried to hide it, he had seen her wince a few times as she soaped up.

"Oh, this feels amazing," she moaned as he wrapped her in a fresh towel. "Thank you, Mal."

"You're very welcome." He dried himself off with his own towel.

"Thank the Mother Goddess my apartment is only ten steps away from yours," she said as she faced the mirror and dried her hair with the towel.

"Hmm? What are you talking about?"

She nodded at the discarded skirt on the floor and smiled wryly at him. "I don't have to worry about getting back to my place tonight without my panties on."

"Your place? Don't you want to stay here?" A strange sensation pooled in his gut at the idea that she wanted to leave.

The towel stilled and she slowly spun round. "You . . . want me to stay the night?" she asked, her voice small and unsure. "I thought maybe you didn't—"

"Of course I want you to stay, ashak'a." He wasn't sure what gave her the impression that he would just tell her to pack up and go home, not after the intense lovemaking session they'd just had. "Stay with me, Jasmine. I want to sleep with you in my arms."

Her eyes went all dreamy. "Then yes, I'll stay."

Chapter Sixteen

JASMINE

Jasmine woke in degrees, her mind and body slowly becoming aware of her surroundings—the extra plush mattress underneath her, the soft pillow her head lay on, the luxurious sheets on her skin, and of course, the distinct male scent that was Mal.

Rolling over, she reached out her hand and felt for—

Nothing?

For a moment, she thought it had all been a dream, but then again, the lingering soreness between her legs told her otherwise. Pushing herself up, she let out a yawn. It was early still, the sun barely peeking through the windows. Her muscles ached deliciously, particularly her inner thighs. After washing off in the shower, Mal had been ready for another round, and she'd obliged, of course. He bent her around like a pretzel, fucking her relentlessly in different positions, before ending with him on top, his arms around her like he was afraid she would disappear, whispering sweet, dirty words into her ears as he came.

Jasmine's knees turned to jelly thinking about it. Who knew the grumpy orc was a master of dirty talk? And his dick . . . Well, she could now confirm it was, indeed, legendary.

I'm glad I didn't wait another day to hop on the Mal train, she thought. But she'd already known sleeping with him was inevitable. And now that it was done, Jasmine wasn't sure what was next.

An ominous feeling crept into her chest. Mal was still leaving in a little over three months, maybe sooner if he got that job with the historical center. But that would also mean she would be the new owner of Fantastic Tails by then. She'd been working hard on her business plan, and she'd managed to save more than she'd initially thought. Tracy had been nice enough to look over her paperwork a couple days ago, and said it was looking good and as long as Jasmine continued on the same trajectory, she might be able to qualify for that loan.

The more she thought about it, the more excited she was at the prospect of finally owning Fantastic Tails. Working there, and now discovering her magical affinity, she knew in her heart this was what she was meant to be doing with her life. The Mother Goddess – or maybe her ancestor spirits – had guided her here so she could meet her fate.

What she had with Mal was only temporary. They'd agreed there would be an expiration date to . . . whatever this was between them.

Great sex, she reminded herself. Really great, awesome, spirit-leaving-your-body sex. But she and Mal were adults, and they agreed, they would walk away from each other without any drama, still respecting each other.

Pushing those thoughts away, she rolled off the bed, then headed to the bathroom to do her business and clean up as best she could, though she realized she was stark naked. Unfortunately, she hadn't hung up her discarded skirt, so it remained in a wrinkled heap on the floor, and her top was still in the living room, along with the shreds of her panties. Looking behind her, she found a shirt hanging over the hook in the door. Pressing her nose against it, drawing in the faint, lingering scent of Mal, she brushed her cheek against the soft cotton before taking it off the hook and pulling it over her head.

Jasmine let the distinct sounds of activity guide her out of the room and to the kitchen. Sure enough, there was Mal, back to her and hunched over the stove, wearing only black pajama bottoms.

Leaning against the doorway, she waited a few seconds before saying, "I thought you said you couldn't cook."

His shoulder muscles tensed in surprise, then he turned to look at her. "I said I don't cook, not that I can't." The corners of his mouth turned up. "You found something to wear."

"I hope you don't mind." She smoothed her hands down his shirt, which went down past her knees.

Switching off the stove, he stalked toward her. "Not at all," he said in a raspy tone. "Come here." His arm snaked around her waist and lifted her up as he leaned down to kiss her. She melted into him, the move so natural she didn't even have to think about it. When he pulled away, she sighed audibly.

"Did you sleep well?" he asked, still holding her up.

"Yeah. Those sheets of yours are amazing."

"They're made of Tartary lamb wool."

"No wonder." Tartary lambs were half plant, half creature that grew from bushes, known for their luxurious soft wool with a self-regulating temperature. "I could have slept for days. I'm so glad I stayed over."

"I hope it's not just my linens keeping you here?"

She traced a finger up his chest. "Of course not. I also like your nice, big firm . . . bed," she teased.

"Is that so?" His eyes turned dark. "Anything else 'big' that you liked about last night?"

"No, that's it—Mal!" She laughed as he whipped her around and then planted her on the kitchen table. Nudging her thighs open with his, he scooted between her legs, pulling her forward so his erection brushed right at her nakedness. "Are we going to do it on every single surface of this kitchen?"

"On every single surface of this house," he growled. He caught her lips between his, giving them a playful nip, his pearly-smooth mouth tusks rubbing against her cheeks. A hand slipped under the shirt, cupped her breast and teased her nipple into a tight bud.

She moaned his name, arching her back as her clit throbbed. Desperate for some friction, she undulated her hips at him, the cotton fabric over his bulge rubbing deliciously at her slickening lips. His mouth found her neck and clamped around it, his tongue licking at her sensitive flesh. Her hands reached for the waistband of his pants, clawing at them to get them off.

A sharp rapping sound made them both freeze.

"Someone's out there." He nodded at the kitchen door.

"No," Jasmine whined. "Tell them to go away."

"Mal!" came a muffled voice. "Mal, it's me, Kap."

"Oh no." She pushed the hem of his shirt down over her knees and struggled to get off the table. "Should I hide in your room? Or go back to my place? I could sneak around—"

"What do you mean 'hide'?" There was a deadly edge to his voice. "Why would you want to hide from Kap?"

"So he doesn't see me here. Wearing only your shirt." Kap didn't need his observation and deduction skills to put two and two together. "He'll definitely figure out we slept together."

"And why in Vorlak's name would I not want him to know that?" There was a crazed look in his eyes, one Jasmine couldn't explain.

Unless he was . . . jealous?

Was Kap right? Had Mal been jealous since the beginning?

The banging became more insistent. "Mal? Are you in there? I can hear you."

"One second," he barked out. "Jasmine, tell me what gave

you the impression that I would want you to hide or sneak out after last night?"

"We didn't talk about what would happen after we . . . you know . . . the third date."

He raked his claws through his hair. "I took you out to dinner on Main Street for our first date. Walked you to and from the shop every day. I've been spending almost every single day with you. What makes you think I wouldn't want everyone to know about us?"

"Oh. Right." She smiled up sheepishly at him. "Sorry, I just panicked. This is all new to me."

His shoulders relaxed. "Me too. For the record, even though I didn't say it, I'm not going to sneak around like teens. We're adults, remember."

"I—"

"C'mon, Mal!" came Kap's voice.

He let out a deflated exhale, then trudged to the door, yanking it open. "What is it?"

"I wanted to check on you. I heard about—" The tree giant stuttered to a halt when Jasmine appeared next to Mal. "Jasmine."

"Kap," she replied.

He grinned at her. "Everything okay?"

"Yup," she said with a pop of the "p". "Are you okay?"

"What are you doing here this early?" Mal asked before he could answer.

"A couple of things, actually. First off, I thought maybe you might want to know that the family you rescued are all doing well. One of the kids had a nasty burn on her palm, but other than that, they're good."

Jasmine pressed a hand to her chest. "Where are they now?"

"On the way to a shelter, as is everyone who lost their home."

"Thank you for telling me," Mal said. "I'm glad they're doing well, and everyone else."

"Thanks to you and the rest of the firefighters."

"You said 'a couple of things'?" Mal asked, a hint of impatience in his voice.

"Well, I gave *someone* a ride with the promise that they wouldn't get close to the fire." He directed his attention to Jasmine. "I said stay in the car, remember?"

"I couldn't, not when I saw that building collapse."

"You could have at least texted me or left me a note. When I came back and saw you weren't in the car, I went crazy. Looked all over for you. I've been texting you and calling you all night, but you weren't picking up."

"Er, sorry . . . I didn't hear my phone." Her screams of ecstasy probably drowned out her ringtone.

"Anyway, had to go back to work and just prayed to the Mother Goddess that you had the sense not to run into a burning building." He snorted. "Now I know why you didn't pick up. Anyway, since I didn't find Mal at the scene, either, I figured you guys left. I'm glad you're both okay."

"Thanks for checking up on us," Mal said. "By the way, any news on what caused that fire?"

Kap's face turned serious. "Nothing solid, but an initial investigation by the Bayview fire chief indicated it's probably due to shoddy workmanship and cheap materials used in that building."

Mal cursed under his breath. "I hate those big corporate developers. Always cutting corners just to make a buck."

"For sure. Anyway, PD nabbed the CEO of the construction company at the airport, trying to catch a flight to Columbia."

Mal crossed his arms. "No extradition to the US."

"Exactly."

"All those poor people who lost everything." Jasmine clucked her tongue. "I hope he rots in jail."

"We're working on it," Kap assured her. "Anyway . . ." He let out a loud yawn. "I should hit the hay."

"Thanks for stopping by," Jasmine said. "I'll see you around?"

"Definitely. You owe me for yesterday," he teased. "As always, I take payment in food."

She laughed. "How about I make you some leche flan?"

"Deal. Have a good morning, guys." He gave them a quick, two-finger salute, then pivoted on his heel and trudged off.

Once they were alone, she turned to Mal. "Sorry again for panicking earlier."

"It's fine. You're fine, Jasmine." His claws brushed her cheeks as he tucked a lock of hair behind her ear. "You're right—we didn't really discuss what would happen after our third date."

"No, we didn't." That ominous feeling wiggled its way back into her chest once more. "Like I said, we should see where this goes and not worry about what's to come." She swallowed the lump in her throat and put on her best smile. "Enjoy each other's company."

"Right. And I want you to know you can be honest with me, Jasmine. And I promise to be honest with you."

"Of course." Jasmine wasn't quite sure where that remark about honesty was coming from or what it meant, but it sounded like a good idea.

"Why don't we finish breakfast and get ready for work?"

"Sounds great."

Jasmine had to admit, Mal's eggs and toast were decent, and she ate more than she usually did at breakfast, perhaps to make up for her increased activity from the night before. After she went back to her place to change into a fresh set of clothes, they made their way to Main Street. Mal convinced her to stop at Brewtique, and when they arrived at the front of the line, Minerva gave a quick glance at their clasped hands but said nothing except to ask for their order. However, once they slid down to the pickup corner, the witch gave Jasmine a knowing wink.

"One large black coffee for Mal, one flat white for Jasmine!" Gary called.

Mal grabbed the coffees from the counter and handed Jasmine hers, then threaded his clawed fingers through hers as they headed to the door. As Jasmine made a grab for the handle, however, it jerked away.

"Ooops! 'Scuse—Jasmine!" Arms wound around her, enveloping her in a cage of candy-sweet perfume, voluminous wavy brown hair, and a cloud of shimmery dust.

Leila.

The pixie pulled away, but held on to Jasmine's shoulders. "Oh my goddess, I haven't seen you in ages! Why haven't you been back to spin class? You're so right, by the way—after two or three more classes, I got the hang of it."

"Er, great to hear."

"And—Oh." She paused, looking Mal up and down. "Val, right?"

"Mal," he corrected.

Her bright gaze flicked down to their linked hands. "I can see why you never called me. But, don't worry, I'm not jealous, I'm thrilled for you, Jasmine." She encased Jasmine in another hug, sending another haze of shiny particles into the air. "See? I'm so excited, I'm getting dust all over you. This only happens when pixies are genuinely happy. So, will you please come back to spin class? I promise, no more hot gargoyle bartenders afterwards."

Mal tensed beside her, and she gave his hand a comforting squeeze. "Er, I'll see if I can make it work, okay?"

"Great! All right, I need some coffee or I'm gonna die. See you around."

"See you, Leila." She tugged at Mal, dragging him toward the door. Before they could exit, however, she heard Leila's distinct voice calling her name. Looking over her shoulder, she saw the pixie hold her hand up in a semicircle, fingers a couple inches apart as she mouthed "legendary."

Jasmine choked on her coffee.

"Jasmine? Are you okay?"

"I'm . . . fine . . ." She cleared her throat and nodded her thanks as she took the napkin he offered. "Went down the wrong pipe."

Once they arrived at the shop, Jasmine proceeded with her morning routine downstairs while Mal finished breakfast duties upstairs, then they went to the office to feed Clawdia. Bowl in hand, she went over to the pen and she barely had time to open the gate before she was hit with a burst of happy emotion, but also that distinct pang of hunger, like she hadn't just eaten a huge breakfast that morning. She quickly let the hatchling out and put the bowl down, not wanting to further delay her.

"She's awfully hungry this morning," Mal observed.

"Oh, I almost forgot to tell you." She relayed what happened the previous night when Clawdia told her about the fire. "It's weird. It was, like, at first she communicated with pictures and emotions, then it was, like—*bam*—I could actually feel the heat of the fire."

"Hmm, sounds like you're gaining more control of your magic."

"You think so?"

"Yeah, it's the only explanation. I'm so happy for you, Jasmine."

"I wouldn't even have discovered my abilities if it wasn't for you." And for that she would always be grateful. "One more thing . . . I also finally posted a picture of her online."

"Really?" A genuine smile spread across his face. "That's great, Jasmine. How did it go?"

"Actually, I'm not sure. I posted it right before I heard the sirens. Let me see . . ." Taking her phone out of her pocket, she opened up the Picstagram app. "Let's see . . . Oh my." She pressed the phone to her heart.

"What's wrong?"

Waving the phone at him, she burst out, "Five hundred *thousand* hearts!"

He steadied her hand. "What?"

"You and Clawdia broke the internet," she laughed. "Oh my . . . all these comments." Despite scrolling and scrolling, she still hadn't reached the end. "They all want more pics."

"Then you should give it to them," he encouraged. "Don't be afraid to share her. She's really special."

"She is."

As if sensing that they were talking about her, Clawdia padded away from her empty food bowl and pawed at Jasmine's leg. "All done?" she asked as she picked her up.

"Why don't you play with her for bit?" Mal suggested. "I noticed she's not sleeping as much as she was when she first hatched. Some extra activity would benefit her."

"But what about the shop?"

"I'll take care of things out there, don't worry." He scratched at his chin. "I'll work on casting a soundproofing spell in here, at least, so she doesn't get bothered by the noise outside. And I'll have to expand her cage soon. In a couple of months, once she's strong enough and you've got her trained, you'll have to let her out of here."

"I know." It was not something she was looking forward to.

"But we'll worry about that later." He leaned down and planted a kiss on her temple, then tickled Clawdia's chin, which made her trill in excitement and squirm in Jasmine's arms. "Take your time."

Jasmine decided not to worry about the future—Clawdia's anyway—and enjoyed her time playing with the little hatchling. Over the last three weeks, Clawdia had seemingly grown into her own personality—spunky, a little bit naughty, but definitely sweet. Jasmine also spent a few minutes doing some training until Clawdia simply didn't respond to treats anymore, indicating she was ready to go down for a nap. After letting her inside the cage, the hatchling curled up into her blanket and closed her eyes.

"Thanks for taking care of stuff out here," Jasmine said to Mal while making a beeline for the counter. She noticed that a bag of canine treats had fallen from the shelf, so she changed her course.

"No problem." He came up behind her. "By the way, I wanted to ask you something."

"What is it?" she asked absent-mindedly as she put the bag back in its rightful place.

"Will you have dinner with me tomorrow night?"

She chuckled and whirled around to face him. "Dinner with you?"

"Yeah." His expression was dead serious. "It is our third date, and since you didn't ask me out, I thought I'd do the asking this time."

"You don't have to—"

"I know. But I want to."

Oh Mother Goddess, she was going to turn into mush right here, between the bags of grimalkin litter and kelpie treats. "Yes, of course."

"Good, I'll pick you up at seven. I'm gonna go to the back office."

Her heart fluttered like a nervous hummingbird as she watched him lumber away. And to think she'd thought her initial crush on him was bad, but now . . .

Get a grip, Jasmine, she told herself. *For goddesses' sake, you've already had sex with him.*

Oh, and what delicious sex it was. She would have to focus on that for now. Just sex. Respectful, hot sex, she corrected. Enjoy each other's company in and out of the bedroom, and at the end of it all, shake hands and walk away.

Chapter Seventeen

MAL

"Are you sure you want to come with me to training tonight?" Mal asked as they locked up the shop.

"Of course. Except for Nick, I've only met some of your squad mates and maybe only once or twice," Jasmine assured him. "Besides, it's probably good to get to know them, just in case anything like the last time happened again."

Her concern warmed his hearts, but he didn't like causing her anxiety. "Don't worry." He smoothed a hand down her back. "Even the experienced firefighters from the other ladders said that had been an unusually large fire for Dewberry Falls. I've been on two calls since then and none of them have been dangerous." One had been an older man who'd collapsed due to heat exhaustion and another had been to help a woman who had been trapped in her car after colliding into a tree.

"Still, I'd like to come and see what you do," she insisted. "I've never been to the firehouse—that was more Vrig's thing."

"All right, if you insist."

They walked back to the house where the truck was parked then drove over to the station. Mal was usually the second one there after Ian, but to his surprise, several cars were already there.

Maybe they all finished work early.

"Hey, guys," he greeted as they entered the station. Everyone, except for Jim, was gathered by the truck, chatting amongst themselves. "I hope you don't mind—I brought Jasmine."

She waved at them. "Hi, everyone."

Mal began the introductions. "Nick, of course, you know. And Ian."

"Hey, Jasmine, thanks for coming." Nick greeted her with a quick hug, while Ian merely gave her a nod and a hello.

"And this is Ven and Sterling."

"You visited Fantastic Tails with your niece," Jasmine stated. "Draasha, right? She still comes in for supplies."

"You remember?" the troll said.

"Of course. I never forget a customer, especially one as adorable as her." She turned to Sterling. "And you stopped by to take Vrig out for his birthday last year."

"Yes, I did. Pleasure to make your acquaintance again, Jasmine."

"And, finally, this is Rafe." Mal nodded to the minotaur. "He joined the squad recently, so you haven't met before. Rafe, this is Jasmine."

"Nice to meet you, Jasmine," he said. "I only knew Vrig for a few weeks, but he seemed like a stand-up guy."

That was perhaps the most Mal had ever heard Rafe say in one breath.

"Yes, he was," Jasmine said.

"Where's Jim?" Mal asked.

The corner of Nick's mouth tugged up. "Yeah, about that . . . we're not really training tonight."

"We're not?" He frowned. "Then why are we here?"

Sterling spoke up. "We have a surprise for you."

"And actually, I asked Jasmine to come," Nick added. "I mean, you haven't said anything, but I assumed that things were good between you after you guys disappeared after the fire and . . ." He nodded at their linked hands.

Mal hadn't even noticed. It was just something he had gotten used to, holding her hand and touching her in general whenever they were together.

"Anyway," the satyr continued. "I thought she'd want to be here too."

"Be here for what?" Mal looked at Jasmine. "Did he tell you what this was about?"

"No, only that I should come too and make up a reason why," she said. "But I am curious. What's this surprise?"

"One sec." Nick looked over his shoulder, toward the office off to the side. "You can bring them out now, Jim."

Them?

Four people strode out the office—Jim, a human woman, and two small girls. "Mal," the fire chief greeted. "A couple people wanted to stop by and say hello."

The woman stepped forward, tugging the two girls behind her. "Hi, Mal, I'm Lisa. Do you remember me?"

Mal scratched at his chin. She was probably in her early forties, blonde and petite, but he couldn't recall meeting her before. "I'm sorry. I'm terrible with faces."

"That's all right," she said with a light chuckle. "The day of the fire was pretty chaotic."

Fire? Was she—

"Mal, Lisa and her daughters were the ones you helped get out of that building," Nick interjected.

"Oh, Mal." Jasmine gripped his hand tighter.

Mal blinked, still unsure how to react. "I . . . I'm sorry I didn't recognize you."

"Between the smoke and the collapsing building, I'm sure

you didn't have time to look at our faces." Bending down, she ushered the two girls—one about twelve years old and the other five or six—forward, both spitting images of their mother. "This is Grace," she said, gesturing to the older girl. "And this is Emily. Girls? Did you want to say something to Mr. Mal?"

Grace stepped up. "Thank you, Mr. Mal, for saving us from the fire."

"I made this drawing for you." Emily waved a piece of paper at him. "To say thank you."

Mal took the drawing, which depicted what he supposed was him—a large green orc figure carrying what appeared to be a yellow umbrella and three small females underneath. Behind them was a building covered in angry red and yellow flames. On top of the paper were the words, "Thank you, Mr. Mal!"

"I like the drawing," Mal said. "You did a great job, Emily."

"That's so sweet," Jasmine said. "I'm Jasmine, by the way." She looked to Lisa. "How are you, though? And the kids?"

Lisa sighed. "We're . . . doing as well as we could be. Thankfully, we were able to move out of the shelter and into some temporary housing. The Dewberry Falls City Council has been great with support so far, and we're told that with the CEO behind bars, we might be able to get some compensation."

"Damned—er . . ." Jim cleared his throat as he glanced at the girls. "I mean, darned greedy bas—rascal."

"He'll get what's coming to him." Nick's face turned serious. "In the meantime, all the victims of the fire will get all the support they need from the Amherst Foundation. Right, Ian?"

His twin nodded. "Of course."

"Thank you," Lisa said. "For everything."

"Mom, Mom, can we go inside the fire truck now?" Emily chirped. "Please?"

She glanced at Jim. "Mr. Halloway? Would that be possible?"

"Of course. And, please, call me Jim."

"That was lovely," Jasmine said as the chief led the family away. "Are you okay, Mal?"

"Yeah, I . . ." Mal's eyes followed Lisa and her girls as Jim led them toward the fire truck. When he had gone into the building to save them, he hadn't had time to think, only to act. And with everything going on in the last two weeks, he hadn't given them another thought. They were safe—that was all that mattered to him—and he didn't think he would see them again.

Jasmine's hand squeezed his once more. "You did a good thing, Mal."

"Because of you, they're alive," Nick added. "See? Aren't you glad you joined us?"

Ian snorted. "He didn't have much of a choice, did he? I mean, you basically volun-told half of us to come here."

His squad mates broke out in laughter. Mal sent Ian a grateful nod, glad that the attention was off him.

"Say, Jim sure is getting cozy with that hot mama," Ven observed.

Jim pointed to something high up on the truck, leaning in close to Lisa.

"Definitely cozy," Sterling said. "Why, I think he's practically preening. Look at him, puffing his chest out."

The fire chief opened the door to the truck, and the girls scrambled in, then he held his hand out for Lisa to help her in. Jim's smile spread a mile wide as Lisa took his hand and thanked him.

Nick whistled. "Wow, I never thought I'd see the day."

"He's been a widower for over ten years," Sterling said. "It's about time. He deserves to be happy."

"Again, all thanks to you, Mal." Nick elbowed him. "He should make you best man at the wedding."

"So, are we going to the Salty Dog or what?" Ven asked.

"Once Jim's done canoodling with Lisa," Nick joked.

"Actually, I'd like a tour too," Jasmine said. "Would you mind, Mal?"

"Not at all."

Tugging Jasmine away from the others, he led her to the back of the fire house. "Did you really want a tour?"

"Yes. But I could sense you getting uncomfortable with the situation," she confessed. "I meant what I said. You did a good thing. I was so mad and worried that day, but if you hadn't been there, they would have . . ." She swallowed hard. "You don't have to be self-conscious about the attention, Mal."

"I didn't do it for attention."

"I know." Brown doe eyes lit up at him. "You did it because it was the right thing to do." Her arms came up around him. "I'm glad you did."

And he was too. "C'mon, I'll give you a quick tour, and then I'm guessing the guys will want to go out for drinks. You don't mind coming along, do you?"

"No, not at all. I really do want to get to know your friends."

Friends?

Mal turned his head back toward the rest of the guys. They were obviously gossiping about Jim and Lisa, who were now deep in conversation, their heads bent close together.

He shook his head. "They're worse than a bunch of grannies at a sewing circle." Still, he rather liked all of them. "So," he said, turning to Jasmine, "let's start with the gear room . . ."

Chapter Eighteen

JASMINE

"Mal, could you hand me the marshmallows, please?"

"Marshmallows?" Mal paused midway as he was about to drive a peg down into the ground. "Why do need them now?"

"I just got the fire going." She waved a stick in the air. "And I want to test it out."

"I'm pretty sure your fire works, Jasmine," he said dryly.

"Mal . . ."

With a resigned sigh, he got up. "Fine. I'll go find them in the bag."

"You're the best."

"Uh-huh," he said before disappearing through the tent flap.

Jasmine smiled to herself, then closed her eyes and took a deep inhale. There truly was nothing like pine-scented, fresh mountain air, and being in nature. Out here, the only things she could hear were the birds chirping, the bees buzzing, and the occasional critter scurrying about.

And she didn't have to worry about obnoxious customers, obstinate suppliers, and demanding creatures.

While she had definitely grown more confident in her

abilities in the last few weeks, it was now like a tap she couldn't turn off. It had been useful in some instances—such as when one of the cerberus pups got sick—but most of the time, it was a lot of noise that drove her to distraction. Thankfully, she'd learned to manage it, but it still took some effort on her part.

"Here you go." Mal handed her the bag of marshmallows.

"Thanks, Mal." She pulled him down for a quick kiss on the cheek. "And thanks for putting up the tent."

"You're welcome. Let me finish it up."

Jasmine opened the bag and stuck a big, fat, fluffy marshmallow on the end of the stick, then held it over the fire. As the gooey confection toasted and turned dark, the smell of sugar filled the air.

This was the best idea ever, she thought. Actually, scratch that—this entire camping trip was the best idea ever. She was glad Mal had suggested it, as she could already feel her stress melting away.

Of course, she wasn't completely ungrateful about the cause of her stress. Fantastic Tails had never been busier, thanks to their newest social-media star, Clawdia. She had become the shop's mascot and even had her own merch. The T-shirts, mugs, stickers, and bags with her pictures on them flew off the shelves, and Jasmine had to keep ordering more. Another time, she posted a video of the hatchling eating her bowl of Ethereal Balance kibble and tagged the company. The owners had been thrilled and offered her a sponsorship deal.

There were, unfortunately, some downsides to fame. A lot of people had been coming into the shop, hoping to get a glimpse of Clawdia. Sadly, she had to turn those curious busybodies away. At one point, she had to put up a sign outside and a post on social media with a picture of a sleeping Clawdia with a caption that read, "I'm still very little and not ready to meet anyone yet. I still can't control my fire and I'm worried that I might hurt someone.

Please be patient." While the hatchling's fans were disappointed and some downright rude, for the most part, their followers were supportive and even lauded their approach.

But Jasmine was nonetheless ecstatic with the positive momentum, and sales were now up thirty per cent from last year. However, she'd been so busy that she was burning out, which is why Mal had suggested a getaway. So, when the next Monday rolled around, they closed up early and drove out to the Twin Mountains Camping Grounds, about an hour away from Dewberry Falls. Jasmine loved camping, plus it was very budget friendly since she already had all the gear. There was nothing like being out in nature, disconnected from the outside world, spending quiet evenings sitting by the fire, and sleeping under the stars.

"Mal!" she called out once the marshmallow's surface turned the perfect dark brown.

"What is it?"

"Here." She swung the stick at him, offering him the toasted confection. "Have a taste."

Mal took a bite. "Hmmm . . . that's good."

She finished off the remaining bit, moaning as the warm, sweet and smokey taste hit her tongue. "You know the best part of camping is s'mores, right?"

"You know the best part of camping for me?"

"What?"

"Going home."

She paused, waiting for him to crack a smile. "Wait, are you serious?"

He shrugged. "I'm not a camping person."

"Not a camping—" Placing her hands on her hips, she stood toe-to-toe with him and looked up. "You don't like camping? Don't orcs spend a lot of time outdoors, like when you march into battles and stuff?"

"Those were my ancestors, back in the days when we were still merciless bloodthirsty hordes hellbent on conquering other lands. Orcs are a much more enlightened people now. Besides, I'm from a builder horde. We build things. Things with four walls, a floor, roof, and preferably a king-sized bed with a mattress topper."

"Then why did you suggest coming out here?" she said, exasperated.

"I didn't. I said we should do a getaway, and you planned this whole thing."

She stared at him, slack-jawed. "If you weren't a camping person, you should have said so. I wouldn't have made you come out here if you hated it."

"I may not be a camping person, but I am a 'want to make Jasmine happy' person."

Her heart flew to the moon. "Mal . . ."

"You know," he said, slipping an arm around her waist, "if you'd wanted to, I could have booked us a stay at a five-star hotel in Bayview. Could have made for a nice staycation."

"Mal, you can't keep paying for things. We already went to Blackbyrd four times in the last two weeks."

"So? I like spoiling you."

Arching her body forward, she pressed her breasts against him. "You can spoil me in other ways, without using your money and—Mal!" she cried out as the world turned upside down.

Mal slapped her ass as he carried her over his shoulder. "I'll show you spoiling . . ."

After a rigorous round of sex in the tent, Jasmine found the energy to prepare a simple dinner of hotdogs grilled over the fire and reheated leftover *kuj'ata* stew. Afterwards, she made some s'mores for dessert, and they sat in front of the campfire.

"How's Clawdia? And the others?"

Jasmine looked up from her phone sheepishly. While she knew this was supposed to be a break from the shop, she couldn't stop herself from checking in. "Sorry, I'll put my phone away."

"Don't apologize, Jasmine. And you don't have to feel guilty."

She sighed. "Am I that obvious?"

"It's all over your face. But just because you need a mental health day, it doesn't mean you don't care for them. And it's understandable you want to look out for them. I take it this is the first time you've been away from Dewberry Falls since Vrig died?"

"Yeah, it is."

"It's normal, then, to want to check in. But don't worry, those gnomes are reliable." They had paid them extra to come tonight to feed the pets dinner and check on Clawdia. "Are they done?"

"They just left," she reported. "And yeah, the gnomes do a good job. Clawdia seems to like them too. They even let her out to play fetch."

"You can take her home in a couple weeks, once the insurance company approves the extra coverage." Mal had already fireproofed her apartment as well, so now they were waiting for the adjuster to come and inspect it. "Which is good, because I don't know how much bigger I can expand that cage."

"I can't wait to have her home." Sure, she wouldn't be able to check on Clawdia during the day, but at least she wouldn't have to worry about her at night, and with the shop only a ten-minute walk away, she could always go home for lunch and take her out. "It would have been nice to have her here with us."

"Once she has complete control over her fire abilities, you can bring her anywhere, even to work."

"True. Hopefully she doesn't bring out the crazies. I've had to block a couple of people online because they think I'm being self-ish, not letting her out. They don't understand that it's still dangerous for her to be around people when she's not fully trained."

"Keep blocking them. You know what's best for her." He handed her a plate. "Here, I made you another s'more."

"Oooh, thank you, Mal." She happily accepted the plate and took a bite of the still-warm confection. "So good."

They stayed up for another hour before they headed into the tent for bed.

The next day, they woke up bright and early, as Jasmine wanted to go for a hike. They followed a trail up one of the peaks, traversing the dense woods and climbing over moss-covered rocks. The air grew cooler as they ascended, and soon they emerged on a high ridge that overlooked an expanse of rolling hills and massive ancient trees. Across the ridge, a craggy obelisk made of rock and granite rose into the sky.

"Wow, it's so beautiful," she sighed. "That's the other peak of Twin Peaks."

"Your ass in those shorts is beautiful," Mal commented. "And your tits are the only 'twin peaks' I want to see."

She smiled wryly at him over her shoulder. "You should be a poet, Mal." He trailed behind her the entire time, and though she could tell he wasn't enjoying himself much, he never complained. "Come here and enjoy the view."

"I am," he said with a grin. Still, he came up beside her and looked out. "Okay, you're right. This is pretty amazing."

"See, I told you. Didn't your dad or stepdad ever take you camping when you were young?"

"Whenever we all go back to the orc homelands, it's basically one big camping trip, but not like this. It's noisy and lots of relatives everywhere. Hated it when I was kid and my parents would drag me there."

"Ah, no wonder. My dad and I went all the time. We loved it." It was the only time she had actually seen her father relax and have fun. In the early days when they'd first arrived in the US, he'd been so stressed about money and paying off the debt he'd incurred to come here and saving for the future. But when they

were out in the woods, with just a fire and a tent, he could dis-
connect and not worry so much.

"Speaking of which, have you spoken to your dad? About
your abilities?"

"Uh, no, actually." She picked off an imaginary piece of lint
from the front of her yoga pants. "I've been busy, and he picked
up some extra night shifts these past couple of weeks." She waited
for him to reply, but he remained silent, thankfully. While what
she said was true, it was a weak excuse. There was no reason for
her not to call her father, except that she was dreading the outcome of that conversation.

They stood side by side, enjoying the view for the next few
minutes. Jasmine stretched her arms above her and yawned. "Oh
Mother Goddess, my muscles are gonna be so sore tomorrow.
Let's go back. You must be hungry. I'll make breakfast, it's the
second-best part of camping."

"Yeah, I'm hungry all right." His gaze dipped down to her
breasts, which had been pushed up by her sports bra. "But for
something else."

"Mal—" He swooped down and kissed her. "I'm sweaty and
dirty," she protested.

"And?" He reached down to grip her ass, pulling her to him.
"I need you, Jasmine." His erection rubbed against her and little
shocks of pleasure zoomed all the way to her core. "Now." Slipping a hand between them, he cupped her pussy through her
yoga pants, his clawed finger teasing at the slit.

"Now?" Moisture gathered between her legs at the thought.
"Here?"

He leaned down to whisper in her ear. "This is my pussy, and
I'll take her wherever and whenever I want."

She bucked against him. "It's yours. Do what you want
with it."

He spun her round, so she faced away from him. A clawed

finger slid between the spandex of her yoga pants and her skin, moving lower. "No panties, huh?"

She nodded. "I pack light."

"Or you were hoping I'd fuck you during this hike." The warmth of his breath tickled her neck. "Lovely, lovely pussy of mine." His large hand covered her entire mound, the pads of his fingers teasing her at her swollen clit. "So wet already." He dipped in ever so carefully inside her, spreading the wetness around her lips. "Do you want me, Jasmine? Want this?" His massive erection pressed against her back, the ridges rubbing at her skin. When did he even take it out of his pants?

"Oh, yes, Mal. Please."

"No need to beg, *ashak'a*." He licked at her neck. "I'll give you what you want." Circling his hand around her waist, he walked her forward a few steps, to the closest tree up ahead. Taking her hands in his, he braced them against the large trunk, the bark rough against her palms.

"Such a beautiful ass," he murmured as he peeled her yoga pants down her thighs.

"Mal, hurry," she whined.

"We can take our time." He lifted one leg to slip the pants off, then the other. "There's no one else around. You can even scream as loud as you want."

She wouldn't dare; her voice would echo down the valley.

"Mal—yes!" A tongue licked at her from behind as claws dug into her skin. He mouthed at her, his tongue fluttering around her folds and teasing at her hole. When he growled against her, she almost came right then, though really, she was halfway there. Only a few more seconds of teasing, licking, and sucking and she was shaking like a leaf as her orgasm ripped through her.

The tip of Mal's cock prodded against her, spreading the slick, natural lube all around her. Jasmine had never been more glad at how different he was, because in this instance, it worked

to her advantage. Still, she had to relax her muscles as he moved
inside her. She bit at the back of her palm as those amazing ridges
massaged her inner walls, making her shudder and grow even
wetter. A hiss escaped her mouth as she pushed back at him.

"Patience," he cooed. "You'll have what you want." The
friction of his ridged cock dragging back had her bracing herself in anticipation. When that first thrust came, she let out a
loud moan.

He began slowly, rocking into her in small movements. However, when she met his thrust with her own, he sped up. His
swift, pounding strokes had her heart racing along. Something
tugged at her scalp—Mal had wrapped her braid around his
hand and pulled, and she nearly came from the sensation.

Her entire world reduced to this moment, his cock moving in
and out of her, his guttural moans, and their skin slapping
together. The orgasm came quick and powerful, as it always did
from this position.

"Mal!"

He slowed his thrusts, knowing how sensitive she was after
coming. She whooped as he pulled out, spun her round, and
picked her up. He faced away from the tree, leaned back on it,
and then planted her on his cock.

Thank the Mother Goddess for sports bras with zip fronts
as Mal easily released her breasts from their confines. Cupping them together, he took both of her nipples inside his
mouth at the same time, his mouth tusks grazing against her
soft skin.

His powerful thighs did most of the work, pounding upwards
and bouncing her on his cock. Hot curls of bliss unfurled inside
her, building up and sending her further and further to the edge.
Her eyes rolled to the back of her head, and she once again lost
the ability to think or breathe as Mal wound her up tighter and
tighter with every thrust.

"Mal . . . Mal . . ." She dug her fingers into his hair, her nails scraping into his scalp in that way that drove him crazy.

Mal roared, his entire body tensing. Somehow, he managed to jerk up into her faster, harder. Her knees dug into his hips as her third orgasm of the morning cleaved through her. Her inner walls clasped at him tightly, the thick ridges pulsating against them as he came. Despite his body shuddering with aftershocks, he managed to hold them up. He let out a deep sigh, kissed her roughly, then nuzzled at her neck.

"If this is what camping is like," he panted, "we should go all the time."

She threw her head back and laughed.

After righting themselves, they hiked back to their campsite where Mal fried up eggs and bacon in a cast-iron pan for breakfast. The rest of the day was spent relaxing, with Jasmine reading a book while Mal took some of the extra firewood they'd brought and practiced his carving skills. In a few hours, he'd made a toy shaped like a bone for Clawdia—which he fireproofed with a simple spell—and a figurine of the hatchling herself, which he gave to Jasmine.

"It's beautiful," she gasped. "You captured her perfectly." Clutching it to her heart, she smiled up at him. "Thank you."

That evening, after a quick dinner of burgers and fried potatoes, they went to bed early as they planned to leave before dawn and head straight to Fantastic Tails to open up.

The next day, as they pulled into the driveway of the house, Jasmine noticed an unfamiliar red sedan parked in front of the house. "Are you expecting any visitors?"

His eyebrows drew together as he too spotted the car. "No. Are you?"

"Nuh-uh."

Cutting off the engine, he unbuckled his seatbelt. "Might be someone visiting the neighbors. That older couple across the street has a passel of adult kids and grandchildren. Someone's always coming over."

Jasmine followed Mal out of the truck. As he lowered the tailgate to start unloading their camping gear, she noticed the red car's driver and front passenger door open. "Mal?"

"Yeah?"

"Do you know them?" She pointed at the two figures lumbering toward them.

"Know who—"

"Mal! Yoohoo, Mal!"

Mal froze, then spun round, his eyes growing wide with surprise and recognition. From their towering statures and their vibrant green skin, there was no doubt the two elderly individuals approaching them were orcs. The male one was about a few inches shorter than Mal, completely bald, with a stockier build and a stomach paunch that hung low on his torso. The female stood at the same height, her thick dark hair arranged into a network of braids down her shoulders and her skin a darker shade of emerald. The wrinkles around her eyes and mouth deepened as her face lit up with a smile, her purple eyes sparkling.

"Oh, son." She pulled Mal into an embrace. "I've missed you so."

"Mom? Karak?"

Son? Jasmine's eyes ping-ponged from Mal to the woman who clung to him.

Mal looked at the male. "What are you guys doing here?"

The male—Karak—grunted. "We were in the area, thought we'd stop by. Morlak tried calling you, but you weren't answering."

"What do you mean, 'in the area'? You live all the way in Vermont."

Morlak released Mal. "Yes, there was—" She stopped short as she finally noticed Jasmine. "Oh, hello there," she greeted.

"Mom, Karak, this is Jasmine," Mal introduced. "My girlfriend."

Her heart stumbled over itself, doing a somersault before it managed to recover. "H-how do you do, ma'am. Sir."

"Girlfriend?" Morlak's eyes grew to the size of dinner plates, then the widest smile broke on her face. "Mal, you didn't tell us you had a girlfriend."

"It's, uh, very new," Jasmine stammered. So new, in fact, that this was the first time she was hearing it herself. "Ma'am, I—" Oxygen cut off from her lungs as she was enveloped in the tightest hug she'd ever gotten.

"Mom, you're suffocating her."

Morlak let go and Jasmine could breathe again. "Apologies, I just got so excited. It's been a while since Mal introduced a female to—"

"Mom," Mal interrupted. "You were about to tell me what you were doing here."

"Oh yes." Her smile faded. "One of Karak's old friends passed away down in San Francisco. He'd been ill for some time now and took a turn for the worse a couple days ago."

"Came to say our last goodbyes," Karak said. "The funeral finished this morning."

"And we realized, well, you're only a couple of hours' drive away, so why not come by for a visit? We tried to call you yesterday but you didn't pick up."

"Your mother was worried," Karak admonished. "And I said we should just come here and see what's going on."

"I didn't have reception. Jasmine and I were camping up at Twin Peaks."

"Understandable, then."

"I'm so sorry, ma'am," Jasmine said. "It was my idea to go."

The couple looked at each other knowingly. "I figured. But

please, Jasmine, call me Morlak, no need to be so formal. You're my son's girlfriend, after all."

Her cheeks heated at the mention of the g-word. "Er, sure. Morlak."

"I hope we're not interrupting," Karak said. "And we should be the ones apologizing for stopping by unannounced."

"It's not a big deal, really. I'm glad you guys came. But we're actually heading to the shop."

"The shop?" Morlak cocked her head to the side. "You mean the pet shop Vrig owned?"

"Mal owns it now, Morlak," Karak reminded her. "And remember, he told us a couple weeks ago that he was staying to get it ready for sale."

"That's right, how could I forget?"

"Jasmine's the one buying it. She used to manage it for Vrig," Mal said. "I'm helping her out while we're waiting for all the paperwork to go through."

Jasmine's mouth pressed into a tight line at the reminder. While the idea that she would own Fantastic Tails still held a thrill, there was an underlying current of unease. Once Mal had transferred everything to her, he would be out of here. She had to keep reminding herself of that.

But he called me his girlfriend. In front of his parents.

Why would Mal do that? Was it a slip of the tongue? Jasmine didn't want to put any meaning into it, but they never talked about what they were, because really, what kind of label could they put on their relationship? They were much more than friends with benefits, but not really committed long term.

Still, his calling her his girlfriend had to mean *something*.

"Would you like to see it?" Mal said.

"That would be wonderful, Mal. If that's okay with Jasmine?"

"Of course it is." Her voice sounded much too bright, so she pulled back a little. "And you have to meet Clawdia."

"Clawdia?"

Mal patted his mother's arm. "Come, it's only a few minutes' walk. We can tell you all about her."

Since Morlak and Karak could only stay one night before they had to drive back to San Francisco to catch their flight home, Mal invited them to spend the day at Fantastic Tails. Jasmine wasn't sure the couple would want to hang out at the shop while she and Mal worked. She tried suggesting that they do some shopping on Main Street or even drive out to a few interesting spots around town, but they insisted on staying.

To her surprise, the older couple didn't mind being stuck inside. In fact, Karak, who Mal mentioned had retired a few years ago, even seemed to enjoy himself as he helped install the brand-new filtration system for the tanks. While the men were working upstairs, Morlak stayed in the office with Jasmine as she entertained Clawdia.

"She's gotten so much better at fetch." Jasmine picked up the ball Clawdia had dropped at her feet. She tossed it across the room, which sent the hatchling scampering off to chase it.

"Oh yes, dragons are so highly trainable and eager to please," Morlak remarked.

"I feel guilty keeping her in here all the time."

"Don't be, you're doing her and everyone a favor." When Clawdia returned, the orc bent down to give her a scratch between the ears, which had the dragon purring in delight. "She doesn't have complete control of her fire. One stray sneeze and she could burn an entire house down. That and she's still vulnerable to disease."

"I hadn't even thought of that." The vet she consulted never mentioned if Clawdia needed shots.

"In the wild, mother dragons kept their hatchlings inside

their lairs for at least two years while naturally building their immune system." She picked up the ball and threw it. "Nowadays, and with domesticated ones, one year is usually long enough."

"You sure know a lot about dragons, Morlak."

"My grandfather used to raise them on his farm."

Jasmine's head whipped toward her. "Really? Mal never said anything."

"I've only mentioned it a handful of times, and of course, that was back in Ghalad-Dur, the orc homelands. In fact, my relatives still keep a few to guard their farms."

Clawdia came back with the ball, but instead of letting go, sat down on her hind legs and began to chew at it. A vision of soft blankets and a sudden feeling of drowsiness came over Jasmine. "She's done and wants a nap." She picked her up and cuddled her to her chest, and Clawdia lay her chin on her shoulder. "My, you're getting heavier." She was at least twice the size she was when she first hatched.

"You know, it's said dragons have a special bond with their owners."

Jasmine smiled down at Clawdia. "I can believe that."

After putting the hatchling back in her pen, Jasmine turned to Morlak. "Do you want to stay in here and sit for a while? I should head back outside. Clawdia won't be waking up until her dinner."

"Am I getting in your way?" Her eyebrows drew together, which, Jasmine realized, looked very much like the way Mal did when he frowned, including that tiny line appearing between them. "I apologize."

"No, no," Jasmine reassured her. "But it must be boring for you to watch and follow me around. Wednesdays are pretty slow for us in terms of customers coming in. I use this time to do stuff like packing orders and posting on social media."

"I don't mind," she said. "Maybe I can help. When Mal's father passed away, I took over his construction business."

"That must not have been easy."

"No, it wasn't." Sadness briefly crossed her face. "It was harder on Mal, though. His father's death kind of upended our lives and he lost that stability children need while they're growing up."

She knew what that was like. "But you both managed."

"I floundered. A *lot*. I was from a farming horde, so I knew nothing about building. But I did my best and got the hang of it. If anything, I would say running the business helped me with my grief. And of course that's how I met Karak. He also owned his own construction firm and we attended the same trade show. I didn't think I would marry again, but he was quite insistent."

"That sounds romantic."

"It was. I mean, as romantic as it gets with orc men." She chuckled, then sent Jasmine a sly smile. "I would ask you where you and my son met, but . . ."

Jasmine's cheeks bloomed with heat. "Yeah. Things just kind of happened between us."

"I understand. When you know, you know, right?" Morlak winked at her. "Maybe in a year or two, Mal can bring you to visit the orc homelands with him. Clawdia would absolutely love it and she can socialize with other dragons."

Anxiety pooled in Jasmine's stomach. She didn't have the heart to tell Morlak that that would never happen. That in about three months, Mal was going to leave the shop and Clawdia.

And her.

"Are you okay, Jasmine?"

She snapped to attention. "Yes," she said in that too-bright tone again. "If you don't mind helping, I do have some orders to pack up. They came in while we were camping and so I need to get them out right away."

She and Morlak spent the rest of the morning catching up with orders, as well as ordering new stock of Clawdia and Fantastic Tails merchandise. The older orc even made a few suggestions for new items, like stuffies for kids and caps for adults. Upstairs, Karak and Mal took a break for lunch, and they all ordered food from the nearby café and ate at the shop.

"I think we'll go check into our motel," Karak said after they finished eating. "Unless you need me to stay and help you with the rest of that installation?"

"No, I got it. Thanks for helping me. The pumps were tricky. It would have taken me hours to figure them out."

"No problem, Mal."

Morlak yawned. "I need a nap. We left San Francisco so early. But we should have dinner tonight."

"I already made reservations at Blackbyrd," Mal said. "It's right here on Main Street. Seven thirty."

"We'll see you both then." He clapped Mal on the shoulder, while Morlak gave him a side hug.

"Thank you for letting us stay and hang around, Jasmine." Morlak pulled her into another embrace, this one less bone-crushing. "I really like this place. Vrig would be so happy to know that the shop will be in good hands."

"And he'd be proud of you, Mal," Karak added. "For the work you're putting in. Now, let's get going, Morlak. We were lucky they even had a room last minute. I don't want them giving it away because we're late."

"All right, all right, hold your water horses, Karak." She smiled and waved at them. "See you later."

"I like your parents, Mal," Jasmine said once the couple had left. "They're super sweet. I mean, your mom is."

"And Karak is Karak," he said with a snort. "But don't let that exterior fool you—he's all mush inside." Mal grunted. "I hope this surprise visit didn't rattle you too much."

"Not at all, and it's nice they get to see you." She paused, hoping he would bring up what he had said earlier.

The g-word.

"Well . . ." He scratched at the back of his head. "All the animals are still in temporary holding tanks. They're probably getting antsy. Gonna head upstairs and finish up."

Disappointment flooded her, but at the same time, she was relieved. Maybe she shouldn't say anything. She wasn't sure she wanted to have that conversation with Mal.

"Uh, yeah, I should start my inventory anyway."

A hand landed on her shoulder. "Are you okay? You sure you don't mind having dinner with my parents tonight? You could always skip—"

"No, no." She patted at his hand gingerly. "It'll be great. Just try and keep me away from that burnt Basque cheesecake," she said, trying to sound lighthearted.

He grinned. "All right. We'll head over around seven fifteen."

"Sounds good." Averting her gaze, she hopped over to her computer behind the counter, then switched the program to their inventory system. "Can't wait."

Chapter Nineteen

MAL

Though his parents' unexpected appearance had initially thrown him off balance, Mal had to admit it was not unwelcome. It had been months since he'd last seen them, and while he really should visit more often, there was never enough time between jobs.

Maybe if he'd come home or called more than just every few months, they wouldn't have just shown up. While initially elated to see them, having Jasmine there had sent him into a panic. True, they said they wouldn't hide their relationship from anyone, but he'd initially thought "anyone" encompassed those who lived within the greater Dewberry Falls area, not his kinfolk. Seeing his parents and Jasmine in the same space was like watching two different universes collide, and, rattled from the shockwave, his flustered brain was not quick enough to stop his mouth from calling Jasmine his girlfriend.

Perhaps even more surprising, was that Mal didn't mind it at all.

He honestly thought he'd run in the opposite direction. But it all felt natural. Even last night, as they had dinner with his parents, as his mother kept saying things like "Mal, your girlfriend is so lovely" or "Jasmine, you sound like a great girl-friend", he could not deny the warm sensation in his belly that spread all the way up to his hearts. Jasmine, ever so gracious, didn't correct his mother. Was she angry that he had called her that? Or did she not mind it? Did she think she was his girl-friend? What would happen in a couple months—weeks, really—once she got her loan and he no longer needed to stay?

But what if I wanted to stay?

The more he thought about it, the more it sounded appeal-ing. It had been years since he'd had an actual home; his apartment in Burlington didn't count as it really was more like a storage locker at this point. Dewberry Falls had not only become comfortable, but somehow the community itself had wrapped around him like tree roots. He even enjoyed his every-other-Thursday-night training with the Volunteer Fire Department and going out on calls.

And then, as always, his thoughts circled back to Jasmine. Beautiful, sexy, and sweet Jasmine, who was now staring at him from behind the register, one eyebrow raised.

"What?" he asked.

"You've been holding that for, like, two minutes." She nodded at the screwdriver in his hand, the tip pressed against a screw in the corner of the shelf that held litter. "I'm no expert, but I think you need to twist it to work."

"Er, yeah." With quick movements, he tightened the loose screw. "There you go. Fixed that wobbly thing. Let me put all these bags back up."

"I can do that." Jasmine trotted over to him. "You're going to be late for lunch with Morlak and Karak."

"Are you sure you don't want to join us? They'd be happy to see you again."

"And so would I, which is why they promised to stop in and say hello when they drop you off," she said. "But you haven't been alone with them since they got here. You guys should have some privacy. Don't worry about me. I'll be okay."

He was always worrying about her, but that was a completely different matter. "All right. Want me to bring you back some pancakes?"

"Yes, please. I can have them for dinner."

Kissing her on the temple, he ruffled her hair. "I'll see you soon."

His parents had stayed at Dreametime Motel the night before, so he suggested they meet at Pamola's Diner. After taking their order, the lamia waitress slid off to put their orders in.

"How was your room?" Mal asked as he took a sip of the coffee.

"Surprisingly great," his mother replied. "Even Karak thought so and he never gets any sleep when we travel."

"It's these damned hotel mattresses," he grumbled. "Never the right firmness, and of course, we usually have to squash two king beds together to even get close to comfortable."

"They put us in this room and it's perfect. Didn't even hit my head getting into the bathroom," Morlak said with a laugh. "The chairs were comfortable too."

Karak looked around them, at the various species occupying each table and booth. "I can see why Vrig settled here. It's nice being not so different."

Mal didn't know why it had never occurred to him until they pointed it out, but it was true. Indeed, that's why the town had been established, as he learned during the Founding Day Festival.

"So, Mal, have you heard back from the Orc Historical Society?"

A pit hollowed out in his stomach at the mention of the historical center job, but not for the usual reasons. "No, not a word," he said, playing with the salt and sugar shakers on the table.

Karak frowned. "I'm not going to have to talk you off a ledge again, am I?"

"No, no, I'm . . ." He searched for the right words as he rotated the glass bottles on top of the red Formica table. "I'm good. All good. If it happens, it happens, if it doesn't, then it's not meant to be."

"I'm glad to hear that." Morlak sounded relieved as well. "I know it means a lot to you. But you can't keep your life on hold for them. If you did get it, Jasmine won't be happy with you being gone for a long time. A girl like that doesn't come along very often."

"Don't get on his case now, Morlak," Karak said in a cautious tone. "We don't even know if they're serious. They've only been seeing each other a few weeks."

"And what does time have to do with it, hmm? Need I remind you how soon after we met that you said you couldn't live without me?"

Karak opened his mouth then shut it.

"Well, son, are you?" Morlak looked him in the eye. "Are you serious about her?"

"I . . ." His hearts collided into each other and then stumbled.

He was stupidly in love with Jasmine.

"That expression on your face answers my question." Morlak smiled smugly. "Have you told her yet?"

"I think he's just discovering it himself," Karak added.

"I . . . I don't know how to say it. Or when." Panic crept in. "What if she doesn't feel the same way?"

"Of course she does," his mother said. "That girl loves you."

"You're more confident about it than I am, then." Did Jasmine love him back? "You're not just saying that because you're my mother, are you?"

"No, I'm saying it because I'm a woman."

"Trust her, Mal," Karak piped in. "She's been in love twice in her life now."

Mal sent his stepfather a grateful smile. Karak had readily accepted Mal as his own, accepted that he came part and parcel when he married Morlak. But another reason Mal appreciated him was that he never tried to replace Mal's father or even erase his existence. Back home, the mantels and walls were still filled with his father's photos and mementos, and Hargoth's portrait sat side by side with their mating ceremony photo.

Morlak's hand covered his. "You should tell her, when the time is right."

"When?"

"You'll know, son," she said.

Before Mal could say anything else, the waitress came by with their order. Though their lunch conversation topics turned to more lighthearted matters, like what happened to the neighbor's cat or the next cruise his parents were planning, Jasmine remained in the back of Mal's mind. His hearts fluttered in anticipation, thinking about what to say to her and when. Part of him wanted to blurt it out the moment he saw her, but another held him back, telling him to be patient and wait for the right time.

As they promised, Morlak and Karak stopped by Fantastic Tails to say goodbye to Jasmine before they drove back to San Francisco. As they embraced, his mother whispered something in Jasmine's ear, and the oddest expression appeared on her face. For a moment, Mal thought Morlak had told her what he'd confessed, but he knew that his mother would never ruin that for him.

"So, that was a nice visit," Jasmine said. "Everything okay, Mal? You seem quiet all of a sudden."

I love you, Jasmine.

"I'm fine," he said quickly. He wanted to say the words out

loud, but they were stuck in his throat. He'd never felt like this with anyone, not even his one serious girlfriend that he'd brought home during the Orc New Year.

"Oh. I was wondering if—" She stopped short, her tongue licking at her lips.

"What?"

"Nothing." She glanced down at her shoes.

"No, really. What is it? Did my mom . . . say something to you? Something bad?"

Her head snapped up. "What, oh no. She would never. She didn't say anything bad, only that she'd never seen you so happy." Her brown doe eyes stared up at him, boring into his very soul. "But, Mal, remember how you said I can be honest with you? And that you'll do the same?"

"Yes." The air from his lungs remained trapped in his chest.

"Well . . . I need you to . . . We have to . . ." She clucked her tongue. "We need to talk about the g-word."

"The . . . g-word?" Confusion sent his head spinning. "What are you talking about?"

"The *word*. That you said. When you introduced me to your parents as your girlfriend."

"Oh. Yeah, uh . . ." He rubbed at the back of his neck. "That kind of just came out. I didn't really know what to say. But what do you think about it?"

She chewed at her bottom lip. "I mean, do we need labels for what we are?"

"No, but . . ."

This was it, this was the time to tell her. Do it, Mal.

His brain, however, told him *not yet*. Like Karak said, they had only known each other for a few months.

Besides, what if Jasmine didn't feel the same way? What if she didn't want to commit to him in the first place? This temporary setup had been her idea. Maybe she wanted to walk away at the end. And the Historical Society could call him at any moment. That job was within his grasp, and if he got it, then he'd have to leave, not just Jasmine, but this life in a small town that had, frankly, grown on him.

"Mal?"

Jasmine's voice jolted him out of his thoughts. He still owed her an answer.

Be honest, he told himself. That's what they promised each other.

"We see each other every day," he began. "We eat nearly every meal together; you've slept in my bed more than yours for the last month. We don't date or sleep with other people. I mean, what would you call that?"

Her face lit up. "I guess I'm your girlfriend. And you're my . . . boyfriend." She said it experimentally, like she was trying it on for size.

But did she like how it fit?

"You're my boyfriend," she stated again, now in a more resolute voice.

"Good." He liked the sound of it, the feel of it. While the l-word remained in his mind, for now, he would take things slowly with Jasmine, even though it killed him not to let her know. Yes, he would keep it to himself for now and tell her when the time was right.

Chapter Twenty

MAL

There was a saying in Old Orcish that translated to, "You could be sitting on top of the world one moment, and then get hit by manticore dung the next."

Karak would recite this quote to his apprentices on their first day of training. It was meant to be a cautionary tale, to always be prepared for anything—delayed or denied permits, budgets blowing up, or a roof you thought you'd sealed properly could start leaking.

Mal, however, had a different interpretation: you can be at your highest point, and life can still find a way to shit on you.

His life was incredible right now. He'd spent most of the last couple of years moving around, going to amazing places and working on some truly magnificent architectural wonders. It was fulfilling, and his peers could only dream of what he'd accomplished. Then he'd come to Dewberry Falls, and while he thought that was a setback, it turned out to be the opposite. Now on top of all his accomplishments, he had a wonderful woman. One that filled every room with sunshine, whose smile could melt even his cynical hearts. Hearing her laugh made his day and seeing her took his breath away. He wanted nothing more than to wake up with her every morning, make love to her, and go to bed with his arms around her.

It was almost too good to be true, and he wondered when that axe would fall.

Right this moment, though, it was difficult to think anything could possibly go wrong. Not when the current expression on Jasmine's face sent his hearts into the stratosphere.

"Mal?" Jasmine's smile could power an entire electric station. "Remember when I said you shouldn't spoil me by using your money?"

"Yeah?"

"Forget I said that." Jasmine threw herself onto the massive double-king-sized bed and let out a sigh as she ran her hands over the luxurious sheets. "In fact, if I ever bring it up, tell me I'm wrong."

Though it had only been three weeks since their last trip, Mal had wanted to take Jasmine away again. The shop had been busier than ever, and Jasmine began to show signs of stress once more. So, this time, he took it upon himself to plan their staycation, and he did it his way, booking a corner suite at the Solstice Pavilion Hotel, right in the middle of the bustling downtown of Bayview City. He also convinced her to close Fantastic Tails for both Tuesday and Wednesday, so they could have a proper mini-break.

"I'm glad you like it." Mal jumped on the bed beside her, then grabbed at her waist. She squealed in delight as he covered her body with his, then nibbled at her neck. As her sweet perfume filled his senses, he reveled in the smell and feel and taste of her. She sighed and melted against him, her fingers lazily raking through his hair.

How he wanted to stay like this forever. For things to always be this way.

But a question slunk into his brain like a slithering serpent that had been hiding in the back of his mind these past few weeks.

Did she want the same thing?

Did she love him too?

And if the Historical Society called him and told him he'd won the bid, could he tell them no?

There were so many times since his parents' visit that he wanted to tell her he loved her, but he just couldn't get the words out. Things were still progressing between them, and they had hit that perfect point—they were still in that honeymoon phase, unable to keep their hands off each other, but also wanted to spend each and every moment together. While that seemed like a positive sign, he should tell her that to him it was the opposite.

What if he scared her off?

What if she didn't love him back?

While his mother might think she knew a thing or two about love, she didn't know Jasmine. Yes, they had been enjoying each other's company in and out of the bedroom, but that didn't mean she was ready for anything more with him. Jasmine was a whole person on her own. She had her own life, her own plans and dreams, and Mal might not fit into them. She was the one who suggested the "see where this goes" arrangement. What if she did that in the first place because she knew he was leaving, and it would be an easy break for them?

That would make things easier when he had to leave, Mal supposed, whether that was in a few weeks or tomorrow. While the Orc Historical Society may have dilly-dallied on their decision, they would expect a swift acceptance, as there were many eager builders ready to take on the job.

"What are you thinking so hard about, Mal?"

I love you, Jasmine.

"Nothing, nothing at all." Mal ran his hand up her thigh, pushing her shirt up so he could graze his claws on her belly.

"Mal . . ." she moaned. "No."

He froze. "No?"

Sitting up, she sat back on her heels. "I mean, not *now*. If we start this now, we'll never leave this room—this bed—until we check out on Thursday morning."

"Oh, we would definitely be leaving this bed. I plan to fuck you all over this room. On that couch, in the jacuzzi, against the window—"

She slapped him playfully on the arm. "Mal, please? I've never stayed longer than one afternoon in Bayview, and that was because Vrig asked me to run an errand at his main bank branch. I want to go out and do some touristy stuff, eat, and do some shopping. All the fun things us sleepy town dwellers miss out on."

"I never figured you for a big-city girl."

"No, but I did live in five major cities in my life. I miss the energy and having stuff to do."

He recalled what she said, about moving around a lot when she and her father first came here, and how she never had time to plant roots. "That must have been tough, having to start again each time."

"Yeah, but I understand. My dad wanted a better life for me. All parents want the best for their kids."

A sudden vision of Jasmine holding a baby popped into his head. Of her playing hide and seek with a rambunctious little boy with green skin. Or comforting a teary-eyed youngling with a scraped knee. The words he'd been wanting to say were ready to spill from his mouth, but he managed to suppress them, because his own parents—and specifically his father—filled his thoughts. Morlak and Karak would be so proud of him if he got the job renovating the lodge. And he knew once he began planning and working on the site his father's and family's legacy would be solidified forever in orc history.

Clearing his throat, he said, "So, have you spoken to your dad yet?"

Her shoulders stiffened. "Haven't had the chance. With the shop and all—"

"I can help you if you want."

"There's also the loan paperwork." Her hands wrung in her lap. "I need to send that off to Tracy soon."

"Want me to take a look at it?"

He'd offered to help her before, but she'd refused, and he respected that she preferred to do this on her own. However, he was confident in her abilities. He even bought that bottle of champagne he promised her and left it chilling in the back of the office fridge, ready to be popped open.

"No, I told you, I can do it on my own."

"It shouldn't take that long. Once you submit it, you'll have time to talk to your dad. I'm sure he'd be so happy."

The look on her face, however, indicated she didn't think so.

"Jasmine? Is that why you haven't told him? You think he won't be happy?" It pained his hearts to know she was still blaming herself for her dad losing the chance at gaining his family's magic. "I told you, it's not your fault he didn't get The Inheritance. You think you don't deserve your abilities because it was meant—"

"Mal, will you stop getting on my case about my dad?" she snapped. A microsecond later, her face crumpled in distress. "I didn't mean—"

A knot in his chest formed. "Shhh . . . it's okay." Wrapping his arms round her, he pulled her close and rested his chin on her head. "We don't have to talk about it. Let's not argue anymore and spoil this time." She was not ready to talk to her dad, and he had to respect that. Still, he hoped that she would find a way to at least stop blaming herself. She deserved more than that.

"So, you want to go see the sights? And out to eat?"

She nodded against his chest.

"All right, I'll take you out."

As he'd promised, they visited all the sights in the city—from the Bayview Natural History Museum to the Historic Old Town to the Siren's Sea Gardens, and ended the day with a big walk up the Lucent Gate Bridge where they watched the sun set. In between, they stopped at cafés and food trucks to snack their way through the city, trying out all the hip and trendy eats. Jasmine had loved the fernflower cakes they bought from a food cart run by an old hippie dryad, while the cloudberry muffins at the famous Night Blooms Café had blown Mal's mind.

Mal was exhausted from their very full day, but at least Jasmine seemed like her normal self again. He didn't like upsetting her. Thankfully, that knot in his chest had eased, though it wasn't completely gone.

"Mal, did you hear me?"

Jasmine's voice jolted him out of his thoughts. "Yes?"

"I asked how you managed to get a reservation here." Jasmine's eyes soaked in the ultra-modern glass-and-chrome dining room of the Obsidian Spire, one of Bayview City's most exclusive restaurants. "They're usually booked up months in advance."

"Called in a favor," he said. "One of my former clients knows the owners of their sister restaurant in Montreal. So, they got me this last-minute table."

"Thank you for doing this and taking me here." Her eyes sparkled as she perused the menu printed on heavy linen stock paper. "Everything looks divine, but . . ." She wrinkled her nose. "How come this menu doesn't have prices?"

"It's all pre-fixed," he said. "And that's the entire ten-course menu."

Brown doe eyes bulged. "We're having all of this?"

"Yes."

She actually let out a little squeak. "You'll have to roll me out of here. But, Mal, this must cost—"

He held a hand up. "Remember what you told me today? About telling you you're wrong if you complain about how I spoil you with money? Well, you're wrong, Jasmine."

"Fine." But she said it with an adorable pout. "Spoil away."

The waiter arrived to drop off an amuse-bouche, then took their orders.

"This really is nice, Mal," she began, taking a nibble at the edge of the tiny lobster-and-caviar bruschetta. "Thank you."

"You're welcome. You deserve this treat." And she really did, with all the hard work she'd been putting in at the shop, for the animals, and for Clawdia. "And you look beautiful."

She tucked a stray lock of hair behind her ear. "Thank you." Her skin was like gold under the soft glow of the mood lighting around them, her brown eyes soft and inviting. Time slowed and the air around them turned soundless. This felt like the moment to tell her.

"Jasmine—"

A soft buzzing sound made her start. "Sorry." She reached for her phone inside her purse. "Might be the gnomes." Glancing at the screen, she went pale.

The tendons in his neck tensed. "What's wrong? Is it the shop?"

"I . . . No." She put the phone face down on the table. "It's Housen Hatchery."

"Housen Hatchery?"

"That's the place that sent us Clawdia." Her fingers skittered at the edge of the table. "They've actually been calling for a while."

"How long?"

Guilt flashed across her face. "About a week now?"

"A we—" His voice rang out in the quiet atmosphere of the

dining room, so he lowered his volume a couple notches. "A week? Why didn't you say anything to me? Have they been harassing you all this time?"

"This is only, like, the third call," she clarified. "And remember what the lawyer said? We're not obligated to tell them about Clawdia. So, I figured I don't have to pick up the phone and talk to them."

"Good." Still, he did not like that they were bothering Jasmine. "If they insist, tell them you want their demands in writing." That's what Nakamoto had advised, to leave a paper trail. "And like I said, I have your back on this."

"I know, thank you, Mal. And I'm sorry to have to drag you into this fight. Don't worry, once I get the loan, it won't be your mess anymore."

Dread seeped into his chest.

She doesn't think I'll be around.

And if he were perfectly honest with himself, he didn't know if he *would* be around.

"Here are your drinks." The waiter placed two glasses of wine in front of them. "Your first course is on the way."

"Thank you," Jasmine said. She glanced at the menu, excitement on her face. "Ooh! That's the caviar spheres with fresh herbs. I can't wait."

Despite the distraction of the sumptuous meal, Mal couldn't stop thinking about why he couldn't just say "I love you" to her. He'd never felt this way about anyone before and he had no reference or experience to guide him in what to do. It was like doing a renovation job without a contract or a plan and not having the right tools for the job.

"This meal was amazing," Jasmine gushed as she finished off the dessert course—a panna cotta sphere literally floating over a pool of mango puree. "Mal, I can't thank you enough. Really."

Seeing her happy was enough for him. "You're very welcome."

After they finished dinner, they took a taxi back to their hotel and headed up to their suite. "I'm gonna get ready. I brought a little surprise for you." She winked at him over her shoulder as she sauntered into the bathroom.

Mal walked over to the bed and sat down on the mattress, loosening his tie and then tossing it aside.

When the door opened, Jasmine called, "Hey."

"Hey, you're—" He nearly swallowed his tongue at the sight of Jasmine leaning against the doorjamb, wearing a white lace bra that pushed her tits up, a skimpy pair of thong panties, and white stockings.

"Do you like it?" she asked as she approached him.

He answered by lifting her up and laying her down on the bed. "You're so beautiful," he whispered against her skin as he nuzzled her neck.

"Mal," she moaned.

He wanted it to be like this forever, to just hold her and be alone with her, without a care for the outside world. His hands roamed over her lush curves and soft skin, memorizing how they felt. Catching her mouth with his, he kissed her tenderly, his lips caressing hers with an aching gentleness that pulled at his chest.

"Need you so bad. Need you." His claws slashed at the thin straps of her thong to expose her to his touch. How he managed to unzip his pants with shaking hands, he didn't know, especially with his cock fully swollen. He pointed the tip at her entrance, rubbing his lube all over before he thrust all the way in. She screamed his name as she raked her fingers down his back.

Despite their hurried start, Mal took his time. He moved with slow, deep movements, kissing and licking and touching, memorizing the feel and smell and taste of her, pouring his emotions into her. While he couldn't say the words out loud, he would tell her this way that he would do anything for her—build her a million hatching tanks, slay her a hydra, walk through fire, just to please her. He wanted to make this moment last, to burn it into his memory so that he would never forget how she tasted, felt, and smelled. How beautiful she was whenever she came around him.

"Mal!" she cried out once more, after what was probably her second or third orgasm. "I can't. You have to . . ."

"One more, ashak'a," he urged. "One more for me."

This time, he picked up his pace, gathering her tight against him as he bucked into her. "Such a good girl . . . You can do it. Squeeze me with that pretty pussy while you come. Do it—come, Jasmine."

She moaned against his chest, her body writhing as her inner walls spasmed around him.

The pressure became too much, all the synapses firing in his brain at the same time. "Jasmine," he growled as he rocked into her. "I lo—" The strangled groan ripping from his throat mercifully drowned out the rest as the pressure released.

Breathing hard, he crumpled on top of her. After a moment, he rolled away and pulled her on top of him. He held her like that, enjoying the feel of her in his arms until she wiggled off.

"Sorry, need to use the bathroom," she called out as she hopped off.

Sighing, Mal stared up at the ceiling. He had almost told her he loved her. How come even then, in the throes of passion, when he let go of everything and was at his most uninhibited, he couldn't say the words aloud?

Grunting, he hauled himself up and swung his legs over the side of the bed. She'd looked so godsdamned sexy in that lingerie that he couldn't even wait to get his clothes off to fuck her. He rose up to right himself, when the soft thud of his cellphone hitting the carpeted floor caught his attention. As he bent down to pick it up, he noticed the envelope icon on the top of the screen, indicating he had an email in his work mailbox. But who would be emailing him at this time of night?

He sat back down on the bed and opened the email app, every muscle in his body tensing as he read the subject line.

```
From: Grok@OrcHistorical.org
To: Mal@TerraFormBuilders.com
Subject: Congratulations, Mal of
Urduk Horde

Dear Mal,

We are pleased to inform you that the
elders have accepted your bid for the
construction of the new Historical
Center. After reviewing many
applications, the elders feel your bid
demonstrated the best combination of
technical knowledge, competitive pricing,
and an appreciation for the preservation
of our culture and history.
    Please find attached the official
contract, as well as more details of
scope of work, requirements, payment
terms, and other important documents.
    Please reply to this email or contact
me at the Historical Society at your
earliest convenience.
    We look forward to working with you.

In glorious victory,
Grok of Harvik Horde
```

Coordinator-in-charge
Orc Historical Society

Mal couldn't breathe as he sat there, reading and re-reading the email. He tapped at the refresh button over and over again, waiting for a follow-up email with the subject "Re: Oops, sorry we made a mistake." But the email confirming that he had, indeed, been chosen remained on top.

He'd done it. After all the work, all the waiting, this moment was finally here.

And now, he didn't even know if he wanted it.

"Mal?"

His head jerked up. "Yes?"

Jasmine padded over to him. "Everything okay? You look like you've heard some bad news."

"What? No." He tossed his phone onto the bedside table like it had been made of hot coals. "Just tired."

The corner of her mouth tugged up, then she straddled his lap, legs hanging off the side of his knees. "You just spoil me so much. Too much."

"No such thing." He cupped the side of her cheek. "You deserve it."

Leaning down, she kissed him, then swung off his legs. "Why don't you get changed and we can go to bed? Slip into something more comfortable, like I did." She motioned down to her pajama shorts set. It was baby blue and had small prints of capybaras. "Not as sexy as the other one I was wearing, huh?"

"You look absolutely sexy and beautiful." And she really was, just standing there, breathing and being her.

She threw her head back and laughed, as if they were sharing a joke. "Oh yeah, I'm sexy all right." She rubbed at her belly. "And look at this food baby right here. I'm surprised you didn't get turned off."

I want to put real babies in there.

"Nothing about your body could turn me off." He pulled her in for a kiss. "But you're right." He got to his feet. "I should get changed."

"Bathroom's all yours."

Mal brushed past her, her perfume still tickling his nose. He closed the door behind him, buried his face in his hands and groaned.

Who knew shit sometimes came in the form of the universe giving you what you wanted?

Chapter Twenty-one

JASMINE

Post-vacation blues had always hit Jasmine hard, but never quite this way. It had been more than a week since she and Mal came back from Bayview City, and yet she couldn't stop thinking about their mini-break. Overall, it had been amazing. She loved being in the city, seeing all the sights and going shopping and trying all the different kinds of food. However, she was also glad to be back in Dewberry Falls, to her own apartment, the shop and the animals, and of course, Clawdia.

However, there was something bothering Jasmine, a notion she just couldn't quite ignore, nor could she put a name to it. A kind of disquiet, like something was not right.

Jasmine opened the drawer under the register and picked up the Clawdia figurine that Mal had carved on their camping trip. She'd gotten into the habit of rubbing it when she was feeling anxious or nervous. Jasmine guessed she'd probably wear the entire thing away within a week if she didn't resolve that suspicion lurking in her mind.

Mal was acting weird.

He'd seemed distracted, distant even, since they came back

from their staycation. Their last full day was busy and they went to more sights and ate all the food they wanted, yet she wasn't entirely sure he was even there with her. And when they returned to Dewberry Falls, it seemed to have gotten worse. The sex was still off the charts, but out of the bedroom, there was a look behind his eyes, something that told her he wasn't quite in the moment with her. This morning when she left, he didn't even walk her to work. Sure, he had an early conference call, but usually he worked around it, whether that meant rescheduling or taking the call with his earphones on as they walked to the shop. He'd also been on his phone a lot, which was unusual for him. While Jasmine would have guessed that maybe he was texting with someone, she noticed that he would hold the device in his hand and tap at the same spot with his thumb, over and over again.

Maybe this was it. They were reaching the point where things were naturally fizzling out and Mal wanted to break up. Their six months was nearly up, and from the beginning, she'd always known that he'd be leaving in that time.

A weight pressed down on her chest, making it hard to breathe. Though she'd known this moment would come, it still hit her like a bucket of ice water to the face.

It's all right, she told herself. *You and Mal agreed to act like adults.*

Then why didn't he say anything? And why was he acting this way? Was it something she'd said or done?

Her mind wanted to dissect and examine all the events that led to this before coming to any conclusion. If Mal really wanted to break up, he would have just done it. He wouldn't act like nothing was wrong on the outside, keep sleeping with her and spending time with her if he didn't want to be with her anymore. What could she have done?

I did corner him about the girlfriend thing, she realized. But he seemed to have taken that in his stride and that was weeks ago. What else—

She slapped her hand on her forehead.

The argument about her father.

That had to have been it, where it all started. But that was such a small thing, not even a real fight. More like a minor tiff, really. She hadn't meant to snap at him, but she hadn't wanted to ruin their getaway by talking about it. Lashing out at him for simply offering to help had been unwarranted and unnecessarily harsh.

That's why he'd been acting weird.

I never said sorry, either.

It was her fault. Was it too late? Did she push him away because of one careless act?

Biting her lip, Jasmine put the Clawdia figurine down, pushed off the counter, then began to pace and plan how she could bring up the topic and apologize to Mal.

How could she make it better? Mal had always been a man of few words. He *acted*. From the beginning, he spoke with his actions. He fixed the sign. He made her that carcinos hatching tank. He gave her Clawdia and kept her safe.

How could I possibly top that?

Her gaze drew back to the wooden figurine and an idea popped into her head. Her hands shook with excitement as she grabbed the computer mouse. Opening up a browser window, she did a search for "apology gifts."

Jasmine scrolled through the options. What kind of gift could possibly convey how she felt? That she was sorry about snapping at him, and she didn't mean to push him away. The gift would have to be something thoughtful and personalized, like how he customized the tank to reflect the shop.

Clicking on the back arrow of the browser, she typed in a new query—"Personalized gifts."

The results were much better, plus she had a lot more choices. However, one caught her eye. She clicked on the photo excitedly.

Perfect.

It had tons of customization options too. After a few minutes, she was done, except for that she needed an inscription on the base. What could she write? "I'm sorry" didn't quite sound right. "I'm sorry for blowing my top when you brought up my father" had far too many characters.

There were so many things she wanted to say to him. Like, how she liked spending time with him. And that he made her feel safe and protected. And that she liked that even though he could be a grump, he was never mean and she thought his grunts were adorable. He was so kind too, especially when he dealt with kids. And so dependable. He made her happy just by being around. She loved the way his eyebrows drew together when he frowned, loved how he remembered her favorite dish at each restaurant. She loved his laugh and his frown and . . .

Him.

Oh Mother Goddess.

She loved Mal.

Jasmine gasped out loud, then covered her mouth with her hands. Why hadn't she realized it before? She'd been keeping that wall up between them to prevent this exact thing from happening, but it was about as effective as trying to keep a baby basilisk from eating a vormynd egg. No matter how many times she told herself that she wouldn't, she'd fallen in love with him anyway.

A laugh bubbled in her chest.

I love him.

And Jasmine couldn't wait to tell him.

But first, she had to finish this order. And now fully aware of her own feelings, she knew what she wanted to say.

After a few taps on the keyboard and a couple of mouse

clicks, she finished ordering Mal's gift. It would take around two weeks to get here. Maybe she could wait to tell him then, when she presented it to him. If she could manage to control herself.

Ring! Ring! Ring!

Jasmine dashed back to the counter and picked up the phone. "Fantastic Tails and Magical Scales, this is Jasmine speaking. How may I help you?"

"Greetings, Jasmine," said the heavily accented female voice on the other end. "May I please speak with Mal of Urduk Horde?"

"I'm so sorry, he's not in today."

"I see. When do you expect him back?"

"Not until tomorrow, maybe? Would you like to leave a message? I can write down your number and he can call you back."

"It's rather urgent," the caller emphasized. "But I suppose this would be the fastest way to communicate with him. All right, please do take a message for me."

Jasmine grabbed a pencil and a piece of paper. "What's your name?"

"Grok of Harvik Horde."

"And what's your message?"

"Please tell him that I would like to confirm he got our email since he hasn't responded . . ."

She scribbled on the paper. "Yeah . . ."

"And that could he please reply as soon as possible if he wants to accept the job."

"Uh-huh." *Scratch, scratch, scratch.* "And which job is that specifically?"

"The new historical center."

"The new—" Jasmine froze, the tip of the pencil stopping in the middle of writing the "w". "I—excuse me? Did you say the historical center? The *orc* historical center?"

"Yes. Why? Has he bid on other historical centers?"

"No, no. None that I know of." She bit her lip. "Uhm, okay, I'll make sure he gets this message."

"Thank you."

Click.

Jasmine wasn't sure how long she'd been standing there with the phone against her ear, but the monotonous dial tone was still droning when she snapped to her senses. Her stomach clenched tight, and her chest contracted, preventing oxygen from reaching her lungs.

Mal got the job.

And apparently, he'd known about it for some time now, but hadn't told her.

What happened to their promise to be honest with each other?

She gripped the edge of the counter, a wave of dizziness washing over her as the blood rushed to her ears at a breakneck pace.

Wait, she told herself. *Don't jump to conclusions.* There had to be a good explanation for this. What if he'd missed that email and hadn't known all this time?

Unlikely, considering how much he'd been on his phone this past week.

"Calm down," she muttered. "There has to be——"

Ding ding dong!

Her head whipped to the door, but before she could greet the customer, her stomach swooped when she saw who it was.

Mal strode in, holding up a white to-go cup in his hand. "Had to take a break. Figured you could use a cup too."

Jasmine's throat dried up and she couldn't speak, not that she had anything to say to him right now. She closed her eyes tight, unable to look at him.

"Jasmine? Are you okay?"

After a deep cleansing breath, she managed to speak. "Grok called."

"Grok?"

"From the Historical Society."

Recognition flashed across his face. "Did she say—"

"When were you going to tell me? Or were you going to even say anything?" That came out snippier than she wanted.

"Of course I was going to tell you."

She crossed her arms over her chest. "When did you find out anyway?"

"I . . ." His throat bobbed. "I got the email while we were in Bayview."

"When we were in Bayview?" How she hated the way her voice pitched high at the end of that sentence, but she couldn't stop herself from continuing. "That was over a week ago. And you never said a word. I thought we agreed to be honest with each other, Mal?"

"I wasn't lying to you." He raked a hand through his mop of messy dark hair.

"It was a lie of omission, then."

He let out a grunt. "Look, I didn't know what to say, okay? I mean, what was I supposed to do? That job means a lot to me. To my family and our legacy. I didn't think they'd choose me after all this time. I'd honestly been preparing myself for the rejection, because of how disappointed I'd be if I didn't win the bid. And then I got that email."

The reality of the situation walloped her in the gut.

He was leaving.

Of course he was leaving. This was his big dream. The chance of a lifetime. To build his legacy, and that of his father.

"Mal, it's fine." Her heart twinged in pain. "Really it is."

"Jasmine—"

"Remember what we said in the beginning? About being adults? We said we would see where this goes and now . . . it went."

"That's it?" His voice turned chilly. "You're breaking up with me?"

She swallowed the emotion scratching at her throat. "Better to do it now before we . . ."

"Before we what?"

Jasmine pasted a smile on her face. "Before either of us got hurt." Though on her part, that sadly was too late.

"What if I did stay, Jasmine?"

Hope fluttered in her, but she squashed it down. "Mal, this is your dream job. What you've been working for, for the past year. Don't throw it all away."

Not for me.

She didn't want another man losing out on his hopes and dreams because of her, not when she could do something about it this time.

If Mal declined that job and stayed to be with her, he'd always regret what he'd missed out on. He'd resent her forever. It would always loom over their heads and frankly, despite loving him, she wouldn't be able to be with him if that happened.

"You really want to end things?"

"That's what we agreed to. You were never going to stay, even if you didn't get the job." It would be different if he'd lost the bid. But his dream was actually about to come true. It was here, served to him on a silver platter.

And she loved him too much to hold him back.

"That's what we said, right? See where this goes, and at the end, we walk away from each other. That was the only guarantee we had. It was the only one I could give you."

Taut silence filled the air between them until he spoke. "All right, if that's what you want." Turning on his heel, he quietly strolled out of the shop for the very last time.

Reality hit Jasmine as soon as the door slammed shut. That hollow pain in her chest spread out, threatening to devour her.

She should have prepared herself more for this day because she always knew it was inevitable, the one guarantee she had offered Mal. She just hadn't thought it could hurt this much.

"You're going to be okay," she said, her voice barely a whisper. Heartbreak and starting over wasn't new to her. She'd been doing just fine on her own before Mal came, and she'd be fine after he left.

Chapter Twenty-two

JASMINE

"Good job, Clawdia!" Jasmine tossed the hatchling a treat as she finished performing her newest trick—spinning around in a circle. "You're doing great." Kneeling down, she rubbed the dragon's chin affectionately. Joy and devotion blanketed Jasmine like a warm coat and visions of more treats danced in her head.

Jasmine laughed. "I'm afraid I don't have any more kibble, but let me see if I can scrounge up something for you, okay? Then we can work on the next trick."

Clawdia trilled and nudged at her thigh, before an image of Mal popped into her head.

For a second, Jasmine didn't know if it was Clawdia's emotions that she sensed or her own. It took all her might not to burst into tears. She'd thought she'd run out of them by now, after two whole miserable weeks of crying.

Clawdia bumped her again, indicating she was waiting for an answer to her question:

Where's Mal?

"I don't know, Clawdia. I'm sorry."

And that was the truth. She hadn't seen him at all since that day they'd broken up over two weeks ago. He didn't show up at the shop, nor did she see him leave or enter his house. Rent had been due the other day and when she'd tiptoed over to slip the check under his door, there was no sound coming from the other side. Had it not been for the lights inside the house occasionally turning on and off, she would have thought he'd vanished into thin air. Nope, just avoiding her.

It was better this way, she told herself for the thousandth time. If she did see him, she might do something rash.

Like confess her love for him and ask him to stay.

"I made the right decision," she said, as if hearing it from her own lips made it hurt any less. The historical center job had been his dream for so long. He'd lost his father so young. Mal had never got the chance to work alongside him or show him all his accomplishments. Over the last few months, she'd seen more of his amazing work, and though he remained modest about it, Mal's talent and capabilities seemingly had no limits. Why he'd even doubted that he would get that job, she didn't know. And why she let herself fall for him when he was going to leave was an even bigger mystery.

A demanding warble and sudden flashes of food, ball, treats, and toys jolted her out of her thoughts. The images cycled over and over again in a frenzied pace. "What is it?" She narrowed her eyes at Clawdia. "Do you want all those things?"

The hatchling skittered away to her pen. Moments later, she came out, dragging her favorite blanket, then set it down by Jasmine before scooting off once more. When she returned, she was carrying her goblin stuffie, and dropped it on top of the blanket.

"Clawdia, are you bringing me all your favorite things because I'm sad?"

Clawdia responded by sitting down on her hind legs, eyes staring up at her adoringly.

"Oh baby . . ." Picking her up, she cuddled the dragon to her. "Thank you, Clawdia." Warmth flowed into her chest, temporarily filling the empty spaces between the pieces of her broken heart. Still, moisture gathered at the corners of her eyes.

Oh Mother Goddess, would the tears never stop?

After another long drawn-out breath, she put Clawdia down. "Let me get you those treats."

Jasmine rooted around in the fridge, trying to find the apples she swore she had stashed in there last week. They weren't on the main shelf, so she pulled the crisper open. To her surprise, the usually empty drawer had something heavy in it. Peering in, she saw a dark, olive-tinted bottle with a distinctive shield-shaped silver label.

What was this doing here?

Dislodging it from the drawer, she held it up and saw a card attached to the neck with a string. She opened it and read the note:

> *Congratulations, ashak'a. You deserve this.*
> *Don't let anyone tell you otherwise.*
> *Love,*
> *Mal*

Her heart nearly dislodged from her chest. Mal had bought this. He'd remembered his promise, that he would buy her champagne once the loan went through.

But I hadn't even submitted the paperwork until yesterday.

When did he buy this?

Ding ding dong!

"We have customers," she told Clawdia. Now that Jasmine had to run the shop by herself, she locked the door whenever she went to check on Clawdia. Her gaze landed back on the bottle and the note attached to it, her mind still reeling about the meaning of it.

Ding ding dong!

"Argh!" Shoving the bottle back in the drawer, Jasmine shut the fridge and turned to Clawdia. "All right, back in the pen for now."

The obnoxious doorbell rang out twice more before Jasmine reached the door. "Good morning! Welcome to Fantastic Tails and Magical Scales," she greeted. "How can I help you today?"

The man on the other side nodded a greeting at her. "Are you Jasmine Gonzalez? The manager?"

"Yes." She eyed him curiously. A little over six feet tall, the burly older man had a thick head of silver hair, a bushy mustache and matching eyebrows. The skin on his arms was a criss-cross of healed burn scars and his dark green eyes reminded Jasmine of a hawk that never blinked. "And who are you?"

"Harry Housen," he said. "I'm the owner of Housen Hatchery."

Her heart pounded a rhythm that rushed to her ears.

This man had come here to take Clawdia away.

Well, he would have to pry her from my cold, dead hands.

"My—our l-lawyer says I d-don't have to talk to you." She reached for the door with shaking hands. "Whatever you need to say, you can do it in writing. Now please leave."

Housen jammed his hand against the door. "Please don't, Ms. Gonzalez. I've been trying to call you for days. Can you give me five minutes?"

"I know what you want to say. No, you can't have Claw—the egg back." She tried to be vague, in case there was a misunderstanding.

"What? You think I'm trying to take the dragon hatchling?"

Okay, so he definitely knew that she had received a dragon egg.

"Isn't that why you've been calling me?" She crossed her arms. "Because you want to take Clawdia? Or sue me for the cost of the eggs?"

"Yes. I mean no." Bushy eyebrows twitched and drew together. "Not quite. It depends." His shoulders relaxed. "Ms. Gonzalez, please give me a moment to explain. There's no need to involve lawyers."

The smart thing to do would be to shut the door in his face. If he insisted on staying, she could always call the police. But then again, she really was curious what he meant when he said "it depends." "All right. Tell me why you're here."

"Yes, it's about the dragon egg we sent to you. My shipping manager discovered the discrepancy when we did our inventory. We looked everywhere, thinking the egg might have been misplaced or had hatched and run off. Perils of the business, I'm afraid," he said with a little chuckle.

"How did I end up with the egg?"

"After checking the warehouse cameras, we realized what had happened—a simple mix-up. One of the new employees put the dragon egg in your package by mistake. Also, your regular customer-service rep, James, went on vacation after he sold you that discounted carcinos egg, so he never followed up. Never even occurred to him that you might have gotten the wrong product, since you never called to complain."

"So, it *was* your company's fault."

"Yes, I'm afraid so."

She placed a hand on her hip. "Which means I can keep her."

"As per consumer laws, yes. We wouldn't have a leg to stand on if we tried to sue you back for the hatchling or the cost of the egg. And it would cost so much more time and money in legal fees if we tried." He raised an eyebrow. "We have this saying in the industry: the only thing more expensive than a dragon egg is a lawyer. In fact, you could sue us for sending you a dangerous animal."

"Like you said, it wouldn't be worth it." But this meant Clawdia was hers—free and clear. That knot of worry she'd been carrying around in her chest this whole time disappeared. "Then what are you doing here? And why have you been calling me?"

Serious green eyes fixed on her. "Dragons are heavily regulated and for good reason, Ms. Gonzalez. We don't sell them at a premium because they're rare. It's because they need a lot of care and training. We can't just let any Joe off the street take a fire-breathing creature home. It's too dangerous. Every potential dragon owner goes through a rigorous background check and must attend mandatory pre-hatching training with us before we even consider selling to them."

"That's actually smart." Vrig would have approved.

Housen continued. "They know what they're getting and we don't sugarcoat it for them. And we conduct regular checks on owners up to two years after hatching. And if we find that they've been mishandling or mistreating the dragon or if the dragon poses a danger to others, then we'd have to get the Department of Magical Enforcement and the Bureau of Animal and Plant Health involved."

She winced. "That doesn't sound fun."

"It's not, believe me. You don't want the feds coming after you."

"So, what do we do now?"

Housen pursed his lips, his silvery mustache twitching. "Like I said, your shop legally owns—Clawdia, is it?—but if you want to keep her and for everyone's safety, you'll have to get the necessary licenses and insurance policies."

"Of course," she said. "The shop is fully insured."

He glanced around at the rows of cages and pens. "And if you want to sell her, that's a whole different ballgame, I'm afraid. I hope you like paperwork. There's a reason it's easier to sell them as eggs."

"Actually, Mr. Housen, my boss gave her to me."

"Gave her to you?" he echoed. "Just like that? He does know how much a dragon egg costs, right?"

"Yeah. But, it's kinda complicated." She didn't want to go over her business—and personal—relationship with Mal at the moment. "But I have my boss's verbal agreement that she's mine, and soon, I'll be the owner of Fantastic Tails as well."

"Oh good," he said with a sigh of relief. "Paperwork'll be simple, just a signed and notarized affidavit. By the way, you should consider joining our training classes. We have a few sessions online, but most people find that face to face is better. When Clawdia's ready, you can take her to my ranch for more advanced courses too."

"Sounds good. I'll definitely look into it. However, I've already been training her."

"You have?" he asked. "How?"

"I watched some online videos. She's very responsive to food and loves to play. I've already taught her sit, wait, lie down, spin, and fetch and drop it."

"Really?" He rubbed at his chin. "Interesting. Say, Ms. Gonzalez—"

"Jasmine, please."

"Then call me Harry. Anyway, Jasmine, do you think I can see your Clawdia? To check on her, see if she's developing properly. I don't just sell dragon eggs. I've been breeding and training them at my ranch for thirty years."

"Sure. I'd love your expert opinion."

Jasmine led Harry to the back office, which had been expanded to twice its size now. Clawdia's crate was also three times larger than it originally was and now took up an entire corner of the room.

"Good spell work here." Rubbing at his chin, Harry examined his surroundings. "Orc handiwork, I bet?"

"Yes," she confirmed. "Mal—the current owner—is an orc."

"Ah, that means you already have the best fireproofing magic on the market. I don't need to send my warlocks over. I trust orc work. You know you need to keep her away from other creatures and the general public for at least a year, right? To build her immune system." She nodded. "Good. May I see her now?"

"One moment." As soon as Jasmine approached the pen, Clawdia got up on her back legs and started scratching at the bars. She did her usual routine of telling the hatchling to wait before she opened the gate. Clawdia leapt out, and sniffed at her, accepting a few scratches on the chin and head before she turned her attention to Harry. Cautiously, she approached the stranger, sniffing at his feet. He, in turn, crouched low to the ground and held out his palm. Three small nuts, a little larger than almonds, lay on top, which Clawdia swiftly scarfed down.

"Spicy Arcane nuts," he explained. "Dragons love 'em. I'll send you a bag."

"That would be lovely, Harry."

"You said you were training her. Can you show me some tricks?"

"Of course. Clawdia," she called, and the dragon scurried toward her. "Let's do some training, all right?"

Jasmine went through the various tricks she'd taught Claudia, plus a few new ones she'd been working on. "She's still getting the hang of roll over."

"Yeah, dragons don't like squishing their wings much." Harry laughed. "I think we're all good here, Jasmine. Thank you for letting me meet her." Bending down to Clawdia's level, he gave her more scratches on the head, which made her purr in delight. "You're a special one, I think."

"I agree."

"And now, I can tell you, that even if I wanted to take her away, I couldn't. She's obviously bonded to you."

"Yeah, I feel like we do share a bond."

Harry shook his head. "No, no, I don't think you understand what I'm saying. Jasmine, you and Clawdia are actually bonded. On a metaphysical level."

"B-bonded?" Her jaw nearly dropped to her feet. "We're connected?"

"Yes, it's rare, but dragons do bond with their caretakers, at least only those with strong magical ability themselves." He narrowed his gaze at her. "Why do you seem so surprised?"

"My magic is something I've discovered only recently. I have an affinity with animals and can sense their wants and needs. I have a connection with all of them, so I didn't think it was any different with Clawdia."

"But your connection with her isn't the same as with the others, right? It's much deeper. More emotional."

Bending down, she rubbed Clawdia's head. A burst of contentment and joy rippled across her chest. "Yes."

Harry tsked. "Even if I wanted to, I wouldn't be able to take Clawdia. It would be cruel to take a bonded dragon away from its caretaker. Well"—he placed his hands on his hips and inhaled a deep breath—"I think I've seen what I needed to see. I should head back. Thank you again, Jasmine."

"Let me see you out."

As soon as Harry Housen left, Jasmine blew out a big sigh of relief. Clawdia was truly hers and they were bonded. Her first thought was to tell Mal, which promptly deflated her jovial mood.

Was he still at home? Had he already left? The lights had been on last night, but she didn't recall seeing them this morning.

Her mind drifted back to the bottle of champagne in the fridge, the contents of the note burned in her mind.

You deserve this. Don't let anyone tell you otherwise.

Mal believed in her. He always had, maybe not right away, but once he threw his support behind her, he'd never wavered. He didn't let anyone pull her down, not even Jasmine herself.

Her heart thumped in her chest.

Jasmine buried her face in her hands. Had she done the right thing, breaking up with him? She couldn't let him abandon his dream. But at the same time, what if she had gotten it wrong? What if he did want to stay?

It was all too much, all too confusing.

Oh Mother Goddesss, ancestor spirits, she pleaded. *Tell me what do. Give me a sign.*

A sudden vibration from her pocket jolted her from her prayers. Checking the screen, her emotions did a full one-eighty when she saw the name on the caller ID. She tapped on the green button and slapped a smile on her face. "Hi, Dad."

"Hi, anak." Jed Gonzalez's face filled the screen, the corners of his eyes crinkling as he smiled. "How are you?"

"I'm good, Dad." Why was he calling? "So, what's up? How are things at work? Busy?"

"Very. You won't believe the shift I had last night."

"Oh? What happened?" Jasmine prepared herself mentally. She had to, because the stories he shared about his work as a nurse could turn pretty graphic. But she supposed it would at least keep her mind busy.

"I'll tell you later. I wanted to check on you."

"Really? You called just to check on me?"

"Yes, I had this feeling . . ." He clucked his tongue. "Call it father's intuition, but I wanted to hear your voice and see your face."

"That's nice, Dad. It's good to see you too."

Was it really intuition? Or perhaps something else at work. Had her prayers been heard and answered? Either way, her father was here. Maybe it was time for her to face her own truth. To address that shadow that loomed over their relationship.

"Dad . . . since you called, there's actually something I've been meaning to tell you." Her heart raced all the way up to her throat.

Jed's brows furrowed. "What is it?"

"I discovered something. A-about myself." Pushing her heart back down to her chest, she scrounged up the words she had been wanting to say. "Dad, I have magical abilities. I can communicate with animals. Sort of, anyway. I can sense what they feel and know what they want."

For a moment, Jasmine thought the video had frozen because Jed went absolutely still. However, her father's face soon broke into a smile. "Really? That's amazing. How did you find out? When? And can you do anything else? Can you heal the animals like your lolo does with his patients?"

"No, it's not like Lolo Joaquin's abilities or anything like that and—Wait, Dad, are you happy for me?"

"Of course I am. I'm ecstatic," he said. "Why wouldn't I be? I can't wait to call back home and tell everyone. My daughter, a magic wielder, who'd have thought?" he said, pride in his voice. "Your Tita Maritess will probably want to put a tarp up in front of their house to tell everyone."

Jasmine couldn't believe it. "Dad, there's something else I wanted to talk to you about."

"What? Wait, do you have a boyfriend already?"

"Er, no." She took a deep breath. "Dad, back when . . . when Lolo died, I overheard you talking to Tito Carlo. About The Inheritance. That you deserved it and the only reason Lolo didn't pass it to you was because I was girl."

"What?" His face was a mask of shock. "Anak, I—" He shook his head. "I'm sorry. You shouldn't have heard that—No, no, I shouldn't have *said* that. I was grief-stricken and angry, losing your grandfather *and* The Inheritance. But that's no excuse for what I said. And no, I don't blame you."

"It's still my fault. You didn't get The Inheritance because you wouldn't have been able to pass it on to me because I'm a girl. And if you couldn't pass it on, then the magic would disappear forever."

"Jasmine, my father was never going to choose me." Jed's mouth pulled into a taut line. "The only thing I ever wanted was to make a difference in other people's lives. I studied my whole life so I could do it. First under your lolo, and then I took up nursing so I could help even more people and give them comfort. But Papa said that was a waste of time. I've thought about it a lot and I think he resented me becoming a nurse because he didn't like that I was learning modern medicine. He was afraid I would waste The Inheritance. That's why he chose your tito instead of me."

Jasmine's words got stuck in the thickness in her throat. "Dad . . . I never knew." All this time, she'd thought she was the reason he never received The Inheritance. That cloud looming over their relationship had only ever been in her head. "Dad, thank you for telling me this." Her entire body lightened, the weight of years of imagined resentment lifting away.

"I'm really sorry for the misunderstanding, anak. But you know I love you, right?"

"O-of course." Oh Mother Goddess, she was going to start crying again. She inhaled a deep breath. "I love you too, Dad."

"And hey, I'm sorry if I keep nagging you about going back to nursing. I just wanted to guarantee your future with a stable career. I love you, so of course I want things to work out for you. But I'm really happy for you, anak. Our ancestor spirits and the Mother Goddess guided you to where you are now. If you didn't find your way there, you might never have discovered your own magic. It's your destiny to be there."

She laughed to herself, thinking of how she'd ended up here. If her car hadn't broken down, she would never have stopped in Dewberry Falls. Never would have taken the job at Fantastic Tails. Never would have met Mal.

Mal.

She should have listened to him about calling her dad. And now she would never be able to tell him, because he was leaving.

What if I did stay?

Jasmine covered her mouth, her chest squeezing tight as a realization spread through her.

Love, Mal, was how he'd signed the note. He'd laid it out for her to see, putting his heart in her hands, risking it without any guarantee.

He loved her.

And she'd pushed him away.

"Oh no."

"Jasmine? What's wrong?"

"Er . . . nothing. But I have to go, Dad."

"Of course. I'll talk to you soon, okay? Actually, I was thinking of coming for a visit."

"That would be great, Dad. Please come anytime."

"All right. Love you."

"Love you too." With shaking hands, she put her phone down.

Mal loved her, Jasmine was sure. And now she had to tell him that she loved him too. She wouldn't ask him to stay in Dewberry Falls. But they could make it work. Lots of people did long distance. If he was willing to do it, then so would she.

But was he still in town? And was she too late or had she crushed his heart so that he could never want her?

Bolting upright, she grabbed her purse and dashed to the door.

Chapter Twenty-three

MAL

Mal closed up his duffle bag, the loud *zzzzzziipp* sealing the finality of it all. He'd packed up his possessions into this one bag, ready to go. His cab would be arriving soon to take him to the airport. He'd be on his way to the orc homelands tonight. Dewberry Falls would be far behind him, a distant memory. It had all been too good to be real, anyway.

Mal replayed all their times together, wondering how he could have missed the signs that she didn't feel anything for him. Jasmine had been sweet, warm, and burning hot for him. And then two weeks ago she'd turned cold. Basically told him to leave.

See you, don't let the door hit you on the way out.

Yet his stupid, stubborn hearts refused to let go and forget about her. He could not erase her from his mind. She was always in his thoughts, his throat aching like he'd swallowed a handful of nails. He couldn't count how many times he'd nearly marched to her apartment to knock on her door and beg for her to love him. To tell her that he'd stay and give up the historical center job. Give everything up for her.

But he had to accept that Jasmine didn't want him to stay.

So he'd accepted the historical center job and made all the arrangements to leave. To his surprise, it wasn't just his breakup that made it difficult to go. Last week, he'd also had to say good-bye to his squad.

Mal thought it would be quick and easy. He showed up for training a couple days ago, so that he could tell his squad mates that he was leaving in person. It didn't seem right to just send them a text message.

"You're leaving?" Nick had exclaimed. Everyone else had taken the news with the same degree of shock and disappointment.

"But why?"

"I told you, I was just here temporarily." Then he had explained about the Orc Historical Center job.

"What about Jasmine?" Ven had asked.

Mal hadn't known what to say so he just shrugged.

Thankfully, Ian had piped in. "It's none of our business. Mal, you'll be missed around here, but congratulations on achieving your dreams. Your father and Vrig would be so proud, I'm sure."

Jim cancelled training and they all went to the Salty Dog for drinks. More emotions churned in Mal, and while his squad mates provided a good distraction, a different kind of emotion roiled within him. He'd come to enjoy spending time with his squad, and once he left, he would never get a chance to see them again.

Slinging the duffle over his shoulder, he walked out into the living room. He hadn't decided what he'd do with the house yet. Putting it on the market now would be cruel to Jasmine. Even though she'd kicked him to the curb, he wasn't about to do the same to her. He left instructions with Howard Nakamoto to deal with everything and contact him once Jasmine's loan went through. In any case, if the shop continued to do well, she'd be able to afford another place at market rate. He'd give her at least a year in the garage apartment before he sold the house.

He should have stuck to his first plan. *Get in, get it done, get out.* Then he wouldn't be walking around every day with a giant hole in his chest, wondering if he was ever going to feel like his old self. He was a zombie, just a shell of an orc, going about his day, but completely dead inside.

Mal tried to distract himself, tried to get himself hyped for the historical center renovation. There were designs to be drawn, meetings to attend, schedules to make. He buried himself in his work, but each time he had space in his brain to think, Jasmine immediately slotted in.

It had been her idea, this thing between them. Of course, she'd guarded her heart and he should have done the same. He'd told her from the start that he was leaving, no matter what. That this was not his home or his dream. That nothing here could ever make him stay, not the community, not the shop, and certainly not her.

The doorbell ringing jerked him out of his thoughts. His taxi was here. With one last look around him, he lumbered to the door.

"Good morning," said the young man on the other side. He was dressed in the distinct blue-and-purple uniform of a national shipping company. "I have a delivery for Mal."

"I'm Mal. But I didn't order—"

"Here you go." He shoved the box into Mal's hands. "Have a good day."

Mal scratched his head as he examined the box. The name of the store on the shipping label didn't ring a bell at all. The box was heavy in his hands and the contents inside rocked to and fro when he shook it. What could it be?

There's only one way to find out.

Dropping his duffle to the ground, he used a claw to rip at the tape, then reached inside to remove a heavily bubble-wrapped package inside. After tearing through the plastic cocoon, he pulled out the mystery item.

"A snow globe?"

Mal definitely hadn't ordered this. The shipping company must have made a mistake. He was about to put it back in the box when he noticed something peculiar about the insert. Holding it up to the light, he peered through the glass. The scene inside featured the cross-section of a building—a pet shop, to be exact. There on the first floor were all the land-based and avian animals and the second floor was filled with tanks of sea creatures of all sizes. He twisted the globe around, to the front of the miniature. Three figures stood under a sign that said Fantastic Tails and Magical Scales. One was a tall orc with a grumpy face and the second, a petite woman with a bright smile. Between them was a small, dark-blue dragon hatchling.

Who could this be from?

Then he noticed the inscription on the base:

This will always be your heart-home. I love you.

A deafening roar rushed into his ears. There was only one person who could have sent this.

Jasmine.

And she loved him.

Why wouldn't she come to his door and say it? He was only ten steps away. Why would she send this to him now?

Unless . . .

A gift like this would have taken time to make. She had to have planned it in advance. Then he'd received that email . . .

Anyway, it didn't really matter when she'd ordered it. Only that she had.

Jasmine loved him.

He had to see her.

Hearts leaping into his throat, he dashed out the door,

making the usually ten-minute trip to Fantastic Tails in half the time. When he reached the door, he nearly ripped it off in his haste. As he tried to enter, something collided into him and a cloud of familiar, flowery perfume filled his nose.

Jasmine cried out as the momentum of bumping into his chest sent her staggering back. He reached out, catching her before she fell, one arm winding around her. He was tempted to keep holding her, but he let go once she steadied herself.

"Thank—Mal?" she said, the shock and surprise in her voice evident. Brown doe eyes grew large as her gaze focused on him. "Wh-what are you doing here?"

"I came to see you," he rasped. Glancing down, he saw her purse over her shoulder. "Where are you going?"

"To see you."

Every molecule of air left his body. She looked beautiful and radiant, and he soaked up the sight of her like an orc starved of fresh water for days. His hearts pulled him to her, and the whole universe fell away.

Her eyes dropped down to his hands. "You got it?"

He'd carried the snow globe with him all the way here. "Jasmine," he managed to croak. "Can we talk, please?"

"I think we should." Stepping back, she made way for him to enter. Once the door closed, he turned to her.

"Jasmine, there's something I should tell you. I shouldn't have—"

"I love you, Mal," she blurted out.

"Godsdamnit." When her face crumpled, he cursed again. "No, no, I didn't mean it like that." He raked his claws through his hair. "I should have said it first. I love you, Jasmine. I've been wanting to tell you all this time. For weeks. And then that email came, and I panicked. I really wasn't expecting it. I was torn between taking the job and staying here. And not just because I fell in love with you, but this town, for some reason, has grown on me. I didn't know what I wanted. Choosing was too hard and I froze up. I fucked it all up."

She reached toward him, placing her small, warm hand on top of his. "I thought I was doing the right thing, letting you go. This was your dream, and I didn't want to hold you back. If I'd told you to stay, you would have resented me for it. It would have been this cloud over us and I'd always be wondering if you regretted it. I pushed you away because I wanted to guarantee your future, your legacy. As someone who loves you, I wanted that for you."

"Jasmine . . ."

She moved first, slipping her arms around his torso, her body melting into his as she pressed her cheek to his chest. He wrapped his free arm around her as finally, after two weeks of torture, he could breathe again.

"You're wrong, you know."

She rested her chin on his chest to look up at him. "Wrong? About what?"

Gently, he disentangled her arms from him and lowered the snow globe between them. Snow and glitter danced around the miniature pet shop before settling down. "This shop isn't my home. And Dewberry Falls isn't, either."

"I know." Her voice turned quiet. "But we can make long distance work." Her teeth worried at her lower lip. "I mean, that's what you want, right?"

"No, no, you're not understanding me." He turned the globe so the inscription was face out. "Remember what I said about orcs having two homes? That ashak'roca is our heart-home, the one we carry with us wherever we are?"

She nodded.

"There's another word we use for our heart-home. Ashak'a. The person who lives in our hearts." He grinned as her face went blank. "You're my heart-home. My ashak'a. I feel most content and at peace with you and I carry you with me wherever I go. I love you, Jasmine."

Her eyes shone bright with emotion. "Mal . . . I love you too."

Reaching for her once more, he lifted her up with one arm and leaned down, kissing her with all the emotion in his hearts. He didn't need the Historical Society job or to solidify his legacy. Jasmine was all he needed and all he ever wanted.

Epilogue

JASMINE

One year later . . .

Jasmine held up a hand to shield her eyes from the glare of the sun as she focused her gaze on the distance. She searched through the puffy, cotton-like clouds floating high above the vast rolling hills until she found what she was looking for.

There.

She spotted the tiny dot on the horizon, a minuscule speck, really, set against a sky-blue background. It grew bigger, coming at her, forming into a familiar shape—four legs, a long tail, and large wings flapping rhythmically. When it was finally overhead, the fully grown dragon drifted down, landing in front of Jasmine, its paws thumping softly on the grass.

"Excellent job, Clawdia. That was the best take-off and touch-down yet." Tossing her a treat, the dragon fledgling quickly gobbled it down. Jasmine rubbed her chin, prompting Clawdia to purr and trill. Pride and joy washed over her like a gentle wave. "Yes, you should be proud. You've come such a long way."

"Indeed, she has."

Warmth pooled in her chest, and she glanced over her shoulder to see Mal walking toward them. "You're home early."

That tiny line between his eyebrows appeared. "I had to get out of there. The elders were driving me nuts, trying to tell me how to do my job." He raked a hand through the mess of his dark hair. "I change my mind about coming here. Let's go back to Dewberry Falls."

Even though Mal had declined their offer, the Orc Historical Society was apparently desperate to work with him. Not only had they been impressed with Mal's skills, but also his passion about orc history and culture. They told him in no uncertain terms that he was the only orc for the job and they would be willing to do anything to have him come on board.

And so, Mal worked out an agreement to come in as a consultant on the project with a crew he had hand-picked himself, working remotely and only traveling to the site every few months. Jasmine hated it whenever he had to leave, but thankfully he was only gone for a week at most. However, after a year of planning, they were ready to break ground, so he needed to stay in Ghalad-Dur for at least a month. This time, he had set it up so Jasmine could come with him, and they'd decided to bring Clawdia along.

Jasmine glanced up at Mal, barely able to keep the corner of her mouth from tugging up. "Go back home? Why? I mean, how bad was it? Were those grumpy elders trying to tell you how to make things more efficient? Were they messing with your system?" she teased.

He shot her a wry grin. "For the record, I never messed with your clipboards. And if I haven't said it, it's a brilliant system and you run a tight ship at Fantastic Tails."

"As I should—after all, I am the co-owner now."

Mal had initially wanted to give Fantastic Tails to Jasmine, but unfortunately her pride wouldn't allow it. So, instead of using the loan she'd eventually gotten from the bank to purchase the entire shop, she bought out Mal for half, and he agreed to co-own with her. They used the remaining money to renovate and upgrade the facilities. Mal also started renting the storefront next door and opened a hardware store and occasionally took on small renovation jobs. Of course, he was still an active member of the Dewberry Falls Volunteer Fire Department, responding to calls every now and then, though so far, no more three-alarm fires, much to Jasmine's relief.

Slipping an arm round her, he pulled her into an embrace, his body relaxing. "I'm just glad I snuck out early. I'd rather be spending the day with you."

"Me too." She pressed her cheek against his chest, and they stood there, arms around each other, just enjoying the moment. It was hard to believe that she'd almost missed out on this.

The last year had been a dream. Sure, there had been some downs, but the ups more than compensated for them. They'd had a few tiffs, but that was understandable considering they spent nearly every moment of the day together. However, they always made up after, specifically with lots and lots of makeup sex.

Jasmine had also officially moved in with Mal a few months ago, though she already spent all her time at his house anyway, so it was more of a formality when he asked her. She loved coming home to a place that was theirs, falling asleep in his arms at night after a vigorous lovemaking session and waking up with his hands all over her, coaxing her in a round of lazy morning sex.

An annoyed chirp interrupted their repose, and impatience snapped at Jasmine.

"Oops. Sorry, Clawdia." She and Mal disentangled themselves from each other. "We're in the middle of a training session," she explained. "Harry said we have to stick to a schedule and routine, or else it'll throw her off."

Once the one-year nesting period was up and she could go

outside, Jasmine had started bringing Clawdia to the Housen Hatchery's dragon-training ranch where Harry himself gave her lessons on further caring for Clawdia. They also worked on controlling her fire, so she wasn't a danger to anyone or anything. Most recently, once she grew to her full size, they'd begun teaching her how to fly. She was a natural at it, of course, though she'd only flown around an enclosed area. One of the reasons Jasmine agreed to come with Mal to the orc homelands was because, out here, Clawdia could fly through the skies freely.

Mal rubbed at Clawdia's chin affectionately. "All right. Sorry for taking away your mommy. Why don't you show me what you've learned?"

Jasmine shook the bag of treats strapped to her hip. "Clawdia," she called. "Heel."

The dragon sat at her left side, eyes sharp and focused. They went through all her tricks, including a few new ones she had learned to do while flying, like catching a ball Jasmine threw in the air and hovering just above their heads.

"She's really good at this," Mal said. "Was that last trick new?"

"Yeah, your relatives taught her that one."

Since they were in Ghalad-Dur, they spent some time with Morlak's horde, who lived on their farm not too far from the house the Orc Historical Society had provided for Jasmine and Mal. Just like his mother, Mal's distant cousins had been warm and welcoming, and she had gone to visit them a couple of times with Clawdia. The fledgling loved spending time there because she got to socialize with other dragons.

"I hope she won't be too sad when we leave here."

"We can't prevent that, but she'll be fine." Clawdia was growing into a strong and intelligent dragon, and every day Jasmine could feel their bond strengthen.

"Speaking of home," Mal began. "How are things at the shop?"

"I spoke to Sophie this morning. She said everything was great."

Now that Fantastic Tails was actually turning a profit, they could afford to hire one full-time employee and a few extra part-timers when needed. Sophie Martinez was a gem of an assistant manager, and the only reason Jasmine even agreed to leave for a month was because she trusted her so much. "But she did say one of our regulars got a bit snippy when they came by today. Apparently, their pet lindworm was depressed and they wanted me to examine him."

Oftentimes, previous customers would come to Jasmine, asking her to check why their pet wasn't eating or sleeping too much or acting out of sorts. While her magic could not heal sick creatures, she could feel if an animal was truly in distress. It made trips to the vet easier, and she loved being able to help the creatures and their owners.

"Clawdia. Come," Jasmine commanded. "I think we should head back inside." She sent Mal a small smile. "It's time."

They walked hand in hand, Clawdia happily trotting behind them, sniffing at bushes and rocks as they strolled back to the house. Jasmine went to their bedroom, washed off and changed into a long white dress and re-did her braid. When she emerged, Mal was already suited up in a gray tunic shirt and matching long pants. He held a white urn in his hands—Vrig's ashes.

"Ready?" she asked.

He replied with a grunt and a nod.

The drive to the Victory Fields was short and somberly silent. Once they reached their destination, Mal parked the car in a small, unpaved lot at the bottom of a hill. From there, they hiked up a dirt path worn away by all the orcs who came here to lay their loved ones to rest. Today, there was no one else around, and only the occasional sounds of Clawdia tittering and chirping as she trailed behind them disturbed the tranquility.

When they got to the top, Jasmine looked out and gasped. "It's beautiful."

The Victory Fields of Ghalad-Dur spread out before them, like an emerald sea dotted with yellow wildflowers. A strong breeze blew by, sending the blades of grass rippling and shimmering and dancing. The greenery seemed to stretch on forever and ever, disappearing into the distance.

"This is where our ancestors celebrated all their conquests and triumphs, back when the world was young," Mal began. "As we transformed and evolved as a species, this place became a place to commemorate and honor those who have gone before us, not just the ones who fought and conquered, but also those who drove us toward a path of peace and prosperity."

"I think Vrig will be very happy to rest here," Jasmine whispered, her throat tight with tears. The grief of losing her friend hadn't gone away, and it never would, but that was what happened when someone you loved passed.

"He'll be joining his ancestors, his parents, and my father." Mal opened the urn and poured its contents out, the fine gray ash raining down on the verdant carpet. The dust scattered, carried away by a passing breeze over the field, before drifting down to become one with the earth.

They stood there in silence, watching the sun slowly dip behind the hills, washing the clouds overhead with the pink and orange hues of sunset. Jasmine could stay here forever, except Clawdia's excited chitters told her it was time to go.

"Someone's impatient for dinner." She frowned. "Hmm . . . that's weird."

"What's weird?" Mal asked.

"I can usually feel her hunger pangs by now." Flashes of sparkles and shiny objects materialized in Jasmine's head. "But she wants something else."

Mal scratched Claudia's head. "I think I know what she

wants." Slipping a hand into his pocket, he retrieved a strip of leather. "I made her a new collar." The silvery tag at the end jingled as he shook it.

"That's lovely, Mal. Thank you."

Mal got down on one knee and fastened it to Clawdia's neck. "I had the tag personalized too, in case she gets lost. Can you check and make sure it's got the right information?"

"Of course." Leaning down, Jasmine slid the silver ID tag to the front to read the inscription:

Will you marry me?

"Mal?" When she turned to him, he was still down on one knee, but he had a black velvet box in his palm.

"Well?" He opened the box to reveal a breathtaking princess-cut diamond ring inside. "Will you marry me, ashak'a?"

"Yes!" she burst out before he could even complete the question. Once he slipped the ring on her finger, she threw her arms around his neck and kissed him with all the love and passion she could muster. He pulled her close and deepened the kiss, and they were both breathless when they broke apart.

"How . . . You . . . When . . ." Her mind scrambled for the words she wanted to say, but the sparkly rock on her finger distracted her. "Mal . . . it's beautiful."

"I'm glad you like it." His grin was ear to ear. "Your dad actually helped me pick it out."

"My *dad*?"

Jed had come to visit them a few times in the last year, and while it had been awkward at first, the two men eventually became comfortable around each other. Her dad told her that he had never seen her so happy, so he heartily approved of Mal.

"Yeah, I didn't know who else to ask. Kap, Nick, and the guys were no help," he snorted.

Jasmine laughed. "When did you even find the time?"

"On my way back from one of my trips here, I stopped by Pittsburgh for a day," he explained. "I wanted to ask for your dad's permission to marry you. He said that it wasn't needed, but he appreciated me asking and gave his blessing. Then we went to shop for this ring."

Her heart had never felt so full. "I love you so much."

"I love you too, ashak'a."

As he leaned down to kiss her, however, a soft trill and insistent clawing made him pause. Clawdia stuck her head between them, rubbing her nose against their shoulders.

Joy and excitement burst across Jasmine's skin like goosebumps. "She's happy." Visions of kibble danced in her head. "And hungry."

Mal grunted, then stood up. "Let's go home then."

Her heart soared higher than Clawdia could fly. Home had always been a foreign concept for Jasmine. After all, what was home to her, when she had been wandering all her life? Was it where she was born or where she chose to settle down?

Now, however, as she stared at Mal's face, his indigo eyes shining with love, she knew that her wandering heart had finally found its home.

Acknowledgements

This book would not have been written or published without some very special people and so I'd like to give my most heartfelt thanks to them. First is my editor at Headline Eternal, Soraya Bouazzaoui, who approached me with the initial idea of a romance set in a magical pet store and then gave me the freedom to run with it and create a brand new world. Next is my partner-in-crime-and-everything-in-between, J, who supported me through all the tears (many, many tears) as I crawled this book toward the finish line while trying to move cross-country and consolidate our two-story house into a single storage locker while wrangling our anxious puppy Jessica Jones.

In the midst of this chaos, my family has been my rock—my parents M and D, and my siblings, and I thank them for continuing to inspire me to work hard. My career and writing life would not have flourished without the following people: my right hand (and left hand, right foot, and second brain) Jannie, who keeps the chaos at bay (even when I'm the chaos); my life-long friends J and L who are fellow writers and always ready to bounce off ideas or just hang out and not even think about our chosen profession; my co-writer Adilyn Andrews, whose wonderful prose and ideas (and deadlines) keep me on my toes; and Mary Meredith, whose messages and stories over the years have

ALICIA MONTGOMERY

kept me feeling grounded and connected in this oftentimes lonely and isolating profession.

Also, my thanks to the wonderful people over at Headline Eternal who made all of this (physically) happen (editorial, art, marketing, PR and everyone in between), thank you for easing the burden of getting the book out there so I can concentrate on writing and for taking a chance on me and Dewberry Falls. And of course, my online community, members of The Den and my newsletter, and my ARC readers, thank you all, for being with me for almost a decade and never failing to support me through your reads, your social media shares, and reviews. You are the reason I do this and at the same time, the reason I'm able to create these new worlds and bring to life Jasmine, Mal, Clawdia and all the characters from my books.

HEADLINE
ETERNAL

FIND YOUR HEART'S DESIRE...

VISIT OUR WEBSITE: www.headlineeternal.com

FIND US ON FACEBOOK: facebook.com/eternalromance

CONNECT WITH US ON X: @eternal_books

FOLLOW US ON INSTAGRAM: @headlineeternal

EMAIL US: eternalromance@headline.co.uk

RAISING READERS
Books Build Bright Futures

Dear Reader,

We'd love your attention for one more page to tell you about the crisis in children's reading, and what we can all do.

Studies have shown that reading for fun is the **single biggest predictor of a child's future success** – more than family circumstance, parents' educational background or income. It improves academic results, mental health, wealth, communication skills and ambition.

The number of children reading for fun is in rapid decline. Young people have a lot of competition for their time, and a worryingly high number do not have a single book at home.

Our business works extensively with schools, libraries and literacy charities, but here are some ways we can all raise more readers:

- Reading to children for just 10 minutes a day makes a difference
- Don't give up if your children aren't regular readers – there will be books for them!
- Visit bookshops and libraries to get recommendations
- Encourage them to listen to audiobooks
- Support school libraries
- Give books as gifts

Thank you for reading.
www.JoinRaisingReaders.com